SHE WAS A VISIO… …HE
LAST T…
TO FIND ON T…

"I shouldn't be here … us are quite alone here, and that's not permissible, according to my companion, Mrs. Forrest."

The entire time she was speaking, Adam had been busy mentally inventorying the trespasser. Her nearly waist-length hair was a marvel. But it didn't begin to compete with her creamy skin, her huge, liquid green eyes, and the pink fullness of her wide mouth.

If this was a dream, he decided he could be content with that. And if it wasn't? If this adorable creature was actually here, actually speaking to him . . .

He held out his bent arm. She grinned, bobbed a fairly saucy curtsy, and took it. He knew then that he'd never smell fresh earth, or see another spring, without remembering how it felt to walk with this lovely, delicious fairy-tale princess. He had gone mad, insane. And he didn't want sanity if it didn't include her . . .

"Kasey Michaels creates characters who stick with you long after her wonderful stories are told. Her books are always on my nightstand."
—Kay Hooper, bestselling author of *After Caroline*

Please turn the page for more raves for Kasey Michaels and her enticing romances . . .

MORE PRAISE FOR NATIONAL BESTSELLING AUTHOR KASEY MICHAELS AND HER CAPTIVATING ROMANCES

"A writing style, voice, and sense of humor perfectly suited to the era and the genre."
—*Publishers Weekly*

Escapade

"A great cast of characters . . . a delightful novel."
—*Southern Pines Pilot* (NC)

"A cast of unbelievably funny characters, a wonderful plot line . . . an awesome book."
—*Rendezvous*

"A wonderful romp with all of Michaels's deft touches of high wit and striking humor, blended with a delightful love story . . . pure fun and wonderful reading . . . vintage Michaels."
—*Belles and Beaux of Romance*

"Sparkling, perceptive dialogue . . . this reader couldn't wait to find out what happens next . . . perfect."
—*Bookbug on the Web*

Indiscreet

"Delicious . . . a thoroughly delightful historical romance. A pleasurable read."
—*Booklist*

"There is so much wit and wisdom in the pages of *Indiscreet* that you'll be filled with wonder, and giggling all the while. Kasey Michaels returns with all the hallmarks that have made her a Regency romance treasure: humor, unforgettable characters, and a take on the era few others possess. Sheer reading pleasure!"
—**Kathe Robin**, *Romantic Times*

"[A] lively romp . . . a well-plotted, humorous story filled with a bevy of delightful supporting characters."
—*Library Journal*

"So appealing . . . brilliantly described. . . . [A] fabulous tale."
—**Harriet Klausner**, *Affaire de Coeur*

"Five Bells! Ms. Michaels keeps the fun coming."
—*Bell, Book and Candle*

Other books by Kasey Michaels

Indiscreet
Escapade

Come Near Me

KASEY MICHAELS

WARNER BOOKS

A Time Warner Company

WARNER BOOKS EDITION

Copyright © 2000 by Kasey Michaels
All rights reserved. No part of this book may be reproduced in any form or by any electronic or mechanical means, including information storage and retrieval systems, without permission in writing from the publisher, except by a reviewer who may quote brief passages in a review.

Cover design by Diane Luger
Cover illustration by Franco Accornero
Hand lettering by David Gatti

Warner Books, Inc.
1271 Avenue of the Americas
New York, NY 10020

Visit our Web site at
www.twbookmark.com

 A Time Warner Company

Printed in the United States of America

First Printing: February 2000

10 9 8 7 6 5 4 3 2 1

To Marianne Willman, mystic and soothsayer.
To Ruth Ryan Langan, angel and mother earth.
To Patricia Gaffney, mischievous sylph.
And to Nora Roberts, a delightful mix of all
of the above.

. . . and here's a mocha latte for someone I owe a big
cup of foo-foo coffee.

I wish I loved the human race;
I wish I loved its silly face;
I wish I loved the way it walks;
I wish I loved the way it talks;
And when I'm introduced to one;
I wish I thought *What jolly fun*.

—Sir Walter A. Raleigh

Book One

A Small Society

By seeing London, I have seen as much of life as the world can show.

—Samuel Johnson

It's worse than a crime, it's a blunder.
—Antoine Boulay De La Meurthe

Chapter One

"The devil you say."

Adam Dagenham, Marquis of Daventry, settled his long, lean body more comfortably against the pillar at the edge of the dance floor and smiled indolently at the man who had spoken. "The devil I do say, sir. You asked the identity of that 'glorious hoyden in the sea-green gown' and I replied: 'my wife'. Now, do you run off, terrified of my wrath, or linger to offer your condolences?"

"My felicitations would be more likely," the gentleman replied in his deep, melodious voice, bowing most formally to Daventry. "Allow me, if I might, to introduce my blundering self. I am Burnell. Edmund Burnell. Late of points south and east, all of them most forgettable, and for the moment residing in London with my dear aunt, the Lady Gytha Jagger. The woman, I might add, who suggested I approach you for my answer when I first inquired as to the identity of—well, of your wife. I imagine she thought she was being amusing."

"Ah, Lady J," Daventry said, shooting a quick glance to the rank of dowagers. He spotted the hatchet-faced old woman waving one gloved and heavily ringed hand and favored her with a slight inclination of his head, acknowledging the hit. "Dear, dear, old bitch. She does enjoy her fun, doesn't she?"

Daventry took one last look toward the dance floor and at his wife. He saw the sparkle of her smile, the overbright glitter in her green eyes, more than a hint of slim ankle as she lifted her skirts and moved with the dance.

Yes. That was his wife all right. Charlotte Victor Dagenham, Marchioness of Daventry. Sherry. His Sherry. And he was her Adam. For their sins. . . .

He lazily, belatedly, introduced himself, then pushed away from the pillar and looked more closely at his new acquaintance, this Edmund Burnell. Tall. Blond. Quite handsome in both his face and dress. Charming smile. Laughing blue eyes. *Intelligent* blue eyes. Likable. Interesting fellow. Very interesting. Well, diverting, at least. God knew Daventry needed a little diversion.

"Crushing bore, this ball, isn't it? Probably the flattest of this short Fall Season. At least of some of us," Daventry said, shooting his cuffs, looking at the man, assessing him even as he smiled. "Burnell? I was just about to go drown myself in some of Lady Petersham's best brandy. Do you care to join me?"

Edmund Burnell frowned slightly, his gaze flitting swiftly to the marchioness of Daventry before he smiled at his new acquaintance. "You'll leave her here? Unprotected?"

Daventry threw back his dark head and laughed. "Unprotected? My wife? You have it the wrong way round, friend. I leave London unprotected. Now, come. We'll drink, perhaps find ourselves a deck of cards. You do play, don't you?"

"Oh, yes," Burnell replied smoothly, following after Daventry, his cool blue gaze still on the marchioness. "I always enjoy a game."

Sherry stood in front of the glass, watching her husband's reflection as he prowled the bedchamber, wanting to leave, knowing he would not. Could not.

It would be better if he did leave. She could scream then. Tear at her hair. Throw herself across the bed and weep until she slept. Dreamed. Woke sobbing.

How handsome he was, even when his face wore the dark scowl that had become so familiar, too familiar. He was angry with her again, of course. He was always angry with her. Disappointed in her. Perhaps even sickened by her.

It hadn't always been this way. Once, he had been amused, intrigued. Once, she had been the world to him. Or so he'd said. But that had been before. Sherry thought of her entire world that way.

Before . . .

And, now, after . . .

"Darling?" she said, forcing lightness into her voice,

a smile to her lips. "Emma has wandered off some-where, as usual, and it would be fruitless for me to ring for her. Could you come help me with my gown?"

Adam's head came up as he stopped his pacing, looked in her direction. "She's done another flit? I don't know why you keep the woman, Sherry. She's worthless."

Sherry lifted her hands to fumble ineffectually with the heavy diamond clasp of the Daventry family pearls, her head bowed so that he couldn't see her face. "She's the only one who can make some manageable sense of this infernal mop on my head, darling. Be-sides, she—she amuses me."

"Oh, well, if she *amuses* you," Adam said, his voice dripping sarcasm. "Far be it from me to suggest you part with anyone—or anything—that *amuses* you. Here, let me get that, before you have six generations of Dagenhams spinning in their graves as you rip the string and beads go flying into mouse holes in the cor-ners."

He used to be able to tell when she was lying. Had he lost that talent, or had she begun to lie better these past months? Or perhaps he simply didn't care any-more. Sherry bit her lip as she lowered her arms, watching in the mirror as Adam stepped behind her, his fingers brushing her neck with fire as he neatly rescued the pearls.

His hands lingered against her skin, searing a light, fluttering pattern she'd feel for hours. In a moment, her fastenings were open, and her gown hung loose from her shoulders. He then moved his attention to the combs in her hair. She watched as the mass of living fire slid from its pearl-encrusted anchors, cascading down, a heavy waterfall of bright color reaching nearly to her waist.

Her skin looked so white against the blaze of hair. So white against the tanned perfection of her husband's hands as he drew her hair away from her shoulders, as his fingers made their way along her skin, pushing the gown from her shoulders so that it puddled in a soft green foam at her feet.

No. He wasn't about to leave her. Everything else had been lost, irrevocably broken. But there was still this, God help them both. Maybe it had been all they'd ever had.

She tilted her head slightly, inviting his kiss against her throat. Longing for it. Praying for it. Offering up her soul in exchange for it.

She closed her eyes.

"There, that should do," Adam said, and she felt the cold evening air reach her as he walked away, turning his back on her, on his own desires. "I made a new acquaintance tonight, darling," he went on as he shrugged himself out of his jacket, tossed it toward a chair already piled high with Sherry's clothing—clothing Emma should have picked up hours ago, put away. "A Mr. Edmund Burnell. Delightful chap. I think he's infatuated with you. But, then, so is the rest of London."

"Except for you," Sherry whispered under her breath. Pinning a bright smile on her face, she stepped away from her gown, remembering the times Adam had delighted in slowly, guided by kisses, divesting her of her undergarments. "How lovely," she then said, walking behind a Chinese screen, ruthlessly wrestling off her remaining finery before slipping her arms into a diaphanous dressing gown. "You should have introduced us, Adam," she continued, moving out from the protection of the screen once more as she tied the satin ribbons at her throat. She gave back pain for pain. "I'm always delighted to meet a new admirer."

She watched as her husband's deep brown eyes flickered betrayingly for a moment as he ran his gaze over her artfully concealed and revealed body.

He wouldn't leave. He wanted to. Oh, how he wanted to. She knew. But he wouldn't leave her alone tonight. Not after she had teased him so unmercifully at Lady Petersham's insipid ball. She had danced, whirled, flirted, enticed, invited. Dancing with everyone but Adam. Dancing only for Adam. Salome, without the veils. *Bring me the heart of Adam Dagenham,* she had chanted fervently as she smiled and danced and flirted and laughed. *Bring me his love, as I've once known it.*

He hated her for the way she acted, but he had left her no other avenue, no other way to fight, and she lacked the strength it would take to surrender. And, even if he hated her, he still desired her. As long as he desired her, she had hope.

"You're right, of course. I should have introduced him to you. Maybe next time," Adam said, reaching for his snifter of brandy. His ever-present snifter of brandy.

He had never drunk more than moderately when she'd met him, married him. She had pushed him into a bottle. Just one more sin he wouldn't forgive her.

She heard his next words through a faint buzzing in her ears. "Yes, I'll definitely introduce him to you. I wouldn't want you to think he's forbidden fruit. We all know your taste for that, don't we?"

Sherry lifted the back of her hand to her cheek as she turned her head from him, recoiling from the verbal blow he'd struck, stifling a sudden sob. "That's all in *your* mind, Adam. No one else's." Then, squaring her shoulders, she turned to glare at him. "Stop it, Adam. Just stop it, all right?"

"Ah, darling, if only I could," Adam said, putting down the snifter and advancing toward her once more. His own cheeks were flushed now, as if with fever. "Wasn't beauty enough, Sherry? Wasn't your every dream come true enough—becoming the acknowledged queen of London Society? Wasn't my heart enough?" She watched, dying inside, as his entire body shuddered slightly, the involuntary movement almost indiscernible. "Why wasn't my heart enough?"

"It was—it is," she told him, made stupid in her need, by the love that became so volatile when mixed with exasperation. "It's you who have turned away—"

"I'm running for my life, Sherry," he told her quietly. "Even as I come to you, inside me, in my head, I'm running for my life. My sanity."

"Then go," she cried out challengingly, her heart aching, her arms empty. "Just go!"

It was his turn to close his eyes, to look away. "Dear

God," he breathed quietly, the anguish in his voice tearing at her, giving her hope at the same time. He looked at her once more, his dark eyes glowing with heat, with want, with emotions she refused to understand. "I'm not that strong."

Against all of her instincts, Sherry backed up a pace, put her hands out to ward him off. For a moment she was the near child she'd been when he'd met her, loved her, changed her life forever. "No, Adam. Please. I'd thought—but, no. Not this way. Please, not this way . . ."

But it was always this way. If not love, then need. If not his heart, then his body. It was all he had to give her. And she would take anything he would give her. Even shame. There had never been shame before, but they'd made love before, created love between them. She didn't know what it was they did now.

Her empty arms were filled with him. Her hands clung as he lifted her, carried her, placed her on the bed where she lay, eyes closed, waiting. The sound of clothing being all but ripped from his body shredded her nerves.

And then he was beside her. His mouth claimed hers. His hands found their way beneath her dressing gown, found her.

She was light-headed before his mouth left hers, traveled to her throat, her breast, robbing her of even the memory of breath. His hands molded her, shaped her to fit his every need, her every desire.

He kissed her. Kissed her breasts. Kissed her belly.

He moved lower, became more intimate. Kissed her again.

"Adam." His name was a curse on her lips, a benediction. A plea for love or, if not love, at least physical possession. Now. Now, before she burst into flame, crumbled into ashes.

Rising as best she could, Sherry frantically beat on his back with her closed fists. Pulled at him, urged him upward, clasped him to her tightly even as he settled himself over her, buried himself deep inside her.

He rocked against her, in her, driving them both. Over and over and over again. Taking them higher, higher. Freeing them from words, from regrets, from memory.

They were together now. One now.

It was all they had left. . . .

Midmorning sunlight wove its way through the ivory-lace curtains, traced dappled patterns on the dish-covered breakfast table of the mansion in Grosvenor Square.

Sherry, always an early riser, had already breakfasted in her chamber and was, Adam knew, even now sunk deep in a hot, fragrant tub. Washing herself clean of him, arming herself for another day of battle.

He had broken his fast alone, at nine, and followed his eggs and country ham with a snifter of brandy in the solitude of his study. But he'd heard the wheels rumble against the snatches of bare tile floor in the hallway a quarter hour ago, and knew he'd find Geoff in the breakfast room.

Lord Geoffrey Dagenham. His younger brother. His beloved, silly, senselessly damaged only brother. His heir until, as the Marquess of Daventry, Adam reproduced himself. Which might be sooner than later if he kept repeating the mistakes of last night.

Adam saw the back of the Bath chair first, its high, stiff back, its caning—the web it seemed to weave around his brother, trapping him in its seat, between its large wheels. He saw the thatch of dark blond hair, then the wide smile Geoff turned on him, the determined cheer in a pair of sky-blue eyes.

Adam's gut clenched. A tic began its work beside his left eye.

"Ah, Adam," Geoff said, waving his brother to a chair. "Looking your usual grumpy self, I see. Don't you ever weary of it?"

Adam took the chair his brother had indicated, the table blocking the sight of Geoff's legs. "Don't you ever weary of that chair?"

Geoff shook his head. "I'm much more weary of your constant references to it, frankly. Besides, I'm not at all attached to the thing. We'll soon be able to smash it into kindling. My latest leech swears it. He may be right, or he may admire the color of all the gold you're stuffing in his pockets, all the money you've stuffed in so many pockets as we languish here in town, on the hunt for miracles. Shall I ring for Rimmon to fetch you a snifter? I'm well aware of how closely our dear butler guards you, how he feeds your new vice. Or is he busy filling brandy decanters? Lord knows that's occupation enough to keep the man busy around here of late."

Adam reached for a cold piece of toast he didn't really want, ignoring his brother's remarks. "Do you plan to go out today? The sun's warm enough. Perhaps some fresh air—"

"Ah, yes, indeed!" Geoff interrupted. "Some fresh air. That should do it. A push through the park, some soft late-autumn breezes, a bit of sun, a giggle or two from the nannies, a stare or three from some comely, nubile young sylphs as they dash by, on the hunt for *upright* men. I do so enjoy my excursions to the park."

"Damn it, Geoff!" Adam exploded, tossing down the uneaten toast. "One minute hot, the next cold. I never know what to say to you, how you'll react. And to see you still talking with her, laughing with her as if nothing had happened? After what she helped do to you—"

"Sherry did nothing to me I didn't do to myself, Adam," his brother interrupted, banging his fist on the tabletop for emphasis. "She tried to stop me. And if your head weren't so thick, and your pride so stiff-backed, you'd see it."

Adam sat back in his chair, rubbed a hand across his eyes. "Oh, yes. Sherry had nothing to do with it. She never encouraged any of those mad starts, the games, the ridiculous dares. And I admit it. I enjoyed them myself. For a time. But then I warned her, warned you—"

"Lie to me, Adam, but not to yourself. You did more than enjoy the games," Geoff broke in. "You joined in with us, at least for a time. You reveled in Sherry, in seeing Sherry happy. How could you help it? She's infectious."

"So, I understand, is smallpox," Adam bit out, shaking his head. "Yes, our flights of fancy amused me, as they were innocent enough. But then we began the races. Those damnable races. The first was a lark. And the second. But then it became dangerous. Our whole *lives* became dangerous. I warned you, I warned you both. It was one thing for you to openly disobey me, but Sherry promised me—*promised* me—she'd put an end to her involvement. And she lied, Geoff. She lied. When I found her with him that day, I finally knew *why* she—"

He stood, the tic now working furiously. "No, Geoff. Don't object, tell me I'm unreasonable. I won't allow myself to beat my head against that particular stone wall this morning. I didn't come in here to discuss any of this again. I certainly didn't come in here to listen, yet again, as you defend my indefensible wife, her inexcusable actions."

"Perhaps you'd be better pleased if you could just cast off the shameless baggage, darling, and have done with it?" Sherry asked from the doorway. "I know I most certainly would oppose a public flogging, but there have been times these past months a scandalous bill of divorce would have seemed almost a blessing. Good morning, Geoff. I'm here to accompany you to the park. If we're lucky enough to find a chestnut man on the way, we can crack our treats open under your wheels when we get down and take our stroll."

Adam stiffened, then slowly turned toward the door. He watched his wife's progress as she floated into the room, dropping a kiss on Geoff's adoring head before seating herself beside him. Geoff took her hand in his, lifted it, pressed a kiss against her smooth white skin.

She appeared both glorious and beautiful in her watered-sunshine morning gown, her cheeks still flushed from her bath, her dark-fire hair a tumble of curls, falling from a topknot that should look silly but that, on her, succeeded in being most eminently becoming, endearingly charming in its simplicity.

Adam died, yet again. It had been like this for more than three months. It was getting so he barely noticed each new death.

"Adam?" his brother jibed as the silence became more than uncomfortable. "If we've given you time enough to withdraw your foot from your mouth, perhaps you'll ring for Rimmon, and your wife and I can be on our way? Oh—do you care to accompany us? You're most certainly invited. Sherry? He is invited, isn't he?"

"Of course he is," she said, plucking at the blanket tucked across Geoff's knees as it began slipping toward the floor. "Adam?" she asked, looking up at him, her eyes so shadowed with unspoken pain that he nearly forgot, only for a moment. But he could never forget for more than that moment. It was his curse, and hers. And Dickie's victory.

"I think not, darling, thank you," he said coolly, already on his way to the hall. "I'll send Rimmon to you as I head out, having promised to meet with Mr. Burnell at White's just at noon. You may remember my mentioning his name to you? We've four invitations awaiting us for this evening, my dear. Feel free to pick and choose among them. Or perhaps you'd like to make an appearance at all four? It makes no difference to me where you choose to disgrace yourself tonight."

He wasn't quite out of earshot when he heard his wife say, quite deliberately, "You know, Geoff, I've been thinking of a small diversion for you. If I were to procure a Bath chair of my own, we could take them both to the top of that lovely, grassy hill in the park . . ."

Adam slammed out of the house, entirely forgetting both his cane and to instruct Rimmon to attend his brother.

Sherry looked around at the park, at the fading, yet-still-magnificent glory of flowers and greenery, and smiled sadly. She adored London, if not her reason for being here during the small Fall Season rather than at Daventry Court, where she, Adam, and Geoff had retired after the King's birthday in June.

How happy the Spring Season had been. Her first Season as a married woman, as the marchioness of Daventry. She had considered herself the most fortunate woman on earth, to have met Adam, to have him fall in love with her, to have become his wife. The Season had passed in a whirl of parties and routs and balls, visits to the theater, silly, absurd picnics with eight hundred or more persons in attendance, revels that began in the early afternoon and lasted well into the evening.

And always, always, with Adam by her side.

She loved to laugh. Adam loved to laugh. Their mad, impulsive courtship had been full of laughter and stolen kisses, from the first. She loved him. Ah, how she loved him. How he'd loved her. All through that magical Spring Season.

And yet? And yet? How afraid Sherry still had been that he would wake one day and realize that he desired her, yes, but that their marriage was a mistake. That he had married a silly, witless child. For all the wrong reasons. That he was bored with her.

She'd put her fears away for the duration of the Season and enjoyed London. But once they'd returned to Daventry Court, to the quiet of the countryside, Sherry's fears had returned. Adam had been so busy with estate affairs that summer, too busy to laugh with her as he'd done in London. She began to think his interest was waning, his love disappearing beneath a mountain of reports on cottages needing thatch and pesky, clogged ditches to be drained.

She sighed audibly, remembering the day she had been sitting beside the stream, worrying about her failings as the wife of a marquess. It had been then that she'd met Richard Brimley, brought the man into all of their lives. . . .

"Well, that sounded heartfelt," Geoff said, touching Sherry's hands as they lay loosely curled in her lap. "Have you changed your mind, sweetheart? Perhaps I have, too. The park is well enough from this vantage point, but I admit to dreading the moment our sturdy coachman stops the carriage and the footman lifts me down into my chair. Strange. I used to rather enjoy making a cake of myself."

Sherry shoved her unhappiness quickly to the back of her mind and turned her brightest smile on Geoff. "Oh, but only think what would happen if Biggs were to drop you? *Plop!* A Daventry on the drive! Why, I imagine I would be crushed in the stampede of young ladies rushing to your rescue. Should I whisper a hint in his ear, do you think?"

"We'd better not. I don't flirt half so well on my arse, sweetheart," Geoff said, but he was smiling now, so that Sherry relaxed. "Still, I don't think I'll ask to stop and have my chair put out, if you don't mind. We'll just keep riding, and I'll sniff up the fresh air as you've told me I should, and I'll tip my hat to the ladies. Much better than tipping my—"

"You've said the word once, Geoff, and that's quite enough," she told him, wagging a finger in his face. "And Adam says I have corrupted you? Ah, he should eavesdrop on our conversations, shouldn't he?"

"Better yet, he should be dropped on *his*—"

"Geoff . . ." Sherry warned.

"Head, Sherry. I was about to say he should be dropped on his head. Maybe it would shake some sense into his brains. To watch him with you, *listen* to him with you—well, I never thought my brother could be so stupid. Thick, that's what he is. Thick as a plank."

Sherry began pleating the long ribbon of her pelisse.

"He did find us together, Geoff," she reminded him, wishing her eyes wouldn't sting so with sudden tears, tears she refused to allow permission to fall. "If only I could push time back, have it all to do over again."

Geoff playfully pinched at her cheek. "What? You mean you can't do that, sweetheart? Well, I'm crushed. I thought you could do anything. Which is why I haven't yet wielded the drawing-room poker on my brother's thick, stubborn head. He'll come around, Sherry. He blames you because he can't blame himself, or me, seeing as how I'm stuck in that damnable chair for the moment."

"Because of me."

"Because of *me*, sweetheart. You begged me not to attempt that last race, told me the course was dangerous in the rain. I must have been insane. We both know Dickie goaded me into it, fool that I was."

"Adam thinks I goaded you into it. He thinks that, after promising him I wouldn't have anything more to do with ... with the races, that I'd handed you my favor and sent you out to be crippled, perhaps die."

"You can say his name, sweetheart," Geoff prodded as the carriage slowed to a stop. "The races were secondary. You promised Adam you wouldn't have anything more to do with Richard Brimley. Dear, deceitful, dangerous Dickie. He certainly did a quick flit, didn't he? I wonder where he's gone."

Sherry's jaw tightened. "To hell, I hope." She lifted her head, realizing that the carriage had stopped, and saw that Lady Gytha Jagger's equipage had come abreast of theirs. Even now her ladyship was all but bouncing herself across the width of the seat, bringing herself close enough for conversation below a bellow. "Why, Lady J," Sherry said, pushing her dark thoughts away in order to be polite to the old woman, "how good to see you this afternoon. You're looking well."

The old woman sniffed, her hatchet nose puncturing the air. "Liar. I look wretched and have always done. Wasn't even pretty as a gel, you know. Passable, I suppose, but never pretty. Never like you, my dear. So, you'll come to dinner this evening? You and that mad, brooding husband of yours? You, too, Lord Dagenham. You don't brood, and I like that. My nephew is in town, you see, and he and Daventry have struck up a friendship."

Sherry frowned, trying to remember the name Adam had flung at her, twice, in the midst of his usual insults. "Mr. Burnell?" she asked hopefully.

"Precisely! Dear, dear Edmund. He was much taken with you last night, m'dear, not that he got to say two words to you. But he and Daventry got on famously, I believe. At least Edmund remarked this morning that he'd be more than delighted if I were to have you all to dinner this evening. You'll come, won't you?"

"Geoff?" Sherry asked as she looked at her brother-in-law, knowing he had so far refused any invitations to socialize. "Adam said I could pick any entertainment I wanted for this evening, remember? It would be good for you to be out and about again. And it would be a small party." She turned to Lady Jagger. "It would be a small party, wouldn't it?"

"Infinitesimal, my dears," Her Ladyship said sprightly.

Sherry bit her lip, looking hopefully to Geoff once more. It would be so good for him to enter society again, concentrate on something other than his injury and her sinking relationship with her husband.

"My goodness, Sherry, you look as if you literally want to *pull* my agreement out of me." He shrugged eloquently. "Oh, why not, sweetheart," he said, looking to Lady Jagger. "We'd be delighted, ma'am. Tell me—do I bring my own carriers, or are your footmen brawny enough to hoist me up your stairs?"

Adam was faintly surprised by the decor of the room Edmund Burnell led him to after dinner, then remembered that once, long ago, Lady J had been married. Strange, though, as the man had been underground and unlamented these twenty years, that she hadn't done the study over in some more feminine fashion.

Or at least opened the windows and let in some fresh air.

The room was oppressively dark. Dark paneling, dark drapes, dark wood. A large room, made small by the dark but never cozy; a high-ceilinged room, whose top disappeared beyond the candlelight, the glow of the fire.

He recognized the mantelpiece as being one designed by Sir William Chambers. It had been carved in a single huge piece of black marble that included matching four-foot-high female figures partially released from the stone, their attire rather scanty, although their hands seemed to be drawn into an attitude of prayer.

Carpets the shade of clotted blood matched the blood-red velvet draperies, their oriental design added to only with vague designs picked out in black and gold.

The chair Adam sat in, however, was completely comfortable. Chippendale had been at the top of his form with chairs, he knew, and this one was no exception, even if its Chinese style did not appeal.

Edmund Burnell sat in the chair's mate, warming a brandy snifter between his hands and smiling, rather enigmatically, at Adam.

"You're waiting for my reaction, I imagine?" Adam said, indicating the room with a languid wave of his right hand, his left fully occupied with its own snifter of dark amber liquid.

"Breathlessly," Edmund admitted on a smile. His golden hair shone in the candlelight, his blue eyes danced in obvious amusement. "Damned dreadful, ain't it?"

"The hangman's retreat," Adam concurred brightly. "Machiavelli's inner sanctum. Nero's music room."

"The devil's den?"

"Yes," Adam said, taking a sip of brandy. "That, too. Are you sure Lady J didn't have her husband stuffed and mounted in one of the corners? It's so dark in here, anything's possible. Oh," he added a moment later, "that was tactless. I know you address Lady J as your aunt, but whether it is by marriage or you're truly her nephew—well, either way, I believe I've just insulted your family. Forgive me."

"No harm done, I assure you," Edmund answered, sitting back more comfortably, crossing one leg over the other. "As happenstance would have it, Lady J is mine. I'm afraid I never met His Lordship. Was he badly oppressed, do you think?"

"Hounded straight into the grave, I'd imagine," Adam said, and the two laughed, then settled themselves again, staring into the fire.

It was comfortable, sitting there with Edmund, a man who was an interesting conversationalist but also knew when a comfortable silence was preferred.

Adam and Edmund had spent a most enjoyable afternoon together, talking of deep things, speaking of nonsense. They seemed to share every interest, every opinion. With most of his friends not in town for the Small Season, Adam had been grateful to have met such a kindred spirit, felt himself lucky to find a friend to lighten his mood, lighten his days.

Edmund had delighted the ladies all through dinner and had thoroughly charmed Geoff, speaking of his travels, the sights he'd seen, some of the outrageous characters he'd met. It was nice to see Geoff smile, to watch him partake in society again, even in this limited way.

Everything would be even more pleasant if there had never been a Richard Brimley. Because Adam really liked Edmund Burnell. A few months ago, he would have trusted the man, trusted his own judgment.

"It's a pity your brother had to retire, Daventry," Edmund said, as if knowing Adam had been thinking about Geoff. "Do his legs pain him?"

Adam frowned as he remembered carrying Geoff down to the carriage, hearing the echo of his brother's sharp rebuff as he had attempted to insist he and Sherry also return to Grosvenor Square. "No—at least he never complains. Although tonight's dinner is the first time he'd been, well, out and about since the accident. It may have been too much for him. And it's a problem with his hip, not his legs, although the result is the same, as he can't walk until his injuries heal."

Edmund nodded, then rose to fetch the decanter from the small table he'd set before the fire to warm its contents. Refilling Adam's snifter, he sat down once more, steepled his fingers, and asked, "It was a fall from a horse, I understand?"

Adam felt the tic begin its work beside his eye and drank deep from the snifter before answering. "No. A curricle accident," he said as coolly as he could. "A stupid accident, as are most, I suppose. An idiotic challenge, a wet course, a splintered wheel—a ditch."

He looked into the fire, seeing Geoff's body crumpled, broken, pinned beneath the overturned curricle. The vision shook him, sickened him, so that he took another deep drink of brandy.

"There was also the obligatory storm that blows up whenever a loved one hasn't returned home and one must go out searching for him. It took hours to find Geoff. The longest of my life."

His eyes darkened at another memory, a memory even worse than that of his brother lying unconscious in the mud. It knocked at the doors of his mind, begging to come in, sit down, laugh at him. "Hours," he repeated, shaking himself back from the brink of that other memory. "He nearly drowned in that damnable ditch."

"I'm sorry if this conversation hurts you, Daventry, and I can see that it does. But I must ask you. Your brother is such a likable fellow. From what you've said, he will walk again, won't he?"

The brandy was warming Adam, soothing him, yet burning deep in his belly. "If there's a God, yes."

"Oh, there's a God, Daventry," Edmund told him, his smile one of almost indulgent amusement. "Most assuredly. A God. A Heaven. A Hell."

"And a purgatory, Burnell?" Adam asked as some of his own good humor returned. He began to relax, became determined to enjoy himself in Edmund Burnell's company. "Does that exist as well?"

Burnell spread both his arms, his grin lighthearted, mischievous. "A purgatory? We're *surrounded* by it, Daventry. Most especially in this room, wouldn't you say? I'm particularly fond of that hideous, grinning gargoyle hanging atop the mirror behind you. If that vision alone isn't enough to make us suffer for and repent of our sins, I don't know what is. Now, let's speak of more pleasant things. Tell me how you met your lovely wife, that dear, delightful creature who is no doubt even now yawning into her hand and wishing the pair of us back in the drawing room. My aunt blatantly cheats at whist, you understand."

"Sherry?" Adam closed his eyes a moment, yet another vision crowding into his brain. How well he could see. Step back, review the past. See her, hear her, smell her, taste her. It was the brandy, of course. Tonight it seemed to heighten all of his senses. He employed it to dull his mind, and, for the most part, it did its job well. But not tonight. Tonight, when the past crashed into his skull with such clarity everything and everyone else disappeared.

How strange. How wonderful. How sad.

The room he sat in was forgotten. Edmund Burnell was forgotten.

"How we met?" Adam kept his eyes closed, his hands wrapped around the snifter, the memories drawing closer, clearer. "We met by accident. Literally by accident," he began, speaking softly, almost to himself, allowing the memories nearer, allowing them in. . . .

O tender yearning, sweet hoping!
The golden time of first love!
        —Johann von Schiller

Chapter Two

It was one of those rare, golden, early-spring days, an afternoon of sunlight following a morning of sweet, gentle rain. Tender green leaves glistened damply as sunbeams danced over them. Freshly scythed grass perfumed the air.

Bees droned lazily overhead as Adam Dagenham, Marquess of Daventry, walked the hills near Daventry Court, his white shirtsleeves billowing in the breeze, his high, tight leather boots protecting him now, as he picked his way across a bubbling stream, agilely hopping from flat stone to flat stone.

He remembered his route across the water, as he had been crossing at this particular place since he was a boy. Except that the stones had seemed larger then, or his feet, smaller.

He was in the middle of the stream, halfway between the bank he'd departed and halfway to the bank he desired, when he heard the shriek. Short. Sharp. Feminine.

He stopped where he was, one foot secure on a stone, the other raised. He held his arms out from his sides, balancing himself rather precariously as he turned his head. He searched out the direction of the scream through the trees, the location of the female.

If he'd had both feet firmly on the stone, he would have been fine. Unfortunately, that wasn't the case.

A moment later, he was sitting rump-down in the stream, his fists dug into the soft, muddy bottom, watching a blur of green and white and vibrant, brilliant, dark red dance across the stones, including the one from which he had lately, reluctantly, departed.

"Oh, my! Oh, my goodness! Did I push you?" On the far bank, the blur of color resolved itself into the form of a heartbreakingly beautiful young woman who was just now pressing her hands against her mouth, ineffectually pushing back a giggle even as she tried to catch her breath. "Well, of course I did, didn't I? I most distinctly remember feeling a *bump* as I flew over the stones. I was minding my feet, you understand. I should have been looking higher, shouldn't I? Are you very wet?"

Adam looked down at himself and the scant foot of water he sat in, then at the female once more. The apparition. The goddess. He resisted the impulse to shake his head, clear his vision. "That, I believe, madam, would depend upon your definition of the word," he said without malice, lifting his hands slightly so that the gentle current could rinse the mud from his fingers. "I'm not soaked. Even drenched. Then again, damp may be too mild a definition. Are you all right? Is someone chasing you? I thought I heard a scream a moment before we, um, *met.*"

"Oh. That." The fantasy, fairy-tale princess—for Adam could think of no other way to describe the beauty who stood before him, stood over him—giggled in a very human way. It was a very infectious giggle; he found himself stifling a laugh of his own.

Which was ludicrous. He shouldn't be laughing. He should be mad as fire. But all the fire he knew was there, in her hair, and he longed for nothing more than to warm himself in its heat. Except, of course, that he was already much too warm. Perhaps approaching delirium. Another rather prudent dunk in the cold water was probably what he really needed.

"Yes, madam. *That,*" Adam said, regaining his feet and his scattered wits as gracefully as a wet, dripping man can. Then, with the least amount of haste he could feign, he completed his journey across the stream, ignoring the stepping-stones as being too little, too late. He splashed through the water without regard to his boots, to stand beside her on the bank. "What was it? Bandits? Great woolly beasts? A bumblebee trying to nest in your hair?"

"It was Bumble, actually, but he's gone," she told him, then shocked him to his toes as she ran behind a nearby tree, only to reappear a few moments later holding one of her petticoats out to him. "Here. Use this to dry yourself." When he hesitated, she waved it in front of his face. "Oh, go on. Don't be a gudgeon. It's old as Moses, and you can't hurt it. And get that spot of mud on your cheek—the left one. Ah, that's it. There! Don't you feel better now?"

"Did—did you say *Bumble*?" Adam finished wiping at his cheek, drying his hands, and made to return the petticoat, which made him feel even sillier than he had in accepting it in the first place. Besides, it was warm from her body, smelled of lavender, and his only other option was to beg she let him keep it forever.

He quickly rolled the garment into a ball and laid it on the bank, wondering when it was he had reverted from a gentleman of the world and into a stumbling, stuttering schoolboy. Better yet, when had he last been called a gudgeon? When had anyone last dared?

The apparition in front of him pushed back a lock of dark red hair and nodded. "Why, yes. I did say Bumble. He's one of the marquess of Daventry's bulls. His prize bull, I imagine. Someone must have forgotten to latch the gate to his pasture, I suppose, and he decided he might like to amuse himself by tossing me in the air a time or two. I didn't linger to ask his intentions. I yelped and bolted straight for the stream. But the trees defeated him, and I'm sure he's gone now. Well, that will pay me handsomely for trespassing, won't it?"

"Someone didn't latch the—" Adam broke off, silently cursing himself. "That was probably my fault, I'm afraid. I was tramping the fields, wool-gathering, not paying attention. Although I could have sworn I'd latched the gate behind me. You could have been badly injured, as could I, considering that I'd stumbled through his pasture without realizing he was in it. Buckfastleigh's Prize isn't known for his ingratiating manners. A thousand pardons," he ended, bowing from the waist, which wasn't easy, considering how his soggy unmentionables stuck to his rump each time he moved.

"Yes, I rather believe—did you say Buck-fastleigh's Prize?" She cocked her head to one side, looking up at him inquiringly. "How do you know that? I most distinctly remember calling him Bumble, which is what Hayes calls him because, much as he loves the sport of the mate, the poor obtuse Romeo has to be helped through the more mechanical moments of the thing."

"Really?" Adam said, knowing his eyes were all but wide as saucers. This all had to be a dream. She had to be a dream. He had fallen on his own, hit his head on a rock, and was now dreaming. He decided he liked the dream. Very much. Even if he ended by drowning. "How—interesting. Except for Hayes, I'd imagine. He probably sees the whole procedure as a terrible bother."

She clapped her hands to her cheeks, which were

now burning quite fetchingly with embarrassment. "I shouldn't have said that, should I? I'm supposed to believe that babies, even bull babies, I imagine, are all discovered in the early morning, beneath the cabbages. Then again, I shouldn't be here at all. Not trespassing, and most certainly not speaking to you. The two of us are quite alone here, you know. That's not permissible, according to my companion, Mrs. Forrest. Except that Mrs. Forrest thinks plum pudding is vulgar and suggestive—how, I don't know—so I really paid her very little attention as often as I could until she finally threw up her hands and left us a year ago. You're the marquess, aren't you? How else would you know Bumble is really Buckfastleigh's Prize. Or care, for that matter. Would you like to step out of the trees and into the sun? You must be cold. You'll dry faster that way, too, although you'll probably begin to itch. I apologize for that, too."

The entire time she had been speaking—and she spoke rather quickly, so he hadn't had all that much time—Adam had been busy mentally inventorying the trespasser. Her nearly waist-length hair was, as he'd already noted, a marvel. But it didn't begin to compete with her creamy skin, her huge, liquid green eyes, the sweep of dark lashes and brows, the pink fullness of her wide mouth.

Her face was small—he was sure his cupped hand would all but swallow her chin and lower jaw—and infinitely exquisite. As was the rest of her. She rose no higher than his mid-chest, putting her at only a few inches above five feet, and her body was one of curves rather than planes and angles. A full bosom, a trim waist, a delicious sweep of hip, the hint of long legs, of feet as narrow and well formed as her hands.

If this was a dream, he decided he could be content with that. If it wasn't? Ah, if it wasn't, if this adorable creature was actually here, actually speaking to him . . .

He waited until she had run down, run out of things to say, then bent to retrieve the petticoat. He held out his bent arm. She grinned, bobbed him a fairly saucy curtsy, and took it. She then allowed him to lead her through the narrow band of trees that had grown up around either side of the stream, and into the sunlight pouring down on a freshly turned field.

He'd never smell fresh earth, feel the sun, see another spring, without remembering how it felt to walk the perimeter of this field with his lovely, delicious, fairy-tale princess. He had gone mad, insane. And he didn't want sanity if it didn't include her.

"As you've deduced that I am the marquess, madam," he said, feeling foolishly formal as the sunlight found her hair, turning it into a halo of reddish gold that all but brought tears to his eyes, "perhaps you'll be so kind as to tell me your name? Mrs. Forrest would undoubtedly say that, at least, was proper."

"Yes, I suppose I should. I'm Charlotte Victor, my lord. My father and I are leasing the cottage to the west of your lands, and have done so for almost the last year. Precisely in the direction we're now walking, just beyond the next line of trees. Mama died, you see, and Papa wished to get away from our home for a while. Away from the memories. At least that's what he tells people. Personally, I believe he's here for the hunting. The man does dearly love the hunt."

"My condolences on your loss," Adam offered automatically, picturing Frame Cottage in his mind's eyes, and recalling that the term "cottage" had always seemed rather too quaint for a fourteen-room structure. Even if the owner had thought it the height of ingenuity to top the slates with a picturesque layer of thatch.

Her grin surprised him. "No, no, you mustn't. You're very kind, but I find it impossible to tell Papa's lie to you, my lord. You'll keep our secret, won't you?"

"Secret?" He was having trouble hearing her, for the blood pounding in his ears. What a pretty mouth she had. If he wasn't actually lying back there in the stream, dreaming, drowning, perhaps Charlotte Victor was in reality a Gypsy, and she had cast a spell over him. There had to be something to explain how he felt. Because he felt as if his life, at the supposedly quite respectable age of thirty, had somehow just begun. He was filled with that life. Fit to bursting.

"Yes, our secret. Mama isn't dead, you see. Not really. She's just gone missing. Well, she's not precisely *missing*. She's gone away. With one Henry Carpenter. Wonderful man. It has all been a bit of a scandal at home, which is why Papa packed the two of us up and took us away. Once he noticed Mama was gone, that is. It was fox-hunting season, and he's rather fully occupied in fox-hunting season."

"I suppose your papa isn't the only gentleman to have misplaced his wife during fox-hunting season." Adam felt a tickle of laughter building low in his throat. He bit his bottom lip as his eyes began to water. Charlotte Victor was beautiful. Charming. Innocent. And he was enjoying her so much he could just eat her up, as he would a sugarplum.

She tipped her head slightly, looking at him. "Mama writes quite often, so I'm not upset, and it's not as if I'm not fully grown and able to take care of myself. She deserves a little happiness. Losing your husband's affection to a pack of hounds and a scrap of vermin isn't something a well-bred woman of any sensibility takes lightly. At least that's what Mama said. I, myself, have no experience in the area, but I imagine she's right. What's this? You're laughing, aren't you? Don't try to stifle it—go on, laugh. It's funny."

Adam, having been given permission of sorts, threw back his head and roared. "Oh, thank you, Miss Victor. I don't remember the last time I've heard such refreshing honesty," he said once he'd recovered. "London is full of lies, you know."

"Really? Well, that is a pity. I'm sure I shouldn't know how to be anything but honest. And you're welcome. I'm glad to have been of service, I suppose, although I've also betrayed myself quite completely as being nothing but a silly country miss," she said, beginning to skip along, her skirts flying out with each kick of her half-booted toes. She all but danced ahead of him on the narrow path, then stopped, turned, looked at him through the fiery haze of wind-kissed curls.

She smiled, unaffectedly shoving the errant locks away from her face, and showing him that she had absolutely no idea she was figuratively punching all the air from his lungs at the same time. His stomach slapped his toes, then shot upward, plastering itself against his windpipe. "I can find my way from here, my lord, if you'll be so kind as to return my petticoat?"

His own probably faintly idiotic smile vanishing, Adam realized he'd begun clutching the petticoat to him as if holding it meant he could also hold on to Charlotte Victor. "Might—mi—" He hesitated, cleared his throat, began again. "Might I be so presumptuous as to invite you and your father to dinner at Daventry Court this evening? We keep country hours, I'm afraid, which includes dining ungodly early. I'd send the carriage for you. At five?"

Adam winced inwardly. He sounded stiff. Formal. And yet stammering, almost pleading. A person would think he didn't know how to offer a proper invitation. Or that he cared, more than he liked to admit, what Miss Charlotte Victor thought of him.

"Why, I'd be delighted, my lord," she responded

with a small giggle, taking the petticoat from his nearly nerveless grasp. "Papa would flay me if I refused. Truth to tell, he's been all but dying for the chance of an invitation to Daventry Court. He's heard your brother, Lord Dagenham, that is, has the most marvelous hounds."

Her answer eased his mind and loosed his good humor once more as he retraced his steps to the stream, and beyond. He'd put the papa with Geoff and send the two of them off to the dogs directly after dinner, while he and Miss Victor took an intimate stroll in the gardens.

It was only as he was sitting in the crook of a conveniently located branch, midway up a similarly conveniently placed tree, waiting for Hayes to engage Buckfastleigh's Prize's interest in something other than stomping on his master, that Adam realized that he had probably just lost his heart.

I do not want people to be very agreeable,
as it saves me the trouble of
liking them a great deal.

—Jane Austen

Chapter Three

". . . brought you together? How very unique."

Adam blinked, and the scene unfolding in front of his eyes once more became the fire in the deceased Lord Jasper's grate. He looked to his new friend, wondering what he might have said to the man, what Burnell had just said. "I—I beg your pardon?"

"I said, how very unique a meeting, Daventry. Having a bull bring you together. And how reassuring to hear that yours is a love match. Not many of those lying about on the ground these days, are there?" He took a sip of brandy, looking at Adam through the distorting glass of the snifter. "Although," he ended, his blue eyes twinkling, "there is a lot to be said for the *matches* based on rather more earthly attraction, if you know to keep them temporary and reward them handsomely with diamonds and the like once the flame has burnt down."

"Ah, yes. I remember that sort of *match,* Burnell. Shall we drink a toast to them all?" Adam pushed himself back from the edge of memory and lifted his glass, wondering how much he'd said, hoping he hadn't said too much. Damnable brandy, it made his tongue run on wheels sometimes. He couldn't remember much past telling Burnell he and Sherry had met by accident. "To lust," he said, earning himself an even wider smile from his new friend, who was suddenly looking past Adam, to the door. Adam's hand stilled in the act of making the toast, and he watched, not seeing but yet *knowing,* as Burnell got to his feet.

"My lady," Burnell said, bowing as Sherry advanced into the room, "how good of you to join us."

Adam could feel her green eyes boring into the back of his skull, and he, too, quickly rose to his feet, turned, and bowed. If a bow could be polite yet still mocking, he had mastered the art of that particular delivery. It was just one more deception in the thousands of small deceptions it now took to be Adam Dagenham. He and Sherry had both become masters of the art, to give her credit—or her share of the blame. The public devotion, laced through with the private condemnation.

"Darling," Adam purred, indicating that she should take his seat.

"Oh, but I can't, dearest," she told him, shaking her head as she spoke, her gaze going straight past his as she directed her next words to Burnell. "I fear we should be going back to Grosvenor Square, Mr. Burnell, as I have just told Lady J. I—I'm worried about Lord Dagenham, truth to tell."

"Truth to tell, my lady," Burnell quipped, taking her hand and bowing over it, "you're fleeing for your life, if I know my aunt. What was it? Whist? She's rather too obvious when she cheats at whist. It's the cards falling out of her sleeve at inopportune times, I believe, that gives her game away. What was it?"

"The ace of hearts," Sherry said, wincing, even as her eyes danced with good humor. "I didn't know where to look as she tried to stuff it back, so I fibbed about worrying for Geoff—which he'd never thank me for, I can tell you—and raced in here to be rescued. I'm so sorry. She's quite a tartar, your aunt, but a lovely woman all the same. Really."

"Don't be sorry, my lady," Burnell said, kissing her hand before releasing it. Reluctantly releasing it, Adam noticed. Sherry had that effect on men, and well he knew it. Once, a lifetime ago, he'd found that male reaction to his wife amusing. "But I must tell you that your honesty is refreshing. Your well-meant but truly transparent fib about my aunt, calling her a lovely woman, when we all know she's two steps from being an incorrigible horror, is beyond refreshing."

Adam watched as Sherry's cheeks turned a becoming pink. "I really should never lie, should I, Mr. Burnell? I'm shockingly bad at it."

"Oh, I don't know, darling," Adam slid in smoothly, just as smoothly taking her arm. "You're probably getting much better at it, with all the practice you've had. Being in Society, I mean."

He sensed Burnell looking at the two of them and wanted to kick himself. He should have known better than to play his and Sherry's destructive game in front of so astute an observer.

But Burnell rescued him neatly. "Good God, yes, Daventry. We all have to tell no end of lies in Society, don't we?" He pulled out his handkerchief, struck a dandified pose, and grinned down at Sherry. "What a fetching bonnet, Lady J," he drawled smoothly. "So original, what with all those green cherries hanging from it to bang against your nose with every step you take."

He turned to Adam, employing the handkerchief again as he performed an elegant leg. "Indeed, yes, Your Highness, that horizontally striped waistcoat most definitely does become your handsome figure."

As Sherry giggled, Burnell pulled a quizzing-glass from its specially made pocket in his waistcoat and stuck it to his eye, looking off into a dark corner of the room. His nose wrinkled and his expression became discreetly shocked, so that Adam rubbed a finger beneath his own nose, trying not to laugh. "That's your wife over there, my lord Sanford?" Burnell continued. "Do tell. You don't say so. Lucky devil, you. Haven't seen such a lovely woman before, I vow it."

He gave an exaggerated shiver as he allowed the quizzing-glass to drop to his waist from the black riband he wore slung around his neck. He looked at Sherry again, winking. "And we all know there's so very *much* of Lady Sanford to *be* lovely, isn't there—almost as much of her as there is of our dear Prince of

Wales? Oh, the lies we all tell! I say to you, my lady, my lord, we should all race home each night and scrub out our mouths with soap."

"Thank you, Burnell," Adam said, and he believed the man knew precisely why he had been thanked. He really could like this man if he allowed himself to do so.

Burnell bowed again. "My pleasure, Daventry. Although now I suppose your truly wonderful wife will never believe that I am telling the truth when I say that I have been very pleased to make her acquaintance this evening."

Sherry's musical laugh helped lead them all to the door and down the hall, where a footman, probably already alerted by her, waited with their wraps. "It has been wonderful meeting you, Mr. Burnell," she said as she raised her hands to her shoulders, pulling her fur-lined cape more closely around her. "Adam? Shouldn't you be running off upstairs, to say good night to Lady J? I'll be fine, waiting here."

"Don't bother," Burnell told Adam, who had turned to head for the stairs. "She's probably already snoring in her chair, as she had her share of wine with dinner." He smiled at Sherry. "My goodness, this honesty of yours must be catching, my lady. I shouldn't have said that, should I? Well enough. Allow me to escort you to your coach. Daventry, if it wouldn't be a bother, would you think to accompany me tomorrow as I hunt out a new tailor? My last one leaves a lot to be desired in the cut of the shoulders, and he's entirely too devoted to buckram padding."

"I wish I could, Burnell," Adam said, finding himself in the position of following along like some not quite lost sheep as Burnell and his wife headed toward the street. "But I'm afraid I'm already committed to meeting with a friend who's coming back to town tomorrow. Another day?"

Burnell stood with Sherry as a footman lowered the steps to the coach. "Another day would be quite fine. But now I'm at loose ends tomorrow, which won't do at all, as my aunt was mumbling something about a day of lending libraries and such. My lady—would you be so kind as to rescue me? We could go for an early-afternoon drive?"

Sherry's gaze flew to Adam's face, but he refused to so much as blink to give her any indication of how he felt about such an invitation. In truth, he didn't know how he felt about it. The man was amusing and hardly seemed dangerous. But Richard Brimley hadn't looked dangerous.

As Sherry hesitated, Adam at last gave a slight nod of his head, at which time she told Burnell she'd be delighted to accompany him if the weather stayed fine.

"That's settled then, for it won't dare rain and spoil our outing," Burnell said, as Sherry stepped into the coach. "Daventry," he said, holding out his hand, giving Adam's a firm shake. "I've enjoyed the evening immensely. I consider myself to live a charmed life, coming to London one week, meeting you and your dear wife the next. In fact, taking into consideration the notion that I should otherwise have Lady J bear-leading me through London this next month, I probably should be kneeling at your feet. Yes, I would kneel there, babbling in all but incoherent gratitude. But you wouldn't ask that of me, I know, for I'd dirty my knees, wouldn't I?"

"Idiot," Adam replied, laughing. Relaxing. "Tell you what, Burnell. Have your drive with my wife, and then meet my friend and me at the Oxford Arms at three. It's in Warwick Lane, quite near St. Paul's. Horrible place, but my friend has some sentimental attachment to it, makes it a point to visit there at least once whenever he's in town."

"I'll do just that, and thank you. Good night," Burnell said, and closed the door behind Adam as he sat himself down on the seat facing his wife.

The coach drove off.

"Why did you indicate that you wanted me to ride out with Mr. Burnell?" Sherry asked, tugging on the tips of her gloves, obviously so that she wouldn't have to look at Adam.

"Why not?" Adam said, leaning back against the cushions and sliding the brim of his hat down low over his eyes. "He's handsome, convenable, clever. He seems clean enough. At least, this way, I get to choose who sleeps in my wife's bed."

Sherry's quick, sharp intake of breath sliced through him like a knife.

"I could kill you for saying that," she nearly hissed. "Don't dare come into my rooms tonight, Adam. I'm warning you. Don't take that chance. I've traveled a long way from the silly child in love I was last spring, to a woman pushed into giving pain as well as feeling it."

"Child, in love. Woman, threatening mayhem. I understand, darling, and I consider myself fairly warned," Adam drawled, hating himself, wanting her. "After all, as you say—oh, so often—you only speak the truth."

"And you hear only lies."

"I believe only what I see," Adam shot back before he could will himself silent. "I heard the lies—even read one of them, didn't I? I *saw* the truth."

"Dickie—"

"Don't!" Adam shot forward on the cushion, his hands braced on its edge on either side of him. He relaxed his grip, took a steadying breath. "Don't," he repeated softly, nearly trembling with sudden passion, a passion alive with hate, born of pain. "Don't ever say his name. Do you understand that? Don't say the man's name. Lie for him, Sherry, cry for him, be glad he left you to face me alone like the coward he was—because I would have murdered him. But . . . don't . . . say . . . his name."

He watched as she sat very still, very straight, her eyes wide, her cheeks pale. He'd gone too far this time, said things they'd only hinted at before, never put into words. If he could draw them back, he would. Cut out his tongue. But he'd said them, said them all tonight for some unfathomable reason. He couldn't take them back. He could only sit, and wait, and call himself seven kinds of bastard.

"You never loved me. Not really. You couldn't

have," she said quietly. "Dickie was an excuse. Even Geoff is an excuse, your own brother. You're using them, both of them. My God, Adam, how satisfying it must be always to be right, never be wrong. Never to make a mistake, never have to listen to anyone else's definition of reason. But you made one mistake in your enviable life, Adam, didn't you? Just that one mistake. Marrying me. What a pity you had to do that, Adam. It's all that stiff-backed honor of yours. If you'd felt you could have had me without marriage, it would have been better for—"

She tilted her head back against the velvet cushions, staring blindly at the roof of the coach. He could see the line of her throat. The vulnerable line of her throat as it worked silently, swallowing tears, swallowing whatever else she wanted to say.

"God, Sherry, what a mess we've made." Adam turned and opened a small, square door that gave access to the driver. "Stop here, Fitzhugh. I've decided to walk." A moment later he was standing on the cobblestones in the dark, his hands drawn up into fists at his sides, watching the coach carrying his wife disappear into the dark.

"Emma? Have you any idea as to the whereabouts of my new gloves?"

"Is I supposed ta?"

Sherry sighed, turned away from the drawer she was in the midst of rearranging from the tangled heap it was into a new, yet-still-tangled design, and looked at her lady's maid.

"There's something not quite right here, Emma," she said, pushing back an errant lock of her bothersome mop of hair. "I do believe I should be sitting on that bench, admiring my stylish self, and you should be over here, looking for my gloves. I may be wrong, but I don't believe so. Do you?"

Emma Oxton pulled a face at her own reflection, laid down Sherry's brush—the one she'd been pulling through her own golden curls—and swiveled on the bench. "I suppose not, ma'am," she said, sighing as she reluctantly rose. "I'm supposin' I should be huntin' up the gloves, ta yer way of thinkin'. Huntin' up the shoes. Huntin' up the handkerchiefs. Huntin' up—"

"Hunting up a broom and a mop?" Sherry suggested, then smiled as she saw the gloves she'd been looking for lying on her writing table in front of the window. "Ah," she declared, swooping across the room and grabbing them up, "you can sit back down, Emma, and continue with whatever it was you were doing. You were doing something, weren't you?"

"Yes, ma'am," Emma said, already seated once more. "I was about to do up m'nails, as it were. Wouldn't want ta scratch yer pretty head when I washes yer hair, ain't that so? Snag at yer hose when I'm turnin' it back rightways after his lordship strips it off yer—not that he don't ruin at least two or more a week, don't he, ma'am?"

"That will be enough, Emma," Sherry said, avoiding the young maid's eyes. "You may retire now."

Once the servant was gone, probably to her own room, where she would sit and stare into her own mirror—the hand mirror she'd boldly taken from her mistress—Sherry slumped onto the side of the bed and put her head in her hands.

She should turn Emma out, sack her, send her on her way without a character. That's what she should do. But she couldn't. Because Emma *knew*. Emma saw the room in the mornings, after Adam had gone. Emma had seen the faint bruises Sherry could never remember receiving as she and Adam loved so furiously, with such intensity, such burning desire to possess each other without any betraying tenderness.

Emma didn't share what she knew with the other servants. She cleaned up the worst of it, the most betraying of it, only saying enough to show that she knew what went on in this room during the dark of the night. And left the rest a shambles.

Sherry was now, as she had been at home before her marriage, in charge of her own wardrobe, her own rooms. Where Mary had been too old, gone beyond doing most work, Emma was young, and unwilling to work. Sherry hadn't minded protecting Mary until the old woman finally realized she was "past it, missy," and went to live with her sister in Dorset. She did mind doing Emma's work. She did mind the implied threat in Emma's growing insolence, her remarks that were much too familiar.

But keeping Emma was easier than letting Emma go and admitting another servant into the rooms, into the horrible little secret that had become Sherry's life, Adam's life.

"Well, this is getting you precisely nowhere," she

told herself bracingly as she stood up and walked to the door. "And the sunshine and Mr. Burnell are waiting."

Sherry tipped back her head, looking up at the sun through the tracery of leaves above her. How pretty it was, so close to London, and yet so wonderfully removed from it at the same time. It wasn't precisely as if she and Edmund Burnell were having themselves a private picnic, but he had spied out the small country tavern sitting just above them, on a slight rise. He had prevailed upon the tavern keeper's wife to provide them with a bottle of wine, two thick, utilitarian glasses, a loaf of bread, and a fat wedge of cheese, then suggested they dine in the open air.

The carriage blanket served very well, spread out across the ground beneath the trio of trees they sat beneath now and, even if the day was chilly, her fur-lined wrap was warm, the sun even warmer. The whole thing was just silly enough to please her, just friendly enough to take her mind, at least temporarily, away from thoughts of Adam and his barbed remarks, his disdain, his distaste—even as he made love to her.

And Edmund Burnell was amusing; he made her laugh. It was so good to laugh again. She needed, almost desperately, to laugh again.

". . . and so I simply raised my nose to a most superior angle—I have the sort of nose for such maneuvers, I'm sure you'll agree—and looked down the length of it as I said, 'My dear, good man. I do believe you're standing on my foot.' "

"You didn't!" Sherry took another small sip of wine. "With him being so frighteningly toplofty? I shouldn't have dared, even if he was crushing my toes. And what on earth did Mr. Brummell say to that? Did he deal you the cut direct—look you up and down, then turn and walk away without a word?"

"On the contrary, my lady." Burnell smiled, a mischievous twinkle in his blue eyes. "He paused in his conversation with the Prince Regent, looked down, saw that, indeed, he was standing on my foot. Beau— I have his permission to call him Beau now, so lovely of the man, don't you think—then leaned toward me and whispered the recipe for his special boot black into my anxious, trembling, and eternally grateful ear."

He emptied his glass and poured himself another measure. "I can't tell you of course. I've been sworn to secrecy. A matter of honor between gentlemen, and all that." He held up the bottle, measuring its contents. "Would you care for more wine before it's gone?"

"You're fibbing," Sherry said, holding out her glass to him. "That never happened, none of it." She looked at him over the rim as she raised the glass to her lips, tipped her head to one side as she examined his face, as if that would help her to see inside his mind. "Did it?"

"Did it?" Burnell teased, cutting her a small wedge of cheese, then pointing to the bread, so that she shook her head, declining that second offer to feed her. "I'm sure I couldn't say. It's that sworn to secrecy thing again, you understand. A pity, especially when forced to hide something from a lady, but there it is. Unavoidable."

Sherry tucked her skirts more tightly around her bent legs and leaned back against the tree trunk. "Very well, then, I have a story for you as well."

"A *true* story? Or am I about to be taken in like a green goose?"

"Of course it's a true story. Now, don't interrupt, all right?" She took a deep breath, held it as she bit her lip, her gaze directed upward as she marshaled her thoughts. "Where to begin? Ah, I have it! I'll begin at the beginning, all right?"

"It seems as good a place as any," Burnell agreed, stretching himself out on his side, his legs dangling off the edge of the blanket, onto the dry, overgrown grass, his head propped in his hand as he bent his elbow. "Begin, madam, and I shall stop you if I have any questions."

Sherry nodded her agreement. "Very well, then. This is a story about my cousin, Little Harry. You'd like Little Harry, Mr. Burnell, he's quite silly."

"Indeed. And I would like him because he's silly, or because we have so much in common?"

Sherry felt herself coloring to the roots of her hair. "Oh, dear. A little of both, I suppose. Now, where was I?"

"About to begin, as I recall," Burnell said, smiling up at her.

"All right. Harry is older than I, by two years, but we always played together as children whenever Aunt Louise and Uncle Giddy-up visited. Well, one day—"

"Uncle *Giddy-up?* Oh, dear lady, please, I beg you. You must draw back from your story about the estimable Harry, and tell me how your uncle came by that name."

Shrugging her agreement, as one story was as good as another, she began, "It was spring, I remember, and I was four. No. Five. It doesn't matter, really, as I'm told I was always disgustingly precocious, even in my cradle." She took another sip of wine, as storytelling could be dry work. "At any rate, it was spring, and I had outrun my nanny and taken off into the woods. Everyone, including Uncle Harry—he was called Uncle Harry then—went off to search for me, sure I would have fallen into a pit or been carried off by Gypsies. Mama was frantic."

"Mamas tend to be frantic. It's a part of their nature," Burnell said, deftly tipping the last of the wine into Sherry's glass.

"If you're going to interrupt me every two seconds . . ."

"A thousand apologies, my dear lady. A million, should you wish it. Shall I cut out my tongue?" He put out his free hand and began searching the folds in the blanket. "I know there's a knife lying around here somewhere. Just a moment, and the deed will be done. Although I warn you, you may not want to watch."

"Wretch." Sherry giggled, quickly locating the knife stuck into the wedge of cheese and holding both above her head, where he couldn't reach. Her nose was growing numb and she put it down to the chill in the air. Which, of course, did nothing to explain how numb her gums and teeth were getting as well. Perhaps she should have eaten more bread, drunk less wine, received more easy affection from her husband so that Edmund's kindness didn't make her desperate heart so happy.

"Now listen," she warned, lowering her voice to heighten the drama of her tale. "I was out there—somewhere. It was growing dark. My parents, everyone, was growing frantic. Mama was crying into her handkerchief. Papa had sent someone off to fetch an article of my clothing, planning to shove it in front of the hounds' noses and set them loose to find me. Which launched Mama into complete hysterics when Uncle Harry said how lovely that would be, as when the hounds found me and ripped my little body into shreds Papa could then cut off my ears and tail and present them to his sobbing sister. My mother, that is. Her hysterics doubled, then doubled again, and Papa, who never really cared for Uncle Harry, turned the air blue with his curses. I saw and heard it all, up there in the branches of the tree where I had climbed hours earlier, then fallen asleep in the crook of two large branches. Their voices woke me."

"You were frightened?"

She shook her head. "I was *angry.* Uncle Harry had made Mama cry. So, seeing as I'd already slept past my tea, and was prodigiously hungry as well as exceedingly angry, I made my presence known and insisted that dear, dear, Uncle Harry be the one who lifted me down from my perch." She smiled at the memory of the rather squat, definitely portly man as she had jumped down, into his arms, nearly sending the two of them crashing to the ground.

"Then, after Mama had done with kissing me, and Papa had done with saying the hounds would, too, have found me as I'd already been good and treed, I insisted that I would only be happy if Uncle Harry put me up on his shoulders and *carried* me all the way home, playing horsy with me, as he had done once or twice before, always under duress. But he had done it. He did it again that day, after Mama told him he'd never slide his feet under her dinner table again if he refused me."

"So, you *rode* Uncle Harry all the way home," Burnell said, grinning. "A fitting punishment for having upset your mama."

"All the way home," Sherry repeated, closing her eyes and reliving those childishly wonderful moments. "I dug in my heels from time to time, used a slender stick I found in my hair as a whip, and called out 'giddy-up, giddy-up' every time he flagged in the slightest. Papa was so happy with me he gave me my very own hound. And the poor man has been Uncle Giddy-up ever since. Although he never visited quite so often after that, but just sent Little Harry along on his own."

"A fine story."

"No, it's not. Not really. It was a silly story. But at least mine was true. Mr. Beau Brummell telling you the secret of his boot polish? I daresay that's what tipped me off, you know. He'd never do such a thing. You should be ashamed of yourself."

"And yet I'm not. Not in the slightest," Burnell said, helping Sherry to her feet, then bending to gather the remains of their impromptu picnic. "I'm the very Devil that way."

Sherry picked up the blanket and shook it a time or two before folding it. "Ha! The Devil is it?" She turned to look at her companion. So handsome, so blond, so very kind and approachable. "You don't have the look of the Devil, Mr. Burnell. No horns."

"I sent them out to be polished," he told her as they walked back to the finely crafted curricle.

"And your tail?"

"My tail? The Devil has a tail? Must be horribly inconvenient."

Sherry giggled. "I agree. How does one sit, with a tail?"

"Gingerly?" Burnell suggested, helping her up onto the bench seat. "But I am the Devil."

"Certainly you are," Sherry said, pushing at her skirts so that he could sit beside her. "Tell me, Mr. Devil, just what is it you do? I've always wondered."

"I enjoy myself, mostly," he answered as he urged the horses forward, back toward the road, and London.

It may have been the wine, or the pleasant afternoon, or the fact that she'd had so little to laugh at recently. Sherry wasn't sure. But she most certainly was enjoying herself. "And how does the Devil *enjoy* himself?"

He smiled at her, his blue eyes dancing. "You'll recall the recent revolution in France?"

"I do," Sherry answered, trying and failing to maintain a sober expression. "*You* did that?"

"I did. I consider it to be some of my best work," Burnell said, winking at her.

Laughter bubbled up inside Sherry, found its way out. "I shouldn't laugh. Those were terrible times in France, even if we're almost always at war with them now."

"That, too."

"What, too? Oh! You mean you're responsible for wars, too? Now you're being ridiculous. Soon you'll be telling me you started the Great Fire."

"No, sad to say, I can't claim that one. The fire began all by itself, in a small bakehouse, I understand. Farriner was the man's name, if I'm recalling the incident correctly," he said as they neatly feathered a corner and Sherry held on for dear life as a curricle coming the other way all but touched wheels with theirs. "Cow-handed idiot," Burnell said, his pleasant voice suddenly ice-hard with anger. "He'll lose a wheel on the next turn and end in a ditch, I can promise you that. Are you all right?"

"I'm fine," Sherry said, but some of the fun and nonsense had gone out of the afternoon. That had been young Baron Gilesen in the curricle, a friend of Geoff's. She'd recognized him in the brief seconds the two vehicles had come close together; she'd seen the moment of fear in his eyes, quickly replaced with the thrill of having so nearly avoided an accident. Like the baron, Geoff had taken a turn too fast, lost a wheel, and ended in a ditch. "But there is no rush to get back to Grosvenor Square, Mr. Burnell. We don't have to fly quite so fast."

He looked at her for a long moment, then eased the horses into a near walk. "How can you ever forgive me?" he asked, laying a hand on hers. "Your husband told me how Lord Dagenham came to be injured. I shouldn't have said anything about a wheel. And I certainly should have been paying closer attention. You've got to be terrified of speed."

Sherry looked down at her hands as they rested in her lap, Edmund Burnell's gloved hand lying on top. "Yes," she said, uncomfortable for the first time since Edmund Burnell had shown up in her drawing room, a bouquet of blush pink roses in his hand, a friendly smile on his face. Was he attracted to her? She didn't think that would be wise, for either of them. "I do like it much better when things move more slowly. I've found that decisions made in haste often are not the right ones, for anybody."

"Of course, my lady," Burnell said, removing his hand as they crested a low hill and began a careful descent. "Ah—look. London awaits. You'll be home and warm shortly, and I'll be on my way to the Oxford Arms to meet the marquess and his friend."

Grateful for this kind offer of safe conversation, Sherry smiled, saying, "Mr. Collin Laughlin. I'm so glad he's come back to town, if only for Adam's sake. You'll enjoy Chollie. He's, well, he's rather unique."

"How so?" Burnell asked, as the countryside dissolved into the lumpy, bumpy outskirts of London.

"Oh, dear. How should I say it so that I don't sound

mean?" Sherry said consideringly, her own eyes twinkling. "I've got it. Let's just say that if you were to tell *Chollie* that you were the Devil, *he'd* believe you."

Burnell's smile, for all his handsome face, appeared absolutely and most endearingly devilish. "Oh, this will be fun, won't it?"

"Poor Chollie. I shouldn't have said anything, should I? Be kind," Sherry warned, then ruined everything by following her warning with a giggle.

"I'm always kind," he answered, and Sherry's smile slid away.

"You seem to be, Mr. Burnell," she said, her now-quite-familiar unhappiness sliding over her shoulders, chilling her as the curricle drove through the shadow of a building placed very near the roadway. "And I thank you for it. I've had a lovely afternoon."

"Next time perhaps we can take my aunt's coach, and Lord Dagenham might join us?"

"Oh, could he? Thank you so much!" Sherry put her hands on Burnell's forearm, giving it a squeeze. How silly she'd been, to think that Edmund Burnell had been flirting with her. He had just been being kind, and had just offered to be kinder still.

And she liked him. She liked him very much. She couldn't allow Richard Brimley to color her life, how she looked at the rest of the world in general or Edmund Burnell in particular. That wasn't fair.

"Shall we do this again two days from now, if the weather stays fair?" she suggested, feeling guilty. "I should be able to bully Geoff into an outing by then."

Burnell agreed, and Sherry soon found herself back

in Grosvenor Square, deliciously sleepy thanks to the wine and the brisk breeze. Taking up the vase of blush pink roses Rimmon had left in the foyer—far be it from Emma to consider it her duty to carry the vase upstairs—she climbed the stairs, deciding a short nap to be just the thing before dinner.

How silly she'd been to think, even for a moment, that Edmund Burnell had been flirting with her. He was just kind. Friendly. Her husband's friend. He saw her as Adam had done in the beginning—as a child to be amused, to amuse in return.

Yes, he'd teased her, especially when he'd given her these perfect roses. What had he said? Oh, yes. "Until this moment, my lady, as I see your simple joy in them, it has astounded me that God should waste such beauty as these roses on mere mortals. And yet even their beauty pales beside yours."

She'd nearly begged off from their ride then, frightened by his words, until he'd smiled broadly and added: "There, now that we've gotten that mandatory social silliness out of the way, shall we go enjoy ourselves?"

Sherry smiled as she remembered Edmund Burnell's smile, his playful wink. Adam had gained a new friend, and she had as well. She was badly in need of friends.

Placing the vase on the night table beside her bed, the heady fragrance of roses enveloping her, Sherry closed her eyes and drifted off to sleep. . . .

The eyes see the open heaven,
the heart is intoxicated with bliss . . .
                              —Johann von Schiller

Chapter Four

It was like a dream, being inside Daventry Court. A fairy tale. Such beauty, such order, such a feeling of stepping from the mundane, everyday world and into a fantasy land where time stood still, where the outside world went away, leaving only those favored creatures allowed inside its portals.

Leaving only Adam Dagenham, Marquess of Daventry.

Sherry had thought of him all that afternoon. How handsome he was. How friendly. How he had looked at her with those dark, brooding eyes that seemed to reach deep inside her, to her heart, her soul.

She'd made a hideous fool of herself, of course, behaving like a hoyden with no sense of who he was, of the respect his station, his very bearing, demanded.

Had she really pushed the Marquess of Daventry into the stream? Oh, she had, she had! And then she'd handed him her petticoat, which had been beyond anything stupid. Childish.

And yet?

And yet he had seemed to enjoy her company, had even invited her father and her silly self to dinner tonight.

How she'd badgered poor old Mary all the afternoon, trying on and discarding a half dozen gowns and finding none of them suitable, and all of them too childish by half. She'd insisted on rosewater for her bath, and she and Mary had taken turns scrubbing her hair with the finest soaps until it squeaked as Sherry pulled her fingers through the long tresses now piled on top of her head, straining to be released from the combs that held the hopefully sophisticated upswept creation in place.

Mary said she looked slap up to the echo, as fine as any London lady, but Sherry wasn't so sure. She wore no lip rouge, no paint on her cheeks, no fine diamonds in her ears. Her ivory gown was provincial in the extreme, with a neckline much too high and a hem that totally hid her ankles. She looked what she was, a country miss who'd never had a Season, a child who was noticeably lacking in town bronze.

So what was she doing here, surrounded by beautiful furniture, fine portraits, vases filled with roses cut from the marquess's own gardens? She didn't belong here. She'd bore the worldly marquess to flinders inside of a minute.

"Papa—don't do that. Behave yourself," she warned in an almost violent whisper as she turned away from the mirror in the Daventry drawing room, disappointed in her reflection, and saw her father hefting a vase in his hand, as if considering its weight and worth. "The marquess will be joining us any moment."

Stanley Victor pulled a face at his daughter, but dutifully replaced the delicate vase. "Made 'em in China eons ago, make 'em now in some county up north or so," he said, interlacing his fingers, then pushing them away from his body so that Sherry could hear each of his big knuckles crack in turn. "Just wanted to see if it were the genuine article. Your mama taught me that trick, looking for marks and such on the bottom, feeling the weight. Could buy a fine pack of hounds for the price of this useless bit of plaster here. Pity."

As Stanley Victor measured everything in hounds, Sherry only nodded and tried to engage her father in conversation more suited to the evening. "Are you hungry, Papa? I'm sure you'll enjoy your dinner," she said, hoping against hope he wouldn't tuck his serviette into his collar or find it necessary to compliment his host's gastronomic offerings with more than two or three discreet belches. She loved her father dearly, but even her mother had said the man had the table manners of a pig bumped up to the trough.

"Hungry, is it, missy? Starved half to death is more like it. Look at that, gel," he demanded, pointing to the mantel clock. "It's already marched past five-thirty. The marquess can't be a hunt man. Any fellow of sense knows we have to sit down within the minute if I'm to finish in time to get my rest and be up with the boys."

The "boys," Stanley Victor's hounds, rose at four, baying and yapping and generally letting the world know it was time for them either to be fed or gotten ready to chase a poor fox across the countryside. This explained why Sherry, whose rooms overlooked the kennels, usually slept with a pillow clapped over her head. She liked the boys, truly she did, but there were days she wished her father were more devoted to fishing than hunting. Fishing was bound to be quieter.

"I'm sure His Lordship will join us shortly," she said now, then turned as she heard footsteps in the hallway. A moment later, a nervous smile pinned to her face and her hands fully occupied with trying to find a place to put themselves that wouldn't look either gauche or idiotic, she watched as a handsome young man entered the room.

"Adam, I don't see why I should be dragged into this bound to be stultifying din—" the young man began, then stopped dead, staring at Sherry. "Well, hello there, dear lady," he went on quickly, recovering nicely, if she didn't count the embarrassed rush of color in his cheeks.

A moment later her hand was lifted to within an

inch of the young man's kiss, then held for a few seconds before he released her. "Dear lady, I am Dagenham, for my sins, and you must be Miss Charlotte Victor. M'brother failed to mention that he'd invited an angel to dine with us, a goddess. Our humble home is more than honored, and I shall have to slay my brother at once, for seeing you first."

He then turned to bow to Stanley Victor, who was looking the stylishly dressed young man up and down with a fairly baleful eye and a slightly curled lip. "Greetings, good sir," he continued, his voice full of fun, of joy and mischief. "You must be my assignment for the evening. How jolly. Would you care for a drink? Lemonade for you, Miss Victor, of course."

"A drink, is it?" Stanley Victor blustered. "Now there speaks a man of sense, even if he does dress like a popinjay. Oh, close your mouth, Sherry, I'm not going to say anything to put you to the blush. Boy knows he looks like a popinjay. He'd have to, stands to reason. Probably even does it on purpose, thinks himself to be right pretty. Don't you, boy?"

"I often find myself to be adorable, yes," His Lordship answered, winking at Sherry, so that she no longer felt as if she had to grab hold of her father, stuff her reticule into his mouth, and drag him back to Frame Cottage.

She watched as the elegant Lord Geoffrey Dagenham strolled to the drinks table, silently marveling at the dangerous height of his shirt points, the intricacy of his cravat. He poured out two glasses of wine and her lemonade, then served them to his guests, his tongue still behaving as if it were hinged at both ends as he prattled on about the weather, his own hounds, the tour of the Daventry kennels he would give her papa after dinner— all seemingly without taking a breath.

He was a handsome young man, almost classically so. His smile was Adam Dagenham's smile, his eyes, although lighter in color, held the same twinkle. His form, tall and muscular, mimicked that of the marquess, and his hair, dark blond to his brother's black, displayed the same tendency to wave, to resist attempts to keep one unruly lock from falling forward onto a smooth forehead.

He was also nearer her age, probably splitting the difference between hers and his brother's. He was still young enough to be silly, to be amused by her unsophisticated ways. Handsome and witty enough to turn any female head, win any female heart. She liked him immediately, was not in the least in awe of him, and felt she could hold her own with him in any conversation. He didn't frighten her, as the marquess frightened her, intrigued her.

And yet Sherry could only see him as a slighter, paler imitation of the marquess. He didn't make her heart skip when he looked at her. Her stomach didn't do a small somersault when he bent over her hand. Her knees didn't turn to jelly at the sight of his smile, the sound of his laugh.

How odd.

Fortunately for Sherry's still-jangled nerves, by the time the marquess entered, apologizing for being late even as he shook hands with her father, Lord Dagenham and Stanley Victor were deep in conversation centering on the "boys," and her father was too busy to disgrace himself further with remarks about the lateness of his dinner.

Unfortunately, also for Sherry's still-jangled nerves, that left her and the marquess quite alone together as they sat near each other on matching couches—she waiting for some kind soul to announce dinner before her heart stopped completely.

The silence in their corner of the drawing room was deafening as Daventry sipped from his wineglass, looked at her over the rim.

She put down her own glass, aware that it was either be rid of the thing or risk spilling lemonade all over her gown. Did he have to look quite so intense? Half so handsome in his dark blue evening dress? So very different from the laughing man who'd just this afternoon sat rump-down in the stream, then used her petticoat to wipe at a smudge on his cheek?

"You're frightened to death, aren't you, Miss Victor?" he said at last. "Why?"

Another young woman might have laughed off his question, or gone racing from the room, crying. Most every other young woman would have dissembled, lied to him, told him he was mistaken, that she wasn't in the least frightened. Frightened? How silly! Why on earth would she be frightened?

"I'm terrified, actually," Sherry answered honestly, dredging up all of her courage so that she looked the marquess straight in the eye. "As to why, my lord, I should think that's obvious. I don't have the slightest idea why I'm here, or what to say. I may even use the wrong fork at dinner." At this embarrassing thought, she leaned forward slightly, anxiously, to add: "There won't be more than three, will there? Mrs. Forrest taught me what to do with three, but beyond that, I'm afraid, I would totally disgrace myself in front of your very proper servants."

The marquess nodded quite solemnly. "Yes, I see your problem, Miss Victor. We can't have that, can we? I know. I'll have the servants shot."

Sherry looked at him for a long moment, then burst into laughter. "Idiot!" she exclaimed, forgetting all over again that this was the important, powerful marquess of Daventry. "We should only have them face the wall, as so not to witness my faux pas. Shooting them is probably unnecessary, although I must thank you for the offer."

"Ah, there we go," Adam Dagenham said, his smile filling her near to bursting with an emotion she found impossible to name, although it was definitely a very nice emotion. "For a moment I thought I'd dreamed our meeting earlier today. Call me a gudgeon, Miss Victor, and I'll be convinced it really did happen."

She picked up the ends of the ribbons tied beneath her bodice and wrapped them around her finger, avoiding his eyes. "I can't do that, my lord," she said, her head bowed as she bit her lip, refusing to giggle at his nonsense. "These surroundings and your title forbid me."

She felt him move closer as he rose from the couch and pulled a low footstool forward, sitting down beside her. "Then I'll burn down these forbidding surroundings," he said, taking her hands in his, rubbing his thumbs across the back of her fingers. "I'll renounce my title and fortune to Geoff over there, although he'd run through every last penny within a fortnight. I'll live beside the stream, and you can come visit me every day, bringing me your smile, your laughter. And perhaps a crust of bread," he added, chuckling, "as I'd probably be starving."

Sherry raised her gaze, unable to look at his hands on hers any longer, unwilling to think how easy it would be to raise their clasped hands, to lay her cheek against his tanned skin. "I think you may be insane, my lord," she said, whispering the words.

"Oh, Miss Victor, I'm convinced of that," he answered just as quietly. "It's a sudden madness that settled on me just today. Isn't it wonderful?"

Wonderful. A lovely description, if incomplete. Frighteningly wonderful was probably more exact, or at least that was the conclusion Sherry reached during dinner. Her father, never shy, dominated the conversation, as she picked at course after course, until the entire parade of elegant foodstuffs was finished and His Lordship suggested Lord Dagenham and her father go straight to the kennels to inspect a new litter of hounds.

"You could be a little more subtle, brother," Lord Dagenham said as Sherry blushed to the roots of her hair—she really had been doing that a lot today. "However, as I'm finding myself unmanned by your mooncalf ways, I believe it's probably for the best that I take dear Mr. Victor away. You're embarrassing, old son, really you are. Miss Victor," he said, bowing, "my condolences. Don't let him drool on you, all right?"

"Eh?" Stanley Victor grunted. He looked to the marquess, then to his daughter, and shook his head, dismissing whatever thought had tried to enter it. "No. Couldn't be," he said, oblivious to anything but his dogs, just as he ever was, then he shook his head again and followed after Lord Dagenham, asking him how many pups the bitch had birthed.

"Well, that was uncomfortable," the marquess said, waving away a footman and holding the chair for Sherry himself so that she could rise, then offering her his arm. "Shall we take a stroll in the gardens? The roses are particularly fine this year; unusually early, the gardeners tell me, and almost shamefully abundant. Perhaps you noticed a few in the drawing room?"

"A few? There were at least four vases of roses, as I recall," Sherry smiled up at him as he pushed open French windows leading to a wide flagstone patio. They'd have conversation now, she knew, and she'd probably embarrass herself, and him. After all, what did she have to say that could possibly interest a marquess, a gentleman used to London debutantes? She could only hope she didn't say anything *too* silly.

"Oh, my," she said a moment later, forgetting her fears as she let go of his arm and hastened to the stone stairs leading down to the gardens.

She tripped down the stairs, holding her skirts above her ankles, and took a half dozen steps into the rose garden, then turned to gaze up at the marquess. "I can't believe there are so many different roses in the whole world, yet alone in one garden. I've never seen . . . never imagined!"

She raced to her right, cupping an immense yellow bloom in her hands. "Why, it's as big as a dessert plate! And here," she said, her gaze falling on a bush nearly as high as she was, its inky dark leaves fitting frames for several dozen blooms as white as snow, each as perfect as a snowflake. "And over there," she continued, lost in the beauty that surrounded her inside the huge, walled garden, "that pink. I've never seen such a pink as that. This isn't just a garden, my lord. It's *paradise!*"

Adam Dagenham descended the steps slowly, his eyes never leaving Sherry's face, never looking at the flowers. Her heart stood still, waiting for him to take her hand, to lead her along the curved paths of the garden.

"Yes," she heard him agree as the buzzing in her

ears grew louder, as her heart pounded not in fear, but in anticipation. "That's just how I would have put it, Miss Victor. Paradise. A veritable Eden. And not a snake in sight. Shall we take that stroll now?"

I answer in the affirmative
with an emphatic "No."
    —Sir Boyle Roche

Chapter Five

Adam was late arriving at the Oxford Arms to meet his friends, and he was still frowning over the memory of Sherry's maid, Emma, as he'd last seen her in the upstairs hall in Grosvenor Square.

She had been carrying a full vase of roses, muttering under her breath as, ignoring him as he stepped out of her way, she headed toward the servants' staircase.

"Ringin' that bell, orderin' me ta take the flowers away. Like it was me what brung them up here? No. I didn't bring them. Think the woman was goin' ta have a liedown, give me some peace. But she rings that bell, then sits there all high-and-mighty in her bed, *orderin'* me to dump the posies in the rubbish . . ."

"Enjoying your own conversation, are you, Emma?" Adam had asked, eyeing the flowers as he stood in the hallway and carefully shot his cuffs. "Is something amiss with Her Ladyship?"

Emma's curtsy was more insolent than respectful, but Adam knew it would do no good to reprimand her. Emma Oxton was a law unto herself in Grosvenor Square, mostly because Sherry let the woman rule her rather than the other way around. He'd have had her gone in the first week, except that Sherry refused to acknowledge that her maid was insubordinate. And lazy into the bargain.

"She says what she don't like roses, m'lord," Emma said, holding out the heavy vase with both hands. "No need to cry about it, exceptin' that she is. I'm goin' now, to toss them in the rubbish."

Crying? Sherry had been crying? Adam reached out a hand to stroke one of the delicate pink blooms, his mind a jumble of memories, only some of them good. "I see," he said, not seeing at all. "Put them in my rooms, Emma, if you don't mind. It will save you a trip down the stairs. You'd like that, wouldn't you?"

The maid shrugged, looking incredibly sly for the lazy slattern she was. "Yes, that would work," she said, then turned on her heels to shamble off to Adam's chambers.

"A moment, Emma, if you would?" Adam called after her, so that the maid sighed audibly, then turned to glare at him. "There will be no more roses in Her Ladyship's chambers. No more roses in this entire household. All right?"

"Weren't me what gave 'em to her," Emma said. "You'd better be tellin' the one what did."

The "one what did," Adam had learned from Rimmon, was his new friend, Edmund Burnell. It had been a harmless enough gesture, Adam knew, as Burnell could have no idea that the roses, however beautiful, might have bothered Sherry. As they bothered him. Which was probably why he'd ordered the maid to put them in his chambers. As a reminder, perhaps even as a sort of penance.

Now, pushing all thoughts of roses and remorse from his mind, Adam pushed open the door of the Oxford Arms and stepped from the bright sunlight into the near dark of the inn, standing still for a moment until his eyes adjusted to the dimness.

"There you are, Adam. I knew I could count on you to get my note to meet here," he heard Collin Laughlin call out, and he turned to his right, heading for the table his friend had secured in the corner of the nearly deserted taproom.

Chollie was looking his same, cheerful Irish self as he had months earlier, when last Adam had seen him. His neckcloth was draped loosely around his throat, his cheeks were flushed, and his eyes shone bright— undoubtedly a result of having arrived earlier than Adam and already having begun some serious imbibing. Adam watched as Chollie shoved his gold-rimmed spectacles back up his nose and stood up, stretching out his arms to give him a hug.

Chollie was a hugging sort of man, which Adam wasn't, but he endured his friend's backslapping enthusiasm because he truly loved this man who had been his friend since Adam had met him at a boxing match ten years previously. He'd met Chollie because Chollie had been in the ring—until he'd been knocked out of it and onto Adam's lap by a wicked punch from some low-browed hulk named the Bruising Blue. Never was there a man less physically suited for the fancy as Chollie, what with his rail-thin body and shortsightedness. But Irish was Irish, and Chollie swore that all Irish were born mad as fire to be alive and therefore spent their lives looking for someone to punch.

"Ah, Adam, it's grand to be seeing you, it is," Chollie said as he retook his seat and gave a whistle to the barmaid, who came running up with another mug of strong ale. "Drink! Drink!" he commanded. "I'm miles ahead of you, you know, and we can't have that."

Adam did as he was bid, raising the mug and not lowering it again until its entire contents had been redeposited inside him. Wiping his mouth with the back of his hand, he grinned at Chollie, shaking his head. "God, man, but it's good to see you again. How was Ireland?"

"Still there, still oppressed by you bloody Englishers," Chollie answered with a wink. "It's thinking about mounting a rebellion I am, except that there's forty thousand others thinking the same thing and all of them wanting to lead the parade, so that we fight more amongst ourselves than we do against the rod lying over all our backs. So we drink, and we sing sad songs and wipe away a tear or two, then go back to drinking some more." He shrugged. "It's hard, boyo, being Irish. Very wet work. Alice! Another round, darlin', if you please!"

Adam knew that Chollie's banter hid a melancholy

heart, and he only nodded to his friend, then picked up his new mug and drank deeply. "This place is falling down, Chollie," he said, looking around the taproom after wiping his mouth once more. "I wouldn't be surprised to see it gone next time you come to London."

"True, true," Chollie answered, sighing. "But this lovely hovel has such a lot of Ireland about it, don't you know. I'll miss it." He noisily blew his nose, then rubbed at his moist eyes.

"You know what I think, Chollie?" Adam said, as Alice automatically replaced their mugs with new ones. "I think that for a race that says being born is a curse, you're still mighty glad to be Irish."

"Not a curse to be born, boyo, a disaster," Chollie said, putting away his handkerchief. "Being born's a calamity, marriage an anticlimax, and death looms ahead as a happy release. Nothing an Irishman loves better than a bruising good wake, don't you know. And speaking of marriage, boyo, how's that angel bride of yours? Couldn't be prettier if she was Irish."

Adam stared into the bottom of his empty mug.

"Oh-oh!" Chollie said, tipping his head to look at Adam. "I'm not liking that dark cloud I'm seeing over your head all of a sudden. What happened, I'd like to know. Last time I saw you, boyo, you were so full of April and May, the two of you. What did you do wrong?"

Adam lifted his head, smiling slightly as he looked at his friend. "What makes you think *I* did something wrong, Chollie?"

"Just stands to reason, I suppose. Being a bachelor

boy as long as you were, and all of that. You gave up that skirt in Covent Garden, I'm supposing, so that can't be it. You did give her up, didn't you?"

"I never *had* a skirt in Covent Garden, Chollie," Adam reminded his friend. "That was you, remember?"

Chollie pushed up his spectacles so roughly Adam was surprised he didn't knock himself over. "God's eyebrows, so I did! Lovely little colleen, with a wonderfully wicked way about her. I wonder if she's forgotten me. Lovely little colleen. And is it remembering her name you'd be, boyo, seeing as how I might need to know that if I think to go back to see her tonight?"

"Sheila," Adam provided obligingly, grateful to have the subject of his marriage abandoned for the moment. "But before you go running off to buy your way back into her good graces with some pearls or whatever, I ought to warn you that a friend will be joining us shortly."

"A friend?" Chollie looked around the taproom. "Here? Must be Irish. Wouldn't be another Englisher alive so little high in the instep as to agree to come to Warwick Lane for a pint."

"Edmund Burnell isn't at all high in the instep, Chollie, although he's definitely English. I'd appreciate hearing your opinion of the man once you two have met. Ah," Adam said, swiveling in his chair and motioning to the man who was standing in the doorway, removing his curly-brimmed beaver. "Here he is now. Behave, Chollie."

"And when do I misbehave, I ask you? Never mind,

boyo, as a litany of my sins would take longer than it takes for your new friend to thread his way through the tables. Big one, isn't he? Big as you, I'm thinking. You don't suppose he favors the fancy? I could do with a bit of bruising about."

"Asking a man if you can punch him is not behaving, Chollie," Adam pointed out, rising to his feet to extend a hand to Burnell as the handsome blond gentleman approached, smiling. "Burnell, good to see you found the place. I'd like to introduce you to my friend, Collin Laughlin. Chollie? Stand up and say hello to Edmund Burnell. Chollie?" he repeated when his friend remained seated, and silent.

"Mr. Laughlin?" Edmund Burnell said, offering his hand. "It's a distinct pleasure."

Adam watched as he put down his mug and stood, offering his hand. "Mr. Burnell," Chollie said, then sat back down again with a thump. He touched a hand to his waistcoat pocket where, Adam knew, Chollie always carried his lucky four-leafed shamrock tightly folded inside a leather pouch.

"Fingering your shamrock, Chollie?" Adam asked, trying not to smile. "Don't tell me you're getting fanciful on me. Last time you did that we ended drunk as goats and sprinkling holy water on our heads so the fairies wouldn't get us."

His friend glared at him for a moment, then turned to Burnell. "It's your pardon I'll be asking, sir, if I seemed rude just now. It's the strangest feeling I had, like I should know you, but I don't. Adam? Call for another mug, would you? Better yet, some brandy all around. Maybe that will open my brainbox."

"If it does, Mr. Laughlin, perhaps you can then open mine, as I really don't recall having made your acquaintance before today. Which is my loss, entirely," Burnell said, slipping out of his greatcoat. "Dashed cold out there, by the way. The sun's gone to hide behind some very threatening clouds, I'm afraid, and we'll probably have rain, or worse, before nightfall. So glad," he ended, turning to Adam, "your dear wife and I had sunshine enough for our drive earlier. I don't remember when I've last spent so enjoyable an hour."

"Two hours," Adam heard himself say, then mentally kicked himself, as Chollie was listening much too closely for his comfort. "And I thank you, as I believe she enjoyed your company as well. She most definitely enjoyed the roses you gave her."

"She did?" Burnell lifted the glass Alice had placed before him and took a sip of its contents. "I was lucky to find hothouse roses. I'll have to send more around tomorrow morning, to thank Her Ladyship for her company today."

"Yes, that would be nice," Adam said, wondering what had happened between Grosvenor Square and Warwick Street that he had suddenly turned so enthusiastically mean. Sherry hated roses now, that was clear, even though she had once adored the gardens at Daventry Court. Was he punishing her, or making sure she didn't take the handsome, likable Edmund Burnell in too much favor? It was a knotty question. "Chollie, did I tell you that Mr. Burnell is staying in town with Lady Jasper?"

"Lady J?" Chollie downed the measure of cheap brandy in one long swallow, smiled at Burnell with some sympathy. "Now that's a woman I *do* remember meeting. Never before met another woman who could so give me the fidgets. It's too late, then, to find yourself some lodgings of your own?"

"Chollie, Lady J is Burnell's aunt," Adam said warningly.

"Is she now?" Chollie, clearly unabashed by his candor, reached for his mug, chasing down the brandy with a swallow or two of ale. "Well, there's no picking your relatives, I always say. Sew your pockets up tight, Mr. Burnell, or else don't play cards with the woman."

"Spoken like a man who has sat at table with my inventive and yet excruciatingly inept aunt," Burnell said, laughing. "How badly did she burn you before she gave herself away?"

Chollie punched at his glasses, his cheeks coloring. "I'd rather not say," he mumbled, shamefaced. "Thought I'd lost my touch, until that ace popped up from her bodice when she took snuff and gave out with a healthy sneeze. No place to look without seeming the fool, you know, when you're trying not to look at some old lady's bosoms. It was a rare Johnny Raw I felt, agreeing to play against her when everyone else all but fell over themselves making excuses as to why they couldn't sit down with her."

"That's my aunt, Mr. Laughlin. Rich beyond anyone's dream, and yet still so greedy as to cheat at cards. Yet, even greed can be amusing, don't you think?"

"Funny as can be," Chollie agreed, "when Lady Greedy-guts is sitting across from anyone but *me*." Then he grinned, his manner becoming even more relaxed as Burnell returned his smile. "Are you in town for long, Mr. Burnell? I usually go about with Adam, here; but he's got himself a wife now, so I'd be pleased of the company if you'd thought to drop by, say, Covent Garden this evening?"

"It's Edmund, please, Mr. Laughlin," Burnell said, grabbing onto Alice as she approached the table to gather up the mugs once more, pulling her down into his lap. The barmaid giggled as he gave her a kiss on the cheek even as his arm came around her waist, his hand provocatively close to her ample breasts. "Covent Garden, you say? That sounds like a fine plan, if several hours in the future. But," he continued, walking his fingers up and over Alice's low-cut blouse, finding the strings that held it shut, "I imagine I can find some way to amuse myself in the interim."

" 'Ere, now," Alice protested, giggling as she slapped Burnell's hand away. "That costs extra, that does," she warned, halfheartedly pulling herself free of his grasp. "Coo, but yer a pretty one, ain't yer?" She ran a hand down the center of his chest, opening her mouth in a small "o" of appreciation and then running the tip of her tongue around her lips. "Free for yer, ducks. Jist give me a moment, awright?"

All three men watched the barmaid walk away, her swaying hips an open invitation. "No woman can resist me," Burnell said, apologetically spreading his arms. "It's because I'm so damnably pretty, I believe. Some might call it a curse."

"I doubt *you* do, Edmund," Chollie said, his own gaze appreciatively following Alice's retreat to the small serving bar in the corner. "You're a man after m'own heart, don't you know, and probably very handy to have around, drawing the females to you as you say. I like that, truly I do."

"Yes, Chollie, I'd somehow sensed that," Burnell said amicably, almost intimately, as he crossed his legs comfortably and leaned back in his chair. "Daventry? I don't suppose you'd want to join Chollie and me as we go off tonight to Covent Garden. I hope to sink ourselves into the depths of depravity—or at least to sink deep into *someone*?"

"Adam?" Chollie said incredulously. "With his lovely bride at home, waiting for him? You said you went driving with the marchioness today, Edmund. Surely you didn't spend all your time minding the horses. You *looked* at the woman, talked to her? Why, and it's lucky I feel to have the lovesick boyo show up here today to drink with his old friend, that's how little he likes being away from her side. Isn't that right, Adam?"

Damn Chollie for heading straight back to the conversation he'd tried so hard to leave before Edmund had shown up at the Oxford Arms. "Don't be indelicate, Chollie," he said warningly, feeling Burnell's interested gaze on him. "Besides, I was never one for

Covent Garden dancers or warblers, if you'll remember."

"Never one for—" Chollie began incredulously, then broke off, clearing his throat. "No, no, of course not. So we won't be seeing you, then?"

"No, Chollie," Adam said firmly, "you won't be seeing me. But you two go along, and try not to catch anything, all right?"

"But we will have dinner together first, won't we?" Burnell asked. "I had so wanted to continue our talk on the pitfalls of ambition, remember?" He turned to Chollie. "We were discussing Pope the other evening over drinks, you understand. Alexander Pope. You may remember that he wrote something about ambition being 'the glorious fault of angels and gods'?"

Chollie shook his head. "Why should I remember that, seeing as how I don't read anything unless it's got a listing of wines and prices on it. And why should angels and gods be ambitious? They can have anything they want, can't they? Angels and gods. What would they be ambitious *for?* Bigger wings? A cloud in a better neighborhood?" He looked to Adam. "Such nonsense. I don't understand you when you start talking deep, you know."

Adam did know that about Chollie, which was why he liked the man so much. Chollie was easy to be with, his simplicity refreshing in an intricate world. But he also liked Edmund Burnell, because he did also sometimes enjoy deeper conversation. And yet, unlike as the two men were, they seemed already to have found something in common—a love of enjoying a good drink and a willing woman. That, in fact, was the limit of Chollie's "ambition." Adam could only wonder, the unbidden thought coming up to trouble him, what was the limit of Edmund Burnell's.

"Oh, have yourself another mug, Chollie," Adam said, winking at Burnell. "We wouldn't want you to hurt your head with too much thinking."

"Then we won't be talking of ambition over dinner?" Chollie asked hopefully.

"Only my ambition to bed the prettiest warbler to grace the stage this evening," Edmund promised, pushing back his chair and rising to his feet even as he signaled to the barmaid, pointing toward the stairs. "And now, rude as it may be, I believe I have some pressing business to attend to, if you don't mind. Where and when shall we meet for dinner, gentlemen?"

"I never had Alice," Chollie said mournfully a few moments later, his gaze following Burnell up the stairs. "Irresistible, he says? Seems so. I can't decide whether to envy the man while I catch the ones he throws back tonight, or think I might not like him overmuch, pleasant as he seems to be. How long do you know him, Adam?"

"A few days," Adam answered carefully as the sound of a giggle, followed by the slamming of a door, reached down the stairs to them. "I found him to be amusing, and we've had a few talks, discussed the world, literature, politics. A very interesting, knowledgeable man. He admires my wife."

"Does he now?" Chollie said, pushing at his spectacles. "Imagine that. And do you?"

"Do I what?" Adam asked blankly, realizing that he had a headache. A very bad headache. A headache so sudden and intense that it hurt to think about Edmund Burnell, and how he was not today the same urbane, intelligent man he'd been the previous evening, but had presented himself as more earthy, perhaps even crude in his sexual desires. A headache so sharp and painful that he'd slipped, mentioned Sherry again.

Did it bother him that this new earthy Burnell so openly admired his unhappy wife? Should it? Had Burnell simply been bantering, teasing, or had he thrown down a gauntlet, warning Adam that he, the handsome, *irresistible* Edmund Burnell, was after his wife? Damn Richard Brimley. Damn the man to hell!

"Well? Are you going to answer me? It's a simple enough question, from a simple man. Do you admire your wife, Adam?"

"I value your friendship, Chollie. Don't make me say something better left unsaid. I'll see you both at dinner," Adam bit out shortly, then, suddenly in need of fresh air, he rose and walked out of the Oxford Arms without looking back.

Sherry stood at the doorway that led from her bed-chamber to Adam's, watching as he stood with his back to her. He was dressed only in shirt and breeches, his boots removed, his jacket, waistcoat, and cravat all tossed onto a nearby chair. He stood very still, staring down at the vase of roses she had banished from her rooms not two hours earlier.

Emma had told her he'd asked for them, of course.

Emma had a way of knowing what to say, how to hurt her. If she had ordered the roses gone, it only had to make sense to Emma that it would hurt her to know that Adam had rescued them from the rubbish heap.

Not that Adam seemed to be taking pleasure from the perfect blooms. He was scowling at them, in fact, so that Sherry was surprised they didn't wilt under his hot gaze.

She didn't like Adam much when he was angry, and she knew he was angry now, although she didn't know why. Angry, and yet also looking so incredibly sad. Defeated.

And she couldn't help him. She had told a single lie, a single small lie she believed to be in his best interests, in Geoff's best interests. One lie, amongst so much truth—a truth he refused to believe, whether she cried that truth to him, or yelled it at him at the top of her lungs.

He had trusted her, delighted in her honesty, had called it refreshing, had said it was one of the many reasons he had fallen in love with her. In love with her? No. Adam had never been in love with her. He'd been in love with love, that's all, in love with his image of what love should be.

Sherry's every nerve jumped as Adam suddenly swept out his arm, sending the vase of roses crashing to the floor, her involuntary sound of dismay betraying her presence even as she turned to flee back to her own rooms.

"No. Stay."

Adam hadn't shouted, but the command in his voice

stopped her. She squared her shoulders, turned to face him.

"I—I was only going to summon someone to clean up that mess," she said, wondering when she'd learn that she lied no better now than she ever had. "But I suppose I can do it. I'll just—"

"For God's sake, Sherry, stop babbling," Adam spat, running a hand through his hair, his dark eyes looking bruised, tortured. He walked over to the bed, sat down on the edge, dropped his head in his hands. "Christ, but my head hurts."

Sherry was shaken. She'd never seen Adam ill, looking any other way but strong, self-possessed, in total command of himself. She bit her lip, thinking to withdraw, then shook her head, knowing she couldn't leave him. Not like this.

She soaked a small towel in water she poured from the pitcher standing on a table in his dressing room, wrung it out tightly, then approached the bed, touching his shoulder. "Here," she said, holding out the towel. "Lie down, and I'll put this cloth on your head. It's cool, and might help soothe you." She caught the smell of strong spirits on his breath, and her lips tightened. "Perhaps if you didn't find it necessary to drink quite so much?"

Adam lifted his head and glared at her for a moment before snatching the towel from her hand. "Ah, yes, just what I needed. A soothing cloth, and a sermon on mending my wicked ways." He lay back on the bed, stretching out his long legs on the coverlet even as he pressed the cloth over his eyes.

Sherry turned to go, but Adam snaked out a hand and caught her wrist. "No. I said I want you to stay."

"Adam, I—"

"Please, Sherry," he said, his eyes hidden by the cloth, but the tightening of his jaw, and the unnatural paleness of his complexion frightening her. Was he simply drunk, or was he really ill?

"All right, Adam," she said, sitting down on the side of the bed as he released her wrist only to hold on to her hand. "For a moment, until you fall asleep."

He didn't speak again, but only began stroking the back of her hand with his thumb, rhythmically stroking, stroking, stroking. She watched as his body seemed to relax on the bed, as the strain went out of his jaw. She silently counted his breaths as she observed the even rise and fall of his chest, tried not to look at the tanned skin exposed above the two opened buttons of his shirt. He looked so defenseless, so young, so much the man she had met and not the man she'd been married to these past terrible months. She bit her lip as a sob caught at the back of her throat.

When she felt sure he was sleeping, she tried to re-move her hand from his grasp; but he wouldn't let her go. In his sleep, he wouldn't let her go. It was only when he was awake that he pushed her away, told her with his expression, with his tone of voice, with pur-posely hurtful, cutting words, that he would be happier if she were simply to disappear from his life.

How simple it would be to lie down beside him. How she longed to do so. She could stretch out her legs, rest her head in the crook of his shoulder, feel his warmth against her body.

When thought turned to action, Sherry didn't know, would never know. She'd gone beyond rational thought in her need to be close to Adam, to touch him, to comfort him.

Her slippers slid off her feet and onto the floor. She lifted her legs slowly, careful not to move too quickly. Still with her hand clasped tightly in his, she lowered herself onto her side, sighed inaudibly as her spine came up against his hip, as the cushion of his arm became her pillow.

Across the room, she could see the roses strewn on the carpet, the dark puddle of water that had seeped into it. Why had he ordered Emma to bring the roses to his rooms? Had he been remembering, as she had been remembering? Obviously, his memories hadn't been happy ones.

Sherry began to cry. Silently. Almost gently. Her sorrow was too deep for sobs. She simply lay there, staring at the windows and the slowly fading light, her tears sliding from her face, onto the fine white lawn of Adam's shirtsleeve.

She didn't know how long she lay there, although shadows had begun to appear in the room by the time she felt Adam stirring beside her. She knew without seeing him that he was awake, that he had removed the cloth from his eyes, tossing it to the floor on the other side of the bed.

Feigning sleep, she lay very still, hoping he'd slip

his arm from beneath her and leave her here, alone in her misery.

He shifted slightly on the bed, turning toward her, his body pressed against her back.

She closed her eyes, silently begging him to leave her.

His fingers gently pushed her hair away, traced a pattern on the side of her throat.

She swallowed, hard, to stifle a weak whimper.

His hand moved lower, sculpting her shoulder, sliding slowly toward her waist, the flare of her hip, exploring her body as it lay hidden beneath the smooth white satin of her dressing gown.

She opened her mouth to protest, but his mouth was against the side of her throat now, his lips warm and soft. His tongue slid along the sensitive flesh behind her ear, dipped inside. Teased.

She turned in his arms, surrendering without words, without the wearying exercise of a battle she knew she'd lose, had already lost. Would always lose.

He kissed her hair, her eyes, her chin, then claimed her mouth. She tasted the sweetness of ale as his tongue invaded her, scraped against the roof of her mouth, slid over her teeth, dueled with her own tongue, sucked at it, drew it into his own mouth.

Both his hands were on her now, molding her, shaping her, dragging her toward the center of the bed, pushing her onto her back.

Her dressing gown fell open, exposing her breasts, and he didn't hesitate in gaining more ground, claiming more territory as his own in this silent war of the senses.

A small cry escaped her at last as his mouth settled over one nipple. Her back arched as he cupped her in his two great hands, lifted her, teased her with teeth and tongue, with talented fingers.

She had gone beyond reason, if she hadn't already taken that step when first she had entered his rooms. Her movements were clumsy, yet effective, and his buttons opened; she felt the bare skin of his chest under her fingers. Becoming frantic in her need, she bit his shoulder.

His hands spanned her narrow waist, he drew circles on her lower belly with his tongue even as one hand slid between her thighs, finding her center.

The frantic need became fluid, and she melted into the mattress, boneless. Without a will of her own.

She allowed her thighs to open, lacking the strength to resist him, to deny her own desires.

How very good he was at loving her body.

Talented fingers slid against her, spread her, teased and nipped and entered her, drowning any thought of shame in a shower of sensation. Colors burst behind her eyes, taking her out of the darkness and into a world filled with reds and bright yellows and blinding, startling white.

She felt him move, raise himself up, fumble with the buttons holding his pantaloons. She smelled the sweetness of ale as he hovered over her, his body no longer touching hers. She didn't breathe, didn't move.

He lowered his head, whispering in her ear. "Tell me

lies, Sherry," he said. "Tell me you were never with him like this. Tell me."

She snaked her arms over his shoulders, tried to pull him down to her. "I was never with him, Adam. Why can't you believe me?"

"Open your eyes."

She shook her head, refusing him.

"Open them, Sherry. Look at me when you lie."

The world grew quiet, with only the rasping of their mingled breaths to tear through the fabric of silence.

Sherry opened her eyes, looked up at him, tried to reach his soul. "I was never with him, Adam. There has only ever been you, will never be anyone but you. I love you."

"Of course you do."

Her heart ached as he smiled. She closed her eyes once more, crying as she held him, crying as he entered her, moved inside her, drove inside her as if to brand her and at the same time erase the touch, the memory, of another man.

And then something changed. Deep inside her. She became numb, with all feeling, all emotion, leaving her, draining away. Leaving her calm, and centered, and completely empty. Desire wasn't enough. Love wasn't enough. Truth wasn't enough.

She didn't need them anymore, and let them all slip away.

She felt no desire building inside her to replace the sweet tension that had come before he'd spoken, before he'd ruined even the studiously built facade of love she had clung to all these months.

When he emptied himself inside her she lay quietly beneath him, an empty vessel, incapable of being filled. As he lay close against her, his body sheened with perspiration, she lowered her arms to the coverlet, their bodies joincd even as she left him there alone. Left him behind as she traveled to a place of emotionless calm deep inside her mind.

He must have sensed her withdrawal. "Sherry?"

Adam rolled onto his side, taking her with him. She didn't have the power to resist him. After all, it was only her body he held. Her body didn't matter. She could even look at him now, dry-eyed, without fear, or hatred, or even love. She had gone beyond feeling anything at all.

He looked at her for a long time, stroking her cheek, still damp from her tears. "Oh, Christ, Sherry, I'm sorry. I'm so sorry. Sherry? Say something. Curse me, I deserve it. But for the love of God, say something."

"Richard Brimley was my lover," she began quietly, her hot, dry gaze never leaving his even as her voice came to her own ears from a strange distance. "It was raining that day and we deliberately sent Geoff off to race a dangerous course just so that we could be alone. We took shelter in the barn. I was with him. I let him touch me. Again and again and again. I let him take me. I wanted it."

The mantel clock chimed out the hour of six, each separate tinkling sound echoing inside Sherry's empty body.

"No," Adam said after an eternity of silence, his voice a rasping whisper of raw, exposed pain as he took hold of her shoulders, shook her, hard. "No, you didn't do that. You couldn't have done that. My God, Sherry, you really didn't do it, did you? All this time! I believed what I saw, not what you said. Christ, what a fool I've been! You weren't lying then, were you? But you're lying now. *Why?*"

"I don't love you anymore, Adam," Sherry told him simply as his hands dropped from her shoulders. She pulled the edges of her dressing gown together and slid from the bed, standing beside it to look at him without love, without hate, without pity. He was a stranger to her, a man she'd only dreamed, but never really known. "I can't feel, I can't care, I can't love. I can't even lie to you and tell you I'm sorry. It simply doesn't matter to me anymore, that's all."

He fell back against the pillows, his forearm pressed over his eyes, and she left him there, her steps steady as she slid her feet into her slippers and walked back toward the door that separated their bedchambers. He heard her softly closing that door behind her. . . .

*O that the beautiful time of young love
could remain green forever.*
—Johann von Schiller

Chapter Six

Even the perfection of his late mother's rose garden paled beside Charlotte Victor's beauty. Sherry, as her father had called her. It was a perfect name for her, for the deep sherry red color of her hair. The sun, hanging low in the sky, seemed only to shine on her as they stood looking down at the rose gardens, bathing her in golden light, setting small fires in that glorious hair, showing the gold mixed with the dark copper. Hers was the only scent he smelled, a mixture of rosewater and homemade soap, of youth and innocence.

Adam knew he was falling, and falling hard. After years of believing he'd never find love, that true love didn't exist, he'd come to believe in love completely. In the space of a day, of an hour, of a minute.

He'd been in love once before, thought he'd been in love once before. How young he'd been, how naive. Melinda had been his everything, and he'd treated her like a perfect, untouchable goddess. She'd agreed to marry him, had told him she loved him, and he'd loved her with all his heart.

Right up until the moment he'd seen his untouchable, lying goddess lost in the arms of another man. A marquess had been a good catch, it seemed, until she'd caught the eye of a duke.

The Dagenham betrothal ring that had been in his pocket, ready to be placed on Melinda's hand that night, now lay somewhere at the bottom of the Thames, buried under nearly a decade's worth of mud. He'd never regretted its loss. He'd danced at Melinda's wedding, congratulated her groom, had watched over the years as Melinda grew increasingly unhappy in her choice. And he'd laughed in her face when she came to him five years after her wedding and offered herself as his mistress.

He was so sure his heart had been hardened against love, that he'd never again look into a woman's eyes and willingly lose himself there.

Until a carefree, laughing young woman looked down at him as he sat in a full foot of water, and called him a gudgeon.

Adam watched, fascinated, as Sherry delicately made her way down the flagstones, holding her skirts above her ankles. She took a half dozen steps into the rose garden, then turned to gaze up at him, her eyes wide and incredulous. "I can't believe

there are so many different roses in the whole
world, yet alone in one garden. I've never seen . . .
never imagined!"

She raced to her right, cupping an immense yellow bloom in her hands. "Why, it's as big as a
dessert plate! And here," she said, pointing to a
bush nearly as tall as she, its inky dark leaves fitting
frames for several dozen blooms as white as snow,
each as perfect as a snowflake. "And over there.
That pink. I've never seen such a pink as that. This
isn't just a garden, my lord. It's *paradise!*"

Adam descended the steps slowly, his eyes never
leaving Sherry's face, never looking at the flowers.
He offered her his arm, and she took it, allowing
him to lead her along the curved paths of the garden.

"Yes," he agreed as he felt himself becoming
complete, after so many years of being half a person, having only half a heart. "That's just how I
would have put it, Miss Victor. Paradise. A veritable
Eden. And not a snake in sight. Shall we take that
stroll now?"

He was nervous, afraid he might frighten her—
would frighten her—if he moved too quickly, gave
her even the slightest indication that he wanted to
kiss her, to hold her, to crush her against him and
never, never ever let her go.

"Augustus—he's our head gardener—told me a
garden like this only comes along once in every
hundred years," he told Sherry, as they picked their
way over the bricked path. "A proper combination

of a wet fall and a mild winter, followed by an early spring and large quantities of sunshine. And his special soil treatments, of course. Nature might be powerful, but without his special treatments, none of which I encouraged him to describe, the garden would simply be lovely, not extraordinary."

"Bone meal," Sherry stated quite unromantically.

Adam's lips twitched. "I beg your pardon?"

"I said, my lord—bone meal. That's what my mama swore by, and our gardens are always lovely, although not nearly as grand as this one. I imagine that's ground-up bones, or something, but you can never be sure just by the name of something, you know. I mean, just think about it. There are so many things we say that don't mean at all what a sensible person would think they mean."

"Such as?" Adam asked, aware that, although he might be falling in love, Sherry Victor seemed not to be noticing his tumble.

"Well," she said, sitting down on a stone bench beside the path, "I imagine Privy Councillor would be one such description that comes to mind. I do believe I read, somewhere, that in olden times the King retreated to the castle privy chamber in order to speak privately with his counselors. The man left to guard the door, allowing no one else entrance, even somehow got himself the title of Privy Watch—out Person or something like that."

"Something like that," Adam agreed, his mind whirling. He was sitting in the most beautiful garden in the world, with the most beautiful woman in the universe, and they were discussing castle privies?

"But the King doesn't meet with his advisors in a privy anymore, now does he, my lord? I mean, you must have been to his palace. They don't meet there, do they?"

Adam scratched at a spot just in front of his left ear. "I seem to recall a large, vaulted chamber, and a quantity of portraits. Perhaps velvet draperies."

"You see? And yet the King's most trusted advisors, undoubtedly most officious and yet privileged persons, go by the title of Privy Councillors. They're probably even proud to have that title." She subsided a bit on the bench, losing some of her stiff, proper posture. "Well, I just know I could never look any of those gentlemen in the eye without falling into giggles and quite horribly disgracing myself."

"I believe I now share that problem with you," Adam said, conjuring up the faces of the Privy Council and imagining them all stuck in a drafty castle privy, whispering secrets to the King, who might have been otherwise occupied at the time. "I'll have to withdraw from Society, in fact, or else make a total fool of myself."

He watched as Sherry's cheeks colored attractively. "I've done it again, haven't I?" she asked, heartbreakingly beautiful in her embarrassment. "Mrs. Forrest says I talk entirely too much, and without ever first bothering to think my words through. Please accept my apologies, my lord."

"Never," Adam answered, taking her hand and lifting it to his lips. "I find you refreshingly frank and honest, Miss Victor, and most totally delightful."

She looked at her hand, being held in his, and then into his face. "You do? How odd."

This particular bit of honesty tickled Adam so much that he threw back his head and laughed, a hearty laugh that melted any lingering ice around his heart. As Sherry stumbled into speech, telling him that *he* was not at all odd, that *she* was probably odd for saying such an odd thing—he wasn't quite sure of her every word, but there were more than a few *odds* sprinkled in her speech—he leaned forward and kissed the tip of her nose.

"Oh," Sherry breathed, looking confused, yet not precisely frightened, even when he took hold of her other hand as well, holding them both against his chest. "Um . . . why did you do that?"

Adam could have said many things then. He could have showered her with easy flattery, complimented her beauty, plucked a bit of poetry from his memory and trotted it in front of her. He could have done so many things, including apologizing for his forwardness. But he found he could be nothing but candid in the face of her own sweet honesty.

"I had to, Miss Victor," he told her, leaning forward and repeating his pleasurable transgression. "In fact, if I don't soon taste your mouth, I may just wither and die."

"Oh," she said again. But she didn't look away.

"I—I thought I was the only one. You—you feel it, too?"

Did she have any idea how her simple honesty affected him? No artifice, no social correctness, no silly, pointless games. She *felt* things, and then she *said* what she felt. What he felt.

"Ah, yes, Miss Victor, I feel it, too. Frightening, isn't it? Whatever *it* is."

"Quite nearly terrifying. A heart really shouldn't beat this fast," she whispered. "It can't be healthy."

"Perhaps if we were to kiss, satisfy our mutual curiosity?" Adam suggested, stroking his thumbs over the backs of her hands, noticing how cold her fingers had become in the gentle warmth of the spring evening. "Then we'd *know*, Miss Victor. We really should know, shouldn't we?"

"I'd like to know, my lord," she told him, withdrawing her hands from his grasp and primly folding them together in her lap. "And, after all, Mrs. Forrest isn't here, is she? Which is a good thing," she added with a rather wicked smile, "as I'm assured she'd have an apoplexy. Yes. Let's do it. Just to see what happens . . . as an experiment of sorts." Sherry slowly shut her eyes, offering her closed mouth to him with a trust and innocence that were all that held him fast to at least one small, ragged edge of sanity.

Adam cupped her face in both his hands, studying her, smiling at the sight of her scrunched-up features. This was madness, but at the same time it was an adventure, a most glorious adventure into

the unknown. Slowly, drawing out the heady anticipation of pleasure, he lowered his head toward
Sherry's . . .

"Ah! There you are, brother. Easy enough to lose
a small army out here, amongst the posies. What's
wrong? Has Miss Victor got something in her eye? I
seriously doubt that, but I'm as willing as the next
gentleman to throw down an excuse if you wish to
pick it up."

"Consider it retrieved," Adam said quietly, releasing Sherry, his fingertips lingering, only for the
barest hint of a second, on her smooth cheeks. He
turned to look at Geoffrey Dagenham, his younger
brother, his most beloved only brother, and a man
he most heartily wished a thousand miles from
Daventry Court. "Surely a visit to the hounds takes
longer than this."

"It could take forever, if Mr. Victor had his way, so
I left him to it," Geoffrey answered brightly. "I think
I've given him pick of the latest litter, but I can't be
sure. My brains started to spin after the first quarter hour of talking bloodlines and points and, with
your pardon, miss, fecund bitches. May I join you?"

"Of course—"

"*Not*," Adam finished as Sherry moved down the
bench and Geoffrey, his smile one of unholy glee,
promptly plunked himself down between them.

The young lord looked to his brother and Sherry
in turn. "Now, isn't this cozy? What shall we talk
about?"

"Oh, I don't know, Geoff. Your impending trip to

our estate in Jamaica, perhaps? You can sail on the next tide, if you hurry," Adam offered politely.

Peeking out from beside Geoffrey, Sherry looked at Adam and giggled. "Jamaica? You have no estate on the farside of the moon, then, my lord?" she asked innocently, showing both men that she was not quite so young or defenseless as either might have believed.

Geoffrey's eyes widened slightly in surprise, then he clapped Adam hard on the back and roared with laughter. "Well," he said at last, sobering, "I can see I'm not wanted here. Or needed. Miss Victor," he said, rising to his feet and bowing, "your servant. And Adam? Someday you're going to have to explain to me why you get all the good luck in the family. And now I'll be off to the kennels again, probably to ruin my new shoes by stepping in something."

As he walked away, Sherry said, "I like him."

"Most people do," Adam agreed. "He's quite good at playing the fool. As a matter of fact, I'm giving serious thought to getting him a belled cap."

"And a pair of those upturned, pointy shoes?" Sherry asked, smiling. "I should think he'd want the shoes as well. Then he could sit in the corner until he was called upon to juggle balls or otherwise amuse you while you're at table. Do you think he could balance a broomstick on his nose?"

"I believe he's already done it or, if he hasn't, an offer of ten pounds for trying the trick would have him racing for a broomstick," Adam said, winking.

"At last I believe someone has found Geoffrey's niche in life for him. But enough of foolish brothers, all right? Now," he said, then turned and took Sherry's face in his hands once more. "Where were we?"

Her intelligent green eyes twinkled, they really did. With mischief. With excitement. With a simple, uncomplicated joy for life he'd forgotten to feel years ago. "Experimenting, my lord?" she prompted politely, then smiled a smile that hit him somewhere in the region of his solar plexus, robbing him of most of his breath.

"Ah, yes," he said, using up what little oxygen remained in his entire body as she once more closed her eyes, drew up her full lips in a pucker that caught him halfway between desire and amusement.

He kissed her forehead. He kissed each of her closed eyes. He kissed that most wonderful, most adorable nose. He watched as her eyes opened in shock as his mouth brushed against her primly pursed mouth. Once. Twice. A third time.

Until that mouth softened under his gentle assault, until a warm, nearly silent breath slipped between her lips and caressed his skin.

She sat very still, her eyes remaining open, brimming with questions he knew he couldn't even begin to answer. At least not tonight.

He tipped his head slightly, kissed her again. Softly. Gently. Raised his head, tipped it again, kissed her again. Butterfly kisses, each one a heart-beat longer than the last.

He took her bottom lip between his teeth, tug-ging gently. He ran the tip of his tongue over her full upper lip, feeling her smile against his mouth, smiling against hers.

And never did either of them close their eyes, not when they were kissing each other, not in between those kisses, when they sat back, looked at each other, smiled at each other, spoke volumes without saying a single word.

His fingers were buried in her hair even as it re-leased from its pins, tumbling down around her shoulders, a warm, living curtain of fire. He stroked her cheeks with his thumbs, dazzled by the smooth-ness of her skin beneath his touch, the warmth of her, the vulnerability of her. The trust she invested in him.

"This . . ." Adam said between kisses, "this is . . . quite . . . incredibly . . . wrong."

"Wrong . . ." Sherry echoed, raising her hands so that she cupped his elbows in her palms. "Yes. Mrs. Forrest . . . Mrs. Forrest would say it is unaccept-able behavior . . ."

"Definitely unacceptable . . ." Adam concurred, sliding his hands down the length of Sherry's slim throat, molding her shoulders to his touch. "Mrs. Forrest is probably a most exemplary woman, a woman of sense. She'd never be caught kissing in a garden."

"No . . . she wouldn't . . ." Sherry said, gifting him

with another telling sigh of pleasure. "Poor thing . . . I feel sorry for her, don't you?"

"We'll send her an invitation to the wedding," Adam said, sliding his arms around Sherry's back, drawing her close against him.

"Yes . . . that would be nice," she agreed dreamily as she nipped at his bottom lip with her straight white teeth, proving that she was a quick learner. In fact, if she learned any more quickly, Adam believed he'd have to leave her where she sat and go throw himself in the pond before he caught fire. Then she sat up very straight, her hands braced on his shoulders, looking wonderfully mussed, her lips moist and even slightly bee-stung from all their kisses. "Excuse me, my lord, but—*whose* wedding? Surely— surely you don't mean *ours?*"

"I accept," Adam said, lifting her to her feet, standing with her, the length of her body searing him from chest to knee, although he didn't hold her, dropped his arms most properly to his sides— as if he'd done a single proper thing since meeting this splendid, precious, fairy-tale princess. He wasn't a drinking man, never had been, but he felt most gloriously drunk at this moment. "Not only that, dearest Miss Victor, but I thought you'd never ask."

"But I didn't," she told him, stepping back a pace. "And, now that I think of it, my lord, neither did you."

"I didn't? Well, I will. Tomorrow. Tomorrow, and tomorrow, and the tomorrow after that. I'll ask until you give me an answer."

"Because—because you kissed me?"

"Because I kissed you. Because I want to go on kissing you, Miss Victor, until the last star dies in the heavens over our heads. Is that too silly and poetic?" he ended, knowing that she—dear, honest princess that she was—would answer him truthfully.

"No," she said slowly, backing away yet another step. "I think it's quite lovely, actually. Um . . . I think I hear my papa calling to me. He likes to be in bed before nine, you know, so that he can be up with the boys. I—I have to go now, my lord." She shook her head, then looked at him as if he was quite the most odd, yet interesting creature she'd ever seen. "I mean, I haven't heard a thing Papa's said in years if I don't absolutely have to, but I really *must* go now. Please?"

"Meet me at the stream tomorrow?" Adam asked—pleaded may have been a better word. "At noon? I'll bring a basket from our kitchens."

She bit her bottom lip for a moment, then nodded, the action alerting her to the fact that her hair, once so carefully piled on top of her head, was now hanging loose over her shoulders. "Mary warned it wouldn't last," she mumbled quietly, pushing at the curls.

"This will," Adam told her, stepping forward, tipping up her chin with his fingertip, and placing a long, lazy kiss against her mouth, a kiss she returned with endearing enthusiasm if not expertise. "At least until tomorrow."

He watched, feeling inordinately pleased with himself, as Miss Charlotte Victor—his own dear Sherry—picked up her skirts and went running back through the garden, toward the house. He followed after her, slowly, stopping to pick a single blush pink bloom from one of the bushes, breathing in its fragrance, tucking it into the buttonhole of his jacket.

Just like any other silly, lovestruck boy.

*He is always right who
suspects that he makes mistakes.*
          —Spanish Proverb

Chapter Seven

Adam opened his eyes slowly, carefully, aware that he was not alone in his bedchamber. As his valet never entered until he was summoned, Adam's heart leapt for a moment, believing that Sherry might have come to him.

Which was ridiculous. Sherry was gone. Gone from this chamber, gone from his life even as she physically remained in this house. He'd made certain of that with his blind, bullheaded stupidity.

"Who's there?" he asked, sitting up, then grabbing at his head, which was definitely in danger of falling off. When would he learn that drinking half the night away did nothing more than destroy half a morning?

"Took a mighty fall off the water wagon, did you then, boyo?" Chollie asked from somewhere in the chamber—there, there he is, Adam decided, as his bleary eyes made out the shape of his friend, sitting in a leather chair beside the fire. "You could have at least sent round a note, saying you weren't going to meet Edmund and me for dinner last night. Bloody bad manners, I say."

"So would I, Chollie," Adam agreed, slowly slipping his legs off the side of the bed, realizing that he was still clad in his shirt and pantaloons. "My apologies to you both. As I'm sure you'll apologize for breaking into my bedchamber."

"You'd have a long wait believing that, boyo," Chollie said, standing up and going to give the bellpull a hearty tug. "I've ordered up a bracing breakfast for you. I had mine already. With Geoff and Edmund. And it's a funny thing about that, you know. Nobody told me Geoff had been injured. Now why, do you suppose, hadn't I heard that?"

Adam scrubbed at his face with both hands, feeling the roughness of his beard, then all but grinding the grit of sleep from his eyes. "Hell's bells, Chollie, give me a moment, will you? I think something crawled inside my head and died there."

"According to that new butler of yours—I don't much like him, by the way—a mighty measure of brandy found its way inside your skull. You've never been a drinking man, boyo, much is the pity, so you probably don't know brandy's the very devil on the head. Better to stick to strong ale if you've got serious drinking to do, and don't you know."

"I'll remember that," Adam said as he directed his head toward the dressing-room washbasin and willed his feet to carry the rest of him there. He bent in front of the basin and poured the ice-cold contents of the pitcher straight over his hair and shoulders, the shock of the frigid water pulling an involuntary yowl of pain from him before he buried his face in the towel Chollie handed him.

He staggered back to the bedchamber and stripped out of his soggy shirt as Chollie obligingly built up the dying fire. He slid his arms into a midnight blue dressing gown before joining his friend, who was once more sitting at his ease in one of the two leather chairs.

"Run your fingers through your hair a time or two, boyo," Chollie recommended. "You look like you've had that black mop of yours combed with a rake. Devilishly unbecoming. Ah, that's better. Now, where would you like me to hit you, I'm asking? A solid body punch, or a clear shot to your jaw? I'm thinking the body punch, as your gut must be doing a fine jig already, with all that brandy sloshing around inside, you understand."

Adam pushed at his still-damp hair, looking at his friend. "I was going to tell you, Chollie."

"And sure you were, boyo. You weren't going to let me just come tripping in here, calling out for Geoff, asking him if he'd like to go wenching with Edmund and me this evening—and find him sitting in that chair, a rug over his knees. When was it you were going to tell me, boyo? St. Tibb's Eve, the last night before Judgment Day? No. That can't be it, can it? Because you've already *made* all your judgments, haven't you? And don't you be going all black-faced on me, boyo. Geoff told me the whole of it just now, after Edmund was gone. Shame on you, Adam Dagenham. Bloody shame on you."

Adam pressed his head against the high back of the chair. "Kill me slowly, Chollie. I deserve every moment of the pain."

"Oh, no. Oh, no, you don't! Don't go making me feel sorry for you, boyo. Not when I'm just building up to a fine tirade. That sweet, dear colleen. Thinking she could have—that she'd . . . well, words fail me, boyo. That they do."

"I was wrong, Chollie," Adam said quietly, opening his eyes because, when he closed them, all he could see was Sherry standing in front of him, telling him she no longer loved him. "I've taken the most beautiful thing in the world, the best thing that ever happened to me, and I've destroyed it. I couldn't believe it, felt I was living a dream, and when I saw her that day . . . Christ! How could I have been so blind?"

"You do penance very well, boyo," Chollie said, as Adam looked at him through slitted, heavy eyes. "I could go about, finding you a hair shirt, but I don't think you *need* it. What you *need,* boyo, is to be telling that wife of yours that you're sorry. Not me. Me, I'm more than a bit put out that I can't beat you into flinders without thinking I'd be striking a man already down. What happened here last night, boyo? Because something did, and no mistake. Something not even Geoff knows about, and there's a boy who'd tell you all he knows at the drop of a hint, and then make up the rest."

Adam needed a drink. He needed a half dozen

drinks. And a month of sleep. "I believed her, Chollie. After weeks, months, of not believing her, I finally listened. But it's too late. She doesn't love me anymore."

"You can be unlovable," Chollie said, standing up and beginning to pace. "There is that. Did you hurt her?"

Closing his eyes, Adam saw Sherry's pinched white, expressionless face, heard her speak again in that frightening monotone, telling him that she couldn't *feel* anymore. "I hurt her, Chollie. I did more than hurt her. I've lost her."

"Then Geoff's right? You never really loved her?"

"Geoff said that, did he?" Adam dropped his chin onto his chest and rubbed at his forehead with both hands. "I thought I did, Chollie. I truly believed I loved her. But I didn't, did I? I wanted her. I possessed her. I made her into a dream of what I thought I wanted, what I believed I needed. I took her innocence, then distrusted her because she let me have it, gave me all of herself. And then I waited, I just waited, until she proved that she didn't really deserve my love. And all of that time, all the time we were happy, through all these last wretched months, it was I who didn't deserve her."

He looked up at his friend through his tears, not the first tears he'd shed since last night. *Good God, am I still half-drunk? How else can I be so willing to make such a damning confession?* "I've ruined everything, destroyed everything. I love Sherry so much, but she'll never believe that. Not now. Not after what I've done.

Oh, Christ. What do I do now, Chollie? What do I do now?"

"I'd start by calling for a hot tub and getting myself dressed and decent," Chollie said, as the door opened and Rimmon himself entered, carrying the breakfast tray. "Because our friend Edmund, our most *irresistible* friend Edmund—and the man is no braggart when he calls himself that, I can tell you after last night—has taken your unhappy wife out for a morning drive. Here, you'll be taking this back downstairs," he said, lifting the brandy decanter off the tray as Rimmon placed it on a table beside the fire. "His Lordship won't be having any more brandy. Not this morning, not ever again. You understand that, my man?"

"I take my orders from His Lordship," Rimmon said, his colorless eyes seeking out Adam, who was eyeing the brandy decanter with some hunger.

Just one more drink. Adam knew he would be all right, if he could have just one more drink of brandy. Him, a man who had never been one for the bottle, not in all his years. Not until his life had fallen apart, until he'd torn it apart. "Take it away, Rimmon," he said at last, "and have my valet order a tub."

"Yes, my lord," Rimmon said, bowing to Adam even as he glared at Chollie. "At once, my lord."

"Salvation seize his soul, but I definitely don't like that man, Adam," Chollie said as Rimmon left the chamber. "Where did Hoggs go, then? Liked Hoggs, I did."

Adam lightly brushed a hand across his face, beating away the remaining cobwebs that lingered in his mind. "What? Oh, Hoggs. Yes, I prefer him to Rimmon, myself. But Hoggs was called away suddenly, something about a sister in Lincolnshire needing him for a few months, as I remember it. It was Hoggs who suggested Rimmon as his replacement for the interim. Hoggs suggested Emma as well, when Sherry's maid, Mary, decided not to come back to London with us. I doubt you'd like her, either, now that I think about the thing. Why do you ask?"

"No reason, I suppose. Hoggs, did you say? Strange." Chollie looked to the closed door, then shook his head, touched a hand to his waistcoat pocket. "Well, never mind. I guess I'm feeling especially Irish this morning, that's all, which just goes to prove that I drank too much last night."

Sherry looked around the large room rather blankly, wondering precisely how she had ended up there, and even why. Her mind was so dull, as if she had been sleepwalking through the day.

She had been out driving with Mr. Burnell. She'd been out driving, then Mr. Burnell had suggested they stop by to visit with his aunt for a few minutes. The woman had been complaining that no one visited her unless at the point of a pistol—which her naughty nephew had considered to be nonsense, as excepting for the fact that he was her nephew, he vowed he wouldn't visit Lady J unless that pistol was also *cocked*.

Sherry had even laughed at that. She remembered

now. Sad and tired as she was, Edmund Burnell had been able to make her laugh.

And now she was sitting in Lady Jasper's drawing room, her gloves in her lap, awaiting the woman, as Mr. Burnell tended to a caller who had come to the servants' entrance, demanding to be seen. He hadn't seemed happy to be summoned, but he'd smiled, politely excused himself, and gone off, leaving her alone.

She was so alone. So very alone.

How lost she was inside herself even as she searched for herself, knowing the essence that was Charlotte Victor had gone missing somewhere, leaving only this sad, unfeeling shell. The outside of her smiled, and spoke, and had even partaken of a very fine breakfast that morning. But Charlotte Victor was gone.

She should go home. To Leicestershire. To her papa. That's what she should do. Papa wouldn't even know she was there, or care overmuch, unless he needed help in the kennels. But it wasn't necessary for her to leave London. Not physically. Her body didn't matter, wouldn't much care where it sat, where it slept. And her mind? Ah, that she carried with her no matter where she went.

Her heart, however, had packed and left the city sometime during the night, and she had no idea where it was now. She'd miss it terribly, if only she could feel anything. . . .

"There you are, you sweet thing!"

Sherry gave herself a small mental shake, then smiled at Lady Jasper as the elderly dame entered the room at her usual near gallop. She had been quite the horsewoman, Sherry remembered, and even if she hadn't been in the saddle in a dozen years, she still walked as if she'd had a horse under her only a moment earlier.

"How lovely to see you, Lady Jasper," Sherry said as she stood for a moment, pressed her lips against the older woman's hot, dry cheek. "Your nephew insisted you wouldn't mind if I made a morning call," she continued at her most formal, automatically saying what had to be said in order to be polite. "As luck would have it, it was a good thing he thought of it. One of his horses went lame just as we were pulling into the square, so that his driver has taken the entire equipage around to the mews, to secure another horse."

"That's Edmund, straight down to the ground," Lady Jasper cackled—she really did cackle, Sherry thought, although she had never heard a cackle before meeting the old woman. She then looked at Sherry with an intensity that made Sherry involuntarily lift a hand to her face, wondering if she had a smut on her cheek. "Luck always favors him. He'd have it no other way. So, you're the one, are you? I'd thought so, that first night, but I couldn't be sure until now."

"The one?" Sherry repeated blankly. She *was* paying attention, wasn't she? What had she missed? "I'm sorry. I'm afraid I don't understand."

"Yes, of course. The *one,* my dear," Lady Jasper said, glaring at the maid who brought in a silver tray loaded down with teapot, cups, and a small mountain of cakes. "Get on with it, Millie. Ever had a horse slow as you, I'd have had it shot. Now," she continued as the maid all but ran from the room, whimpering, "where were we? Oh, yes. I think my nephew is smitten with you, my dear, in his way, of course."

"Smitten with—" Sherry closed her mouth with a snap, realizing that she'd been repeating everything Lady Jasper said. "I don't think I have given him any reason to—"

"No, no! You haven't encouraged him, m'dear," Lady Jasper interrupted. "Edmund needs no encouragement, I assure you. And he's impossible to resist. Unless you're in love with your husband, that is, and who in London loves her husband, I ask you? Certainly no one of my acquaintance, not in forty years of watching this mad dance we call Society. I certainly despised mine most thoroughly. Sugar, m'dear?"

"Um . . . yes. Yes, please," Sherry answered, holding up her cup so that her hostess could spoon some sugar into it. "Thank you. Um . . . surely you didn't just say you didn't like your husband, Lady Jasper?"

"That's true enough, m'dear. I said I *despised* him. Most thoroughly."

"Yes, of course. But, if I might ask, my lady—why did you marry him if you didn't love him?"

Lady Jasper looked at Sherry for a moment, then a grin all but split her face in two. "Why? Ah, you may be married, but you remain an infant, don't you? Why does anyone marry, m'dear? For money. For station. Mostly for money, I'd say. Daventry is positively up to his handsome neck in it, isn't he? Give him an heir, m'dear, that's what he wants, and then he'll let you alone, and you can do what you wish. I tried, but the Devil was in it, and none of the babes lived to see breath. That, and old age, are my only sorrows. You have to be very careful what you ask for, you understand. Don't limit yourself when the chance comes to strike a bargain."

Sherry knew her jaw was at half cock, but she couldn't seem to close her mouth, or think of a thing to say. Lady Jasper was a strange woman, everyone knew it, but she'd never believed the woman to be out of her mind. Until now. "Um . . ." she said at last, wishing she felt more in command of her own senses at the moment, "thank you, my lady. I'll—I'll remember that."

"Giving advice, Lady J?" Edmund Burnell asked as he strode into the room, a spring in his step, a becoming smile lighting his handsome face. "My deepest apologies for deserting you, ladies. An unavoidable interruption, I'm afraid. But it's all taken care of now. I'd commissioned someone to do something for me, and he came to apologize, for it seems he couldn't do what he was told to do and felt he personally needed to come inform me of that fact. Infernal creature. Do you have a problem with your servants, my lady?"

Sherry immediately thought of Emma, whom she had last seen trying on one of her favorite bonnets. The tub had still sat in front of the fireplace, damp towels were laid over chairs, and Sherry had been forced to locate her parasol on her own, but Emma had seemed perfectly content. Emma, who knew when her mistress slept alone, and when Adam had come to her during the night, leaving evidence of the frenzy of their passion. Their passion, never their love.

Well, that was over now. Everything was over now. And, if Lady Jasper was to be believed, servants would see nothing out of the ordinary if a husband and his wife lived separate lives. Perhaps it was time she dismissed Emma. If only she knew how to go about the thing.

"I'm afraid I haven't quite gotten the hang of how to be a proper mistress," Sherry said after a moment, shrugging. "In fact, I believe I'm rather intimidated by them, as town servants are so very different from our simple country servants, who seem almost to be members of our small family. I've only had one maid before coming to London this time, and she had been a part of our household since before I'd been born."

"Excuse me, sir, madam."

Everyone turned toward the doorway, where the Jasper butler stood just on the edge of the carpet, looking to Edmund. "The person is back, sir. The one who was here yesterday, if you take my meaning. I said you weren't receiving, but—well, sir, I couldn't budge the person, sir."

Sherry watched as Edmund's face turned hard, all planes and angles as his temper came close to the surface for a moment before retreating behind his bright smile. "You and I will speak privately later, Midgard, I assure you. Put the person in the tradesmen's anteroom. I'll be there shortly. Excuse me again, dear ladies," he then added, rising and bowing to both of them. "I seem to have made a mistake in stopping back here, as I'm suddenly in such demand."

Sherry only nodded, then drank deep of her now-tepid tea, wincing as she realized that Lady Jasper had put at least three measures of sugar in the cup. She sat still and let Lady Jasper smile at her, believing she heard a woman's voice raised shrilly before a door closed heavily somewhere in the house.

". . . has to beat them away with sticks, poor boy," Lady Jasper was saying as Sherry brought herself back to attention. "Go to the window, dear, and peek out to see if there's a crest on the carriage. I'll wager a monkey to a hatpin you'll see the duke of Westbrook's crest. Melinda Hatchard always was a fool, no matter that she's a duchess now. Go on, there's a good girl," she ordered, as Sherry reluctantly got to her feet, embarrassed for the duchess of Westbrook, or whoever it was who had been so desperate as to come to Lady Jasper's house, seeking out Edmund.

"Yes, it's the duke of Westbrook's coach. I recognize the crest," Sherry said a few moments later as she turned away from the window, cringing at the sight of Lady Jasper's horsey face split in what could only be termed an unholy grin.

There was so much Sherry didn't understand about London Society, and the duchess of Westbrook's behavior in coming to see Edmund Burnell headed the list at the moment. "Are—are you saying that the duchess and Mr. Burnell . . . that is . . . surely—"

"Oh, sit down and drink your tea, m'dear," Lady Jasper interrupted, and Sherry gratefully retook her seat, even as she wished herself back to the day before she'd met Adam at the stream, back to her innocence. "I suppose Edmund danced with Her Grace a time or two, that's all. Whispered a few bits of nonsense into her willing ear. But you know how it is when a woman gets to believing herself to be in love. They do the strangest things."

"Yes, they do," Sherry agreed quietly.

"And the gentleman who has caused all the ruckus—if we can even call such a person a gentleman—isn't in the least upset when he realizes that he's left another heart behind him, crushed under his heel. Edmund included, I'm afraid. The duchess would be your witness to that." Lady Jasper leaned forward in her chair, motioning for Sherry to do likewise. "What do you say, m'dear? Shall we turn the tables on Edmund? Strike a blow for all womankind?"

"Strike a—no, I'm through with repeating whatever you say like some simple-witted gudgeon," Sherry declared flatly, falling back on honesty because it was the one thing she felt she had left to her. "Lady Jasper, just what is it you're trying to say, have been trying to say ever since you first walked in the door? You really must tell me plainly. Otherwise, I'm afraid you could drop hints until they rain down on us both from the ceiling, and still I wouldn't understand. I'm a simple country miss, for all that I may have a husband and a grand title now. You're simply going to have to be more clear. Plus," she ended, taking truth all the way to its limits and perhaps a step or two further than necessary, "I really haven't been attending you all too well, for which I must most sincerely apologize."

Lady Jasper fell heavily back against the cushions of her chair, staring at Sherry. "Lord, you are simple, aren't you? Oh, not simpleminded, m'dear. I certainly didn't mean that. But you have no notion of intrigue, do you? Although I do see that your rather brutal honesty might seem refreshing to many of the jaded. For myself, I've never scrupled to use honesty when a good wile would do. I doubt many would ever think of it. Interesting. That's probably what attracted Edmund to you, beyond the fact that he's got quite an eye for beauty. Honesty. Not something the boy has been exposed to all that often." She gave a wave of her hand. "Go on, m'dear. Do it some more. Say something else honest."

Sherry sighed and shook her head. "I think I'd like to go back to Grosvenor Square now."

"Yes, yes, that's good," Lady Jasper prompted, rubbing her hands together. "You want to go home. I can understand that. But that's enough honesty for now, m'dear. Now we'll talk about Edmund, and how you're going to teach my naughty nephew not to trifle with a woman's heart."

"No, Lady Jasper," Sherry said, rising, holding her gloves tightly in her hand. "No, I'm not going to do that. I have no reason to do that. I like your nephew, even if you don't. I don't know why you don't, but it's clear to me that you'd like nothing better than to see him unhappy."

"Of course I want to see him unhappy, you silly little chit. He's the very Devil," Lady Jasper gritted out quietly, shooting a quick, nervous glance toward the doorway.

"He's the—oh, Lady Jasper, how silly!" Sherry sat down again, giggling. Poor, dotty old woman. "Well, of course he is. He told me so himself, as a matter of fact. But he didn't start the Great London fire. That began in a bakery, I believe. Mr. Burnell," she said, seeing Edmund enter the room once more, "you've got your very own aunt calling you the Devil. Shame on you."

"Shame on Lady J, rather," Burnell said, holding out his hand, so that Sherry rose, taking it, more than ready to continue their ride, or do anything other than remain there, listening to Lady Jasper, who most definitely had lost half her mind to old age and general meanness. "Dear Aunt, you never will forgive me for enjoying myself, will you? I suppose you've been busy telling Her Ladyship that I'm a thoroughly wicked man? I assure you, I did nothing to encourage the duchess."

"Now *that* is evil," Sherry scolded, shaking a finger in his face. "The poor duchess of Westbrook is owed anonymity, at the very least." And then, as Edmund raised one well-sculpted brow, a half smile lighting his handsome face, she said, "Oh, dear. I shouldn't have said that, should I? I peeked out the window, if you must know. Have you totally crushed her heart beneath your boot? Because that would be wicked."

Burnell pulled her arm through his, patting her hand. "I was kindness itself, my lady, I assure you. I merely told her my heart was otherwise occupied, and there was, alas, no room for her."

"Ha! You don't have a heart, nephew," Lady Jasper said, and Sherry turned just in time to see the old lady pouring something into her tea, then secreting the silver flask again somewhere on her person. Had she been drinking tea all this time, or something stronger? Was she drunk? She did seem to be slurring her words. "Or a soul, I imagine. Does the Devil have a soul?"

"Why, I'd imagine the fellow's got millions of them, dear Aunt, with more of them falling to him every day," Edmund said, leaving Sherry for a moment, to bend and kiss Lady Jasper's cheek. "Now excuse me, please, as I escort the marchioness back to Grosvenor Square. Why don't you take a small nap, Aunt? I believe your tongue could use the rest."

Sherry bade Lady Jasper good day, her mind tumbling over itself with questions as she allowed Edmund Burnell to escort her back down the stairs and out to his open carriage. "Your aunt is the strangest woman I've ever met," she told him once he'd handed her up onto the seat.

"She's the *unhappiest* woman you've ever met," Edmund corrected, and Sherry silently agreed with his assessment of the lady who was, after all, his aunt. Who should know her better than her own nephew? "She doesn't much care for men, even those in her own family, sad to say. I also believe she's discovered, after forty years of believing otherwise, that money and social position are not the roads to complete happiness."

"Is there anything that assures us complete happiness?" Sherry asked, snapping open her parasol as the carriage pulled away from the flagway and made a wide turn inside the square, heading back to the main thoroughfare. "Other than perfect love, which doesn't really exist."

"Oh, my, that sounded heartfelt, my dear lady," Edmund said, taking her hand in his. "And, yes, I do believe I see a hint of sadness in those lovely green eyes, a deeper hint even than I saw when first we met. Well, we can't have this, can we? May I be of assistance in any way? You've but to ask and, if it's within my power, I promise to give it to you."

Sherry remembered Lady Jasper's declaration— perhaps her warning—that Edmund held her in some affection other than brotherly concern or platonic friendship. Which was above everything silly, because Edmund was Adam's friend, and had been before she had even met him. Friends didn't betray friends. Richard Brimley had never been a friend. "You could consent to being my escort at Lady Winston's masked ball, I suppose, since my husband calls such affairs silly and refuses to attend. But first you'd have to help me decide on a costume. I had thought to wear a simple domino. You know—a cloak and half mask. But I feel a sudden urge to lose myself in a small fantasy. Do you have any suggestions?"

"A masked ball?" Edmund's grin took years off his face, making him seem no older than Geoffrey. "Oh, I can think of several ideas for costumes. If you'll allow it, I'll send something around for you by tomorrow morning. It will be my gift, to thank you for your kind invitation."

Sherry considered his words. She'd spoken impulsively and already regretted her invitation. Edmund seemed much too eager, and she had no idea if Adam planned to attend Lady Winston's ball with her—just that she couldn't bear the thought of seeing him right then, talking to him. "I don't know that it would be proper for me to accept such a generous gift," she said, lowering her parasol to cover her sudden confusion. Edmund was such a dear man, but she couldn't be attracted to him, no matter how kind he was when she was so in need of kindness. She couldn't be attracted to anyone. Could she?

"I'll send Daventry the bill, then. I'm sure he wouldn't mind," Edmund said cheerfully. "Not only that, but I'll find a costume for Lord Dagenham as well. I'm quite sure I can convince him to join us. In fact, I believe I shall insist upon it. Much better than a simple ride in the park. The boy needs some fun."

Mention of Geoff—so kind, Edmund was, so endlessly thoughtful—served to dissolve the last of Sherry's misgivings, and the matter was settled before the carriage pulled up in front of the mansion in Grosvenor Square.

Adam knocked on the closed door separating his bedchamber from Sherry's. Just that spring it had been the door connecting their two rooms; a door that had never been closed, giving him a view of her bed, that never had been slept in through all of the Spring Season. Separating. Connecting. It was all a matter of one's viewpoint.

Sherry opened the door herself, a silver-backed brush in her hand, her eyes looking at him without rancor, without passion, without any emotion at all. In fact, it was as if she were looking straight through him.

He'd gone out this afternoon in his curricle, looking for her. In the park. Along the main thoroughfares. But there had been no sign of Edmund Burnell's carriage. Where had she been? What had she been doing? Why did he think he might still have the right to ask those questions?

"Geoff and I missed you at dinner this evening, and I thought I'd stop by and see how you are feeling. May I come in?" he asked, his hands bunched into fists at his side, because otherwise he would have taken hold of her, held her, tried to shake her into some sort of reaction. Any sort of reaction.

She just looked at him for another long moment, nodded, then turned, walked back to sit in front of her dressing table, and began brushing her hair.

He followed her to the dressing table, standing behind her, longing to put his hands on her shoulders, aching to bend down, kiss the top of her head. "I've come to apologize, of course," he said stiffly after a few moments, then winced as he heard his own voice, the empty words.

"I accept your apology, Adam," Sherry said with unshakable calm as he watched her reflection in the mirror, watched her tip her head, pulling the brush through her long curls. "We've both made mistakes. I think that's clear now."

"Yes. That's very clear now, Sherry."

"For a long time it wasn't. Not to me. Not to you."

"I suppose not."

What else could he say? What else could he do? He stepped to one side of the low bench and dropped to one knee. "Sherry, don't do this. Please. I'd cut off both my arms if it would help."

Sherry put down the brush, but still didn't turn to look at him. "You didn't believe me, Adam. You all but leapt at the chance not to believe me. And not all that much has changed, has it? You still believe that I'm at least partly responsible for Geoff's accident. I am, you know. That was the lie I told, saying I didn't know where Geoff was that day, not giving you time to find him, dissuade him from his recklessness. Because I did know. I knew he'd gone off to race. So it doesn't matter what you chose not to believe or forgive. The lie, or the truth. Either way, I'm responsible."

"No." Adam took her hands in his, held them tightly, winced inwardly when he felt how icy-cold they were. "All the scales have dropped from my eyes now, darling. I'm seeing clearly now, and for the first time in my life. I'm responsible, Sherry. For *all* of it. Your only mistake was in loving me when I didn't deserve your love. Geoff, out to disobey me after I'd tried to run his life, made his own decision, then dragged you into lying for him. And I *wanted* to believe what I saw, for my sins. Lord knows I couldn't believe in my own happiness. We were living a dream, darling, you and I, and I knew it. The dream was too perfect, a fantasy that had nothing to do with really living our lives, really loving each other. Somewhere, deep inside of me, I knew it had to end. I believe you sensed it, too. The dream had to end."

"And it did," Sherry said, pulling her hands free of him as she rose, walked to look out the window overlooking Grosvenor Square. She looked so fragile as she stood there, achingly beautiful, sadly vulnerable. "How gratifying for you to be proved right, Adam, one way or another. Yes. I knew the dream couldn't last. I had already seen it slipping away once we'd left London and gone back to Daventry Court. You'd married a child and begun to regret it. Why else do you think I played with Geoff, played with those terrible races, if not to gain back your attention any way that I could?"

"Sweet Jesus," Adam mumbled under his breath, whether as a curse or in prayer he didn't know. He'd worked this all out in his head, through all of a drunken night and a long, sobering day, but hearing Sherry say the words rocked him all over again. "I don't deserve anything but your disgust, Sherry, but I want to try again. Begin again. We can't pretend the past didn't happen, either of us. We can't blink our eyes or snap our fingers and have all the hurt go away, all the terrible words, the unhappy months—"

"Geoff's accident?"

He nodded, sighing. "Yes. That, too. But I do love you, Sherry. More now than ever. It's a real love, darling, not a dream, a fantasy. If you believe nothing else, please believe that. Give me time to show you I mean what I say."

She was silent for a long time. Adam suffered through several levels of Hell during that silence, would have offered his soul to anyone who could make his words sound more believable, help to soften Sherry's heart.

"It may be too late. I can't feel anything, Adam," she said at last, her voice low, almost a whisper. She turned, looked at him, her eyes dry, distant. "I believed I loved you. But I don't know now if I really did, if what I felt was really love. I don't know that I'll ever feel anything again."

He took a quick step toward her, but she held out her hand, the defensive gesture stopping him with the power of his own guilty conscience, his shame for how badly he'd treated her, how shabbily he'd served their love.

"I won't touch you, Sherry. I promise. Not until you want me to touch you, to hold you. Just let me be near you, here in London, once we've gone back to Daventry Court for Christmas. Let me court you, as I should have courted you from the beginning. Slowly, giving you time, time I didn't allow you. Everything happened in such a rush, much too quickly. There's so much we know about each other, and so much more we don't know, have never taken the time to learn. I think I can make you feel again, darling, earn your love again. Because I'll never believe you didn't love me. I can't believe that, Sherry, and still want to take another breath. Just, please, darling, give me that chance. Give us both that chance."

"For the child," Sherry whispered, her hands going protectively to her belly. "I'll do it, Adam, but not for us. I doubt either of us deserves a second chance. Only for the child."

"The—the child?" Adam sat down on the dressing-table bench, his knees suddenly not strong enough to keep him upright. This was too much, and he didn't know how to react if he couldn't hold her, kiss her, know that she was as happy about the idea of a pregnancy as he was. "Sherry? There's to be a child? You're sure?"

"Yes, I'm sure, and have been for more than a month," she said, her voice at last taking on some emotion, although it was not the one he'd longed to hear. "And, before you ask, Adam, it is yours. Now, if you'll excuse me? I'm tired, and I want to go to bed. If you want, you can begin courting me, as you call it, in the morning. Thursday night, however, Edmund is escorting Geoff and me to the masked ball at Lady Winston's. Good night, Adam."

Adam stood, a flash of anger shooting through him as he remembered Chollie's warning that the handsome, likable Edmund Burnell was "irresistible" to the ladies. Who could be more vulnerable to the man's charms than his own unhappy wife? He shook his head. "No, madam, Edmund is *not* escorting you to Lady Winston's. He may *join* us at the ball."

"Whatever you wish, Adam. I really don't care. Although I must say that ordering me about is a strange way of courting me," Sherry said, shrugging, her indifference maddening him, frustrating him beyond his own comprehension.

Adam opened his mouth, to apologize yet again, but something stopped him. Pride. It stuck in his throat, stuck hard, so that he was unable to swallow it one more time. He'd come to Sherry, the penitent, on his knees. He'd damn near crawled to her. Now she was dangling a child in front of him and at the same time waving Edmund Burnell beneath his nose.

"Pleasant dreams, Sherry," he said shortly.

He then turned on his heels and left the chamber, quietly closing the door behind him, leaning against it, trying to recapture his breath, ease his heart back into its usual slow, steady beat. It would be another long night, but a sober one. He hoped he would live through it.

*Don't let your heart depend on things
that ornament life in a fleeting way!*
        —Johann von Schiller

Chapter Eight

Sherry had never thought much about her appearance, or thought much of that appearance when she did happen to catch her reflection in a mirror. She was a girl-child, which meant she already had one stroke against her, according to her papa. Her mama, not one for looking at anything other than her own misery and ways to alleviate it, had let Sherry grow rather on her own, leaving her only daughter to the mercies of Mrs. Forrest, who was not the most humorous of women. She certainly had not been the sort of woman to encourage vanity of any sort.

Sherry had built her own life as she grew, befriending whom she liked, and she liked almost everyone. Her friends ranged from the lowest scullery maid to the stiff, powdered ladies forced to sit in her mama's drawing room as all the husbands went tearing around the countryside, chasing help-less vermin. She welcomed everyone who was nice to her and paid little attention to herself as being anything more than the daughter of the house.

She lived a carefree life, unfettered by ambitious parents, and had grown to her nineteenth year without giving much thought to the effort involved, or to what would happen the morning after the night she last laid her head on her pillow and drifted off to dreamless sleep.

She'd thought about a Season, but never seri-ously, especially once her mama had done her flit with Henry Carpenter the previous summer. She'd thought about marriage, about babies. But, again, never seriously. She most certainly had never spent a sleepless night thinking about one particular man. She hadn't given more than a moment's thought to how she looked to a man, if she might appeal to a man in *that* way.

That's what Mrs. Forrest had called it—*that* way. When Sherry had once pressed her further, asking her precisely what way *that* way was, the older woman had given the longest sermon in her life, one filled with words like "duty" and "progeny" and "they can't help themselves, base creatures that they are."

All of which meant less than nothing to Sherry now, as she paced the bank of the stream, watching her skirts kick in front of her with every step, feeling her blood running strangely hot in her veins as her stomach fluttered, rather pleasurably, with nerves.

She was a child. No, a woman. A young woman? Yes. That was it. She was a young woman, a young lady. Nineteen. Not yet on the shelf, but close enough to it to be able to see her spinster's cap lying there, waiting for her. There were neighbors back in Surrey who'd already been married for three years, had already been mothers for two of them. Someone had looked at them in *that* way.

Why hadn't she paid more attention? She'd always wandered off when talk of handsome young men and balls and engagements made her yawn behind her hand. She hadn't been ready for such conversation, had no interest in it, frankly. She most certainly didn't believe herself ready for marriage, and for sitting in a drawing room gossiping about fashions and paint pots and other people's unhappiness while her husband devoted himself to a pack of hounds and falling asleep in his pudding after drinking his dinner. She was much too involved in being Charlotte Victor; student of the world closest to her, reasonably devoted daughter, and eager child in search of what Mrs. Forrest had termed "simpleminded pleasures."

Just four and twenty hours ago she'd been indulging herself in an enjoyable tramp through the lovely countryside, with not a care in her small world or a thought to her future.

What had happened to her? How had it happened? When had her appearance not only become important to her but a curiosity to her? She never remembered being this conscious of herself as a female, this unusually *aware* of her own body. Was it because of the way the marquess of Daventry looked at her? Stared at her? What did he see that she'd never seen? Was she really pretty? A person should know that, she believed, if that person paid attention. Why had she never paid attention until yesterday afternoon?

She felt like a plant that has lain dormant over nearly nineteen winters, sleeping and unaware, only to find itself suddenly forced through the surface of life and immediately encouraged to flower.

Sherry stopped pacing partway between a large willow and a flowering bush she didn't recognize, and sat herself down on the grassy bank, pulling off her shoes and hose in order to dangle her feet in the cool water.

He'd kissed her. Again and again. She'd allowed it. Again and again. Encouraged it. Had liked it very, very much.

How could she have done that? There was a word for girls like her; she'd heard it a time or two. *Fast.* That's what she would be called if anyone knew she'd allowed the marquess to kiss her. There were probably worse words for a girl who wanted him to kiss her again today, and hang the consequences.

He was quite entirely above her touch, of course. Older. So very intelligent. Titled and sophisticated and horribly important. Able to say witty things without effort, tease her about marriage and laugh at her in the same breath.

He couldn't really be interested in her. Not simple, uncomplicated, barely aware Charlotte Victor. Not in Charlotte the girl, or in Sherry, the sometimes dreamer. Happy, probably horribly shallow, naive, silly Charlotte Victor, who found her greatest happiness in simply *being*, not *accomplishing*. Why, her greatest aspiration, before yesterday, had been to explore more of the countryside and perhaps find another private, shady spot in which to read her book.

For all of the quite respectable, upper-class blood that flowed through her veins, she couldn't be more of a country miss if she had straw in her hair and a milk pail in her hand. She might know of the existence of the Privy Council, but the marquess of Daventry had probably met them all, knew all their names, was routinely invited to dine at their houses.

What could he possibly see in her? Except *that*.

Which wasn't so very terrible, Sherry decided, smiling as she kicked at the water with her bare toes. *That* was very nice, actually.

Did that make her "fast"? Yes, it probably did. Did she care? No, she decided, she probably didn't.

"I would wish Geoff here with his paints, to capture the way you look, Miss Victor, with the sun shining down at you through the trees, except that I'd rather not share this moment with anyone. No— don't move, don't change a thing. Please. Just let me look at you."

Sherry sat very still, her hands braced on the bank, her right leg extended above the water, her bare flesh exposed almost to the knee. Then she tipped back her head, looked up at the marquess, and laughed. She'd been worried about seeing him again? Worried about what she'd do, what she'd say? How silly! Joking with the marquess of Daventry, teasing with him, was as natural as breathing. "You could always have a statue commissioned, my lord. You could call it *Girl Shivering with One Foot in Cold Stream*."

"Well, in that case, Miss Victor," Adam said, extending a hand to help her to her feet, "I suppose you should be allowed to move. I remember how cold that water is, you know. Lord, but it's wonderful to see you again. I woke this morning, half-believing I'd dreamed the whole thing."

"And this isn't a dream?" Sherry asked, wondering when it was that she'd learned to look up at a man through her lowered lashes, how she knew that this simple maneuver held a power potent beyond imagination.

"Not if Geoff's unmerciful teasing at the breakfast table could be taken as an indication that, yes, he did catch me out last night in the rose garden, making a fool of myself."

Sherry blinked at him. Once. Twice. "Making a fool of yourself?" she asked quietly. "How?"

His smile lit her world, that small, silly world she'd lived in so long, never knowing it hadn't contained the full brilliance of the sun. "By letting you leave, I suppose. Why did I let you leave me, if even for a moment?" He raised a hand to her cheek, allowed his fingers to drift softly over her skin. "Dreams, especially those very rare real-life dreams, should be held tightly, or else they slip away."

Looking up at him through her lashes had been the limit of Sherry's expertise in this new world of flirtation, of dalliance. "I—I think I'm frightened, my lord," she said honestly, blurting out exactly what was on her mind. Truth, her mama had told her more than once, was Sherry's greatest failing.

"Yes," he said slowly, his hand falling back to his side, a small frown marring his smooth forehead, clouding his dark eyes. "So am I, Miss Victor. So am I. Are you hungry? I've brought a basket, as promised."

She watched him as he retrieved a blanket and wicker basket from a spot just on the other side of the trees. He spread a thick plaid blanket on the ground, then motioned for her to sit down.

How handsome he was, even more so in a simple white shirt and tan breeches than he had been last night, when he'd been clad in more formal, fashionable attire. She liked him better this way, with his dark hair slightly rumpled by the breeze, without the starch and correctness of evening dress. He wasn't nearly so formidable, although he was twice as impressive.

"I'll do that," she said quickly, as he moved to open the basket. "You go over there, behind the willow tree, and bring back my contribution. You do like cakes, don't you? I—I rose rather early this morning, and badgered Cook into allowing me use of her kitchen."

He raised one dark, winged brow. "Are you saying, Miss Victor, that you have baked us some cakes? Surely I'm mistaken."

"No," Sherry said as she knelt over the basket, reaching into it and pulling out a large napkin folded over a roasted half chicken. "I'm very good at cakes. Not quite as talented with a piecrust, I'm afraid. Papa says he could sole his boots with my piecrust. But you'll like these spiced cakes, I promise. I put raisins in them."

Adam put the small basket holding a half dozen round, icing-dribbled cakes on the blanket, but not until he'd lifted the top of the basket and breathed in deeply. "I can see there's a good deal I don't know about you, Miss Victor—Sherry, if I might. I think we're already miles beyond 'Miss Victor' and 'my lord,' don't you?"

"Mrs. Forrest would have said miles and miles, my lord. All the way past the most distant boundaries of Perdition, as a matter of fact."

"Adam. My name is Adam, Sherry."

She felt herself blush, which was beyond anything ridiculous. She'd kissed the man, for heaven's sake. She could certainly say his name. "Adam," she said quietly, handing him the bottle of wine from the Daventry cellars she found tucked into the side of the basket.

Rather than taking the wine, he closed his hand over hers, held it fast until she looked at him. "I don't know about you, Sherry, but I think if we were to kiss, just one time, we'd both relax a little. As it is, I can feel your tension, and I'm worried you'll run away in another minute. Although your retreat would be a bit hindered, until you could find your shoes. Has anyone ever told you that you have beautiful ankles?"

Sherry curled her bare toes, drawing her legs more fully under her skirts. "I doubt a kiss is going to do anything to relax me, Adam, if you insist on talking to me this way. Or does everyone speak this way in Society? I don't know whether to take you seriously, or if I should laugh and say things like 'La, sir, you do flatter me so.' "

She frowned. "Except that, remembering my lessons from Mrs. Forrest, I don't believe gentlemen should say the word *ankles* in front of ladies. We're supposed to pretend such things don't really exist. I believe we're supposed to put forth the notion that we have two long sticks with wheels attached to them under our skirts, and that's all."

"Wheels?" Adam's grin lit her universe. "Well, now, that does it, Sherry. I have to kiss you now. You're simply too delightful for me to do anything else."

She put out a hand, placing it against his chest as they both knelt on the blanket. "No," she said, even as she longed to throw herself into his arms. "I met you yesterday, Adam. You met me yesterday. Since then, my entire world has turned upside down and inside out, until I don't know who I am, or who you are—not that I ever did, of course. I don't know what's right or wrong, or much care. So you're going to have to help me, all right?"

He took hold of her hand as it lay against his chest, stroked it. "Help you, Sherry? Gladly. I've said it a thousand times before, or more, but for the first time I truly mean the words. I am your servant, madam."

She felt tears pricking at the back of her eyes, blinked them away. "Are you teasing me, Adam, Marquess of Daventry? Am I losing my heart to a moment's madness as the peer amuses himself while being bored in the country, waiting for the Season to begin? Because I believe I'd rather stop now, run away now, than to continue this."

"Continue what, Sherry?" he interrupted. "Continue being here with me? Continue feeling what we're both feeling? Because I'm mad for you, you know. Completely and utterly mad for you. And I doubt I could *stop* any more than I could halt Buckfastleigh's Prize if he took it into his head to have himself a piece of that delicious chicken I've got absolutely no hunger for at the moment. I'd much rather feed on your mouth, my sweet, confused love. That wasn't particularly flowery, especially mentioning the bull, but I'm feeling a little light-headed at the moment, Sherry, so I hope you'll forgive me."

"Stop it, Adam, all right?" she demanded, pulling her hand free and rather ungracefully getting to her feet so that she could stare down at him. "Stop it right now, please. I'm sorry I can't tease and flirt, but I never learned how. I never cared to. Why, you won't believe it, considering how *fast* I've been, but I never even kissed a man until last night. What? Well, I hadn't! Are you laughing at me? You *are*— you *are!* You're laughing at me. What are you laughing at? Stop that! I haven't said anything even remotely funny. Adam!"

She was on the blanket again somehow, she wasn't sure how she had gotten to be there, lying on her back. Adam was on his knees, leering over her, still laughing, his eyes shining, his posture intimate, but not at all threatening.

"Don't move," he said, shifting his weight for a moment, picking up something, holding it in front of him, a rather abashed look on his handsome face. She saw the small basket she'd packed with cakes, the sadly crushed basket, imagined the ruined cakes inside it. "Ah, Sherry, I'm so sorry," he said, the corners of his mouth twitching rather adorably. Was there anything about him, this so sophisticated gentleman of society, that wasn't adorable? "I seem to have put my foot in it this time—or at least my knee. Will you forgive me?"

Sherry felt a bubble of laughter rising inside her. "I suppose that might be another way of looking at the old saying about not being able to both have your cake and eat it, too? I mean, you can have your share, Adam, but I seriously doubt you'll want to eat it now."

He tossed the basket away—Sherry thought she heard a small splash—and placed his hands on either side of her head, tangling his fingers in her unbound hair as it spread around her on the blanket. "This is wrong, and yet it's so right. I know I should be going slow, courting you. But I can't do it. You're too precious, and I'd rather slit my own throat than go through weeks and months of silliness when we both know what we want. We do, don't we? Mad and crazy as it is, we *do* know. If you feel what I'm feeling, let me kiss you now, Sherry. One kiss, that's as far as I can trust myself, and we'll go see your father. I've already sent off to London for a special license. I can do that you know. I'm the marquess of Daventry, thank God. But I really believe I need to marry you before the week is out, my darling Sherry. I really, really do."

She believed him. She believed every word he said to her. How could she do anything else?

"But, as I pointed out last night, Adam, I haven't asked," Sherry teased, any remaining misgivings melting away beneath the heat of his gaze. Yes, it *was* possible to tease and still be quite serious at the same time. It was possible to love, and to laugh, and to want nothing more than this man, this moment. It was possible to embrace a dream. "Neither of us, as a matter of fact, has asked the question."

"Perhaps not," he said, lowering his mouth toward hers as she saw all of her tomorrows in his eyes, "but I believe we both know the answer."

Appearances are often deceiving.
—Aesop

Chapter Nine

Sherry awoke smiling, her mind still wrapped in a lovely dream. She was loved, she was cherished, she was . . .

She pressed a hand to her mouth, stifling an involuntary dry sob.

She was *awake*.

Perhaps if she closed her eyes, and wished it enough, she could go back to sleep, back to her dream. Back to the time Adam had loved her, to the time she'd loved him.

Had either of them really loved? *Really?*

If she really loved him, she'd forgive him. If he really loved her, he'd never have believed she could have betrayed him with Dickie. If they'd been anything other than foolish dreamers, desperately trying to make their impossibly romantic paradise last, perhaps they would have had time to know what love really is.

Now, he was sorry. Now, she couldn't forgive him. Couldn't forgive herself. Couldn't forgive the dream.

Was it really too late? People who can't feel don't fall asleep crying, wake smiling. People who don't care shouldn't feel a small leap of the heart at the thought that maybe, just possibly, there was hope. That there had always been hope.

Always been love.

A love based on a dream—even Adam had said so. A marriage forged by a mutual passion before either of them had time to think, to reflect, even to learn anything about the other person except that they were both quite certain they couldn't exist without each other.

And now there was to be a child. Her child. Adam's child.

Sherry rested her hands on her still-flat belly, felt a tear slide toward her temple, lose itself in her hair.

She could still feel.

And it was time for her to grow up. Time for her to take charge of her life. She was a woman now, no matter that she had entered this marriage as a silly child. She was soon to be a mother. There were dreams, and there was real life.

Real life was Geoff in pain. Real life was hurting, and living, and being true to yourself so that you could be true to others, most especially to your husband, the man you loved. Real life was truth.

Real life, Sherry thought, sighing, was also Emma Oxton, who had just entered the bedchamber, shuffling her feet, her expression its usual faintly hostile smirk.

It's past time to wake up, Charlotte Victor Dagen-

ham, time to grow up. Start small, Sherry told herself. *And then build from there.*

"Emma?" she said, sitting up in bed, pushing at the mound of pillows behind her. "I'd like my breakfast now, if you please. Served to me right here in bed, because I think *that* would please me. In fact, I'd like it served to me in bed every morning, served at precisely this time. What time is it?"

"Clock's on the mantel," Emma said, halfheartedly poking at the fire, which she'd nearly allowed to go out. "Yer goin' ta make me track all the way back down two sets of stairs, just ta bring yer breakfast when there's a whole mess of breakfast waitin'? Waitin' in the *breakfast* room. That's why they calls it that, I imagine. No, ma'am, I don't think so. What put such a hair up yer nose, anyways? Uh-oh. His Lordship weren't here last night, were he? Maybe tonight, hmmm?" she ended, winking in a way that made Sherry feel dirty.

"Emma," she said, sliding her feet over the edge of the bed and standing up very straight, looking at the woman, staring her down. "You're dismissed."

The maid nodded, sitting down in one of the small, upholstered chairs in front of the fireplace. "Good. I knowed yer'd change yer mind and see the right of goin' down ta breakfast."

Sherry rolled her eyes, wondering just how distracted she must have been since coming back to London, ever to have put up with such insolence. "No, Emma, I mean you're dismissed. Discharged. Let go, as of this moment. I'll see that his lordship's secretary arranges for a final payment of wages, but there will be no letter recommending your services to an unsuspecting world. I'm not that accomplished at fibs. Which is probably a good thing," she said, softening just slightly, "as I really don't think you were born to be a maid, Emma. You're very pretty, too. Perhaps a future treading the boards? Or—or, perhaps selling things in a milliner's shop? But, no matter what, you can no longer work here. Is that understood?"

The maid blanched. "Yer doesn't mean that, ma'am. Yer can't."

"Oh, Emma, but I do. You're incompetent, unwilling to learn, and seem to believe that you're in charge here. You're not. I certainly can blame myself for allowing this impossible situation to go on for as long as it did, but it can't continue any longer. You're dismissed."

Emma's expression lost its fear, filled itself to the brim with cunning as she stood up, jammed her fists against her waist. "And that's it? You'd turn me off with no character? I'm not *good* enough for the little country baby turned whore? Oh, why so shocked? You think I didn't hear about it? About *Dickie* Brimley tossing up your skirts and your husband finding you together, playing the beast with two backs while his only brother lay trapped in a ditch?"

"How dare you!" Sherry's palms itched to slap Emma's face. "Where did you hear such a lie?"

"Servants talk," Emma told her casually, picking up Sherry's new shawl and draping it around her own shoulders. She picked up a pearl brooch that hadn't been put away, pinned the shawl closed at the bodice. "Turn me off, *missy*, and all of London will know. Whose bun do you have slowly baking in the oven? That's what they'll ask. Oh, yes, I know about that, too. Isn't it your *maid* who cleans up after your monthly flux—the flux you haven't had since I've been here? And His Lordship? He won't be able to stand for the gossip. Not him. He's too proud. Proud as Lucifer. We'll see who's ordering who about then, won't we—*whore*."

Sherry held on to the bedpost as she sank unsteadily onto the side of the bed. "Your speech . . ." she said, wetting her dry lips with a nervous flick of her tongue. "What—what happened to your speech?"

Emma stuck a diamond-encrusted comb into her hair, pocketed more than a few pots from the top of the dressing table, then turned to Sherry, raising her hands as if in alarm. "Lawks! Criminy! Wot happened ta the maid's speech?" She walked over to Sherry and bent down, going nearly nose-to-nose with her. "Look at those eyes, would you? Innocent enough to turn a person's stomach. So sweet, so damned pure. So bloody stupid! But you won't get me into trouble with him, I can tell you that, whore. I'm here, and I'm staying, or else the babe's branded a bastard, I promise you. Bah!" she said, stepping back. "I don't know what he sees in you. I truly, truly don't. This should have been over months ago. But he keeps dragging it out, dragging it out. And for what? For *you?*"

As Emma turned to leave, Sherry grabbed onto her wrist, held her fast. "What are you talking about,

Emma? *Who* are you talking about? Someone put you in this household, didn't they, made certain you'd be put in this household? Was it Dickie? Was it Richard Brimley? Dear God, it has to have been Dickie. *Why?* To watch me? To watch my husband? Geoff? It's another game, isn't it? Another terrible game. Where is he, Emma? What is he trying to do? I want to talk to him. I *have* to talk to him."

"Let . . . me . . . go," Emma ordered slowly, her face a mask of cold fury, each word she uttered even colder, harder. Her eyes seemed to glow, her gaze was so hot in that cold face, so intensely hot. "There's a smart girl. Now why don't you get yourself dressed, big girl that you are, and go eat some breakfast. I'll be taking a small nap in my room. *Ma'am,*" she said as Sherry released her, then watched as the maid—no, never the maid—slowly walked out of the room.

Sherry pressed shaking hands to her mouth. She'd awakened from a dream this morning and entered into a nightmare. Richard Brimley was back in her life.

"What have you there, Geoff?" Adam asked his brother as he walked into the drawing room, thinking about a snifter of brandy, although he'd settle for a single glass of wine.

"A puzzle," Geoff said, holding up a wooden sphere that seemed to be constructed out of more than two dozen small, variously shaped wooden pieces. "Edmund sent it round. I'm to take it apart, then try to put it back together again, so that it looks the same as it does now. Edmund's note informs me that it is possible, but not probable. I'm deciding whether I want to try it, or simply tell Edmund I took the dratted thing apart and had it all back together in five minutes flat."

Adam took a sip of wine, then placed the glass on a table, relieving Geoff of the sphere, hefting its weight in his hand. "He'd only ask you to do it again, in front of him. Or hadn't you thought of that?"

Geoff's mischievous smile was infectious, always had been. So Adam smiled, too.

"Oh, I see," Adam said, handing the sphere back to his brother. "I'm to be your witness, aren't I? Clever, Geoff. Very clever. I won't do it."

"No, I rather thought you wouldn't. And asking Sherry would be a pure waste of breath. Never met a person less suited to fibbing, even in a good cause."

Adam's mood, not really good when he'd come into the room, sank a notch. "If you'd thought of that before you asked her to lie for you, we might be in better shape now. All of us."

Geoff began dismantling the sphere, pulling out different pieces of wood, each a unique shape, and laying them in his lap. "I was going to run that race, Adam. That day or the next, wet roads or dry. I'd become obsessed with those races. So were you, for a time."

"I was running a different sort of race," Adam said quietly, picking up his wineglass again, taking another sip of the pale liquid. "I lost, by the way, even as I won," he ended, lobbing the wineglass into the fireplace with only halfhearted force, watching as it shattered against the andirons.

"Sherry never loved Brimley, Adam. She was fascinated, I'll grant you. So was I. So were you. It was a crazy few weeks. Heady. Exciting. Stupid."

Adam sat down, knowing Geoff hated looking up at everyone. "Where do you suppose he went? I even hired a Bow Street Runner, but to no avail. It's like he dropped off the edge of the earth."

"Earth's round, brother, like this sphere," Geoff said, then grimaced at the pieces in his lap. "Perhaps not this sphere. Not now, anyway. But I know what you mean. He was there, and then he was gone. Poof!"

"Leaving you in a ditch as he pawed my wife," Adam bit out, knowing that even now, months later, he could choke Richard Brimley to death without a thought to the consequences. "I'll never forgive him."

"Yes, he may have sensed that," Geoff said, holding up two of the pieces, one shaped like a house with a curved roof, the other in the image of a dog. "For a while there, I thought you were going to murder me. Did I tell you I can stand now?"

Adam was immediately shaken out of his bad humor. "You can what? Geoff—why didn't you tell me?"

"I just did, brother mine. I think this new man you've set on me has discovered my problem. It's my pelvis, you see. I looked it up in one of your books. Quite a big bone, Adam, and fairly important, as it turns out. I broke it. Probably into more than two pieces. Knocked those pieces around a bit. Best thing I could have done, it turns out, was lying down and staying down. But the bone is healing now, and I can stand again, with a little help. Just don't ask me to walk. Not yet."

"When?" Adam asked, staring at his brother with an intensity of purpose that should have had the younger man on his feet and skipping around the room.

"When?" Geoff repeated, smiling. "When I can stand the pain—*stand* the pain—less than I can content myself in this chair, I suppose. He's bringing me canes today, as a matter of fact. Two of them, one for each hand. God, Adam, you're not weeping, are you? I told Sherry this morning, and she all but ruined my new jacket with her tears. Maudlin bunch, you are, when I'm handing out good news. We always knew I'd walk again someday. Or at least hoped it."

Adam brushed at his cheeks with the back of one hand. He felt hope again. Such intense, nearly over-whelming hope. "We're going to get it back, Geoff. Everything we lost. We're going to get it back. It's going to be like it was before—for you, for Sherry, for all of us. I can feel it."

Geoff shook his head sadly. "No, Adam. We're never going to get it all back to the way it was. I wouldn't want to, would you? It was too good, too per-fect to last, to be real. Like a dream. Very unlike this sphere. Look at the pieces, Adam. A tree, a small bust of Shakespeare or some dead poet—and I think this one is a cat. Yes, a cat, licking its paw, although part of its back is obviously also the outside of the sphere. They're amazing pieces. They're real. I can hold the pieces in my hand, enjoy each cleverly shaped one, even if I can never get them back together again to the same perfect way they were before I took the sphere apart, examined it, held the pieces in my hands. Lord, that's profound, especially for me. But perfection doesn't exist, Adam."

"It did. I thought it did. I wanted to believe in it, believe in the dream," Adam said quietly, almost to himself. He looked at Geoff. "How did you get so wise, little brother?"

Geoff smiled. "Lie in a bed staring at the ceiling for a month, brother, then sit in a chair for another. Gives a person more than enough time for thinking deep thoughts. But that's enough for now, as I refuse to be maudlin today. Did I tell you I'm going to Lady Winston's masked ball with Edmund and Sherry? Outmoded, costume parties, but there's little enough amusement in the Small Season, so it might be fun. You won't believe the costume Edmund had sent over along with his little puzzle. It's the most clever contraption. I'm to go as the throne of England. All gold and gilt, with my head sticking out as part of the decoration. Clever, yes? As long as no one decides to sit in me."

"Especially one of the inevitable dozen portly Henry Tudors we'll be seeing there," Adam said, disliking the fact that he disliked the notion of Edmund Burnell becoming such a large part of life at Grosvenor Square. Which was ridiculous. The man was harmless enough. Quite likable. Amusing. Rather like Richard Brimley. . . .

"Adam? What's wrong? Your face suddenly resembles a thundercloud. I thought you and Sherry were beginning to—well, you know what I thought, what I'm hoping. Surely it isn't Edmund? You're not going to judge Edmund by the same ruler we all so belatedly used to measure Richard Brimley?"

"No," Adam said, standing up and smiling down at his brother, shaking off his dark thoughts, his ridiculous, dark thoughts. "No, of course not. I simply remembered that I don't have a costume. A simple domino is out of the question, not when my brother is going to appear as the throne of England. I think I'll go hunt up Chollie, and the two of us can cudgel our brains for ideas. I'll see you at dinner, all right?"

"Help Chollie if you want, but Edmund sent round rigouts for you and Sherry as well, you know. Good man, Edmund," Geoff told him, wheeling after Adam as he walked toward the hallway. "I had Rimmon peek inside the boxes."

"And?" Adam asked, feeling his jaw set into a tight line. Burnell was going too far, even in the name of friendship.

Geoff's grin reached all the way to his mischievous eyes. "According to the note Rimmon found, you're to be the fabled King Arthur. Which doesn't mean *you* can sit in me. Oh, give over, Adam. Smile! I like Edmund. What's wrong with that?"

"He wants you to like him, Geoff," Adam said, feeling that a curtain drawn closed over some great revelations was slowly beginning to draw back, giving him a view of the stage where his life was playing out. "He wants us all to like him."

"And that's bad?"

"I don't know, Geoff," Adam said, suddenly anxious to meet with Chollie, speak with Chollie. "I honestly don't know anymore."

"Leaving Sherry to be Guinevere," Chollie said, sitting back in his chair, peering at Adam over his spectacles. "Interesting tragedy, I suppose. We Irish had it first, don't you know. We're very good at tragedies. You English bollixed it all up with round tables and swords stuck into stone and all that rot. But we had it first."

"My apologies, Chollie. In fact, I apologize for every Irish twig crushed by an English boot, every Irish tree now holding up an English roof. But this is getting us nowhere. I was asking you about Edmund Burnell."

"Yes, but that's the devil of it, Adam. I don't know what you want me to say. Do I like Burnell? Very much. We had us a fine time the other night, drinking, singing, wenching. He knows all the songs, Adam. Even verses I forget once I'm three-parts castaway and feeling particularly maudlin. And even then, with the both of us more in our cups than out of them, he went off with two—*two*, Adam—lovely ladies hanging on his arms. Left me sprawled out, filled with wine and wishes, but with no way to make more than the spirit willing. Ah, Adam, he's the man I could be if I were more of a man. Prettier, with more coins jingling in his pockets, and with a winning way about him even this Irishman envies. His mother must have been Irish. It's the only explanation."

"It's one explanation, Chollie," Adam said, rubbing at his forehead. "I only wish I could think of others. But there's something, *something*—" He stood up, looking toward the door, suddenly wanting to be outside, in the cool, crisp air. He might think better, outside. He might think, rather than simply react to the nagging feeling that something was wrong. Very wrong. Was he fated to forever measure each new friend with Richard Brimley's yardstick? That was no way to live a life.

"It's not like you to be so suspicious, boyo," Chollie pointed out, draining his glass and joining Adam as they both walked out of the club. "You've talked to me some, but there's still a mess of talking to be done, I'm thinking. What happened this summer, to change you so? To make you go around peeking under your bed, like an old woman looking for demons?"

Adam clapped his hat onto his head, pulled his greatcoat more closely about him as they walked down the flagway. "Demons under the bed, Chollie? I'll leave that to people like you, who routinely feel geese skipping over your grave. I'm just wondering if Burnell will be taking me aside in a week or so, telling me all about some fantastic bubble I should be investing in with him now that we're such fast friends. I'm only wondering if I should have my valet sew my pockets shut." It was a lie, but a reasonable one.

He waited for his friend's reaction.

"All right, boyo," Chollie said after a bit. "I'll admit it. Edmund Burnell is too perfect. There. I've said it. Too friendly, too open with his money, too willing to be anything and everything I want him to be. And nobody's perfect, Adam. Nobody. Perhaps he is after your money, seeing as you're obscenely rich. He certainly can't be after my fortune, as I barely have any. And is it thinking he's being fast friends with me, with Geoff, with Sherry, in order to get you to liking him more, trusting him more? There have been worse scoundrels, more devious plots."

"Sometimes, Chollie, there's no plot at all. Just a love of trouble."

"Well, now, there you've got me, boyo. I'm not so deep as to see the point of trouble for trouble's sake. There's always a reason. It's just up to us to find it. You'll want my smiling face and open ears at Lady Winston's tomorrow night, I'm supposing? Guarding your back, as it were?"

"I can't think of anyone else I'd trust more, Chollie," Adam said, as his carriage drew to the curb and Biggs jumped down to open the door, pull out the steps. "Now, come on back to Grosvenor Square with me, and we'll have my valet cut a good five inches of material from my black domino for you, so that you don't trip over it while you're guarding my back."

Chollie shook his head. "A domino, Adam? Do you think I'm so lacking in imagination, then? No, if we're going to make bloody fools of ourselves, you can count on me to hold up my end of the farce. Now, go home, boyo. Think pleasant thoughts. I'll see you Thursday night."

"How will I know you?"

Winking, Chollie said, "Oh, boyo, not to worry. Arthur recognized his wizard at once. You will, too."

"Merlin? You'll be Merlin?"

"In the Irish tale—the *first,* you'll remember—I do believe he was a magical leprechaun. But I'll make do, I'll make do."

Sherry hadn't wanted to enter the Bond Street shop, but Emma was insistent, vowing that she'd find what she wanted there.

Was Dickie waiting for her inside the shop?

She'd left Grosvenor Square with Emma as her companion, at Emma's suggestion, and believing that the woman was going to show her something she really did not want to see. Yet needed to see. Needed to know.

It was dark inside the shop, even in the midst of what passed for a sunny English day, and it took some moments for Sherry's eyes to adjust to the dimness.

And then she saw her. Standing in front of the counter, being assisted by a young male clerk, at least two dozen bolts of cloth spread out for her inspection. Tall, beautiful, demanding. The duchess of Westbrook. Edmund Burnell's spurned lover. The woman who had once held Adam's heart. A woman Sherry didn't want, need, to see. Coincidence could be stretched just so far, and this time coincidence snapped.

"You knew this," she accused Emma. "You knew she'd be here. How?"

Emma didn't answer, but just brushed past Sherry, nodding to the clerk, then passing through a hanging curtain and into a room at the back of the small shop. Leaving Sherry very much alone, which was ridiculous, for she'd been longing to be shed of the woman. It was just that she suddenly felt safer when she could *see* her.

Sherry looked at the clerk again, having realized that he and Emma must know each other. He excused himself from the duchess and stepped out from behind the counter, smiling at Sherry.

"My lady Daventry," he said, his tone and smile proper for a clerk, his eyes those of a hunter who has just spied out the prey he'd been seeking. "How good of you to grace this humble establishment. I'm sure I could have had the package delivered, but now that you're here . . ."

"The package?" Sherry could barely make her mouth form the words. His eyes. They were Dickie's eyes. She was looking at a stranger, and seeing Dickie's eyes. How could that be? "You—have a package for me?"

"A gift, actually," the clerk said, as the duchess turned, looked, approached.

"Lady Daventry, how good to see you," Melinda said, her gaze traveling Sherry's length, as if measuring her. "How is our dear bride? Such a fuss this past spring, with Daventry springing his bride on us all without warning. There were more than a few unhappy faces when first we heard, as I believe the betting books were fairly weighted on the notion that dearest Adam would never marry. Are you here alone? That's not done, you know. Even for milk-and-water pusses from the country. Only naughty ladies of immense consequence, like myself, dare to come to Bond Street unescorted."

"My—my maid accompanied me, Your Grace," Sherry said, feeling very much the child. The awkward child. The duchess of Westbrook was a work of art, even if small lines of unhappiness had begun to etch themselves on either side of her full mouth. She could imagine Edmund being attracted to her, could not imagine him rebuffing her.

"Whatever, my dear," the duchess said airily, gesturing to a bolt of silvery cloth spread over the counter. "That's the one, dear boy. And the blue velvet as well. Have the materials sent to Madame Yolande and the bill delivered to Mr. Burnell, as usual. If he rips it off, he pays for the replacement. With Mr. Burnell's appetites, dear boy, you'll soon be able to afford a larger establishment at the more fashionable end of Bond Street."

Sherry winced. She hadn't been schooled in hiding her reaction to heavy-handed hints like the duchess's that she was Edmund Burnell's lover. Besides, she was still looking at the clerk, still seeing Richard Brimley's eyes, feeling much like she was standing in Hell, looking at Heaven. Or the other way round. . . .

"I said, Lady Daventry," the duchess said with heavy emphasis, "have you made the acquaintance of Mr. Edmund Burnell? He's staying in London with his aunt, Lady Jasper. Fascinating man. Horrid old woman."

"Yes," Sherry told her quietly as the clerk went behind the counter once more, began rerolling the bolts of material. "My husband introduced me to Mr. Burnell. I agree. He's a most, um, fascinating man."

The duchess moved closer, so close that Sherry could smell the wine that soured her breath. "One mention, one word, of what you saw at Lady J's, my dear, and it will go badly for you. Do you understand?"

"I don't—"

"Oh, please, don't even attempt to dissemble, my dear. I know you were in the drawing room. Edmund made sure of that. He takes great pleasure in waving other women in front of my face. He enjoys hurting people."

Sherry couldn't help herself. She asked the question. "Why would you want a man who would do that to you?"

The duchess threw back her head, laughed heartily. "Either Daventry is very good in bed, or totally inept. Either way, I can't believe you just asked that question. Edmund hasn't had you yet, has he? No wonder he's in such a foul temper. I'll have to go see him, tweak him. Good day, my dear. You should probably be running along yourself, as it must almost be time for your porridge."

I don't know what's happening. I don't want to know. I want to go home, Sherry chanted inside her head as Emma reappeared from the back room, a large, flat box under her arm. *Please, please. I just want to go home.*

Sherry looked toward the counter, but the clerk was gone, an older woman taking his place, already showing bolts of cloth to another customer, one Sherry hadn't even noticed entering the shop.

"Time to leave, little innocent," Emma said, dragging Sherry by the elbow. "You can open this once we're back in the carriage. It's a present. A very special present."

Sherry shook off Emma's grip. "No," she said firmly, her heart pounding, her voice shaky, but her resolve suddenly quite firm. She took the package, because not knowing what was inside could only be worse than knowing. "No more games. I don't know what's going on, Emma, but I'm not playing anymore. Your belongings will be bundled up and waiting for you in the kitchens. Find your own way back to Grosvenor Square."

Emma's eyes slitted evilly. "He won't be happy," she warned tightly.

"Who, Emma? *Who* won't be happy? Dickie? That was a cousin, or a brother, or someone inside that shop. Wasn't it? Did you all really believe I wouldn't recognize those eyes? Or is that someone Edmund Burnell?" She leaned close to the maid, all but spitting out her words. "Either way, tell them the game is over, Emma, whatever mad, elaborate game it is. I've lost everything once. I won't lose it again. Do you understand?"

"Oh, I understand, little idiot," Emma said, drawing herself up so that she was nose-to-nose with Sherry. "And one day you will as well. I'm going to enjoy that." And then she turned and walked back into the shop, leaving Sherry alone on the flagway.

"M'lady?" the footman prompted as Sherry stared at

the door to the shop, seeing the name for the first time. *Oxton's.* Oxton was Emma's name. A cold shiver raced along Sherry's spine.

"Yes, yes," she said, feeling hysteria mount up inside her, trying to beat it down. She handed the footman the package, which he returned to her once she was settled inside the carriage.

She stared at the box for a long time, an endless, frightened time, then opened the lid.

She heard Dickie's voice then, heard it inside her head as she told him he was mad, insane: "Yes, I know. Otherwise, little doll, this would be over now. Instead, it is just beginning."

The large spray of very dead roses spilled onto the carriage floor as Sherry slid sideways in a swoon.

Adam bounded up the stairs two at a time, and slammed down the hallway before bursting into Sherry's bedchamber. "Sherry? Are you all right? Rimmon told me—"

"I'm fine, Adam," she told him from the depths of the high, wide tester bed. "Mrs. Clement took me very much in hand when Biggs summoned her, and I've been cosseted enough for any three women. Mrs. Clement says women in my delicate condition are prone to bouts of dizziness in the first few months."

"The child," Adam mumbled through numb lips, thankful for his housekeeper, who was a calm, competent woman. "I hadn't thought about the child. Of course." He approached the bed, sat down on its edge. "I'm sorry, Sherry."

"Sorry? For what? I want this child, Adam. I want this child very much. I can understand if you don't, but I do."

Adam winced, knowing he'd put yet another foot wrong. Once, they had talked for hours, laughed for hours. Now he couldn't seem to say anything that made Sherry happy. "Where's that maid of yours? Rimmon told me you came back unescorted."

Sherry's gaze slid away from his even as her cheeks paled. She looked so small in the large bed, so young, so vulnerable. "I—I dismissed her. I should have done it sooner, but today just seemed to be the time I chose. Mrs. Clement is sending for her niece, Dorris, to replace her. She said it was about time, too, but I think making the sign against the evil eye when she mentioned Emma's name was perhaps a shade too dramatic, don't you?"

Adam was upset, more than upset by Sherry's faint, but that didn't mean he'd lost his wits entirely. "I never liked that woman. Lazy, insolent. But you insisted on keeping her, so I let it alone. She did something, didn't she? Something that upset you?"

"No!" Sherry pressed her hands to her cheeks, probably to hide the guilty coloring she must know he'd learned to recognize. "Well, yes," she said, dropping her hands as he tipped his head, looked at her expectantly. "She purposely directed me to a shop owned by one of her family. At least I think so, as the name painted on the window was Oxton. If she had said as much, that would be one thing, but I decided she was, um, overstepping. She was rather belligerent when I pointed that out to her and . . . and, well, I dismissed her."

A lie for a lie. Did she believe admitting to one lie made it easier for her to dupe him with the second one? Poor Sherry. She was cursed with the inability to be even the slightest bit devious. A truth he had learned too late, but a truth nonetheless.

"And the dead roses, Sherry?" he asked quietly, taking her hands in his, holding them, squeezing them slightly. "Is that what your maid's family sell in their shop? Dead roses?"

"Oh, God," Sherry breathed, closing her eyes. "Adam, could you send Mrs. Clement to me, please? I'm feeling faintly muzzy again, and she said she'd bring me tea. And I'm to remain in bed for the rest of the day, which is probably a good thing, for I'm really quite sleepy."

"Sherry? What's happening? I don't blame you for not trusting me. God knows I've been an ass these past months. But, please, darling, talk to me now. Something's going on. Something I don't understand. Let me help you, darling. Let us help each other."

She looked at him. With love in her eyes. He prayed it was love in her eyes. But without a drop of trust. "Emma was a maid, Adam, not the Devil incarnate. I dismissed her then, silly thing that I am, swooned when I felt guilty about doing something I should have done weeks ago. The box was Emma's, not mine. I have no idea why it contained dead roses, any more than I know where she is now. Nor do I care. And I think it very mean of you to press at me when I'm not feeling quite well. If you'd ring for Mrs. Clement now?"

Knowing when he was beaten, not that one battle was the war, Adam left and made his way down the servants' stairs, hoping to find the footman in the kitchens. He grabbed the youth by the ear, dragged him out to the mews, and ordered two horses saddled at once.

"We goin' somewheres, milord?" the footman asked, speaking around a lump of apple wedged into his cheek.

"You're taking me to Bond Street," Adam said as the two horses were brought out. "To the shop her ladyship visited this afternoon. You do remember its location, don't you?"

"Yes, milord, that I does," the footman agreed, and they were off.

An hour later, having twice ridden the length of Bond Street, they returned to the mews, the footman still shaking his head, still apologizing. "I coulda sweared that was the shop, milord. A draper's shop, that's wot it was. Mayhap if we wuz ta go back onct more?"

"No need, no need," Adam said, dismounting, handing the reins to a groom. "Thank you for your time."

They'd gone directly to the draper's shop, the footman firm in his belief of its direction, only to find an empty store. No name on the glass, no goods on the shelves. He'd humored the footman, riding the length of Bond Street with him, but he knew they'd found the correct shop.

Adam opened the door to Sherry's chamber, finding the draperies closed against the faint light outside, the entire room in shadows. He walked to the side of the bed, looking down at his wife as she slept, whispered to her in the darkness.

"It's a game, isn't it, darling? A dangerous, dangerous game neither of us wanted to play, one for which neither of us knows the rules. We never did. He's back, isn't he? Richard Brimley is back. He's playing the game again. You know it, I know it. We just don't know why."

Adam found a chair, carried it over to the bed, sat down, took one of Sherry's hands in his. He was prepared to stay with her all through the night, protecting her from demons he couldn't understand. "Ah, sweetheart, if only we could go back. If only we could begin again. It was all so wonderful. Such a perfect dream. I'd gladly sell my soul to have that dream back again . . ."

Book Two

A Dangerous Game

*It is the function of vice to
keep virtue within reasonable bounds.*

—Samuel Butler

Soft eyes look'd love to eyes which spake again,
And all went merry as a marriage bell.
                                        —Lord Byron

Chapter Ten

"Such haste, Romeo, is unseemly," Geoff said as he sat sideways in the Sheraton armchair, his legs dangling over the side as he watched his brother being shaved.

"Really?" Adam accepted a warmed towel from his valet and rubbed it over his jaw, then stood, inspecting himself in the mirror over the dressing stand. He usually shaved himself, but this was his wedding day, and he was nervous as any bridegroom. He didn't plan to start this most important of all days by bleeding all over his cravat.

"Oh, yes. Truly. I may even have read that somewhere," Geoff continued happily, for he'd been drinking since early that morning, by way of celebration, as he'd told Adam. "Wait, I have another one! Not Romeo, though. Seems my school days weren't all spent working most diligently to avoid learning anything. Congreve, I believe, or one of those dead poets. Yes, he's the one. How did he say it? Something about marrying in haste, only to repent in leisure? There's probably a few *fies* and a *'tis* in there somewhere, but it hurts my brain to get round those words. Anyway, brother, you know the girl a week. If that's not haste, I don't know what is."

"Perhaps I worried you'd try to steal a march on me," Adam said as he slipped his arms into the waistcoat his valet held out for him. "There is that."

"As if there's a chance of that happening. Not that you're more handsome, mind you. Lord knows I'm the only one who inherited any looks in the family. Unfortunately, you inherited the title. Now you're probably going to reproduce yourself a half dozen times, so that I'll never again be able to toddle around London with the words *heir to the title* reverently whispered after me as I pass."

"Is that what they whisper?" Adam said, teasing his brother, who was doing such a fine job of teasing him. "I had thought they were whispering 'there he goes, the younger brother of that most marvelous marquess of Daventry.'"

"Marvelous, is it? Hah! Think, man, think what you're doing to me. I can't be sure, considering the fact that I'm more handsome, younger, and quite a wit, but I may just be losing much of my consequence thanks to *your* losing a bout with Cupid. God, no wonder I'm drinking. I thought this was a celebration, but perhaps I'm drinking to the passing of a dear, dear boy. Me, that is. Moving out of the shadow of the title, and fully into obscurity. Ah, the misery." He held out his empty glass. "Pour me some more wine, would you, brother? My mouth's too dry to summon a suitably affecting, anguished moan."

"I think you've had enough, as you're supposed to be bearing me up as I suffer through my last hours as a carefree bachelor. Keep me from bolting, running out through the back of the chapel, or whatever it is bridegrooms do when they realize they're about to trade their freedom for a yoke around their necks."

"A yoke around your neck? Oh, Sherry would appreciate hearing that, I'm sure." Geoff scrambled to his feet. "I think I'll just go tell her. Right after I pour myself another glass of wine."

Adam watched his brother pour two glasses of wine, accepted the one he was offered. "Do you really think I'm making a mistake, Geoff?"

"Do you, brother?"

Adam sank into the tall chair, waving his valet out of the room. "I'm mad for her, Geoff. From the moment I first saw her, I knew. I just knew."

"You knew what, Adam?"

"That I had to have her."

Geoff cleared his throat, but didn't speak.

"What?" Adam asked, looking at his brother. "Go on. Say what's on your mind."

"You had to have her, Adam? I see. Then we're not speaking of love here, are we? Having her is owning her. Possessing her. I think I'd feel better if you'd drop a few I *love her's* and I *adore her past all rea-soning's* into this conversation. I mean, I like Sherry. She's quite a sweet, innocent, loving young crea-ture. She probably believes you love her."

"Of course I love her," Adam said testily, grabbing his favorite old jacket from the back of the chair and punching his arms into the sleeves. There was time and enough for his valet to return, to help him with his cravat, his bridal clothes. He felt a sudden need to be out of this room, perhaps to take a walk through the gardens, breathe some fresh air. "Bloody hell, Geoff, I never said I didn't love her."

"And she's from a respectable family, not to men-tion that her father would probably feed your liver to his hounds were you to consider any other arrangement with Sherry besides marriage. Still, it would have been easier if she'd been a housemaid, or a dancer in London, I suppose. I've *had to have* a few of those myself, but it wasn't necessary to jump into a parson's mousetrap in order to do so, thank God. You're blowing hot right now, brother, hotter than the outskirts of Hell on a windy day. What hap-pens when that wind blows itself out? Are you left with only those empty words—*of course* I *love her?*"

"Go away, Geoff," Adam said, sinking onto the chair once more. "Take the decanter with you, but just go away, all right? The vicar will be here at two, and you can meet me in the chapel. In the mean-time, I believe I'd find more brotherly *support* in your absence."

"You won't ever hurt her, will you, Adam?" Geoff

asked quietly, laying a hand on his brother's shoulder. "You've snatched her up, carried her off on every young maiden's dream, if I know anything at all. Don't ever let her fall, all right? Because I don't think I could forgive you that, big brother or not. If I've ever met an innocent, it's Charlotte Victor. After Melinda, after all your years spent enjoying those not so innocent ladies of London, I think it's Sherry's innocence and honesty that you want, even more than you want her. The devil of it is that you have to destroy a part of that innocence you crave so much in order to possess it."

Adam rubbed the back of his hand across his mouth. "You know something, Geoff? I believe you're probably the most intelligent person I know. And I'm the least intelligent, because it took me until today to realize that fact. I was probably too busy rescuing you from your latest bout of recklessness, I suppose. Now go away. You've given me a lot to think about. A lot to think about . . ."

Sherry looked toward the small mountain of luggage standing in the foyer of Frame Cottage, knowing that their entire contents were totally unsuitable for a London Season. And yet, before the day was out, that's where she and her unsuitable wardrobe would be. In London. In Grosvenor Square. In her husband's town mansion.

Her husband. In less than two hours, Adam would be her husband.

Oh, God.

Perhaps if she ate something? No. Her stomach would surely go into revolt if she ate anything, even so much as a dry crust of toast.

She was dressed, ready. As dressed, and as ready, as three days of mad preparation could make her.

Her papa was nowhere to be found, unless she wished to go out to the kennels, a thought she suppressed as quickly as it had risen into her head. He'd been delighted with the match, of course, and had all but fallen on Adam's neck, profusely thanking him for wedding the Victor hounds to the Daventry hounds. That's how her papa saw the thing, Sherry knew, but she had lived with the man all of her life, and hadn't expected more.

If only her mama were here. She'd fuss over her only daughter. They'd giggle and plan and speculate about the gaiety of the London Season. And her mama would tell her about Adam, about what Adam would expect from her once she was his wife, once he didn't have to say "enough for now, sweetheart," and take her hand, and walk with her, walk away from their kisses . . .

She loved him. She was sure of that.

As sure as she could be.

"The gardener from up at Daventry Court sent these on over, love," Mary said from somewhere behind Sherry, so that she turned around quickly, nearly coming to grief as she forgot that her new shoes, purchased yesterday in the village, had small heels on them.

"Oh, Mary, they're beautiful!" Sherry reached toward the bouquet of blush pink roses, the circlet of palest pink rosebuds, almost afraid to touch their perfection. "Let's go into the drawing room, shall we? There's a mirror in there."

The circlet of roses had been fashioned around ribbon-wrapped wire, purest white ribbon that also bunched and hung from the back of the circlet, hanging as long as Sherry's unbound hair. Mary placed it on her young charge's head, low, over her forehead, then stood back, wiping a tear from her eye with a corner of her apron. "Oh, Little Miss," she said on a sob, "that's just what was needed. Now you're an angel."

Sherry smiled at this silliness as she took up the nosegay of roses held in place by a cone-shaped, silver filigree holder, and turned to look into the mirror. "Oh, my." she said a moment later, stepping forward slightly, unsure that she was seeing her own reflection.

Her gown was new, but necessarily simple, as the village seamstress had only three days and two assistants to help her. It was more of a slip than a real gown, made of softest white muslin, with a demurely scooped neckline that tied shut. In a moment of inspiration, the seamstress had sewn four graduated tiers of faux pearls to each shoulder, and they hung down nearly five inches onto Sherry's arms, giving the illusion of sleeves without the work of setting those sleeves into place.

There hadn't been time for fittings, so there hadn't been time for a cleverly constructed bodice. The gown fell straight from her shoulders and gathered neckline, with only a white-and-gold-satin rope loosely tied around her waist, rather in the way of a monk's habit. In fact, the entire gown had been made with no more measurements than Sherry's height, and even that hadn't quite worked out, as the gown was about three inches too long, so that it dragged a bit as she walked.

And yet?

"I do look rather nice, don't I, Mary?" Sherry said, turning to smile at her maid, at her dear friend who wouldn't accompany her to London. "Oh, Mary, do you think he'll approve? The marquess is more accustomed to satin and diamonds and—"

"He'd be a blind man to say anyone has ever looked more beautiful, Little Missy," Mary interrupted brusquely. "And a heathen indeed not to cherish you. Now, go sit down right here and wait while I find your papa and scold him until he agrees to get out of his boots and into decent clothes. A bath would be beyond even my scolding, I know, so you'll just have to be taken down the aisle by a man who smells of wet dog, or worse."

"Yes, Mary," Sherry said obediently, waiting until the maid had gone off in search of her papa, then uncrossing the fingers she'd held behind her back. Picking up her skirts, she went into the hallway, passing the mountain of luggage without a backward look, and ran out across the grass, toward the stream.

It was a crazy idea, and she'd probably end with

her new satin slippers ruined and green smears on her hem, but she just had to go to the stream. Had to be alone. Had to think.

Because she couldn't remember what Adam looked like. She wouldn't be able to identify him by his voice. How tall was he? She couldn't remember. What color were his eyes? Brown, surely. A brown nearly black in its darkness, especially when he looked at her, brought his head closer, bent to kiss her, set her insides to shivering.

Sherry picked her way through a line of trees and into the open field, walking quickly. Beginning to run . . .

She didn't know his full name. Certainly a marquess had more than a single name, probably an entire string of them. Perhaps the vicar would recite them for her during the ceremony, at the same time Adam learned that her second name was Amelia.

Charlotte Amelia Victor.

Stranger.

Stranger marrying stranger.

She ran faster, her skirts hiked up past her ankles, the streamers on the circlet of roses flying out behind her.

How had this all happened? How had she come to this day, her wedding day, the day she'd give herself over to a stranger for the rest of her life?

Perhaps if she didn't go back to Frame Cottage, but just stayed at the stream, dangling her toes in the cool water, nobody would think to look for her there.

What would everyone do then? Her papa? Adam? Would they mount a search, as her parents had done the day she'd hidden in a tree and heard her Uncle Giddy-up suggest she was soon to be torn apart by her papa's hounds?

What was her fate to be this time?

A sob tore at her throat. Too fast, too fast. It was all happening too fast. She didn't know Adam. Not really. He didn't know her, couldn't know her. She barely knew herself. After all, hadn't she been born only a few days ago?

Sherry slackened her pace only slightly as she dashed through the line of trees that edged the stream, then slammed to a halt in a patch of sunlight when she saw him. He was standing with his back to her, informally dressed in a dark blue jacket, his hands clasped behind his back, his head lifted, staring up at other dusty shafts of sunlight threaded down through the trees on the opposite bank.

"Adam?"

He turned slowly, as if he couldn't quite believe he'd heard her speak. "Sherry?"

She pressed a hand to her mouth as her stomach dropped to her toes. He looked so young, with his jacket hanging open, his shirt collar undone, his cravat nowhere in evidence. A lock of midnight-dark hair fell forward over his forehead, above slightly unfocused eyes. Darkest brown eyes, just as she remembered.

"My God, Sherry," he said quietly. "Look at you.

All in white, with your skirts trailing off behind you in a tumble of sweet grass and wildflowers. You're like an angel escaped from Heaven. So young. So innocent. I must be out of my mind."

She bent her head, plucking at the flowers in the nosegay. "What are you doing here, Adam?" she asked as a single tear splashed onto one perfect rose.

"Fighting with myself," he answered, and she saw his boots as she kept her eyes downcast, as she felt him moving closer, closer. His hand was on her shoulder now, his touch fairy-light, yet holding her in place, making it impossible for her to move.

She closed her eyes, her senses coming alive as he traced his hand along her shoulder, slid his fingers over the silly cascade of faux pearls, set fire to her flesh as he skimmed her flesh, took her hand in his.

She raised her head, looked at him through her tears, felt the living pulse of power leap between them even as she knew she didn't understand that power. Only that it frightened her.

"I can't let you go, Sherry," he said, stepping closer, bending his head so that his lips brushed her throat. "You've overrun my head, my soul, my reason. I should wait, be patient, give us both time. But I can't. Not when I look at you, not when you look into my eyes, not when I know that my entire life changed the moment you entered it. And, after today, it will change again, for both of us. You're frightened, aren't you, darling? I'm frightened."

There were words, thousands of words, tumbling over themselves inside Sherry's head, but she couldn't seem to force any of them past her lips. Instead, very simply, very honestly, she lifted Adam's hand, kissed it, pressed it against her cheek.

A moment later she was crushed inside his embrace, and all her misgivings closed themselves away behind a locked door in her mind.

"Married in buckskin breeches and shirtsleeves! Married in boots, with your cravat looking as if you'd tied it in three seconds, blindfolded. Married on the bank of a stream—the vicar won't forgive that bumblebee sting soon, let me tell you, brother. Married to the sound of birdsong and cowbells and yapping hounds, and with everyone made to stand about in the grass and watch you all but eat Sherry up with your kisses before the two of you did your flit, leaving me to deal with a weeping maid and a man gleefully pointing out that his prize bitch was just then in the process of being covered by my own Ripping Jack. Damn, Adam, but my hat's off to you. It was fantastic!"

Adam sat in the Grosvenor Square drawing room, a glass of wine dangling from his fingertips. He looked at his brother, who had finally arrived, a full two hours after he and Sherry had entered the mansion. Sherry, exhausted from their three-hour drive, was upstairs, taking a bath and a small nap before they'd share a late dinner in his rooms. An intimate dinner in his rooms.

"No, Geoff," he told him. "It would have been fantastic if you hadn't followed after us. Tell me, where is Sherry's papa? Not with you, I hope."

"What? And leave his boys? No, you have no fears there, Adam. Although Sherry's maid, Mary, decided to come along at the last moment. That was jolly, sharing my carriage with her. She doesn't travel well, old Mary don't, but she wasn't about to let her baby go without a proper good-bye. You'll have the good woman in residence for the Season before she retires to her sister's house in Dorset, which is small, but they should all manage well enough. Would you like to know the names of her sister's children, and *their* children?"

Adam's lip twitched in amusement, knowing his brother would probably have taken the reins from the driver and raced his way to London if the maid hadn't been along for the ride. "My apologies, I'm sure."

"Accepted. I'm just happy to be here, even if we did arrive at a snail's pace and with my left ear all but burned off with Mary's nonstop conversation. But I won't be a bother, I promise. There's a multitude of rooms in this pile where I can hide myself while you and Sherry . . . well, you know. Besides, the Season will be starting soon. You don't expect me to stay locked up at Daventry Court, do you? I want to help you introduce Sherry to Society, watch people's faces as I do it." He poured himself a glass of wine, then sank into a chair, crossing one leg over the other. "Ought to be grand fun."

"But not at my wife's expense, Geoff," Adam said in warning. "We have to go about this slowly, for Sherry's sake. Get her outfitted correctly, introduce her to a few new faces at a time, guide her way."

"You could engage a nanny for her, I suppose," Geoff said, his voice taking on a hard edge. "Put her in leading strings. Have her learn the names of our most influential hostesses by rote."

Adam took a sip of his own wine. "Don't be facetious, Geoff. You know what I mean."

"I do, I do," Geoff answered, nodding. "We're about to toss an innocent infant to the wolves. The fact that those wolves have titles like 'countess' and 'duchess' means less than nothing. Will the lovely Melinda be in town, do you think?"

"Melinda?" Adam shook his head, rising to his feet, off to take his own bath, ready himself for the evening. "That's long over, Geoff. I have no fears there. I just want Sherry to be happy, that's all. So we'll do as I've planned. Outfit her, ease her into Society by way of a few small parties, and then host our own ball here at the very end of the Season, when she's confident of her ability as a hostess. I had just sent off an announcement of our wedding to the newspapers when you arrived. Everything will be fine. London will love her."

"As you do?" Geoff called after him. "Love her, that is?"

"Just as I do, brother," Adam said very definitely.

*   *   *

Mary's unexpected arrival in Grosvenor Square had delighted Sherry, who had been more than slightly intimidated by the Daventry housekeeper, Mrs. Clement, who had seemed to disapprove of her. She'd arrived without a maid, without notice, while wearing wilting roses in her hair and clad in an unfashionable gown with grass stains on its hem.

And giggling.

She probably shouldn't have been giggling.

But Adam had entertained her for the entirety of their journey, telling her mad tales of the foibles of London Society, teasing her whenever she slipped into silence, stared out the window of the rapidly moving carriage. He'd just told her about his friend Chollie's sadly failed sartorial experiment with puce-velvet and high-heeled shoes as they'd arrived in Grosvenor Square, and she'd still been laughing at Adam's description of the man as being "part peacock, part slice of plum pudding" as Mrs. Clement had been introduced.

"So? What do you think, Mary?" she asked now, spreading her arms wide to take in the entirety of the massive bedchamber that could have swallowed her childhood bedchamber three times over and still had room for half of her papa's kennels. "Do you suppose I'll become lost in here often? Should I tie a mile-long string to the bedpost and my waist before I dare to enter my dressing room, for fear I'll never find my way back?"

"I think you should explain to me how you didn't

stay where you were put and how I had to be pushed into a bumping carriage with Mr. Victor and dragged across bumpier fields to see you standing there, grinning like the village idiot and telling me you were about to be wed, barefoot, to a man without the decency to wear a proper jacket," Mary ground out as she flounced around the room, tipping open baggage until she located Sherry's old white-cotton night rail and dressing gown.

"Here," the sensible old countrywoman said, tossing both articles in Sherry's general direction. "You're shivering in that towel, Little Missy, and indecent, too, while you're about it. Strange woman, that Mrs. Clement, to leave you all but jay-naked like this while she went to calm some kitchen crisis. It's a good thing for you I decided to come to London for a space, that it is. Did you know that Lord Dagenham can sleep with his eyes wide-open? He even snored, right in the middle of me telling him how my sister Joanie's Maryann's second son, little Davy, broke his two front teeth falling out of an apple tree last year."

"Imagine that," Sherry said, tongue-in-cheek, then quickly dressed herself in her old, familiar clothing and gave Mary yet another hug, for she was truly happy to see her. "And you'll really stay for the entire Season, Mary? I'd be most grateful. I'm rather frightened, you know. This house is so *big*. All of London is so *big*. And noisy." She wrinkled her nose, grinned. "And it really doesn't smell all that grand, does it?"

"Like your papa's kennels at high noon in the middle of summer," Mary agreed, closing, then arranging the mound of luggage behind a screen in the corner of the room. "There, that's all right and tight for now. We'll do the rest in the morning, Little Missy, and don't think you'll be finding your way out of honest work now that you're a marchioness, or whatever. I didn't raise you to be lazy, that I didn't, or to go off chasing dreams, like your mama. Never a lick of sense, that woman. Here you are, a wife, and where is she? Nowhere we know, that's for certain. And what am I supposed to do, I ask you? What am I supposed to say to you? He'll be strutting in here anytime now, knowing things you don't know, saying things you've never heard, wanting—"

"Mary, please," Sherry said, giving the old woman a quick kiss. She knew what Adam would be "wanting." She'd grown up fairly innocent, but she'd grown up in the country. She wasn't ignorant of what went on between a man and a woman. "I'm fine. Truly. Adam's my husband now, and I love him very much. Very much, Mary. I trust him, and he would never hurt me. I believe that."

"Thank you, darling," Adam said, pushing open the door she'd already learned connected their two bedchambers and walking into the room. "I knocked, but I don't believe you heard me. Mary, is it? I'll be taking Her Ladyship to my rooms now, where a fine dinner awaits us. If I have your permission, that is?"

The old woman dropped into a creaking, clumsy

curtsy. "Yes, my lord," she said, looking to Sherry, who only smiled and nodded. "I, um, I suppose I'll just go off downstairs now and find that Mrs. Clement. We two should talk, I'm thinking. Let her know the straight of things."

"Yes, Mary, you do that," Adam said, holding out his hand to Sherry. "Come along, darling. Are you famished? Our chef has quite outdone himself, and on such short notice. I doubt either of us has eaten all day."

Sherry looked down at her dressing gown, which covered her even more modestly than did her makeshift wedding gown, shrugged, and allowed herself to be led into her husband's bedchamber. Willingly. Almost eagerly.

She totally forgot to say good night to the woman who had almost single-handedly raised her from an infant, all the way to the advanced age of just past nineteen, when she had become a wife. . . .

A soft rain that had deigned to wait until evening fell on the mansion in Grosvenor Square as Adam gently pressed Sherry back against the pillows of the Daventry marriage bed.

Candles kept any hint of gloom from the large chamber, throwing its far corners into intimate darkness, so that the bed became the center of the chamber, the center of their world.

Her hair lay like a dark halo against the white of the pillow, her green eyes were wide and alert, and faintly apprehensive. She'd laughed through dinner, he'd made sure of that, but now her smiles were gone, and the mood had turned intense.

"Are you all right, darling?" Adam asked, easing himself down beside her, knowing her body was as taut as a bowstring, barely touching the mattress. "It's been a long day, all in all. Would you rather go to sleep?"

"I—I don't think so," she said, and he smiled. At her honesty, at her sweet flush of embarrassment. He wouldn't ask her to say more, for he wouldn't embarrass her more. Because he knew. He knew she was afraid, yet eager. He felt much the same way himself.

"You've only to ask me to stop, Sherry," he whispered against her ear. "That's all. If I frighten you, if what's happening frightens you, just tell me to stop. All right?"

"I'm not a child, Adam," she said, then gasped audibly as he took the lobe of her ear between his teeth, stroked it with the tip of his tongue. He ran his tongue down the side of her throat. "Well, that's—that's . . . nice . . ."

He smiled against the base of her throat.

"But I'd really like you to kiss me, Adam, if you don't mind."

He chuckled, low in his throat, then raised himself up, looked down into her face, her wide green eyes. "Your servant, madam," he breathed, then pressed his mouth against hers, slid an arm across her waist.

So virginal, so bridelike, yet so quick to flower beneath his carefully controlled, amorous assault. She returned his kisses in full measure, slid her arms up and around his shoulders, sighed a time or two, relaxed against the soft mattress.

He kissed her hair, her forehead, her eyes, her most delectable nose. He kissed her fingers as he held her hand, kissed her shoulder as he lifted her slightly, slid her arms free of that ridiculous dressing gown.

He longed to worship her. Wholly. Completely. But knew he had to go slowly, keep himself under control even as he longed to go spinning off into an unknown galaxy of familiar and yet somehow alien sensations.

Her breasts rose and fell with her deep, uneven breathing as he looked deeply into her eyes, slowly drew open the ribbon holding her night rail closed, hiding her from his sight, his touch.

"Stop," Sherry whispered as he pushed the material away, cupped her firm breast in his hand.

Adam froze even as his palm burst into flame, looked at her.

"I like our kisses. Very much. I like that, how you're touching me now. I didn't know you were going to touch me, but I'd hoped so. And it's everything I thought it would be," she whispered. "How did I know? Why on earth do I want this? Why do I like it so much?"

He moved his hand on her, skimmed his palm across her nipple, felt it tighten into a hard bud. He bent his head, took her nipple into his mouth for a few moments, tasting her, teaching her, then lifted his head and asked, "How do you feel now, Sherry?"

"How do I feel?" She closed her eyes, took a deep breath, released it slowly. "Even better. Light. Liquid. Heavy. Faintly frustrated, as if there should be more even as I'm enjoying what I feel. And free. Very, very free. Nice. But I'm not quite sure why."

He withdrew his hand, pulled her night rail back into place, then shifted himself onto his side so that he could look down at his wife. "Physical love, Sherry," he said, choosing his words carefully, "is the most personal expression of love. My loving you, and you loving me, means that we want to be together. Be close. With no secrets, no barriers between us, not even physical ones. As a reward for loving each other, I suppose, Nature has created pleasure in that personal intimacy. Animals mate by nature, without understanding, in order to reproduce. Men and women," he paused, seeking the right words, knowing that he sounded stiff, formal. "Men and women mate because of their love for one another."

"And to reproduce," Sherry said matter-of-factly, brushing a stray lock of hair away from her face. "And because they like it. My papa certainly doesn't love Maisie, one of our maids at home, but that doesn't stop them from . . . well, you know what I mean. I just don't understand why I never felt this way before, felt this *need* before I met you. How does a person know if what they feel is love, or just a need to . . . to mate?"

"I don't know," Adam said, touching the tip of his finger to one corner of her mouth, watching as she smiled at him. "I suppose that's the gamble we all take when we tell ourselves we're in love."

"True love lasts a lifetime, and beyond," Sherry said with the conviction of innocence, placing her hand over his. "This—what we're doing now, are about to do now—is only a part of that love. A rather nice part," she ended, smiling again. "And I do love you, Adam. I'm sure of it. I was afraid this morning. I'm sure you know that. But I know now. It's all right. I do love you, very much."

"And I'm quite convinced I love you, too, sweetheart. But is that what's still troubling you? Are you trying to separate the two things in your mind? Because they can't be separated, Sherry. I can't love you without wanting to *make* love to you."

"Make love," Sherry repeated, sighing. "Making love. Yes. That's what we're doing, isn't it? Taking our bodies, and making love of them, creating love with them." She put a hand on his shoulder, drew him closer. "I'm not afraid anymore, Adam. Not even a little bit. I want to create love with you. I think we'll make love very well, don't you?"

"I imagine we'll be extraordinary at it," Adam breathed against her mouth even as his hand brushed the night rail away once more and he cupped her breast, began to rub lightly at her nipple with his thumb. "Simply extraordinary."

And she became liquid for him. Melting and re-forming under his hands; opening to him, flowering, whispering sweet sighs, touching him tentatively, then with more assurance.

Her very innocence fired him, intensified his own reactions. Never had he been so aware of the differences between man and woman, the subtle as well as the obvious. She gave through love, and the sensation followed the love, intensified because of it. She felt for the moment, yes, but gave herself for a lifetime. His desire was more physically driven, had always been more ephemeral. A pleasure of the moment, the hour, without a thought to more than that pleasure.

Except that now he felt Sherry's love. She gave him the gift of that love, of her innocence, and considered her own pleasure to be a natural part of that gift. Not a mountain to climb, an end to achieve, an explosion of physical desire to be sought, experienced, enjoyed for the moment.

This was more, so much more.

This was commitment. Total and complete. She didn't so much love him as comfort him, shelter him, envelop him within the haven of her love until he became a part of her. Emotionally, physically, until he believed himself to be inside her head, thinking her thoughts, feeling the sensations he was causing.

She cried out, once, more in shock than pain, then wrapped herself around him, soothing him as he panicked, believing he'd hurt her. She was all giving, all love, and he felt tears stinging his eyes as he took what she gave him, knowing he could never give her enough in return. Not if they both lived another five hundred years. He would always be in her debt, for this gift of unconditional love, this gift of innocence.

Afterward, as she snuggled against him beneath the covers, as the fire died in the grate, as the rain washed away the last minutes of their wedding day, Adam tried to come to grips with this new sensation, this feeling of dependence he'd never felt before.

He was almost angry with her, even as he loved her. Because he couldn't live without her now. He'd given her his heart, his entire being, and she'd accepted it, given him back that love in equal measure.

They were responsible for each other's happiness now. Each held the other's heart, the other's future, in their hands. It was wonderful. A perfect dream of a perfect love.

And yet dangerous . . .

On with the dance! let joy be unconfined;
no sleep till morn, when youth and Pleasure
meet to chase the glowing hours with flying feet.
                                    —Lord Byron

Chapter Eleven

There could be nothing more intoxicating than a London Season, unless it was dancing and loving your way through that Season on the arm of your most wonderful husband.

That's what Sherry told herself a dozen times a day, sometimes even pinching herself to be sure she wasn't dreaming her happiness.

Adam was at her side day and night. Introducing her. Protecting her. Laughing with her.

They'd played country-bumpkin tourists, visiting the Tower and other points of interest Sherry vowed she simply must see. Adam never flagged, never yawned a single time, never pointed out that once a person has seen London that person doesn't necessarily harbor a burning desire to visit some areas of it again.

In fact, Sherry quickly learned that most of those

in Society hadn't even seen the world's most magnificent metropolis a single time. They lived in Mayfair, partied in Mayfair, and the rest of London simply didn't exist for them.

To Sherry, this was like standing outside a shop filled with wonders and only being able to see what was displayed in the window.

Adam called her a Student of Life, and smiled indulgently when she pleaded with him to tour a local brewery. He stood by, watching over her, as she sampled greasy gastronomical horrors hawked by street vendors. He paid for the string of "pearls" she bought from a small child for the grand price of three shillings. He pointed out exotic personages strolling Bond Street, kept a whole day free so that they could visit Astley's Circus, and agreed to stand in the stalls at the theater one evening so that she could join the young bucks tossing oranges at the stage.

It was heaven, or as close to heaven as two people could get while still earthbound. They played all day, made love every night. Laughed, kissed, and laughed some more.

Adam cherished her.

She adored him.

Everything was perfect. More than perfect.

"I'm afraid I'm going to have to leave you alone for a space today, darling," Adam said over breakfast one morning. "Estate business."

Sherry was still fairly lost in a happy fog that had

a lot to do with some early-morning lovemaking that had been especially sweet. "That's all right, Adam," she said as she spooned jelly onto a piece of toast. "I believe I'm capable of amusing myself for one afternoon. Although I doubt it will be by applying to Mrs. Clement for a lesson in counting linen. Does it bother you that I'm such a happy failure in things domestic?"

"I'm devastated, actually," Adam said with a grin. "Just think, I could have married Mrs. Clement, the complete housekeeper."

"Instead, you chose a silly little girl who'd much rather watch people walk up and down the flagways than ride herd on footmen and upstairs maids. I hope you've got a good staff, darling, or else they could all be robbing you blind without my ever knowing it." She sighed, knowing she didn't want him to answer her next question honestly. "Do you think it's time I sat down with Mrs. Clement and pretended to be mistress of this household? I will admit that, at times, I feel more than a little useless, perhaps even superfluous. Except that Mrs. Clement wants me to pick menus, and I haven't even *heard* of some of the foods she suggests, much less tasted them. She's rather disappointed in me, Mrs. Clement is."

"You'll never be superfluous to me, darling. You're the most important, most necessary person in my life." Adam reached a hand across the table, and Sherry took it in her own, let him squeeze it. "You'll do what makes you happy, darling, and that's all you'll do. There's time enough for counting linens and choosing menus. For now, you're to enjoy yourself. Agreed?"

Sherry nodded, biting her bottom lip. There was something wrong in what Adam said, but she wasn't quite sure what it was. Something in the way he treated her, in the way she encouraged him to treat her. As if they were playing at life, at love, even playing at being married.

She'd have to talk with Mrs. Clement this afternoon, sit down with the housekeeper, ask her to explain exactly what it was a mistress of a London mansion should know. Throw herself on the woman's mercies, that's what she'd do. Adam would be proud of her, and she'd even be proud of herself. After all, she was a married woman now. It was time she behaved like one.

"Adam, I—" she began, only to be cut off by a bellow that sounded much like that of a wounded animal caught in a trap.

"*Daventry!* Where are you, Daventry? Don't try to hide, for it'll do you no good. I swear by the hole in my old coat, boyo, I don't believe what Hoggs just told me. Bracketed? You? What happened? Who held the pistol to your head? *Daventry!*"

Adam touched the linen serviette to his lips, then carefully folded it and laid it on his empty plate. "That would be one Mr. Collin Laughlin, my love," he said, slowly rising to his feet and turning toward the door. His grin was positively boyish. "Prepare to be hugged."

"Hugged?" Sherry didn't believe the man who was just now bellowing at the top of his lungs sounded much like the hugging sort.

"Yes, it's a failing of Chollie's, although he's a good egg for all of that. But Irish, you understand, and with a flair for extravagant emotional displays when the spirit moves him. I believe, for my sins, he's about to be moved. Chollie? In the breakfast room, man, before you shout the walls down on us."

A whipcord-thin, bespectacled gentleman about the same age as her husband suddenly appeared in the doorway, as if he'd taken a great giant leap from the hallway in order to be sure his was a grand, startling entrance. His brown hair hung nearly to his shoulders, unbound and rather unkempt, and his clothes looked as if he'd run into them on his way somewhere, glad to have met them but not impressed enough to pay them more than cursory attention. His nose, rather large, appeared as if he routinely used it to knock down doors.

His long, thin face split in a truly unholy grin as he spied Adam, and he leapt at him, fists clenched. The two exchanged a few blows, none of them actually landing, then the Irishman gathered a clearly delighted Adam in a bear hug, lifting the larger man completely off the floor.

"Ah, boyo, but it's grand to see you!" Chollie exclaimed before putting Adam down, then grabbed onto Adam's head and planted a loud, smacking kiss on his cheek. "Now, where is she? Where's this conniving female who tricked my poor boyo into— good God, man—*marriage?*"

"She's sitting right here, Mr. Laughlin," Sherry said, "and enjoying herself very much. It isn't often I've seen Adam so lost for words. Darling, did Mr. Laughlin squeeze all the air out of you, or do you have enough left to introduce us?"

"Glory be to God," Chollie said in awful, hushed tones, backing his way to the end of the table, then walking around it to take Sherry's hand, lift it to his lips. "It's a vision I'm seeing, that's what it is. A vision of loveliness. That hair, that smile. Hair so glorious there has to be some good Irish blood in there somewhere." He straightened up, glared at Adam. "You've always had the devil's own luck, haven't you, boyo? No need to ask if it's a love match, I'm thinking. You both look almost insufferably happy. Adam? May I?"

"If I said no, would it stop you?" Adam asked, seating himself once more and reaching for the coffeepot.

"No more than an upheld hand would stop a charging cavalry regiment. My lady? Would you stand?"

"If I said no," Sherry teased, winking at Adam, "would it save me?"

"Not a whit. I must hug you, my lady. My heart demands it."

And hug her Chollie did. And pick her straight up

off the floor. And whirl her around a half dozen times, until she was breathless and giggling.

"I'll die a happy man now, boyo, having done that," Chollie said, falling into a chair once he'd seated Sherry once more. He pulled out a large white handkerchief and wiped it across his forehead, then began fanning himself with it. "Now, tell me all about the thing, if you please. When you met, how you met, when you were married, why I wasn't informed, much less invited. Not that I'm complaining, don't you know, but a little begging for my forgiveness wouldn't come amiss."

"Please accept my apologies, Mr. Laughlin," Sherry said, placing a cup of steaming coffee in front of him. "It was all my fault, I'm afraid."

"How so?" the Irishman asked, scooping enough sugar into his cup to allow the spoon to be stood on end in it.

"I compromised the poor man."

Chollie stopped in the act of licking the back of the spoon and stared at Adam. "Poor fellow. That must have taken all of two seconds' resistance before he gave in."

"I was powerless in her hands," Adam said, spreading his own hands, then sighing deeply. "Bewitched, Chollie. Why, I'm under her spell still, nearly a month later. Have you no pity for your dear friend?"

"Not a lot," Chollie said consideringly, then grinned at Sherry in a way that somehow made the thin, scraggly Irishman look like a cheery, chubby leprechaun. "Not just a love match, but two completely besotted creatures. You will let him out to play from time to time, won't you, my lady? Either that, or take pity on this poor man and allow him to hang on to the fringes of your lives? I could land in trouble otherwise, if left to wander the Season on my own. I often do fall into bumblebaths, don't you know."

"What Chollie's trying to say, my love, is that he gains his greatest pleasure in punching and otherwise pummeling his fellowman. He considers it good sport. Isn't that right, Chollie?"

Chollie dropped his head onto his chest, dramatically spoke into his badly tied cravat: "They won't let me in Gentleman Jackson's Boxing Saloon anymore, blast their hides. Playing at the fancy, dancing around, barely landing a blow—what sort of sport is there in that? Give me a man good with his fives, a jolly nosebleed, a split lip, a bruised eye. Knock me down, get me up, knock me down again. Ah, there's the life."

Sherry was fascinated. "You enjoy being knocked down, Mr. Laughlin?"

"Chollie, please, m'darlin' girl, if your husband doesn't call me out for being so familiar. And to answer your question, I don't mind being knocked down. As long as I get to do some knocking down of my own. Remember Simpson, Adam? Bled like a stuck pig when I broke his pretty nose for him. Ah, it was a grand sight, that. Just grand."

"Are you in town for the rest of the Season?"

Adam asked, changing the subject just as Sherry was about to ask if Adam had ever knocked a man down, made him bleed.

"That I am, boyo, that I am," Chollie said. He finished his coffee and stood up, bowing to Sherry. "It's a fine time we'll be having, too, I'm thinking. A rare, fine time, my lady."

"Sherry," she corrected, offering her hand, which he kissed yet again. "But please don't rush off. Adam has a meeting with his solicitor in a few minutes, and I'll be left to my own devices until at least three. Isn't that right, darling? Perhaps Chollie and I can take a drive, if he's free, then join us for dinner?"

"So that you can ask me dozens and dozens of questions about this naughty husband of yours, and what he was like before you met him? I wouldn't miss it."

"Nothing too shocking, Chollie," Adam warned, excusing himself and heading off to his meeting. "Remember, my wife is a lady."

"No, Adam," Chollie called after him, "she's an angel. She'd have to be, to have taken you on. Since it's too late to warn her off, and put in a good word or two for myself, I suppose I can sing your praises a bit. It's a hard job I've put before me, but you must have a redeeming quality or two, boyo. Could you be giving me a hint as to one I might mention?"

"I haven't beaten you into a jelly yet. That alone should qualify me for sainthood."

"Yes, there is that, boyo, there is that. Sherry, my

darlin' girl, shall we be off? I've just remembered a story about your dear husband and a certain curricle race that had much to do with the two of us, copious quantities of imbibed wine, and a temperamental pair of horses no sane man would ever put in the traces."

"Really?" Sherry said, taking Chollie's arm as they followed a muttering Adam through the doorway, into the hall, and most happily consigning Mrs. Clement and household duties to the back of her mind. "I must say, I never before realized my husband had such an adventurous nature. Now, please, go on . . ."

Collin Laughlin was a most entertaining companion, and Sherry spent a happy, laughing afternoon listening to him tell tales about his fairly singular life as well as a few of his and Adam's adventures. She hadn't thought about her husband as being the sort to play pranks on his friends, or indulge in silly curricle races, or spend long nights in low places, drinking deep and singing sad songs.

There was so much she still had to learn about Adam. He spent his time entertaining her, so that she hadn't given much thought to what he might do without her, how he had lived before she'd entered his life. She was younger, with less of a history, almost no history. Hers was a life just beginning. Adam had come into his title, had been grown, and moving about in Society, while she was still learning her sums in the schoolroom.

"What does he like, Chollie?" she asked her new friend as he tooled his fine curricle through the gate and into the park for a quick circuit before returning to Grosvenor Square.

"Adam? You, I'm thinking," Chollie answered with a wink. "What's troubling you, darlin'? You've got a look so dark on you all of a sudden I can barely see your pretty eyes."

This was ridiculous. Sherry barely knew Collin Laughlin, and here she was, about to tell him things she barely dared to think to herself. "I—I don't want to be boring to him," she mumbled half under her breath. "It's well enough here in London, with all the excitement of the Season, but when the Season's over? When we go back to Daventry Court? Well," she ended, summoning a bright smile, "let's just say I don't know that Adam will have so much time to devote to me then, or want to, for that matter."

"And are you wanting to be joined at the hip day and night then?" Chollie asked, tipping his hat to a couple in a passing vehicle. "Sounds uncomfortable."

Sherry shook her head, knowing she wasn't being clear, wasn't expressing herself well. "I know nothing of politics, Chollie. I like paintings, and the theater, and good books, but I don't know why I do, or believe it necessary to commit lines of Shakespeare or Milton to memory. I know nothing of running a single household, let alone a mansion in London or Daventry Court. And there are other estates, I've been told. I don't even know the names of those, or where they're located."

"What do you know, then, Sherry?"

She blinked, for her eyes stung with sudden tears. "I know that I love Adam with all my heart," she said honestly.

"But you're thinking that's not enough?"

"It should be, shouldn't it?" she asked as Chollie laid a hand on hers, gave her fingers a short, bracing squeeze. "Are you at all superstitious, Chollie? Do you ever think something is too perfect, and that it can't possibly be real? Can't possibly last? That, just possibly, you didn't do anything to *deserve* being quite so happy?"

Chollie's grin was infectious. "Ah, so there is some Irish blood lurking about somewhere in your past, darlin'. I thought as much. Happy as can be on the outside, even enjoying himself a time or two, that's an Irishman for you. But always sure nothing will ever succeed, that no good luck will ever last. You must love my boyo very much."

Sherry bit her bottom lip, nodded.

"Here you go then," Chollie said, reaching into his waistcoat pocket and pulling out a small leather pouch. "Reach inside, darlin', and you'll find two finely folded papers. Each one has a four-leafed shamrock pressed inside, for good luck, don't you know. I don't need two when one's enough. You take one, all right?"

"Oh, I can't take your good luck, Chollie," Sherry protested feebly, even as she longed to tuck one of the shamrocks up inside her reticule. "That wouldn't be fair."

"Darlin'," he said, leaning closer to whisper his next words, "I've got a drawer full of the things. Never let it be said this Irishman goes out on the road without a bit of his luck with him and more at home, waiting. That, and my beads and holy water and such. Put your faith in God and His church, I always say, and then make the sign against the evil eye and spit in your shoe for luck. Ah—" he said, quickly averting his head. "Don't look, darlin', for it's Lady Jasper heading straight at us. All the shamrocks in the world don't work with that one, and no mistake. Gambles you know, and cheats. Even sat on my handkerchief, not that it helped the one time I was fool enough to play against her. Here, we'll turn off before she spies us out."

Sherry held on to the seat with both hands as Chollie all but cut over the grass in his eagerness to avoid Lady Jasper, and looked back at the woman as her open carriage drove past. "She appears innocent enough," she said, turning back to Chollie, immediately putting the memory of Lady Jasper out of her head as she asked, "Why would you put a handkerchief on your chair?"

"To change the fall of the cards, of course," Chollie answered in all seriousness. "We were in company, so that I couldn't blow through the deck while shuffling for the next deal, or take a walk all around the table, or even turn my chair about and straddle it. Strange lot, Englishers. Do some of the silliest things, like rising at the crack of dawn to chase foxes and the like, yet look down their noses at serious business like superstitions. So I was left with sneaking my handkerchief onto the chair and sitting on it. Which helped not a jot, don't you know, because the lady was cheating me all hollow. Worse luck even than being dealt the Devil's four-poster bed."

Sherry was thoroughly intrigued, not to mention amused by Chollie's dismissive comment about her papa's ruling passion. "The Devil's four-poster bed? What would that be, Chollie?"

"The four of clubs, of course," he told her. "Never win with that card in your hand, I'm telling you. Not that Adam believes in any of this, mind you. Should have heard the fuss he kicked up the night I tried to stick a pin in his lapel before we played as partners at White's. We lost, of course, but he wouldn't admit it was his fault. There's a wealth of good sense outside that boy's head, don't you know. Doesn't believe in luck. Doesn't believe in the little people, the fairies who steal you from your bed to take you off to their fairy forts, or in ghosties or banshees or none of it."

"Chollie?"

"Yes, darlin'?"

"I don't believe in that sort of thing myself. I just thought I ought to tell you that."

He patted her hand. "But you'll be keeping the four-leafed shamrock, darlin'?"

She clutched her reticule close. "If you don't mind, yes. Yes, I will."

"I thought as much, darlin'. A bit of luck tucked away never hurt anyone, don't you know. After all, it's only the Devil's children who have the Devil's own luck. It's shamrocks and holy water for the rest of us. I could be getting you some beads of your own, if you want. But it's just loving Adam that will keep him happy, to my way of thinking. Just loving him with all your heart. And now," he said, falling into a broad Irish brogue, "seein' as we're done with all of that, tell me, darlin'. Is it a sister you'd be havin'? A female cousin with those same sweet green eyes? And if you have, would you be puttin' in a good word for a poor Irishman in need of his own darlin' angel now that his best friend has gone and deserted him for matrimony?"

"Oh, Chollie," Sherry said, laughing, her niggling worries banished yet again, swept away by the happiness that seemed to come to her so easily these days. "Adam hasn't deserted you."

"No, darlin', he hasn't," he told her, serious once more. "Adam isn't the deserting sort. A truer friend was never born. It's the same with you, darlin'. If you have his love, you have it forever. So, we'll not be talking more about the boy being so foolish as to change his mind, now will we?"

"No, Chollie, we won't be talking about that again. I promise." Sherry leaned over and kissed her new friend on the cheek. "But I will be counting linens tomorrow, I believe. Just so that I can tell myself I'm useful. That's not being silly, is it?"

"Anything that makes you happy, darlin', can't be the least bit silly. Now, how about we get shed of the park and I'll introduce you to some of Gunther's best ices? Has Adam treated you to one yet?"

"No, I can't say as he has. Are they delicious?"

"Ah, shame on Adam, stinting on your London education this way. What is Shakespeare, compared to a Gunther ice? It's a taste of pure ambrosia, darlin', that's what you're about to have. It's a fine thing that I've come to town, that it is. We're going to have a splendid romp this Season, darlin', the three of us. A splendid romp!"

"May I have the pleasure of this dance, Lady Throgbottom?"

Adam smiled as Sherry turned to him, her head held high as she peered down her pert nose at him.

"I don't believe we've been introduced, sirrah," she said haughtily, then unfurled her fan and began to wave it, hiding her smile behind the silk-covered ivory sticks.

He raised one eyebrow imperiously. "We haven't? But I am Buckfastleigh. Baron Buckfastleigh. I assure you, everyone knows of me."

"Baron Buckfastleigh?" Sherry's green eyes were dancing with delight. "Yes, I remember now. Impeccable lineage, as I recall, although country-bred. Your reputation precedes you. Very well, sir. I'll dance with you."

"You are too kind, Lady Throgbottom." Adam executed an elegant leg, flourishing his handkerchief before holding out his arm so that they could walk onto the dance floor for the waltz that had just begun.

"Lady Daventry gives a most delightful ball, doesn't she, Baron Buckfastleigh? I do believe I have not seen such a crush in all of the Season."

"It's her husband's consequence that draws the masses," Adam told her as they dipped and whirled, and dipped again. "A good man, Daventry. And he didn't stint on anything, as some do. Good music, good food." He leaned closer, all but leering at her. "Good company."

"Then you're enjoying your evening, sir?" she asked as they glided across the floor.

"I'd enjoy it more if you were to accompany me outside, into the gardens."

She tipped her head, hiding her blush. "La, sir, but surely you jest. I am a married woman, and my husband watches me closely. He's very jealous, you understand."

Adam looked down at her, resplendent in ivory silk, her vibrant hair a tumble of curls threaded through with pearls. She'd been the sensation of the Season, so popular he'd nearly had to make an appointment in order to see her of late. Chollie adored her, all of London adored her. But no one more than he. She was his dream, his reality, his every wish come true.

Would she be happy back at Daventry Court,

away from the gaiety of the London Season? He'd done his best to make her life a living fairy tale these past weeks, knowing she deserved all the happiness he could give her in return for making him the happiest of men.

"Your husband is the jealous sort, my lady?" His hand tightened on her gloved fingers. "With great reason, I'm sure. There's not a man here tonight who wouldn't put a knife in my back to be where I am right now. You walk through a room and leave a dozen broken hearts in your wake. Never have I seen such a heartless beauty."

Sherry's chin came up as she gave herself over to the game. "Children. Little boys," she told him, shrugging. "I don't even see them. But you, Baron Buckfastleigh? I wonder."

"Meet me on the far end of the balcony in ten minutes, my lady, and put your wonderings to rest," Adam suggested, leaning close so that he could whisper the words.

"A kiss stolen in the moonlight? How tiresome. Such a long Season it has been, with this the last night before my husband drags me back to the country. And all you offer me is a stolen kiss? I vow, I kiss in the moonlight so often. Is that all you can suggest, Baron Buckfastleigh?"

Adam leaned closer, whispered in her ear.

"Oh my. Yes, that is interesting. A fitting climax to my first Season, I'm sure. But—but my husband? Do I dare? Do you dare?"

"A pox on the man," Adam said, curling his fingers into the small of Sherry's back, feeling her shiver of response. "Your blush is most becoming. Have I shocked you, dear lady? Has your husband never made wild, impassioned love to you in your hostess's garden at midnight?"

"Adam, surely you aren't suggesting—I mean . . . my dear Buckfastleigh, you have no idea of my husband's creative mind." She sighed theatrically. "Of course, that's when he was a younger man, and more vibrant, shall we say. Now, a pipe, his slippers, a hound at his feet. This is my husband. I grow so . . . *restless*."

He stopped near the edge of the dance floor even as the musicians played on, dropped his hands to his sides before he abruptly pulled her completely into his arms, kissed her hard on the lips, and shocked half of the *ton* straight down to their toes. "Ten minutes, my lady. As we dare."

Adam watched as Sherry walked away, smiling as he decided that Lady Throgbottom had quite a nice *bottom*.

"That's the Devil I see peeking out of your eyes, boyo," Chollie said, walking up to him and handing him one of two glasses he carried. "The air is so thick with whispers that I nearly had to fight my way over here, gasping for a breath that didn't include swallowing down mention of the two of you. Shameless man. It's not done you know, being so obviously in lust with your own wife. It's surprised I am the poor child hasn't melted under your hot looks. And that kiss? Boyo, it's proud of you I am, and no mistake."

Turning to look out over the dance floor, and seeing more than a few interested stares and dropped jaws, Adam muttered, "Perhaps, Chollie, if you were to yell *fire*, all these tiresome people would go home, and leave me alone with my wife. You could lead them out."

"Adam?"

Adam turned to see his brother Geoffrey approaching, wearing a grin so wide he knew the young man had something wicked to say. "What is it, Geoff? Have you been complimenting Miss Wicks on her bosoms again? Just because she nightly puts them on display is no reason to believe she won't take offense, go running to her brothers so that one of them pounds you into the ground, then forces you to propose marriage to the silly chit."

"Sally Wicks parades her bosoms more often than fair England shows its colors, Adam, and I'm probably the only man in Mayfair who hasn't seen her gown at half-mast," Geoff answered, then winked. "Although tonight may just be my lucky night. As to her brothers, they want nothing to do with her. Why, Barry Wicks told me himself that his sister has a child tucked away somewhere in Somerset, if you can believe it. Why else do you think she's set her cap at old Carruthers? Seventy if he's a day, and her last chance at respectability. Speaking of which—"

"Here we go, boyo," Chollie whispered, "the libertine about to give a lesson in prudity. This will be as good, don't you know, as hearing the Devil give a sermon on the evils of pride."

"Adam," Geoff said, shooting a quelling look at Chollie, "do you have any idea what a spectacle you're making of yourself this evening? This is *your* ball, you know, and you've spent the entire evening ignoring your guests and casting calves' eyes at your wife. No less than five gentlemen have pulled me aside, begging me to make you stop, as their own wives are suddenly demanding similar attention. Lady Winslow went so far as to stomp into the card room and drag Lord Winslow out of there by his ear. They're waltzing now, and a more pitiful sight I've ever to see. The man dances as if he's got a pole stuck up his——"

"Point well taken, Geoff," Adam broke in as Chollie went into whoops of laughter. "It's obvious to me that you're much more sober than I. So, seeing that you, too, are a Dagenham, you have my permission to take over as host for the remainder of the evening. I may return in time to stand at the top of the stairs and wish everyone a good riddance. Then again, I may not."

Geoff positively blanched. "Are you out of your mind, man? Me? What do I know of hosting a ball?"

"And what would there be to know, I'm asking?" Chollie laid a heavy hand on Geoff's shoulder. "The bunting's up, the guests have all been greeted, the candles are glowing, the wine is flowing, the violins are sawing away. Other than to remind the servants to flush lovers out of the shrubberies in the gardens, I'd say you've less than nothing to do."

"But—but—" Geoff looked to Chollie, then to his brother once more. "What are you going to do, Adam? Tell me that, at least. Just because half the men here are drooling on your wife whenever you step more than a foot away from her—well, that's no reason to leave your own ball. Asquith couldn't have been serious when he said he would leave his wife in a heartbeat if only Sherry would dance with him again."

Adam shook his head. "Sherry can't help being the sensation of the Season, Geoff. Unlike Miss Wicks, she does nothing more to attract foolish gentlemen than to be her own sweet self. Although," he added, "I won't say I'm unhappy that we'll be returning to Daventry Court in the morning. Now, if you'll excuse me?"

"Chollie?" Geoff bleated.

"Let's go see if the wine is flowing freely enough, shall we, boyo?" he suggested, winking at Adam as he gave Geoff a friendly push to get him moving. "And then we can search out Hoggs, and you can throw yourself on his mercies. A good enough man, Hoggs. He's sure to know how to go on. Adam?" he then said, turning back to his friend once more. "I'm off to Ireland in the morning and won't be seeing you again for a while. But it's been a grand Season, more than grand. Say my good-byes to Sherry, if you will. Give her a kiss for me, boyo, among the dozens you give her every day."

"I'll do that, Chollie," Adam said, sad to part from his friend, but knowing that he had less than two minutes to find his way to the end of the balcony. "Have a good journey."

"I always do, knowing I'm going home, don't you know." He smiled, then gave the still-reluctant Geoff another playful push. "Come on, boyo, don't you know when you're not wanted?"

Adam watched them go, then neatly avoided old Lord Quigley—the man could talk a hole in a bucket—and slipped out through one of the French doors, on his way to paradise.

She was standing in a shaft of moonlight that had found its way through the trees and onto the balcony. She had her back to him, her head lifted on the slim column of her throat as she watched the stars. She looked so young, so heartbreakingly beautiful.

But when he addressed her as Lady Throgbottom she turned to him, her green eyes alight with mischief, and he took her hand so that, together, they could race down the steps and into the night-dark gardens of the Grosvenor Square mansion.

"Did you see my husband, Baron Buckfastleigh?" she asked as he led her behind one wonderfully wide-trunked tree and began nibbling on her neck. "As I said, he's terribly jealous. And quite a monstrous good shot."

"I'd heard," Adam mumbled against her ear, tickling her lobe with the edge of his tongue. "So I threw him down the stairs. He won't bother us, I promise."

"Poor Throgbottom," Sherry said on a sigh as Adam freed one breast from her low-cut bodice, cupped it in his hand. "He was always so clumsy. Shall I look good in widow's weeds? I've never before worn black, you understand."

Adam's mind drew him an achingly clear picture of Sherry's ivory skin caressed by finest ebony silk, her dark red hair spilling onto her shoulders. He moved his lips down her throat, across her chest. Found her nipple.

"Baron Buckfastleigh!" she objected, playfully pushing his head away even as she ground her hips against him. "I am in mourning."

He shifted so that he could slide a leg between her thighs, lifted a hand to lightly pinch her exposed nipple between thumb and forefinger. "I know, Lady Throgbottom," he said, grinning at her as she did her best to look indignant even as a contented sigh escaped her parted lips. "I'm here to ease your suffering. You must be quite distraught." He waggled his eyebrows at her. "Perhaps if you were to lie down?"

She slid her arms around his neck, pulling him close, nipping at him with her teeth. "No need, dear baron. You may not have noticed, but your breeches are undone, and I believe lying down might only be considered a shameful waste of time."

Adam dropped a hand to his breeches, shocked to realize that she was right. She was getting rather good at this, the shameless minx. When, a moment later, her hand somehow found him, released him completely, he decided she'd gone beyond the rather good, and had graduated to the excellent.

"I may not be Hayes, Baron Buckfastleigh," she told him as he felt control slipping away from him and worked to hurriedly bunch her skirts up around her waist, "but I believe I can be of assistance if you should require it."

"Oh, madam, you shall pay for that insult," Adam threatened, laughing even as his passion grew. Her gown wouldn't defeat him. The chance of being caught making love to his own wife in his own gardens in the midst of his own ball didn't give him a moment's pause. With the handy tree trunk as his ally, with the cover of the shrubs and a moon conveniently sliding behind a similarly convenient cloud, Adam bowed to impulse and urgency, lifting Sherry against him, reveling as he felt her silk-encased legs lift, encircle his waist.

This was wild. Wanton. Idiotically impulsive and wonderfully abandoned.

He held her tightly, kissed her madly, poured his seed into her in an explosion of passion that should have been heard inside the ballroom.

At least it appeared as if his triumphant shout could be heard in the gardens.

"Dickie? Did you hear that? We're not alone. Quickly, hand me my petticoat!"

"Oh, my God, Adam," Sherry whispered, her arms and legs clasping him in a vise that nearly robbed him of what little breath his exertions had left him. "We're not alone out here."

"Shhh, darling," he whispered back, afraid to move so much as a hair for fear of giving away their location, exposing his wife to the embarrassment of being caught out in a most revealing circumstance.

Besides, he recognized the voice, as it was one he'd heard before. Too many times before. The woman was Melinda, he was sure of it. While he had been making love to his wife, the duchess of Westbrook had been having her own tryst in the gardens. Except that the duke of Westbrook was not named Dickie.

"Just stay still, sweetheart," Adam whispered in Sherry's ear, and the two held their breath as Melinda's companion spoke, his tone amused, laughingly wicked.

"If you were to unwind your legs from my neck so that I could get up off my knees, dear lady, I imagine I'd be delighted to honor your request. Otherwise, I can see no way to help you."

"Damn you, Dickie, this isn't funny!" Melinda exploded, her anger obviously blinding her to the fact that, if she could hear someone else, that someone else most probably could hear her as well.

"Oh, on the contrary, my sweet, this is fair bordering on the hilarious. Now, put this on, and let's be out of here, shall we? I have a carriage waiting.

Unless you'd like to return to the ballroom with grass stains on your lovely rump?"

"That's where I wanted to go all along. It's you who wanted to play slap and tickle in a damp garden. Damn you, damn you, damn you, Dickie!"

"Yes, you said that. Now, are you ready to adjourn to my lodgings so that we can be damned together?"

There was more rustling, a few more curses from the lady and pithy comments from the gentleman before the night was quiet once more.

Spent, his legs turned to butter, Adam and Sherry sank to the ground in a tangled heap, laughing and kissing and holding on to each other like guilty children.

"I shouldn't be laughing," Sherry said between kisses. "We were very nearly caught out. The marquess and marchioness of Daventry, making wild love in their own gardens in the midst of their own ball. Did you recognize their voices, darling? Do you know who they were?"

Adam hadn't recognized Dickie's voice, or his name. Not that it mattered. And he wasn't about to tell Sherry that the woman had been none other than the duchess of Westbrook, once very nearly his wife.

"Do we care?" he asked, helping Sherry as she tried to smooth down her gown, even as both of them knew they'd soon be sneaking up the servants' stairs to find other clothing. "However, if you want to worry about anything, my darling, perhaps it would be in helping me dream up a workable reason why we greeted our guests in these clothes and will be bidding them *adieu* in another two hours wearing something entirely different."

"We were caught outside on the balcony in a sudden rainstorm that lasted only a minute?" Sherry suggested as, hand in hand, they made their way through the gardens and toward the kitchen entrance.

"We insulted the chef and he pelted us with cream tarts?" Adam offered as they tiptoed through the kitchens, three maids and two footmen—plus their French-only-speaking chef—all turning their backs and pretending they didn't notice their disheveled lord and his lady skulking past.

They mounted the stairs and ran down the hallway, flying into Adam's bedchamber and slamming the door behind them. He looked at her, she looked at him.

He smiled.

She giggled.

This is how he wanted her. Alive. Happy. Laughing. Loving. With never a cloud in her sky. "Oh, the devil with it, Sherry," Adam said in mingled exasperation and rising excitement, reaching for her. "Let Geoff offer our excuses."

Arm! Arm! It is—It is—
the cannon's opening roar.
                              —Lord Byron

Chapter Twelve

Sherry sat on the bank of the stream, dangling her bare toes in the cool water. Bees buzzed overhead. Birds sang in the trees. The stream bubbled along, singing its own sweet song. Flowers dipped their bright heads in the warm breeze.

It was so good to be home.

And this was home. Daventry Court, the most beautiful spot on all the earth, the most magical, the most perfect.

Her papa was gone, having traveled back to Leicestershire to supervise the construction of new pens for his hounds, enclosures patterned after those at Daventry Court. He'd waited until Sherry and Adam returned, then shaken Adam's hand until her poor husband's arm was nearly ripped off, kissed the air in the vicinity of Sherry's cheek, and then—yoicks!—bolted away.

He'd taken Mary with him, so that the maid could gather up any belongings left behind in Leicestershire, promising then to pay for an inside ticket on the mail coach heading to Mary's sister's house in Dorset.

Sherry missed Mary more than she did her papa, which gave her an occasional pang of guilt, which quickly passed because she was so entirely happy. She'd had a wondrous Season as the marchioness of Daventry, and now she was at home in the country with her husband, settling down into an easy, relaxed life that left plenty of time for sitting beside streams, dreaming daydreams.

She'd brought one of the household account books with her today. The novel she'd carried with her at the last minute, however, had proved more interesting, so that she'd spent a lazy hour reading of the exploits of Jane Gooding, governess. It was much more exciting than putting herself to sleep perusing neatly written columns of numbers having to do with the price of candles and the number of housemaids it took to give Daventry Court a good cleaning each spring and fall.

She really had to get stern with herself and begin to learn how to run a household. Adam certainly knew his responsibilities and, in fact, had been busy almost from morning to night ever since they returned from London.

Geoff, pleading his case by saying that he wouldn't be the heir above another year, had absented himself from Adam's daily rides over the estate. He'd also refused to look at a single ledger or interview so much as one prospective new worker. Adam grumbled about his brother's defection a time or two, then simply shrugged and went back to work.

Adam liked to work. Sherry had come across him more than once during her long, ambling walks over the estate, finding him wielding a shovel with a will, or stabbing a pitchfork into a bale of straw, and even helping out at the gristmill.

Everyone on the estate adored him, from the lowest cottager to the estate manager, who had told Sherry he'd never worked for a more knowledgeable or able man. "Almost as if he wasn't one of the gentry, my lady, while he's ears and head above any of his neighbors. Why, over to Aimsley Manor, Lord Aimsley don't even know iffen he grows wheat or beets. Lord Daventry? He helps plant 'em!"

Sherry smiled as she thought about all of this, then frowned as she wondered if Adam realized that they had barely spoken for the past weeks, except when they met at a single meal during the day—and when they went to bed at night. Not that there was a great deal of talking once they were in bed. She might have had nothing much to add to conversations that were fairly one-sided, and that dealt mostly with estate business, but he didn't seem to notice that lack once he was holding her, once he was kissing her.

He asked her, every day, if she was happy, if she was enjoying herself, if there was anything she wanted, anything she needed. And he frowned when she told him she'd spent yet another day wandering the estate, stopping to sit and read a book, finding an hour to play with some of the children in the small village, spending a morning in the kitchens, baking apple tarts. Her wants were so simple she felt silly telling him about her day, and believed Adam would find her to be silly as well if he had to listen to her prattle on about such mundane things.

So she *simply* told him each day that she was happy.

And she *was* happy. Really she was. A bit lonely, perhaps, when she'd never been lonely before, even if she'd often been alone. Adam might invite her along for a ride once in a while, when he knew he wouldn't be too busy, but he didn't want to bore her with estate business. He'd told her as much.

This made sense to Sherry, as she was sure she wouldn't want to bore him with a recitation of her duties—when she remembered to perform them. She seriously doubted that he would want to accompany her as she toured the rooms with the housekeeper, commenting on how fine everything looked when that conscientious person looked to her as if it just might be time she mumbled something flattering about beeswax or some such thing.

Still, for as lovely as the country was, and as happy as she was, Sherry was beginning to worry that Adam didn't see her as his wife. Which was ridiculous, because she was his wife. They'd said their vows, right here, beside this very stream. She was his wife, he was her husband.

Except that between being lovers and ignoring each other—the former being how she saw their marriage, the latter being how she'd seen her parents' marriage—she was beginning to believe there might exist something that was *different* from either of those unions.

Adam cosseted her, tried to amuse her, gave her lovely gifts, laughed with her, teased with her.

She did her best to please him, wanted only to please him.

They never argued, never spoke seriously about anything at all.

They simply loved each other.

Shouldn't there be something *deeper* than pleasure?

Perhaps when they had children of their own . . .

"Well, hello there, dear lady. Doesn't this make for a most delightful, bucolic scene?"

Sherry quickly pulled her feet out of the water and tucked them beneath her skirts as she turned around to see a man standing on the bank above her.

"Oh, I'm sorry. Forgive me, did I startle you? I should have realized you were miles away, made my presence known by crashing through the trees like a loose bull on the run or some such thing. Daydreaming, were you?"

Sherry couldn't find her tongue. It was there, somewhere, stuck inside her head, but it wouldn't work, wouldn't push out any words. Because the man she was looking at was so singular, so unique, that she thought she must be dreaming him.

Tall, as tall as Adam, as dark as Adam, he had a face that could only be called angelic. Eyes as blue as a summer sky, long, dark lashes, a smile that could melt ice in the dead of winter. He was dressed in London's latest fashions, his cravat an intricate marvel, his superfine coat fitting him like a second skin. What on earth was such an elegant creature doing tramping the fields of Daventry Court?

"Ah, a silent beauty," the man said, smiling so that the sun seemed suddenly to shine ten times brighter than it had before. "And rightly so, as you have no idea who I am. I should rectify that, I suppose." He bowed, elegantly. The word kept circling inside Sherry's head. *Elegant*. He was simply *elegant*.

"Yes," she said at last, feeling suddenly defensive and, for the first time, very much the marchioness. "Introductions most definitely would be in order, as you're standing on Daventry soil. That said—who are you, sir, and what are you doing here?"

"I am Richard Brimley, my lady, come to rusticate in the country for a few months," he intoned, holding out his hand to her, to help her rise, which was something she most definitely didn't want to do. At least not until she could locate her hose and shoes. "Which is the same as to say I've a need to outrun my tradesmen's bills until the next quarter, but we won't pay any attention to that, shall we? I've just rented a most wonderfully appointed domicile someone with a flair for the ridiculous has dubbed Frame Cottage. And you're the marchioness of Daventry, of course."

"There's no of course about it, Mr. Brimley," Sherry told him, surreptitiously shoving her balled-up hose into her pocket and pushing her still-damp feet back into her shoes. She couldn't decide if she liked Mr. Brimley or not. He was so smooth, so very sure of himself, so obviously confident he was making a first-rate impression on her. The fact that he was doing just that only upset her more. "How would you know who I am?"

There was his smile again, battering down any defenses she might have tried to build, taking all of her new, titled consequence and blowing it off his hand like so much rice powder, reducing her to what she still felt herself to be—a slightly simple child. As sophisticated as a dairymaid, for all of her London Season. "I may be new to the neighborhood, my lady, but my locally retained staff has already informed me of the lovely Lady Daventry. Hair like dark fire, a beauty beyond compare, and a most honest, straightforward disposition one might even call blunt. So? Am I wrong?"

"No, Mr. Brimley, you're not wrong about my identity, and I thank you for your compliments if they assisted you in coming to a correct, if only somewhat flattering conclusion," Sherry said, still ignoring his outstretched hand as she clambered to her feet. Had she ever felt as gauche, and yet so possibly intriguing? Feminine? "I must return to Daventry Court now. Would you care to escort me?"

"It would be my honor, madam," he said, bending down to retrieve her account book and her novel, tucking both under his arm. "I had dared to hope, but you would have had every right to order me from the property, never to return. You are too gracious."

"Belatedly gracious, I believe, sir. Please forgive me for being so impolite, but you did startle me, you know."

"Yes, and I could have been a highwayman, couldn't I? Or a Gypsy king come to steal you away, hold you for ransom?"

"A Gypsy king, Mr. Brimley?" Sherry said, relaxing more and more under Richard Brimley's friendly gaze. "You aspire, then, to royalty?"

"Of a sort, my lady, of a sort," he replied, holding out his arm. This time she took it and, together, they walked out of the trees and toward the small bridge that crossed the stream a quarter mile in the distance. She would have told him about the stepping-stones, except she didn't picture the man as the sort who would chance muddying his highly polished boots when there was a less risky way to cross over the water.

"You were in London, Mr. Brimley?" she asked after a few moments. "I don't believe I saw you, and I believe I saw most all of the world there during the Season." What she didn't say was that, among the hundreds of names and faces that had been presented to her, she was sure she would have remembered Richard Brimley. He had the face and figure and air of easy confidence that would make him easily recognized in the midst of a multitude of lesser mortals.

"A brief visit only, actually, my lady," he told her as he helped her over a patch of rough ground. "Only long enough to renew a few old acquaintances, I fear, but my time was delightfully spent, I assure you. In fact, I attended your ball the last night of the Season, not that I'd been invited. But when a friend dared me to accompany her, I could not decline. Naughty, aren't I?"

"A friend?" Sherry looked up at him, caught the devilish glint in his liquid blue eyes. "I shouldn't ask this friend's name, should I?"

"You could ask, my lady, but, as a gentleman, I fear I would have to decline to answer. We arrived late and withdrew early, I will say that, and so most unfortunately I was denied the opportunity to meet my host and hostess. Would your husband have tossed me out on my ear, do you think?"

"Adam isn't quite that starchy," Sherry told him, remembering how little of their own ball the host and hostess themselves had attended. "I only hope you enjoyed yourself."

"Oh, I did, most definitely. I always enjoy myself in London Society, and feel very much at home; amid kindred spirits as it were. In other words," he said, winking at her, "I find London deliciously naughty."

"And the countryside, Mr. Brimley," Sherry asked, "how do you find it?"

He looked at her for long moments, until she felt a blush rising in her cheeks. "Delightful, my lady. I find the countryside absolutely delightful. Tell me, do you play?"

Sherry blinked in confusion, and to rid herself of the insane idea that she might be in danger of falling under some fairy spell. What a pity that she had left Chollie's four-leafed shamrock in her rooms. She'd never known a man could be so beautiful. "Do I play? Do you mean cards, Mr. Brimley?"

"No, my lady. Although I do enjoy a good game of chess, I find cards boring and predictable. What I meant, however, was do you play—at life? Do you enjoy life? Do you enjoy the simple pleasures of dancing alone in the middle of a field of wildflowers, moving to the music inside your head? Do you gaze at the full moon and wonder what it would be like to take flight, see the other side of it? Can you stay very still and stare at a deer for hours, without once wishing to put an arrow through its heart? Do you dare anything, try anything, just to feel the joy of life it gives you? Do you *live*, my lady? Do you dream? I think you do. I have a sense about these things, you understand."

Sherry removed her hand from his arm, shaken to her very core. How could he so carelessly guess so much about her? "Do you sense, Mr. Brimley, that you are entirely too personal with your questions?"

"A thousand pardons, my lady," Brimley said, his

handsome face earnest, yet still smiling. "I've always been one to rush my fences, often to my sorrow. But I sensed a kindred spirit in you, from the moment I first saw you. We are life's wonderers."

"Wonderers? You mean wanderers, don't you?"

"No, my lady. *Wonderers*." He took her hand, laid it on his bent arm once more, patted it companionably. "We look at the earth, and wonder. We look at people, and we wonder. We look at beauty, and we wonder. How did the grass get so green? The sky so blue? Where did all this lovely diversity come from, and why, how? Are we a part of it, or is it a part of us? And why, oh why, are most mortals so unimpressed with any of it? Why don't they see what we see? Why are they so ungrateful, and so unhappy?"

"Oftentimes," Sherry said hesitantly, "oftentimes I imagine they're just too busy."

"Oh, yes, too busy. Too busy to look up at the sky. Too busy gathering and grabbing and lusting for more and more and more. God wasted all this beauty on mere mortals, that's what I think."

Sherry smiled, believing herself to actually be having an intellectual discussion. Adam had never discussed anything with her in this way, spoken of ideas, of notions. "Are you saying, then, Mr. Brimley, that the Lord should have planned a shorter week during the Creation? Perhaps stopped after the birds and the trees, and left Man totally out of the perfection of His creation? It's an interesting theory, I suppose."

"Indeed, it is. Think about it, my lady. The earth is

perfection itself. Without Man there to clutter it up, that is. What has Man brought to the earth, madam? Wars, pestilence, petty jealousies, coal fires, insatiable greed, evil in all its forms. You and I, we see a deer. We watch it, savor its beauty, while others look at the same deer and see"—he grinned down at her—"dinner."

"Man has to eat, Mr. Brimley," Sherry pointed out rationally. "And, even if Man didn't exist, there are other predators who look at a deer and see their dinner."

"True enough, I suppose," he said, sighing. "But animals don't kill for sport, do they, once their bellies are full?"

"No, I suppose they don't," Sherry answered as they paused at the steps leading up to the sprawling gardens. "But do you really think the world would be perfect if we humans were erased from it? If we'd never been here in the first place? Who would appreciate all its beauty, if Man had never been created?"

"God and his Angels, my dear," Brimley said, lifting her hand to his lips, then smiling at her. "Of which, I am assured, you are most certainly one. A beautiful, unspoiled angel."

Sherry tilted her head to one side, then smiled. "You're funning with me, aren't you, Mr. Brimley? Just talked round and round, in a huge circle, in order to compliment me? Surely there are more direct ways?"

"A circuitous route, my lady, is eminently more

enjoyable for some of us. But have I done it? Have I wormed my way into your good graces? Intrigued you, made you believe that we all could spend a most enjoyable summer, laughing, and playing, and perhaps even thinking deep from time to time? Dare I even hope that I will be invited inside Daventry Court, to meet your esteemed husband and his brother, Lord Dagenham? I will perform party tricks for them as well, should you wish it."

"You have left me no choice but to invite you inside, Mr. Brimley," Sherry responded with her usual honesty. "Otherwise, how should I ever be able to explain you to my husband? You are quite singular, you know."

"One of a kind, my lady," he agreed with a smile so boyish and appealing that Sherry giggled. "There will never be another like me, I assure you."

"Sherry? Who is that with you?"

She turned at the sound of Geoff's voice, then motioned for him to come down the steps, join them. She made the introductions quickly, and just as quickly Geoff invited Richard Brimley into the house for a glass of wine and some conversation.

Sherry smiled as she followed the two men into the house, knowing Geoff had been at loose ends since returning from London, and believing that Richard Brimley's curious and intriguing presence may just be the perfect solution to her brother-in-law's ennui.

And her own?

No. She was happy. Really, she was happy.

*   *   *

Adam put down his wineglass and clutched at his stomach, doubled over with laughter at Richard's unexpected joke at the Prince Regent's expense. What made the joke, one he'd heard before, so much funnier was that Sherry quite obviously hadn't the faintest idea what Richard's mention of cherry brandy had to do with anything, so that her polite, puzzled smile sent Adam into whoops all over again.

As Geoff leaned over to whisper in Sherry's ear, explaining the Prince Regent's recourse to cherry brandy in order to try to screw himself up to the sticking point—quite literally—on his wedding night to an unappealing bride, Adam turned to grin at Richard. "You're a bad man, Dickie. A very bad man. And now I believe my brother is corrupting my dear, innocent wife."

"Oh, I very much doubt that your sweetest Sherry is easily corruptible, my dear Daventry," Richard said in that easy way he had of complimenting and at the same time giving the feeling that he was speaking of something deeper. "In fact, I believe I'm counting on it."

"Counting on it?" Adam shook his head. "I don't understand."

Richard's smile was devoid of artifice. "It's simple enough. I have never before met a woman so marvelously invulnerable to my charms. You may not have noticed, being a man and all of that, but I'm rather pretty."

"I have a friend who'd offer to break your nose for you, make you less pretty," Adam said, grinning.

"Why, thank you, Daventry, I'll give that some thought. It's a curse, you understand, this pretty face of mine. My winning manner, all of it. Caused me no end of female troubles. But Sherry doesn't care about any of that. She only laughs at me, and considers me to be her good friend. It's refreshing, having a female as a friend, such a boon companion over these past weeks. But you hold her heart, my dear Daventry. Completely and totally. It must make you very proud."

"Grateful would be a better word, Dickie," Adam said, motioning for his friend to rise and follow him outside, into the lush rose garden, leaving Sherry and Geoff behind to gossip, something Geoff enjoyed very much. "I've been meaning to ask you something these past weeks," he said, once they were standing on the flagstones, looking down at the profusion of perfect blooms that seemed to glow in the moonlight. "You don't have to answer me if you don't wish to but, when you were in London did you perhaps make the acquaintance of the duchess of Westbrook?"

"In your gardens the evening of your ball, you'd have to mean, as I was only in London for the one night? Oh, dear. I do recall a noise, and my companion's concern that perhaps we were not alone. Was that you, then, sharing a bit of romance and moonlight with your own wife? How wonderfully romantic of you," Richard responded, grinning at

Adam over the top of his wineglass. "But for shame, Daventry, asking me to betray a confidence, compromise a lady's honor." His grin widened. "Which I just did, didn't I? Thank goodness Sherry, bless her, appears not to have made the connection."

"Which I pray she never will, as she'd probably then be too embarrassed ever to see you again," Adam said, smiling a little at the memory of what had been a most enjoyable evening. "Tell me, are you rusticating to hide from tradesmen, or from the duke? If it's the latter, it may ease your mind if I were to tell you that he has long since ceased caring what his wife does."

"Poor Melinda," Richard said, sighing theatrically. "Such an unhappy creature, so unsatisfied with her lot. Someday, if I feel in the mood for tears and trembling lips, I shall have to ask her what she wants. Although I believe I know."

"Everything?" Adam suggested, pulling two cheroots from his pocket and handing one to Richard. "That's what she has always wanted, you know. Everything."

"Yes, most people do," Richard agreed, accepting the cheroot, then bending to light it from one of the small flambeaux that hung against the wall. "Money, power, beauty, good luck, health, the destruction of their enemies. Fame. Immortality. No one is ever completely happy, totally content."

"I am," Adam said, drawing deep on his own cheroot. "I can't think of a thing I'd want different in my life. Not a single thing."

"And Sherry," Richard said, nodding. "She feels the same. In fact, my friend, the two of you are almost sloppy in your perfect happiness. Geoff said as much to me yesterday as we were trying out his new pair when you were called away to tend to that wagon that got stuck in a puddle, or some such thing. Have you even seen Geoff's new pair? They're smack up to the echo, Daventry, just ask him."

Adam felt the familiar pang of guilt that assailed him whenever he thought about Geoff. Between the unusually heavy press of estate business—there seemed to be a new emergency every day of late— and the hours he spent with Sherry, there was precious little time for brotherly companionship these days. If he had a regret, Geoff was it. "I'm grateful Geoff has your company, Dickie," he said, blowing out a thin blue stream of smoke. "My marriage has made a few fairly drastic changes in our lives, all of them at my brother's expense, unfortunately."

"I enjoy his company," Richard said, sticking his cheroot between his teeth, smiling around it. "In fact, all three of us have been having quite a jolly time while you labor so dutifully in the fields. Did Sherry tell you about our picnic the other day? She goaded Geoff and me into building kites and racing across the field with them. Geoff ran into a tree."

Adam laughed. "You mean his kite got tangled in a tree, don't you?"

"No," Richard answered, his grin wicked. "Although Geoff might try to tell the story that way one day. The truth is, he was so busy watching his kite that he quite forgot to pay attention to where he was going. Then the kite got caught up in the tree."

Adam tossed his cheroot out over the balustrade, watched its glow as it arched high, then dropped into the gardens where Augustus would no doubt find it the next morning, and shake his head sadly at the discovery. "I would have paid a monkey to see that," he said consideringly. "You know, Dickie, I think I've been neglecting my brother shamelessly, don't you? What do you say we plan something for tomorrow? Can you suggest anything?"

Richard smiled, tossed his own cheroot after Adam's. "Oh, I suppose I could think of something. After all, I promised your wife I'd be court jester for the summer."

"You did?" Adam asked. "Why?"

"Why? My goodness, Daventry, do you know you suddenly resemble a thundercloud? I don't in the least mind amusing your brother and your wife while you go about the business of being lord of the manor, or whatever it is you do. In fact, I'm having quite a marvelous time, even better than I could have hoped when I first rented Frame Cottage."

Adam leaned against the balustrade, his head dropped against his chest as he inspected his toes. "I've never had a summer this busy," he said, speaking almost to himself. "One problem tumbling on top of the next, all of them requiring my presence.

During the Season, I could be with her every day. Sherry assures me she's happy, totally able to amuse herself, but she's so young, and without a drop of experience at running a household like Daventry Court." He looked up at Richard Brimley. "Not that she wants to, you understand. Tell me, what do you and Sherry and my mischief-loving brother do all day, Dickie?"

Richard shrugged. "Besides watching Geoff run into trees, you mean? Well, I suppose we just amble, and talk, and inspect the world. There's a lot of it out there, you know, other than your cultivated fields and the rest. And we have fun, just for the sake of it. Tomorrow, for instance, Geoff has challenged me to a curricle race, to show off his new pair. To get into the spirit of the thing, Sherry has kindly gifted Geoff with her colors, which he'll wear on his arm as I beat him all hollow. Mere children's games, Daventry, I promise you, while you do all the serious work. I'd be ashamed, if I weren't enjoying myself so thoroughly."

He tipped his head, looking at Adam curiously. "Hasn't Sherry told you all about it? The race, I mean, and the rest of it?"

She hadn't, actually. She didn't tell him much of anything. Sherry only told Adam that she'd had a lovely day, and then he'd tell her a bit of estate business, all of it boring, and then they'd fall into bed and make love, which was of infinitely greater interest than walks around the estate or crop thinning. They were very good at making love. They weren't, it now occurred to him, quite so proficient at talking to each other.

Adam pushed himself away from the balustrade, heading back toward the doors to the drawing room. "You know what, Dickie," he said as he stopped, to allow the other man to walk through the doorway ahead of him, "I have a fairly decent pair of my own. What time is this race tomorrow? I think it's time I taught your pretty face a little humility."

Adam smiled as Sherry burrowed closer against him beneath the covers, the two of them happily tired and replete after making love. He kissed the top of her head, slid his fingers into her hair. "Happy, love?" he asked automatically. All he wanted from life was that Sherry be happy.

"Ummmm," she mumbled, sliding her arm across his waist. "That, I believe, sir, would depend upon your definition of the word," she then said teasingly, taking them both back to the day they'd met, as he'd sat rump-down in the stream, and she'd asked him if he was very wet. "I'm not sad. Not in the slightest bit melancholy. Then again, happy may be too mild a definition."

Adam slid down the pillows slightly, to grin straight into her face. "Give me a few minutes to recover, minx, and I'll see what I can do about making you ecstatic."

She smiled, put a hand to his cheek. "Oh, Adam,

I do love you," she said, then kissed his mouth. "So very, very much."

He picked up a lock of her long hair and twirled it around his fingertip. "Tonight, Dickie said nobody seems content with their lot in life. That they always want more. Until I met you, darling, I would have agreed with him."

"But not now?"

"Not ever again. Daventry Court, my title, everything could disappear tomorrow, and I wouldn't miss it. As long as I still had your love."

Sherry pressed her cheek against his palm. "That's also what Dickie says."

Adam tensed. "I beg your pardon?"

She looked at him curiously for a moment, then giggled. "Oh, no. No, Adam. I don't mean he feels that way about *me*."

"Well, that's a relief," Adam said, lying back against the pillows once more. "For a moment there, I thought I'd have to climb out of this nice, warm bed and go kill the fellow."

Sherry sat up, reached for the dressing gown that still somehow managed to remain lying at the bottom of the tangled covers, and slipped into it, covering her most delightful nakedness. She left the bed, returning a few moments later with two half-filled glasses of wine.

"Dickie's very deep, isn't he, for all he tries to pretend he's silly and shallow?" she asked, handing one of the glasses to Adam, who now sat propped against the pillows, bare to his waist beneath the covers, looking at her in wonder. He thought they had been about to make love again, and now it appeared they were going to have a talk. He'd wanted to talk, but he also wondered if he really wanted Richard Brimley to be the subject of their conversation. He'd wanted to tell her he planned to join them tomorrow for the curricle race. And yet, suddenly Richard Brimley interested him more.

"Deep? I'd say he's muddled. Telling you he'd give up everything, gladly, for true love, and telling me that no one is ever happy, always wants more, even if they have everything good in abundance. Don't you find that contradictory?"

"No, Adam, I find that sad," she told him, taking a sip of her wine. "It's because he lost at love. He's become jaded, cynical, and whatever other words you can think of to describe a sad, sad man. He told me all about it."

"Oh, he did, did he?" Adam sat up more fully, holding out his arm so that Sherry could lean against him. "And now you're going to tell me, aren't you? Unless that would mean betraying a confidence?"

"I don't think so. Besides, Dickie told it to me as a fairy tale, or an epic poem like those Mrs. Forrest used to insist I read, pretending it didn't happen to him at all."

"So perhaps it didn't, darling. Perhaps he was simply telling you a story. Did you ever think of that?"

Sherry twisted around to look up at him in that

long-suffering way of women who know that men can never understand anything unless it has something to do with war or crops or hunting dogs. "Do you want to hear this, or don't you?"

"I am hanging on your every word, darling," Adam teased, kissing the tip of her nose. "Now, to begin. Once upon a time . . ."

"Wretch," she countered, sitting back against his shoulder once more. "All right. Once upon a time there was perfection. Complete happiness. Beauty. Truth. And the most perfect creature in the midst of all this perfection and truth and beauty."

"In other words, Dickie was in love and seeing the world through a lover's eyes. Yes?"

"I suppose so. He was so happy, so in love with this perfect creature. There couldn't be a more perfect happiness. Until one day, one horrible, terrible day, this perfect creature decided there should be more. That it wasn't fair that this perfection be seen and enjoyed by so few. That this perfect happiness, this perfection, must be shared."

"She cheated on him with another man. Another *several* men," Adam put in, believing he was acting the role of translator for Richard Brimley's fairy tale, or parable, or whatever name Dickie wished to give such romantic nonsense in order to impress his tenderhearted wife.

He gave out a small "oof!" as his wife's elbow found his unprepared and unprotected midsection.

"Oh, I'm sorry, Adam, for it's not really your fault. I'm not telling it right, that's all. To hear Dickie tell it, he lived in a sort of paradise, and that his most perfect, wonderful creature—yes, dearest block-head, I'm sure he meant a woman—opened the gates of that paradise to those Dickie considered inferior and undeserving."

"I'd consider them dead, if they tried to infringe upon *my* private paradise," Adam said, draining the last of his wine.

"Yes, darling. You'd be ferocious, and I thank you," Sherry said, giggling, but then sobering again. "Well, to hear Dickie tell it, he couldn't stay and watch as his perfect world was despoiled—that's what he said, despoiled—and so he left, never to return. Sadly, he says he has devoted himself ever since to making this most perfect creature—yes, Adam, the woman who betrayed him—realize the mistake she made in letting others, those inferior others, into her paradise. Happily, he still seems able to enjoy himself very much."

She snuggled against him. "I wonder who it was, don't you? I mean, Dickie is certainly the prettiest man I've ever seen—except for you, darling, of course. Who would ever choose somebody inferior to him, choose someone else *over* him? Well, who-ever this woman was, she broke his heart most thoroughly, I can tell you that. In fact, I don't think he likes anyone anymore, most especially himself."

"He likes you well enough, pet," Adam told her, taking the empty wineglass from her and putting it down next to his on a small table beside the bed. "He told me as much. He enjoys Geoff. Perhaps his broken heart is healing a bit this summer. I'd like to think so, now that you've told me his sad tale. Because he's quite likable in his own way."

"And he likes you, darling," Sherry said, sliding her leg over his, maneuvering herself so that she lay half on top of him, smiling up into his face. "But that would be because you are perfect. You are, you know. Completely and absolutely perfect. Except that I believe you should be kissing me now." She rubbed her body against his provocatively, and he knew she could feel his immediate response. "Yes, you definitely should be kissing me now."

Adam happily obliged, and all conversation trailed away into giggles and deep breaths and wondrous sighs, and he entirely forgot to tell her that he'd planned to join them the following morning for the curricle race.

Chapter Thirteen

Sherry didn't know whether to be delighted or dismayed when Adam made his appearance at the end of the drive that led onto the road outside Daventry Court. She was happy to see him, that was certainly true. She was happy that he'd found time away from his seemingly endless estate business to "play," as Dickie termed the thing.

But would he think them all foolish? Childish?

Geoff was already wearing Sherry's pale yellow scarf tied around his arm, "milady's favor," he said. He'd just handed her a single, long-stemmed yellow rose in return as Adam drove up in his curricle, two magnificent gray, stamping, blowing horses in the traces. It had all seemed so lighthearted and romantic a moment ago, but now it just felt silly.

Except that Adam entered into the game immediately, glaring down at Geoff and demanding the two of them race for the honor of wearing Sherry's "favor," and might the better man win.

"The better man obviously has already done, brother," Geoff said, then kissed Sherry smack on her parted, thoroughly surprised lips before winking at her and climbing up onto the seat of his curricle. "All that remains is to see who is the better driver. Dickie?" he then asked, calling to Richard Brimley, who was just then escorting Sherry safely to the side of the road, "if you'd be so kind as to give the signal for us to begin?"

"Oh, but Dickie was going to race as well," Sherry said, looking to Adam. "But you can't possibly race three-across, can you? The road is almost too narrow for two."

Richard lifted her hand to his lips, smiled at her. "Let them go, my dear. I am certainly not one to come between brothers, at least not recently, and not while I'm on my best behavior. We all know how badly that can end, don't we?"

He walked to the center of the roadway, for a groom had already pulled his curricle and horses off to one side, clearing the road for Adam's equipage. "The route, Daventry, is fairly simple. To the smithy at the beginning of the village, where the road widens enough for a turn, and back. Other than that, if you've a mind for mischief, there are no rules." He extracted a snowy white handkerchief from his pocket and held it aloft as he stood between the two curricles, just ahead of the eager horses. "At my signal, gentlemen?"

* * *

Over the course of the next month, the curricle races at Daventry Court became almost legendary. Everyone knew about them, everyone attended, more than a few tried their hand at attempting to best Geoff, or Dickie, or the marquess himself over the length of the race. New rules were made up almost daily, new courses plotted, new dares thrown out and accepted.

Daventry Court seemed to settle itself from its rash of cottage fires and overrun drainage ditches and cracked millstones and broken equipment, leaving Adam free to indulge himself with as much enthusiasm as his brother, Dickie, and his ever-laughing, happy wife.

They'd flown kites. They'd spent a rainy afternoon in a scavenger hunt that took them from cellars to attics inside the house, hunting down objects like the housekeeper's second-best apron and an iron kettle with a hole in its bottom. They'd helped Sherry prepare lemon tarts in the kitchens—an afternoon that ended with Adam having to raise the wages of his temperamental French chef or else lose the man entirely. It hadn't been the invasion of his kitchen that had upset the man, but when Geoff had initiated a flour fight that ended with the four of them looking much like ghosts and the kitchen reduced to a shambles—well, Adam believed it was a very good thing Sherry didn't understand a word of French.

Daily, Adam fell more in love with his wife. He'd

seen her as wonderful, beautiful, irresistible. The most straightforward, honest, generous woman in the world. But she was more. So much more. She could be silly, profound—even profane, when her chosen hen was beaten at the last minute in a race with Geoff's prize pullet. She discussed politics and philosophy, not using the hackneyed arguments others learned in books, but from the perspective of a person who lived life, looked at it simply, through the most innocent of eyes, studied it from her own unique angle, then reduced the world to its clearest, purest form.

In short, he didn't just love his wife anymore. He didn't merely desire her with all his heart and soul. He liked her. He really, truly, honestly *liked* her.

So did Geoff. So did Richard Brimley. So did everyone who came to Daventry Court to play and laugh and dance and enjoy themselves. Sherry, it seemed to Adam, had found her element, and reveled in it. He never again heard her lament her sad lack of domestic skill, for she had found her milieu. She made people happy.

Only Richard Brimley equaled Sherry in popularity, perhaps even exceeded her. There wasn't a woman he couldn't charm with his beauty, a man he couldn't win with his free and open ways.

But Adam enjoyed watching his wife shine, enjoyed seeing his friend conquer country society.

For this perfect month, this flawless slice of time in this exquisite place, the outside world no longer existed. Adam had the best wife, the best brother, and the best friend any man could ever have.

Perfect. A pure paradise.

He wasn't sure when it all began to fall apart.

It began slowly, insidiously.

It started with jealousy.

Geoff laughed a little too hard when he was around Sherry. Touched her too much. Kissed her unnecessarily. Looked at her too deeply when he thought no one else was watching.

At least that's how Adam began to see it as he enjoyed another race, another game, another pleasant dinner party—but not as much as he previously had been enjoying them.

It had been Dickie who'd first pointed out Geoff's seeming infatuation with Sherry. Dickie who had jokingly teased that Adam had a rival for his wife's affections, then had pointed to Geoff, who had been in the midst of whispering into Sherry's ear while resting a hand on her shoulder.

"A coltish infatuation, I'm sure," Richard had said, as Adam frowned into his wineglass. "Why, I'm half in love with her, myself. As is every man within five miles of Daventry Court. You should be proud, Daventry. Flattered."

"She doesn't encourage anyone," Adam answered, watching as Sherry giggled, then asked Geoff's advice before she played down her next card as she sat across from the squire, a man who wore the doomed expression of a dedicated gambler who knew his partner was not in the least devoted to winning the hand.

"She doesn't have to, Daventry," Richard pointed out, for the man only spoke the truth. "I've come to believe it's her honesty that is most attractive. Having some experience with less than honest women, I feel I have a right to say this, you understand. You're a lucky, lucky man, Daventry. Sherry would rather die than tell a lie. Not that she'd be very good at it. Not with that sweet, open face. I tell you, Daventry, she almost makes me believe again."

"Believe?" Adam turned to look at his friend. "Believe in what, Dickie?"

He smiled, a strange, faraway look in his eyes. "Just believe, Daventry. Just believe." He shook his head slightly, involuntarily, then pointed with his wineglass. "Ah, here comes Geoff, and with a naughty gleam in his eye, don't you think? He didn't like losing that race to Simmons yesterday. I'm willing to wager you my own pair that he's come up with a new twist in the course, just to advance his odds."

"I don't think I'll take that wager, Dickie," Adam said wryly. "I'm afraid I made the mistake this morning of telling Geoff about a race my friend Chollie and I ran outside London years ago, in my own grasstime. I should have known better than to reminiscence in front of Geoff."

"I say, you two," Geoff began a moment later, as he joined them, putting a companionable arm around his brother and his friend. "Who cares to drop the handkerchief tomorrow, and who wants to be my guide?"

"Your guide?" Richard looked at Adam, who was shaking his head. "Your guide for what?"

"It's simple," Geoff went on, stepping back from his friends in order to snag a glass of wine from the tray the butler was carrying to the ladies. "Tell him, Adam."

Adam sighed fatalistically, remembering his youth, and one of the most embarrassing episodes from that carefree time. "It was the way Geoff set out the racecourse today that reminded me," he told Richard as the three stood propping up the mantel, watching the other occupants of the room as they milled about, laughed, and generally enjoyed themselves. "I stupidly remarked that I'd once raced such a course blindfolded, with a friend up on the seat beside me, guiding me. The fact that both my friend and I were three-parts drunk at the time lends no hint of respectability to the telling, either. We ended upturning over the edge of a barrel as I tried to feather a corner."

"Isn't that famous, Dickie? You must admit that it seems more fun than just our usual races. Simmons has already agreed, and his cousin will act as his guide. We'll both run the course with our curricles, one after the other, and the fastest time with the fewest nicked barrels wins. Sherry has already volunteered to time us. In fact, I believe she's as excited as I am. She's a real brick, Sherry is."

"And you want me to be your eyes for you,

Geoff?" Richard asked, winking at Adam. "You'd put that much faith in me?"

"Well, of course. Dash it all, Dickie, you're my friend, ain't you?"

And that's how it really began . . . or kept on beginning. Who could say when it all really began, or why.

The blindfolded races proved a huge success with Geoff, and with the other younger gentlemen who'd made Daventry Court their second home as they waited out their return to London, or to Scotland, or a trip to their favorite hunting boxes.

Not content to confine their races to courses set up on Daventry Court land, they'd soon abandoned the now-boring design of barrels. They'd begun racing the narrow, twisting country lanes blindfolded, and often drunk, with an equally castaway guide shouting out "turn ahead, to your left," or "farm wagon approaching," or—in the case of Billy Simmons and his cousin—"cow in the road! Turn left! No! Right! No! Bloody hell, Billy—*jump!*"

After Billy Simmons was carried home on a fence gate, his leg broken, Adam sat Geoff and Sherry down and ordered the races to stop. Sherry agreed with him; Geoff did not.

Two days later, with Geoff holding the reins, and Dickie sitting beside him, a small child nearly came to grief under the wheels as they careened through the village at top speed.

Adam sat Geoff and Dickie down together, and ordered the races to stop.

Richard Brimley listened politely, then stood up, looked down at Adam in a way that chilled him to the bone. Smiling, yet without a hint of good humor. "How amusing. You assume that you are in charge here, Daventry. Nothing could be further removed from the truth. Now, and from the very beginning. This isn't about silly races. It's a *game*, Daventry, my game. Played by my rules. And it goes on. Trust me in this, it goes on, until I decide to end it." Then he turned on his heels and left the house, clearly with the intention of never returning.

Adam stared after Richard's departing back. "What the devil was *that* about?" he asked his brother.

But Geoff wasn't speaking to him, obviously sure that Adam had destroyed what had been a wonderful friendship, a most singularly enjoyable summer. He'd stormed out of the room, petulant as a three-year-old, and took himself straight to Sherry, trying to enlist her support in convincing Adam to apologize to Dickie.

"Why are you being so hard on them?" Sherry asked, watching Adam as he paced the carpet in their bedchamber.

"Why are you so intent on defending him?" Adam countered, stopping in front of her, glaring at her as he spoke.

"*Him*, Adam? Who are you talking about? I'm talking about Geoff and Dickie. But you're not, are you? You're talking about Dickie. Why just him? Isn't Geoff equally as guilty? Or is he less guilty because he's your brother?"

"He's less guilty because he's an *idiot!*" Adam shouted, his hands balling into fists at his sides. "I*m* an idiot. Why didn't I see it? Why didn't I know?"

Sherry tucked her feet under her dressing gown as she sat on the bed, nervous beyond measure at seeing this new, angry side of her husband. She'd once thought married people should argue from time to time, not just exist in some happy daze of loving. But this wasn't an argument. This was a man who looked ready to do mayhem. "You really believe what you've been telling me, don't you? You believe that Dickie was never our friend? That this whole summer has been a lie? A *game?* That's ridiculous, darling. Why would he do that? Why would anyone do that? What would he *win?*"

Adam subsided on the edge of the bed. "Christ, Sherry, I don't know. Looking back . . . thinking back over conversations we've had . . . I can see that Dickie has been playing his own game from the very beginning, playing the piper while we all danced to his tune. Hinting to me that Geoff might be in love with you—"

"What?" Sherry shot to her knees, staring at Adam in total disbelief. "Well, now I *am* angry. That's absurd, Adam, and you know it." She sank back on the bed with an exasperated groan. "I don't believe this, Adam. I truly don't. Next you'll be saying *Dickie* is in love with me."

"No, I don't think he is," Adam said quietly. "As a matter of fact, I'm not even sure he likes us. Any of us. We're just part of his game, very helpful pawns, actually."

"*What* game?" Sherry asked, sitting up once more, laying a hand on her husband's shoulder. "Adam, you're frightening me, do you know that?"

"I don't mean to frighten you, but I'm afraid it's unavoidable." He turned and took both her hands in his, trying to explain. "There are people, darling, unhappy or bored or just simply *mean* people in this world. People who, as children, pulled the wings off butterflies, or set blinded mice inside a maze, just to watch them try to struggle back out again. People who make mischief for mischief's sake. People who dislike their fellowman so much that they spend their entire lives trying to prove those fellow men inferior to them, lesser than them, unworthy of them. Flattering others into stupidity, turning brother against brother, wife against husband—country against country, if you want to broaden our discussion. I don't, frankly. I just want you to understand that Richard Brimley is not our friend. He's dangerous. Worse than that, after all these weeks of hiding behind a smiling, affable face, he now wants me to know he's dangerous."

"By saying what he said to you today?" Sherry nodded, not totally understanding—she doubted she ever would understand totally—but remembering what Geoff had told her earlier. She also remembered Dickie asking her, oh, so long ago, if she liked to "play." At the time, she had thought him silly. But now? After what Adam had just told her? "Maybe this is another game? A silly challenge of sorts, to see who has more control over Geoff— you, or Dickie?"

Adam leaned closer, kissed her. "No, darling. He wants to see how much control he has over *me*. I made some inquiries this afternoon of Seth Frame's solicitor in the village, and found that Brimley paid twice the normal price to rent Frame Cottage, successfully ousting a family from Sussex who had wanted to tenant the place for the summer months. This, after telling us he was here to hide from his creditors in London. He came here on purpose, Sherry, sought us out. Sought me out. He found a way to be at our ball in London. You didn't know that, but I did, probably because he wanted me to know. It doesn't make any sense, but the man wants to hurt me. Through Geoff. Through you. It's the only possible explanation."

"You're frightening me, Adam," Sherry said, laying her head on his shoulder. "But if you're so afraid of Dickie we should leave here, that's all. Go back to London, or to one of your other estates. At least until you remember why Dickie wants to harm you. Had you met him before, and just don't recall? Or perhaps he has a cousin, or a good friend—someone you insulted in some way? Adam, as your wife, I should know this—but do you gamble?"

He smiled at her. "Have I ruined Brimley's cousin or whoever at the card table? Is that what you're asking? Do you think Brimley would then try to drive a wedge between Geoff and me, perhaps even between you and me, by thinking up such an elaborate scheme? No, darling. This isn't revenge. It's a *game*, remember? Richard Brimley saw me, probably in London, disliked me for some reason, and decided I was the sort of person he'd enjoy toying with, possibly even destroying. I'm his butterfly, his blind mouse. I'm not afraid of him, even if I don't understand him. I'm only worried about Geoff, and about you. Promise me you'll stay away from Brimley, all right?"

"I promise," Sherry said as clearly and earnestly as she could when, inside, she was shaking with a thousand unnamed fears. "But do you really think he'll be back, after the way he stormed out of here today? He's as good as thrown down the gauntlet, or whatever you want to call it. He has to know he won't be welcome at Daventry Court."

"Which will make my stubborn, angry brother twice as welcome at Frame Cottage," Adam grumbled against her hair. "I've ordered Geoff never to speak with the man again, and after more screaming and invective than either of us will want to remember, he's agreed. I just pray I can believe him. If the three of us can remain solidly together on this, Brimley's game will be over."

"Without us ever knowing why he began the

game at all, what his motives were, what he'd hoped to win?"

Adam smiled sadly, feeling old, older than anyone else in the world. "Without us ever knowing why he began it at all, yes. But he's already won, Sherry. Because we'll always wonder, won't we? We'll always wonder why, we'll never trust anyone else quite so much again. We'll have, in a way, become almost as cynical and distrusting of our fellowman as he is. For someone like Richard Brimley, that alone is a victory. God knows it's certainly our loss."

Sherry had every intention of obeying her husband, even if she didn't truly understand him. If he didn't want her with Dickie, she would stay away from the man. Give up the fun they'd all had before the races turned dangerous, turn her back on the whirl of society around them—a whirl that continued, even if it no longer included the residents of Daventry Court.

Estate business once more occupied Adam, seemingly from early morning to late into the evening. The steward fell from the roof of a barn and would be in no condition to run the estate for several weeks. A particularly nasty infestation of bugs had closed the gristmill for over a week as Adam oversaw the workers scrubbing the huge building from top to bottom, and burning the grain that had been scheduled for the wheel. Packets seemed to arrive daily from London, all of them containing papers that needed Adam's immediate attention.

Leaving Sherry very much to her own devices, just as she had been before Dickie's arrival on the scene. And she missed him. Missed his smile, his jokes, the excitement of being in his presence.

As the days passed, and as Geoff routinely began to disappear for hours at a time, and as Adam was occupied with estate matters, Sherry began to re-think her husband's strange description of Richard Brimley, of Brimley's motives, the danger Adam be-lieved Dickie presented to them.

It was all so silly. Adam's rules had made them virtual hermits at Daventry Court, while the rest of the countryside enjoyed themselves as before. The races continued, the parties, the picnics. If Dickie had planned to "destroy" Adam, surely he would go on about doing it, not spend his days in the same carefree way, playing at life, enjoying life, clearly without a thought to Adam or Geoff or her.

Adam was jealous of Dickie. That's what Geoff had said, and that's what Sherry slowly grew to be-lieve, much as she didn't want to think her husband could be so venal. He was jealous of Dickie's popu-larity, his brother's affection for the man—and per-haps even worried that his own wife found the man too attractive by half.

No matter what the reasons, no matter what Adam said, the end remained the same. Sherry was once more alone at Daventry Court, at loose ends, walking the estate, dreaming her solitary dreams. Only the innocence was gone . . .

"Geoff? Where are you going?"

Adam's brother turned to Sherry, his smile somewhere between defiant and guilty. "Oh, no, sweet sister. If I tell you, and if Adam asks, you won't be able to summon a creditable fib. Just forget you saw me, all right?"

"You're going to see Dickie, aren't you?" Sherry took hold of his arm, trying to keep him from leaving. "You've been sneaking around meeting with Dickie and the others behind Adam's back for two weeks while he's so very busy. Haven't you?"

He shook off her hand. "And if I have? What of it? Dickie's the best friend a man could have, and a damn sight better than my missish brother, telling me where I can go, who I can talk to, what I can and cannot do." And then he smiled. "We're having another race. Do you want to come along? I know it's raining a little, but that just adds to the sport, don't you think? Dickie said you're certainly welcome. I think he misses you."

"I miss him, too," Sherry admitted, patting Geoff's cheek. "I can't believe one silly argument has grown into such a wide breach between Adam and Dickie. I've often thought, if I could only talk to Dickie, ask him to explain—"

Geoff all but pounced on her. "There's my girl! Adam's gone God knows where, so he'll never know. Come with me, Sherry. Meet with Dickie, talk with him, watch me race. We've set up the most smashing course."

"I'll have to write a note for Adam, in case he comes home," she told him, and Geoff waited impatiently while she penned a lie having to do with visiting the squire and his wife, then propped it on Adam's desk. It felt wrong, lying to Adam, even on paper, but with any luck at all she'd be home in ample time to retrieve the note.

Geoff then pulled her after him, willy-nilly, gathering up cloaks and hats and other whatnots as they went, and before Sherry knew it she was sitting up beside Geoff in his curricle and on her way.

Dickie was waiting at the crossroads, sitting in his own curricle, a huge black umbrella over his head. He hopped down from the seat when he saw Sherry and ran to her, his smile as beautiful as ever, his expression open and loving and so genuinely friendly that Sherry spared a moment to wonder if her dearest husband had somehow lost his mind these past weeks.

"Sherry!" Dickie called out, pulling her down from the seat and giving her a hug before setting her on her feet in the muddy roadway. "What on earth are you doing here? Geoff, you rapscallion, how could you drag your lovely sister-in-law our in this downpour?"

"It wasn't a downpour when we left Daventry Court," Geoff grumbled, looking about as if to locate something or someone who had gone missing.

"Where is everyone? Don't tell me they're afraid of a little bit of damp?"

Sherry took out her already damp handkerchief and wiped rain from her cheeks, her nose, her chin. "Damp, Geoff? We're likely to drown in this. The race can wait for another day, can't it, Dickie? Why don't we all just take shelter in that barn over there until the worst is over? We can talk, sort out a few things?"

"I don't know, Sherry," Dickie said consideringly. "I was to race Geoff here for my pair. He wants them badly—don't you, Geoff? We're here now, and it's a short course. All he has to do is drive from here to the next crossroads, pick up one of the flags I've already placed there, and return so that I can try to best his time. I know I shouldn't take more than ten minutes to complete the course, although I can't vouch that Geoff will take less than a quarter hour. Surely, Sherry, you can stand in the shelter of the barn for that short time?"

"Say yes, Sherry," Geoff pleaded earnestly. "Especially now that Dickie has all but said I won't be able to beat him. Your bonnet's ruined, so you can easily sacrifice one of your ribbons as my favor. I always do best when I'm wearing your favor. Please, Sherry? We've come this far."

They were already quite wet. They could be back at Daventry Court within the hour. And Sherry did very much want a few minutes alone with Dickie, so that she could talk to him. If he was Adam's friend, she wanted to know that. If he was her husband's enemy, she needed to know why.

"Oh, all right, Geoff," she said, pulling off her bonnet and stripping it of its bright blue ribbon. "Here. Now, give me your pocket watch and wait for my signal. We'll watch for your return from the barn."

"I've missed you," Dickie said, as Sherry held the timepiece in her hand, watching as Geoff sprang his horses and rode out of sight. "I've missed your smile, your laugh. I hadn't thought I would, but I did. I do. But I knew you'd come to me, eventually. They all do."

She swallowed down hard, turning to him, seeing a fire in his eyes she'd never noticed before this moment. And she knew, knew in that instant, that she had just made the biggest miscalculation of her life.

"I think you've mistaken my reason for being here, Dickie," she said quietly, wishing she were able to look away from him, from the beauty of his form, the compelling attraction of his smile. It was like looking into the face of an angel. A very naughty angel.

"No, my little doll," he said, leading her inside the barn, out of the rain. "It's you who have mistaken your reason for coming here. I'm temptation, little doll, and even you cannot resist temptation, the lure of the forbidden. Daventry made his biggest mistake when he forbade his so innocent wife to see me again. The eternal lure of the forbidden fruit. You'd think someone named Adam would have learned, wouldn't you? But he didn't. I counted on that, and Daventry didn't disappoint me, even if the predictability of men is a disappointment in itself."

Sherry yanked her arm free of Richard's hold, more angry now than afraid. "Stop it, Dickie! No more games! Just stop it! I don't know what you're saying, or what you think you know, but I'm not going to stand here and listen to another word of this nonsense. I don't know this game, I don't know the rules, but I do know that you're a terrible, terrible, evil man. I'll wait for Geoff outside, and then we'll be leaving."

"Look at me. Adam doesn't see you as a real woman, but I do. Look at me, Sherry. Look at me. See me. See yourself."

Richard said the words quietly, but the command was heavy in his voice. Unavoidable. Impossible to disobey.

Her eyes swimming with tears of frustration and fear, Sherry did as she was bid. She turned, looked at Richard Brimley.

She saw beauty.

She saw adventure.

She saw temptation.

She saw danger.

And she was unable to look away.

"I meant to have you, little doll," she heard Richard saying, his voice sounding far away now, yet luring her closer to him. "From the beginning, I meant to have you."

"From—from the beginning? When was that, Dickie? In London?"

"Sshh, no questions. I could have you now, Sherry, will have you soon. You're still delicious, but Daventry now intrigues me enough so that the game gets more interesting the longer it runs, don't you agree?"

"I—I don't know what—"

"Of course you don't. How could you? So innocent. So incorruptible, so loyal. I gave you so much. But no one is entirely happy with paradise, are they? They all can be tempted. Even you, little doll, even you. But you aren't ready yet. The stakes aren't high enough yet, are they? So we'll play a little longer, you and Daventry and I, until I tire of the game. In the end, you'll choose me. They always do. But it has to be your choice."

"You're mad. Insane. I wouldn't choose to cross the street with you."

"Yes, I know." He moved closer; cupped her chin in his hand. "Otherwise, little doll, this would be over now. Instead, it is just beginning. I've raised the stakes, you see. Now I want you both."

And then he kissed her. As she stood there, unable to move, too frightened and confused to run, he kissed her. Not in anger, as she'd supposed, or even in lust. He kissed her tenderly, almost as if he cherished her. He kissed her so sweetly that she began to respond, even against her will, pushing him away only as she heard the horses drive up, signaling Geoff's return.

Except that it wasn't Geoff who cried out, "I should have known! You *bastard!*" and leapt down from his curricle, to run toward the barn.

It was Adam.

Adam was very accomplished with his fives, as good a boxer as Chollie. Possibly better. So how he came to find himself lying with his head in Sherry's lap as the world slowly came back into focus was beyond him. He'd had enough anger, enough fury inside him to mill down a dozen men. Yet he hadn't landed a single punch before Richard Brimley had felled him with a fist that had seemed to appear out of nowhere, knocking him straight into unconsciousness.

"Adam? Adam, are you all right? Oh, God, I thought you'd never wake up!"

He looked up at Sherry, at her tear-stained face, and something inside him went very cold. "Let me up, Sherry," he said. He rolled away from her, slowly got to his feet. "You didn't go with him?" he then asked, looking around, seeing that Richard Brimley was no longer in the barn with them.

"Go with him?" Sherry scrambled to her feet. "Are you out of your mind? Why would I go with him?"

"How long?" Adam rubbed at his aching head, exercised his stiff jaw a time or two. "How long have the two of you been meeting? How long, Sherry? Or did I imagine that kiss? Did I imagine that you weren't kicking at him, fighting to escape his arms?"

"It wasn't like that, Adam," Sherry said, her tears enough to melt his heart, if he'd still had one somewhere inside him. But he didn't. He'd known, known from the beginning. Some things are just too good to last. Too perfect to exist outside of a dream. And now the dream was over. For whatever reason, Richard Brimley had proved that to him.

"No, of course it wasn't, Sherry. It never is," Adam said dully, looking past her, out into the driving rain, the gathering darkness. He felt slow, sluggish, as if he were trying to swim through a huge bowl of honey. "Where's my idiot pawn of a brother? One of the grooms said you rode out with him."

Sherry looked blank for a moment, then reached into her pocket, pulling out his brother's timepiece. "He's been gone for almost thirty minutes," she said, looking at Adam in panic. "The course could be driven in ten. Dickie said so. My God, Adam—"

What followed was a nightmare within a nightmare.

The drive through the sheets of gray rain. The turns and twists, the backtracking, trying to find the correct roadway out of a half dozen that branched off in every direction. Sherry's tears as she sat beside him, telling him she was wrong, that he was right, that Richard Brimley was a monster, that she loved him, she loved him with all her heart and soul, would never betray him.

Then there was the wreckage, and the screams of

the horse that hadn't died when Geoff's curricle left the road, tumbled into the ditch on top of Adam's only brother, pinning him, crushing him.

There was Sherry, kneeling in the ditch running nearly wild with rainwater, holding Geoff's head above the rushing water, keeping him from drowning. There was the eternity it took for Adam to find enough help to lift the smashed curricle from his brother's body; leaving Sherry and Geoff alone for all of that time; praying to any god who would listen to let his brother live. Just let his brother live.

The next morning, as Sherry sat vigil with a blessedly unconscious Geoff, as the sun broke through the clouds to start another perfect day in this most imperfect world, Adam returned from the deserted Frame Cottage and walked outside to stand looking out over the garden.

A garden full of dead roses.

"Some sort of blight struck 'em down, my lord. I cain't explain it, but they'll all have to come out. Enough ta make a man weep. A garden like this one. Won't see another like it, none of us. I'm that sorry, I am," Augustus said, tugging at his forelock before going back to his shovel, digging out one of the bushes at the roots. "A blight, my lord. Has to be that."

Adam turned and walked back into the house.

Book Three

Good and Evil

Hell is a city much like London—
A populous and smoky city.

—Percy Bysshe Shelley

La vieillesse est l'enfer de femmes.
Old age is a woman's hell.
—Ninon de Lenclos

Chapter Fourteen

Adam told Chollie the whole of it, from the first day he'd met Sherry beside the stream until the moment he'd seen the empty shop on Bond Street and known, just known, that Richard Brimley was back in their lives.

He didn't spare himself in the telling, letting Chollie know what a fool he'd been, how he'd been duped, how shabbily he'd treated his wife, the woman he loved above his own life.

"Have you spoken with Sherry again since asking her about the dead roses?"

Adam shook his head. "She's too upset. And I can't blame her. Not after the hell I've put her through. But we both know what's happening. Richard Brimley is back, playing his game again."

Chollie took a drink from his glass, sat back, crossed one leg over the other. "It would be helpful, I'm thinking, if you were to know why he was ever around at all. A game is it, Adam? I've never heard of such a game."

"I agree. It's time we stopped calling it a game. Anyone who would go so far as to insert his own people into my home, to spy on us, to make Sherry's life miserable? That person has passed miles beyond playing games."

"And yet that fellow Rimmon is still here," Chollie pointed out. "Worse, he's still breathing. Which means you have a plan, boyo, doesn't it?"

"No, Chollie. It means I don't have the faintest idea what to do, so I'm doing nothing, for fear of making some fatal misstep."

Chollie stood, began to pace. "Richard Brimley. Dickie Brimley. I thought I knew the whole world one way or another, but I've never heard the name. What does he look like?"

Adam smiled ruefully. "He's pretty—that's out of his own mouth. And I suppose he is." He closed his eyes, tried to conjure up Richard Brimley's face. "Dark hair, rather unique blue eyes—a chin a little too feminine for my tastes. Rounded, you know, like Byron's. Yes, that's it. He rather reminds me of Byron—without the dark, brooding moods, or the poetry. The women were mad for him. Except for Sherry. She simply liked him. He made sure everyone liked him."

"Rather like Edmund Burnell, except in his looks, of course," Chollie said thoughtfully. "In fact, very much like our new good friend, Mr. Burnell. Have you asked Edmund if he knows this Brimley person? Not that it would do any good if the two of them were friends, would it, for he'd only lie to you. You've already thought of that, haven't you? Of course you have. Sweet Mary, Adam, I don't have geese walking over my grave today, don't you know. They're fair dancing a jig on it."

Adam came to a decision. "Then pack them up, Chollie, and have them dance along with us, all right? We're on our way to see Lady Jasper."

"Lady J?" Chollie pulled a face, blessed himself. "Must we?"

"Think about it, Chollie. Lady J is Burnell's aunt. If he's a part of this, Lady J's a part of it. She's just the sort to enjoy tearing the wings from butterflies."

Sherry walked through the morning in a daze, trying to sort out the events of the past days, the past months, and having no success. She disliked keeping secrets from Adam, but he'd been so quick to leap to all the wrong conclusions before, about her, about Dickie.

Except that Adam knew. He had to know that Dickie was back, knew that the man was playing his infernal game again. They both knew.

It wasn't fair. They'd been to hell, and were coming back. Both of them. Less trusting, less open with each other, but slowly finding their way back. They'd never have the perfection, the dream they'd once lived. Never again. But it had been Adam who had said it: *Dreams, especially those very rare real-life dreams, should be held tightly, or else they slip away.*

They hadn't held on tightly enough, either of them.

Either that, or it was impossible for any dream to last forever. How could a person exist only within a dream? That wasn't real life, was it?

"This isn't real life either," she told her reflection as she looked into the mirror in the drawing room, seeing herself looking pale, drawn, as if she hadn't slept in months. "I just wish I knew what it is. *Why* it is."

"Mr. Edmund Burnell to see you, my lady," Rimmon said from the doorway, and Sherry nearly jumped out of her skin. "Shall I show him in?"

"Yes, yes, of course," she told the man. "No. Wait a moment, Rimmon," she added hastily. "I believe I'd like a private word with you first."

"Ma'am?"

Sherry looked at the butler, visually inspected him. Did he look anything like Emma Oxton? Was there any hint of Richard Brimley in his eyes? No. No, there wasn't.

"As you've probably heard by now, Rimmon, I dismissed Emma yesterday. Did she return for her things?"

"I'm sure I wouldn't know, my lady," Rimmon said, bowing. "The comings and goings of lesser servants are not my concern. Perhaps if you were to inquire of Mrs. Clement?"

Sherry screwed up her courage. "No, Rimmon, I'm asking you. You are the person who recommended that Emma be taken on as my personal maid, aren't you? When you yourself were hired, when Hoggs so very unexpectedly had to leave his post. Where is Hoggs, Rimmon? I forget."

Rimmon's dark eyes narrowed into slits. "Lincolnshire, my lady. With his ailing sister."

Sherry sat down, spread her skirts around her. She was thinking clearly now, more clearly than she had in months. A trickle of sweat running down the side of Rimmon's cheek lent her even more bravery. "Ah, yes, I remember now. His sister. She took ill quite suddenly, didn't she?" She lifted her head, stared straight at the butler. "How much did that lie cost Richard Brimley, Rimmon? What price did Hoggs put on his loyalty to my husband?"

"My lady isn't making sense," Rimmon said, turning to look toward the hallway, as if measuring the space between his current position and safety. "I'll call Mrs. Clement."

"No, Rimmon, don't bother. I'm sure my husband will be asking you the same questions shortly. Perhaps you'll be more able to remember when *he* asks you," Sherry said, holding her hands together in her lap, so that they wouldn't betray her with their trembling. "You may go for now, and send Mr. Burnell to me."

Rimmon looked ready to say something else, then merely bowed and withdrew. A few moments later, Edmund Burnell entered the drawing room.

"Well now, dearest lady, what have you been up to?" he asked, tossing his hat and gloves onto a chair. "That butler of yours came running down the stairs as if the hounds of Hell were after him, his face as white as chalk, and told me to find my own way up the stairs. Bolted straight past me, out the door. Left me to carry my hat and gloves up with me as well. Did you discover him sliding silver spoons into his pockets?"

"Something like that, Edmund," she said, indicating that he should use the bellpull to summon someone from belowstairs who might then bring them refreshments. "Thank you, you did that well," she said, as he sat down in a chair near her. "I should ask to engage you to replace Rimmon, if you'd be so kind as to furnish me with several letters of reference."

"What? You'd need more than my handsome face? My winning ways? I'm crushed, Sherry," Edmund said, his expression so sad she couldn't suppress a small giggle.

"Ah, Edmund, thank you. I had begun to think I might never laugh again. Are you here to see Adam? He and Chollie went off somewhere about a half hour ago, I'm afraid."

Edmund looked at her curiously. "You've argued, haven't you? You and Adam?"

Sherry looked at her hands, noticing that she was turning her emerald-and-diamond wedding ring round and round her finger. "No," she said, looking up at Edmund, "Adam and I haven't argued. Not that you should have asked such a question."

"How can I not?" he asked, rising from his chair and coming to sit beside her on the striped satin couch, taking her hands in his. "A man would have to be blind not to know that the two of you are unhappy, even as I'd have to be blind not to know that you're very much in love with each other. Oh, I know I'm speaking of things you believe to be none of my concern, but I can't help myself. I like Adam, very much. I like you, my most sweet Miss Giddy-up. Even in the short time we all know each other, I feel that we could be great friends. And so, as a friend, is there anything I can do to help? Anything, Sherry. Anything at all. You've only to ask."

Sherry wet her suddenly dry lips with the tip of her tongue. She was tempted, so very tempted. Tempted to rest her aching head on Edmund's strong shoulder, pour out her heart to him, tell him all about Emma, and the dead roses, and the clerk who looked so much like Dickie, about how much she loved Adam even as she feared he would turn from her again—all of it.

But Richard Brimley had done his work well. Just as Adam had said, it was now difficult for Sherry to trust her fellowman. Dickie had betrayed them. Hoggs had betrayed them. Where once she looked at the world and saw friends, allies, she now saw distrust, lies, the possibility of being hurt. Once again, being hurt.

And then she remembered something. Remembered someone. A person who seemed, somehow, connected both to her and to Edmund Burnell.

"Tell me about the duchess of Westbrook, Edmund," she heard herself say as she politely withdrew her hands from his warm clasp, and watched a measure of her own shock at her words register on his face.

"Melinda?" Edmund rallied quickly, smiling and wagging a finger in her face. "Naughty puss, I thought we were going to pretend that moment at my aunt's house never took place."

Sherry felt hot color run into her cheeks. For all that

she was trying to be a sleuth, she certainly lacked a good deal of sophistication. Which didn't mean she hadn't learned how to lie without giving herself away. She'd learned a lot in the past four and twenty hours, none of it making her happy, all of it putting her on her guard, lending her the strength to be devious, even duplicitous, if she could save Adam from more hurt.

"No, I'm not talking about that, Edmund," she said with a wave of her hand. "I understand *that*. I was just wondering how you met, if you met her through mutual acquaintances, for instance. She's, um, Her Grace is quite good friends with Richard Brimley. Do you know the man?"

"Brimley?" Edmund looked quite blank as he seemed to search his brain for Richard's name. "No," he said at last. "I don't think I've ever been introduced to him. Melinda and I met through my aunt. Lady J knows my needs, you understand, and my tastes. There, now we've both been horribly frank and possibly naughty. And here's the tea tray, just in time to save us both from more embarrassing truths."

"I'm sorry, Edmund," Sherry said once the footman had put down the tray and disappeared. "I can't imagine what has gotten into me, really I can't."

"You're unhappy, Sherry," he told her as if he had the answer to every problem in the world. "And, since you won't let me help you, I can only look forward to the masquerade tonight, at which time I should at least be able to entertain you. Don't you think I shall make a dashing Sir Lancelot to your Guinevere?"

"Yes, I can imagine we'll all be quite dashing."

Sherry smiled weakly and took a sip of tea, the hot liquid burning her tongue. She closed her eyes and wondered where Adam was at that precise moment.

Lady Gytha Jasper wasn't looking well, not that she had ever been a beauty, even in her youth. But her smile was strained as Adam and Chollie entered the room after being announced, especially as her butler, speaking in stern rather than affectionate tones, reminded her that she wasn't to tire herself with a visit longer than fifteen minutes.

"Don't push at me, Midgard, I'm not dead yet," she barked at the man, then waved him out of the room before holding a finger to her lips as she looked at Adam. "Don't talk, don't say anything," she warned in a whisper.

Chollie turned to Adam, spoke quietly. "Wanting a square, ain't she?"

"Quiet, Chollie," Adam warned as Lady Jasper rose from her seat and tiptoed to the double doors to the hallway, then threw them open wide. Midgard, who was standing just outside, his body bent as he appeared to have been listening at the keyhole, pulled himself up stiffly and walked away. Lady Jasper cackled, then slammed both doors shut and locked them, pocketing the key in her bodice. "Now that's interesting."

"How so? He's her keeper, that's all. She needs one. I tell you, boyo, she's dotty in the head, and it isn't today or yesterday that it happened to her. Wasting our time, that's what we're doing."

"About time you got here, Daventry," Lady Jasper

said once she'd come back to the couch, sat down once more. "Drinks for us all first, then we'll talk."

"First sane thing the woman's said." Chollie moved sprightly, heading for the drinks table. "I wouldn't be sorry to get a glass of wine. Adam?"

Adam nodded, then split his coattails and sat down on the couch opposite Lady Jasper, looking at her assessingly. She had a story to tell, that much was obvious. But was she insane or simply frightened? "You say you've been expecting me, Lady Jasper? Why?"

"Why, the fool asks," she said, all but grabbing the wineglass out of Chollie's hand, then downing its contents in one long gulp. "Fill it again, boy," she demanded, holding the glass out to Chollie. "This is going to be dry work."

"Adam?"

"Just do it, Chollie, all right," Adam said, putting his own drink, untouched, on the table between Lady Jasper and himself. She immediately helped herself to it. "Lady J? Where do you want to start?"

She cackled again, so that Adam wouldn't have been surprised if she soon laid an egg. "That's not it, Daventry. It's where I want to start *over*. Did you ever want to do that? Go back, start over? I'd bet a monkey you do."

Adam's jaw tightened. "Yes, Lady Jasper. I know the feeling. Tell me about Edmund, please. Tell me about your nephew."

"Nephew! Hah! That's a rare joke, isn't it? He's no nephew of mine. He's the *Devil*. Haven't you figured that one out for yourself yet? I thought even an idiot could have figured that out by now."

Chollie, who had been sitting pretty much at his ease on the couch beside Adam, leapt to his feet, his face as red as fire. "Bad manners to you, woman!" he shouted. "Is it after making fools of us you are? Come on, Adam, we've better things to do than sit and listen to such moonshine. Tempts fate, it does, talking wild like this."

"Oh, sit down, you bloody Irisher," Lady Jasper commanded wearily. "Pull out your beads and count them, or shove them in your mouth—but be quiet. This is serious business, and I haven't much time before the bastard comes back and Midgard greets him at the door to say I've been skulking around behind his back. That's the only trump card we hold, you know. Edmund doesn't know what's happening until sometime *after* it happens, and he gets to see it from a distance. Regular storehouse of knowledge about things that have been and knowing how to use them for his own ends, but with no real control over what's happening, what will happen. Irks the fellow no end, especially now that I've figured it out. Took me a lot of years, but I figured it out."

Adam, who agreed that Lady Jasper was as bat-filled as a belfry, nodded as if he understood. "That would explain why Edmund—why the *Devil*," he corrected as Lady J looked ready to interrupt, "found a way to insert two spies into my house. Emma Oxton, and Rimmon, our butler. Interesting."

Lady Jasper's hawklike face rearranged itself into a

sneer. "Don't laugh at me, boy, or I'll leave you to swing on your own. Except I can't, can I, and still save myself? I need you, curse my luck. Those weren't spies, you dull sot, they're the Devil's own helpers."

"Wine isn't going to do it for me, boyo," Chollie said, rising, heading for the drinks table. "Would you be wanting some brandy before I gulp down the whole decanter?"

"Stop right where you are, Irisher," Lady Jasper commanded, then handed him a small black book she had pulled from her pocket. "Open this to the place I've marked, and read the page for me. You do read, don't you, Irisher?"

Chollie took the book, turned it over in his hands, looked to Adam. "I don't like to say this, but the geese are waltzing again, boyo."

He then opened the book to the place Lady Jasper had marked, and began to read aloud. "'Mankind is beset by many minor devils, lesser demons. Fear them, do not call them forth, for only the Devil himself can control them once they are loosed. They are his servants, not ours, brethren, and it is best you should know this. Believing that you can call them forth for your own purposes is the height of folly, and a sure road to disaster. They are the Devil's own. Furthermore, only a master of magic would ever dare to call on the Devil himself, for—'"

Chollie slapped the book shut. "Well, that was lovely, wasn't it?" he said, pressing a hand against his vest pocket. "Now can I be getting that brandy, do you think?"

"Open it again, you dolt, and read the names."

"Names?" Chollie choked out the word. "I'd rather not, actually. Never can know just who's listening, don't you know."

"Give me the book, Chollie," Adam said wearily, and his friend quickly complied. Adam opened it to the marked page, his eyebrows lifting as he saw that the book had been handwritten, the pages yellow with age and looking to have been much handled. He read the passage Chollie had just recited, then ran his fingers down the column of names listed as being "infernal names." He began to read some of them aloud: " 'Abaddon . . . Astaroth . . . Balaam . . . Beherit . . . Dagon . . . Diabolus . . . Emma O . . . Gorgo . . .' " He stopped, looked at Lady Jasper.

"Yes, yes. Emma O. Go on," she prompted, casting a quick glance toward the locked doors.

Adam ran his finger along the page, quickly turned it over to the next one. Where he found Midgard, found Rimmon. He tossed the book onto the table. "That proves nothing, Lady Jasper," he said with all the conviction he could muster. "London gentlemen— idiots all—have been playing at devil worship for decades. There was the Hell-fire Club, for one, and about a dozen more. Dabblers in the black arts, fools with nothing better to do with themselves than to scare themselves to death—and find excuses for wearing masks and bedding women. It's as I've said all along. A game. What we came here to learn, Lady J, are the rules. The motive. The hoped-for prize. So, again, my lady, tell me about your nephew. Tell me about Edmund Burnell."

He took a deep breath, hoped he would gain some reaction from the old woman with the next name he mentioned. "Tell me about Richard Brimley."

"Edmund, Richard. It makes no never mind." Lady Jasper leaned forward, motioned for Adam to lean forward as well. "They're the same person," she whispered hoarsely. "They're the Devil, Daventry. He's the Devil. Learn it, know it, or you and your so-innocent little wife are destined to be forever damned. Like me."

Adam felt Chollie collapse onto the cushion beside him, even as he continued looking deeply into Gytha Jasper's dark, burning eyes. "Go on," he said, his voice so quiet it could barely be heard above the chiming of the mantel clock. "I'm listening. Perhaps if you were to start at the beginning?"

"That's my book," Lady Jasper said, motioning toward the black-leather-covered volume that seemed to throb with a life of its own as it lay on the table. At least Chollie seemed to think so, for he took a cushion from the couch and covered the thing up so that no one could see it. "Don't remember where I got it, it's been too long, but I was young then, and stupid. I read what I had your idiot friend read just now, but I didn't believe it. So I summoned him. Summoned the Devil."

Chollie quickly touched a hand to his forehead, his chest, his left and right shoulder. Then he spat on the floor.

"It isn't hard at all, you know," she went on. "He's

more than happy to come. I called on all the devils of hell one after the other, the crown princes, as it were. Lucifer. Satan. Belial. Leviathan. And the next day? Well, the next day Edmund Burnell came knocking on my door."

Adam held out his hands, asking her to be silent for a moment. "Edmund Burnell, Lady J? When was this?"

"Forty years ago," she said, sighing. "And, before you interrupt me again, I'll tell you that he looked nothing like he does now. Didn't call himself Edmund Burn-in-hell then, either. I've seen him so many times, when he's come *collecting*, and he never looks the same, never has the same name. But he's always pretty. Stands to figure, doesn't it? I mean, he was once God's favorite archangel, if you've been reading your Bible, and let me tell you, boy, I have been. Makes sense that he'd be the prettiest one."

"That does make sense, doesn't it, boyo? If you could look like anything you wanted to, who'd want to have horns and a tail, I'm asking?" Chollie leaned forward, rested his elbows on his knees, clearly captivated. "Go on, Lady J. You tell a good tale, so far. You called forth the Devil. Then what happened?"

"This happened, you drooling dolt," Lady Jasper said, spreading her arms to include the whole of the room, the whole of her town house, the whole of her life. "Or did you really think I got that old idiot to marry me for my beauty, my nonexistent dowry? I got everything I asked for and nothing I didn't. Made a few mistakes there, let me tell you. And all I had to do was trade my soul for the whole of it. Now I want it back."

"After you made the trade, had yourself forty good years?" Chollie asked, winking at Adam. Clearly his friend was caught between his superstitions and his love of a fine joke. "That doesn't seem fair to the Old Boy, now does it?"

"Let the woman talk, Chollie," Adam whispered, as Lady J took recourse to her wineglass once more. Confession might be good for the soul, but it also appeared to be a thirsty business, just as she'd said. "She recognized Richard Brimley's name. Mad as a hatter or not, she knows what we need to know."

"If you say so, boyo," Chollie shot back at him. "But I don't like all this talk about Old Nick. This whole thing is giving me a grand case of the fidgets."

It seemed clear to Adam that Lady Jasper had finished her tale, sketchy as it was, so he felt free to ask her a few questions. "Why is Dickie—why is Edmund after us? After my wife and me?"

"You'll have to ask him that," Lady Jasper said, waving away the question. "Maybe because, unlike me, you aren't such easy pickings. But what makes you think he's after you, too? What you really need to know is how to thwart him. Thwart the Devil. Do it and, according to that book, anyone he's come to collect this time is free as well."

"Meaning you?"

"Meaning me," she answered, smiling. Her smile was most unpleasant. Adam would rather strike allies with a cobra. But, he thought, only with an ounce of humor, *needs must when the Devil drives.*

"So, how do we thwart the Devil, as you call it?"

"Tie a dozen rosaries around your neck?" Chollie offered.

There was the sound of a carriage being halted outside, followed by the opening and closing of the front doors on the ground floor.

"It's him!" Lady Jasper exclaimed, turning a sickly pale gray. "We're just visiting, that's all. Aren't we? Just visiting, and waiting for him to return."

"Of course," Adam agreed, afraid she would have an apoplexy if he didn't. "But tell me, quickly, please. How do we thwart the Devil?"

She shot a look toward the door, then searched inside her bodice for the key, tossed it to Chollie so that he could undo the lock. "Love, Daventry. Something few of us have. Pure, unselfish love. Never faltering, never wavering. I've thought and thought, and it's the only answer. It's the opposite of every human vice that draws him to us, us to him. Make that wife of yours fall back in love with you, want babies. A happy woman who has everything she wants doesn't need the Devil. Think about it, Daventry. Think, and act."

"Well, other than scaring me out of a year's growth, what good did that do us, boyo?" Chollie asked, as they rode back to Grosvenor Square.

"Only a year, Chollie?" Adam teased absently, remembering every word Edmund had said during their short visit, every expression, every smile. "He knows,

Chollie. He's not the Devil—Lord knows Lady J has lost her mind to believe such nonsense—but he knows we're onto him. Him, and Richard Brimley, and whoever else might be involved."

"Involved in *what*, boyo?" Chollie asked, turning on the seat to look at Adam. "You know nothing more than you did before. Maybe less. Because, like it or not, and I most certainly don't, unless Lady Jasper is telling the truth, there's no good reason for anyone to go to such extremes to destroy just you. Which, if I heard her right, isn't true at all. He—they, whoever— is also after Sherry."

"I know that now, and I'd like to kill both Brimley and Burnell at this point. But are you willing to say then that Edmund Burnell is the *Devil*, Chollie?"

His friend puffed out his cheeks, shook his head. "All I'm saying, boyo, is what my dear mama used to say. Seeing as how I've never met this Brimley fellow, then it's better the devil you know than the devil you don't know." He laughed, hollowly. "I wonder what she'd say about a whole host of devils mucking about, don't you?"

"Know one, Chollie, and know them all. At least Lady Jasper says they're all the same person, entity, whatever," Adam reminded him, then slapped a hand against his forehead. "Would you listen to me? I'd half expect you to believe Lady J, Chollie. But not me. Not me."

"Then maybe you *do* believe her, or are at least thinking about believing her?" Chollie rubbed a hand against his waistcoat pocket. "I don't thank you for saying that, boyo. Truly, I don't. Um . . . do you think your man could drop me by that small Catholic church in Spigot Lane? I've a sudden need to light a brace of candles, I do. Been a long time between visits, but—" He stopped speaking, his eyes wide as saucers. "Wh–what's that? Sweet Christ, boyo, never say you did that!"

Adam turned the small black book over and over in his hands. "Do you think I'll be sent screaming down to Hell for taking this, Chollie?"

Chollie took the small leather bag from his pocket and gave it a kiss. "It's slapping you straight into Bedlam that could happen, that's what I'm thinking. What are you going to do with that terrible thing?"

"I'm going to read it, Chollie, of course. What was it your dear mother said? Better the devil you know? I think she was right. If Dickie and Edmund are playing at some new sort of Hell-fire Club devil worship, devilish games, or whatever in—excuse me for this, Chollie, but—whatever in *hell* they're doing, at least I should know the rules."

Sherry all but paced a hole in the drawing-room carpet as she waited for Adam to return from wherever he and Chollie had gone off to more than an hour earlier.

How could he have left her alone like this?

Didn't he know?

Didn't he care?

Court her. That's what he'd said. He was going to court her. Hah! That was rather difficult to do, when they never seemed to so much as be in the same room at the same time.

And what would she tell him, when he finally did come home? That she'd all but chased Rimmon out of the house? How was she going to explain that to him?

She couldn't keep taking to her bed, pretending that the child made her faint. She and Adam had to talk sometime. Sometime soon. So how was she going to explain the dead roses, dismissing Emma? Explain questioning Edmund as if he were an enemy, not a friend?

How was she going to explain any of it? She didn't understand anything herself.

"Where is everyone? No Edmund, no Chollie, not even Rimmon. Here I am, ready to be wept over, and congratulated, and there's no one about to see me. Except you, of course, sweetheart. I think you'll do."

Sherry whirled around to see Geoff standing just inside the doorway, leaning heavily on a pair of canes. "Geoff!" she exclaimed, her fears forgotten as she ran to him, gathered him close in her arms. "I can't believe it! You look wonderful. Wonderful!"

"Taller, certainly," he said as she backed away, stood looking at him in wonder. "Now, if you don't mind a few weak whimpers and some rather grotesque expressions on my otherwise adorable face, I think I'll hobble on over to that chair and sit myself down before I fall down. Would you be so kind as to fetch me a glass of wine? It dulls the edges of the pain."

Sherry hastened to do as he'd asked, kneeling beside him as he stood in front of a chair for a moment, then dropped, all at once, onto the cushions. "Ahhh, that's better. The leech says I'll be improving every day now, if I'm good." He smiled at Sherry. "I wonder if I'll improve twice as fast if I'm bad, don't you?"

"Gudgeon," Sherry accused, handing him the wine-glass. "Does it hurt very much, then?"

"Ah, pity. Just what I like to see in my dear sister's eyes. Yes, pet, it hurts quite a lot. My muscles cry out to be sat down, left to rot as they've been doing, but I must ignore their imploring voices. Again, that's what my leech tells me. He also tells me I'm not to sit in that Bath chair again, as that sort of coddling is all behind me now, should have been behind me a month ago. Do you mind, Sherry? That means I'll be giving tonight's masquerade a miss, as I don't think I could manage these canes for the entire evening."

"The masquerade?" Sherry frowned, having forgotten the evening's entertainment for a moment. How could she have done that? How could she *not* have forgotten it, when she considered how full her plate already was, how muddled her mind always was with things much more serious than a masquerade ball. "Oh, no, Geoff, I don't mind in the least. In fact, I am not at all excited about the evening. Perhaps we could all stay in with you and just play chess or some such thing?"

"No, no, don't do that, sweetheart," Geoff said, patting her hand. "Edmund would be most disappointed, seeing that he went so far as to gather up costumes for everyone. I really feel someone must attend."

Sherry's smile faded. It was ridiculous, really, but

she agreed with Geoff. They were rather beholden to the man, since he had gone to so much trouble. Just as if he wanted to be very certain they'd attend tonight's ball. "Oh, yes. Edmund. Of course. He did mention something earlier, when he was here. I believe he's very much looking forward to the evening."

"And you aren't? That would be a pity, darling, as I also find myself quite looking forward to the evening Edmund seems so anxious for us to have together. Are you saying you're still unwell?"

Sherry watched as Adam strolled into the room. He seemed very much in control of himself, confident, very unlike the frightened, angry man who had come to her rooms last night, demanding to know about Emma Oxton and dead roses. She couldn't seem to take her eyes off him.

She wet her lips, looking to Geoff for a scant moment, then quickly back to Adam. "No, I'm feeling quite well, actually." She mentally shook herself, unable to believe what she was seeing in his face, although she'd been wishing for it with all her heart, for all of these past long, dark weeks. "But look—Geoff is walking with his canes today, Adam. Isn't that wonderful?"

"He already saw me, early this morning," Geoff said, lifting his wineglass to his brother. "And straightaway offered to buy me a new curricle and pair, if I promise to behave myself in the future. It's probably unnecessary to tell you that I promised to never be such a sad nodcock again, is it?"

When Sherry didn't answer, he looked up at his

sister-in-law, and then at his brother, who were looking at each other. "I say, is anyone listening to me at all? No. I didn't think so. Adam—I say, *Adam.*"

"What is it, Geoff?" Adam asked absently as Sherry felt her eyes welling with tears. Because her husband was looking at her with such love, such wonderful, sweet love that she could almost feel his arms around her. He'd looked at her this way a lifetime ago, and she'd never forgotten it. "Can it wait? Because, if you'll excuse us, my wife and I are going upstairs now."

"Just what I was about to suggest," Geoff grumbled, as Sherry got to her feet, then bent down to kiss his cheek. He gifted her with a wink. "Go on, sweetheart, go with your husband. Seems like today is going to be rather glorious all around, doesn't it?"

Sherry took Adam's hand when he stepped forward to offer it and allowed herself to be guided out of the room, up the stairs to his bedchamber. They didn't speak. They didn't look at each other.

It was like the first time, Sherry decided as Adam closed the doors to the bedchamber behind him. The very first time they'd met. There was a charge in the air, an almost tangible something that shot between them, drew them to each other, made them comfortable with each other and yet nervous and excited and nearly giddy.

"You've forgiven me, haven't you?" Adam asked at last, as Sherry stood in front of the fireplace, looking down at the flames. "For all my stupidity, my bull-headedness, for all of the living hell I've put you through these past months, you've forgiven me. Why?"

He loved her. Man to woman, he loved her. As she loved him. The past disappeared. All the hurt, all the tears. The future wasn't clear, but they would face it together. Because she was a woman now, no longer a silly, romantic child.

She spoke as a woman now, from her heart, as Adam walked closer to her, as he took her hands in his, as he lifted each of her hands to his mouth, kissed them. "Because I love you," she said, a new strength entering her, taking hold. "Because I've always loved you, even when I hated you. Because I finally know what real love is, and real love takes in the bad as well as the good."

She took a deep breath, let it out slowly. "Because I think I've punished myself enough for allowing Dickie to kiss me that one time. Because we've both suffered enough for our stupidity, our sins. Because the sun is shining and Geoff is walking and our baby is growing inside me and I want and need you more than food or air. Is that enough, Adam? We'll never have that perfect dream again, I know. But is what we have now enough? Perhaps even better, more real?"

"More than enough. More than I deserve. Most definitely better," Adam whispered quietly, pulling her completely against him, so that she dissolved into tears as she laid her head against his chest, all the anguish and pain and fear of the past months dissolving as she felt his arms go around her in love. Holding her. Cherishing her.

He kissed her through her tears, pressing butterfly kisses against her hair, her eyes, the tip of her nose, her mouth. Tentative, not teasing, kisses. Getting to know each other better kisses. There was no sudden flame of desire between them, no great passion flaring up to consume them. They simply kissed. They simply held each other.

They simply loved. Made love. Created love. . . .

Wherever God erects a house of prayer,
The Devil always builds a chapel there,
And 'twill be found upon examination,
The latter has the largest congregation.
                                    —Daniel Defoe

Chapter Fifteen

"This is nice," Sherry said sleepily, snuggling closer against her husband in the wide bed as they both slowly woke from their nap.

"Nice? Is that all you can say?" Adam teased, kissing her hair. "I'd thought I'd been much better than *nice*. Did you dream about me?"

"I did," she said, tilting back her head so that she could look up at him. "That's probably why I woke up, don't you think? Being awake and alive is so much better than living in a dream."

"And eminently better than existing in a nightmare," Adam said, "which is what we've been doing, haven't we? Sherry—"

She raised her hand, pressed her fingers against his mouth. "No, not another word. Not another apology, all right? It's over now, Adam. Whatever mistakes we made, they're in the past. Nothing can hurt us more than we've hurt each other. Not as long as we know we really love each other. Each other, Adam, not just the dream of love."

Adam longed to let it go, allow Sherry to convince him that there was nothing to talk about, nothing to worry about—nothing to fear. He longed to believe that now that they'd found each other again, found their love again, nothing could hurt them.

But she was wrong, and she also knew she was wrong. Because it, whatever that *it* might be, was far from over, as much as they both might wish all the ugliness away.

He had to tell her about Edmund, about Dickie, about the game. Not that he'd tell her about Lady Jasper and her horrible little book. And he most certainly wouldn't say anything about Lady J's ridiculous assertion about Edmund being Dickie and the two of them both being the Devil.

"Sherry, darling," he said as she moved her fingers from his lips, drew them down over his chest, drew lazy circles on his bare skin, "we have to talk, all right? Not apologize—talk."

Her hand stilled. Her body, that had been so fluidly draped against his, stiffened perceptively. "Talk?" She sighed, a long, deep, sad sigh. "Yes, I suppose we do. About Dickie. I want to will him away, but I can't." She sat up, dragging the sheet with her, covering her breasts. "You know he's back, don't you?"

Adam saw the fear in her eyes and felt an insane urge to leap out of the bed and go tearing through the bowels of London until he found Richard Brimley, then rip the man's guts out and feed them to the bastard.

But that wouldn't do them any good, and Adam knew it. Tamping down his murderous urge, he left the bed and pushed his arms into a dressing gown, then held Sherry's out to her. "Yes, love. Richard Brimley is back. As a matter of fact, I believe he came to London from Daventry Court, and has been waiting here for us, waiting for us to walk back into his game."

"His game," Sherry repeated, sitting down on the rug in front of the hearth, staring into the flames. "That's all it is for him, isn't it? Destroying people is a game to him. I can still remember the day he asked me if I liked to *play*. How foolish I was, how naive. I said yes. I actually invited him into our lives."

She turned, looked at Adam. "Emma was part of Dickie's game, Adam. And Rimmon. I—I confronted him this morning, and he took to his heels. I'm sorry now that I did that, for you might have been able to batter him into telling us where Dickie is hiding. Chollie says you're quite good with your fists."

Adam sat down beside Sherry, pulled her head against his shoulder.

She sighed, relaxed against him. "Except that now I don't want you to find Dickie, Adam. I just want him to go away, leave us alone. I don't want to see him, don't want to know why he picked us to play his game on, don't want you to beat him into flinders. I just want him gone."

Adam decided to test his wife's knowledge of what

he believed they both knew. "And Edmund, darling? Do you want him gone as well?"

She pulled away from him, looked up into his face in surprise, shock. "You think so, too? I thought I must be imagining things, looking too hard at anything that seemed even the slightest bit suspicious. But you think so, too? You think Edmund and Dickie are playing the game together now?"

"Well," Adam said lightly, hoping his friend would forgive him for putting Lady J's insane words into his mouth, "Chollie has a different theory. He believes Brimley and Burnell to be one and the same person. The Devil, actually. The Devil, come to carry our souls away."

Sherry's hands protectively covered her abdomen. "That's not funny, Adam. I told Edmund that if he told Chollie he's the Devil, Chollie would believe him. But that's not funny. I shouldn't have thought it was funny when he tried to tell *me* he's the Devil."

Adam took hold of Sherry's shoulders, holding her away from him. "What are you talking about, Sherry? Are you telling me that Burnell *told* you he's the Devil? When?"

"When? When we took a drive outside the city, I believe. Why? What does it matter? He was only teasing. He was really quite funny. I mean, think about it, darling. The *Devil?*"

Adam smiled. It wasn't a natural smile, but it was the best he could offer. "You're right, darling. Devilish, perhaps, but not the Devil. However, I'm quite convinced that Burnell and Brimley are both playing the game. Brimley from the shadows this time, Burnell out in the open. Very much in the open, if he's going about telling you he's the Devil. In fact, he seems almost reckless, as if he wants us to believe there's something more than human about him, now that I think of it."

"This game, Adam," Sherry said, frowning. "It's just what you thought it was back at Daventry Court, isn't it? Mean people being mean for the sake of their own meanness. Pulling the wings off butterflies, placing blind mice in a maze—seeing happiness and setting out to destroy it just for the satisfaction meanness finds in making others as unhappy as they are themselves. That's our crime, you know, Adam. I've thought and thought, and that's our crime. We were happy. So very, very happy. How Dickie must have hated seeing us so happy. That's sad. Horribly sad."

"He almost destroyed us, and you're feeling *sorry* for him?" Adam shook his head, not able to believe his own ears. "But I see we're thinking along the same lines. Brimley saw us together, probably in London during the Season, and decided to destroy us, just to prove that he could. He came to Daventry Court to destroy us. He's here, in London again, to finish the job, even enlisting Burnell and more of his friends to make sure he gets the job done right this time. And you feel *sorry* for him?"

But Sherry wasn't listening. She had been, Adam was sure, for a while. Except that something he'd said must have intrigued her mind, taken her off somewhere, to relive a clearly unpleasant memory. "He said," she began slowly, biting her bottom lip. "That last day . . . when I told him he was mad, insane—he said something I've been trying to forget ever since. I thought I had forgotten. But now I remember."

She looked into Adam's eyes, her own eyes flat with fear. "He called me his little doll, Adam. How I hated the way he said that. And then he said . . . and then he said that he knew I thought he was mad, because otherwise it would be *over* now."

She closed her eyes. "But it wasn't over, he said. He said it was just beginning. That he'd raised the stakes, that now he wanted us both." She opened her eyes once more, tipped her head, looked at Adam searchingly. "He'd wanted to seduce me. That's what I finally realized that day in the barn. He wanted to seduce me in order to hurt you. And it was all so strange. Much as I wanted to turn away from him, run away from him, I couldn't move. It was as if I was drawn to him against my will. I—I let him kiss me. I'll never understand that, never forgive myself for that."

Adam pulled her against his chest once more, trying to soothe her. "That part *is* over now, darling. Over, and forgotten."

She pushed away from him, pressing her palms against his chest in order to keep her distance. "But it isn't, Adam. If I had let him seduce me, *then* it would have been over. Or at least that's what Dickie believed when he began his game. But he changed his mind. He wanted—*wants* us both. He said as much. My God, Adam, do you think he wants us dead? Has he gone that mad?"

"No, no," Adam assured her quickly. His head was

pounding, it was so full of contradictory thoughts, impossible explanations. "He's still playing the same game as before, darling. He just decided he was enjoying it, and wanted to drag it out. His friends wanted to play as well. And Edmund is Richard Brimley's friend, Sherry. There's no mistake in that, I'm sure. Which," he ended, sighing, "leaves us with the masquerade tonight."

"We won't go," Sherry said shortly, her chin coming up belligerently. "We will *not* play their game anymore, Adam. And if we won't play, they'll eventually give up and go away. Go pull the wings off some other unsuspecting butterflies."

Adam shook his head. "No, Sherry, you don't mean that. Think about it a moment. The party tonight is a masquerade. A perfect place for Dickie to appear, without really showing himself. If we don't find him now, confront him now, we'll never be free of him. Do you really want to live the rest of our lives looking at each new face we meet with suspicion . . . with dread? I can't live like that, darling. Neither can you. Brimley wants us at the masquerade, but he doesn't know we're onto him at last. That's our trump card, darling. And I fully intend to play it. If you'll help me. Are you up to helping me? Helping us?"

"Play our trump card?" Sherry repeated, shivering. "How? How do we play it? And of course I'll go with you. Did you really think I'd let you confront him alone? What must I do?"

Adam's smile was slow, seductive. She was his Sherry. His dearest, sweetest, bravest Sherry. He loved her beyond reason. But this was something they had to do. Taking into consideration all that he believed, and mixing it generously with all that Lady Jasper believed—they had to continue with the game.

"First, I want you to promise me you won't accept anything Burnell or anyone else might offer you tonight."

"Offer me?"

"Offer you, yes. Most especially if anyone offers you help. Say thank you very much, you'll think about it, but *don't* accept it. All right?"

"I have no idea what you're talking about, Adam. Truly I don't."

"That's all right, darling. Neither do I. Now, secondly," he said as he stroked her pale cheek, "we're going to have to pretend that the two of us are still very *unhappily* in love."

"That might not be impossible, if you keep telling me things like this. Adam, I—"

He cupped her chin in his hand, kissed her. Kissed her long, and deep, and with all the love in his heart. Kissed away her questions, hopefully some of her fears.

Slowly, he pushed her back onto the carpet, divested her of the dressing gown, began to worship her body.

He kissed her breasts, her belly, thrilling to the thought that their child was even now growing inside her.

Her hands soothed him, her love words inflamed him, and soon they were lost in passion, a passion born of love and, quite possibly, of the realization that they were still in danger.

For all they now knew, there was still so much they didn't know. They clung to their love for each other, for it was the only true thing in the world.

Whether it was the lack of other pursuits in this, the Small Season, or whether Lady Winslow was simply an exceptional hostess, the masquerade ball seemed to be proving a marvelous success.

The Winslow ballroom in Portman Square was littered wall to wall with eye-patched Lord Nelsons. It had been gifted with at least a dozen Cleopatras—one of them had brought her own small barge that a servant toted along behind her everywhere she went. There were a sprinkling of Romeos and their giggling Juliets—actresses from Covent Garden, most probably, sneaked into the ball by daring young peers, all well hidden behind their masks.

And, as had been predicted, a person couldn't go more than a few feet without bumping into a portly Henry Tudor carrying a greasy chicken leg along with him.

There was also one lady who had chosen to attend dressed as the widow of Sir Walter Raleigh, which role, to make the thing more authentic, she embellished by also carrying with her a wicker basket that supposedly held her dearly departed's cutoff head. The fact that the real widow had actually done that, for a space of almost fourteen years, did nothing to endear the unknown woman to Sherry once Adam had explained the reason behind the basket.

But, in Adam's opinion, Sherry stood out among all

the feathers and jewels and various ridiculous folderols with the historical purity of her costume. In fact, she looked as if she had just stepped out of one of the ancient tapestries kept at Daventry Court.

She was clad in the simplest of fine, long-sleeved woolen gowns, colored a soft green. A jeweled girdle was slung low around her waist, a similarly jeweled dagger tucked into the girdle. Her feet were covered by deerskin sandals that allowed her to float across the floor rather than walk, or so it seemed, and a simple gold circlet denoting her rank as queen shone dully amid her long, loose, dark red curls.

As Arthur, Adam was dressed a little more formally, but Edmund Burnell had provided him with a quite comfortable long, straight tunic and heavy leather girdle encrusted with faux jewels. He wore soft, deerskin boots and had a dark purple woolen, ermine-tipped mantle draped about his shoulders, clasped at the front by a pin whose center jewel was as large as a finch's egg. His crown, although higher in the points than Sherry's, was also a dull gold, without ornamentation.

And he was, of course, carrying his sword in a sheath hanging from a second leather girdle around his belly.

He was rather surprised that Edmund had allowed him the sword, but it only convinced him that Burnell and Brimley had no idea their plan had been for the most part exposed. They felt no danger from Adam. They were too busy arrogantly continuing their game.

And, to Adam's mind, growing increasingly reckless.

He took another sip of wine. He'd had a glass in his

hand from the moment he'd bowed over Lady Winston's hand in the receiving line and then left Sherry where she stood so that he could make a great business out of calling out for a drink.

Servants had been more than happy to keep him generously supplied from that moment on, especially as he gifted each man with a coin for every new drink—drinks he sipped from a bit, then managed to pour away into potted plants Lady Winston had so conveniently littered throughout the rooms.

He glowered behind his mask, standing on the edge of the floor as Sherry danced each dance, then sat out the first intermission with Julius Caesar—if that wilted green thing around the man's bald head could be considered a Roman crown of laurel.

Chollie joined him just as he'd poured yet another drink into a pot of hothouse orchids. Adam watched as his friend hitched up his own bright green girdle, which showed every sign of slipping off the Irishman's nonexistent hips.

"He's late," Chollie said unnecessarily. "And this beard itches like a sack filled with fleas," he continued, reaching up to scratch under the long, white beard that matched the shoulder-length white wig he also wore. "Wish Geoff had come along. I could have used the seat, and no mistake."

Adam smiled at Chollie's nonsense, then remembered his role. As he'd been more than drunk more than a few times since his return to London, it had seemed the most convincing role to play. He slapped his friend most heartily on the back, nearly staggering him, then laughed loud and long, attracting more than a little attention to himself. As long as he had that attention, he staggered a step or two himself before manfully, drunkenly, pulling himself upright once more.

"Do that again, boyo," Chollie warned, adjusting his wig, "and I'll forget you're supposed to be bosky and wipe your nose for you. Ah—here we go, boyo. I doth think Sir Lancelot doth approach, forsooth, and all of that nonsense. At least we all can recognize each other this way, being knights of the Round Table and all of that rot. I've got your back, all right?"

"I'll mind my own back, Chollie," Adam said, lifting his empty wineglass to his lips. "You watch Sherry, you understand. If Brimley's here, he'll go to her sooner or later. God damn, Chollie, I wish I could think of another way. I also hope, frankly, that he does show up. Then we'll know if there really are two of them."

"We have to know, boyo," Chollie agreed with a shiver. "One way or the other, we have to know. And I pray God there are two of them, and that they're both human enough to bleed when I mill them down. Here, stick these beads in your pocket, if you've got one. Ma had them blessed in Dublin." Then he walked away before Edmund, dressed quite handsomely in white and blue and odd pieces of chain mail, called out a greeting.

"Good evening to you, Sire," Edmund said, bowing from the waist, then grinning at Adam from beneath a simple eye mask. "I'm dreadfully late, I know, but dearest Lady J's costume proved somewhat of a bother. That's her, over there, with the bent halo tipping over her eyes. But it was the wings, you know. Had the very devil of a time getting them to stay on."

Adam looked across the room and saw Lady Jasper battling her way through a crowd of other costumed guests, slapping at Henry Tudors and belled fools as her large, white wings got tangled up with chicken legs and ribboned canes. "You picked that for her, I suppose, Edmund," he drawled, then manfully suppressed a hiccup. "Considering that you picked everyone else's costumes?"

Edmund's white teeth flashed again. "Guilty, Daventry. I always like to give everyone just what they think they want. One way or the other." He turned his gaze to the dance floor. "Now, where is our dearest Sherry? Ah, there she is. I've said it before, and I'll say it again tonight. She's glorious, Daventry. What a lucky dog you are."

Adam tossed his empty wineglass into a potted palm. "Lucky, Burnell? Is that what you call it? Do you see anyone carrying a tray of drinks?"

"Better than that, Sire," Burnell said, taking Adam's unresisting arm. "I've gone so far as to find us a round table, and then supplied it with two full decanters of brandy. Interested? Or do you want to spend the night standing here, watching our fellow creatures make bloody fools of themselves?"

"More than interested, Edmund," Adam said, willingly going along with Burnell. "I'm not much in the mood for frolic tonight, I suppose you could say."

"It's Sherry, isn't it?" Burnell asked as he closed the door behind Adam, sealing the two of them in one of the small antechambers lining the ballroom. "I spoke with her earlier today, and I couldn't help noticing—as I have before—that she's not quite happy. The two of you are at odds somehow, aren't you, for all your show of being the contented couple?"

"That's none of your concern, Burnell," Adam gritted out as he splashed a quantity of brandy into one of the two snifters, then collapsed into a chair. "I won't discuss my wife with you."

"No. No, of course not, dear friend," Burnell agreed quickly, pouring brandy into the second snifter, then sitting down across the table from Adam. "I've overstepped, and I'm sorry. Please, forgive me."

Adam gave a dismissive wave of his hand, dropped his chin onto his chest. "Everything's so much easier at the beginning of the thing, isn't it, Edmund? We see so clearly, or so we think. We know what we want." He gave a short, derisive laugh. "We *think* we know what we want . . ." He allowed his voice to trail off as he lifted the snifter to his mouth. He drank deep, sending up a silent prayer that he'd be able to hold on to his mind as he downed enough brandy to be convincing.

"Oh, dear," Burnell said, pouring more brandy into Adam's snifter. "It's like that, is it? If I remember the words correctly, I believe it was Joseph Addison who said, 'there is nothing we receive with so much reluctance as advice.' He was most probably right, hmmm?" He smiled. "In which case, dear friend—and this is only a suggestion, and not an offer of advice—I propose the two of us sit here quietly, and long enough to get very, very drunk. It's either that or I have to trip back into the ballroom in this ridiculous costume. I have no idea what ever made me think a costume ball would be enjoyable, do you? But first, if you'll excuse me for a few minutes, I believe I'd better check on my aunt's whereabouts. She may look angelic enough tonight, but I assure you, looks are more often than not quite deceiving."

"That's the truth, all right, Burnell. Deceiving." Adam lifted his snifter in salute, silently agreeing to the plan, then watched as Edmund walked out of the room.

"Your turn, Sherry, I suppose," he whispered as his gut clenched. "Chollie, don't take your eyes off her for a moment."

Sherry moved along the dance floor, touching hands with gentleman after gentleman in the line, smiling and dipping and doing her best to pretend to enjoy herself even as she was inspecting each masked face. Was this one Dickie? This one? This one?

Lady Winston had to be either delighted or appalled by the success of her masquerade ball, which was quite a bit more *lively* than any social engagement Sherry had attended during the Spring Season. Even young Baron Gilesen, with his arm in a sling after a fall from his curricle, seemed to be enjoying himself.

There was more laughter, for one thing. Definitely the wine was flowing more freely than usual. And, safe behind their masks, the gentlemen were being freer with their speech—and their hands—than most of them would have dared if the ladies could see their faces.

Not that every woman in attendance could be called

a lady. Adam had warned Sherry that masquerades were a perfect excuse for men to foist ballet dancers and mistresses on an unsuspecting society, and he hadn't been wrong. She'd laughed out loud as she'd passed by one young, masked lady dressed quite elegantly as Marie Antoinette as she leaned over an eyepatched Nelson and trilled, "Cor, ducks, but this is the life, ain't it?"

Yes, this was the perfect place for Dickie to show himself—without showing himself. And once he had, and once he'd been goaded into telling her why he was here and just what he planned to do, well, then they'd have him. All she had to do was to ask a few questions, listen to the answers, then beg to meet with him tomorrow. After that, Sherry really didn't much care *what* Adam had planned for the man.

Just so it would be over. Finally, finally over.

She'd come to the end of the line of dancers, to very nearly the end of the dance floor itself, when a tall, slim man dressed very much like Adam, but all in black, took her offered hand and then quickly escorted her off the floor and through the doors leading to a slice of balcony.

She had disappeared so quickly, so silently, that she was nearly numb with the shock of it, sure that Chollie hadn't seen her go.

"Guinevere, it is I, Mordred. You know the legend, my dear? He, rather more than Lancelot, was the death of Arthur," her companion drawled from behind his eye mask, to which a length of black silk was fastened, so that it hung down over his nose and mouth. But she could see his eyes in the light of the full moon that hung over London on this strangely clear night.

Oh, yes. She could see his eyes. She knew his eyes. She'd never forget them.

"Dickie," she breathed quietly, swallowing down her sudden panic now that the expected had so unexpectedly happened. She tried to tug her hand free of his, but it was useless to fight his greater strength, so she gave up. She didn't want to do anything that might make him happy, make him feel that he held more power over her than he already did. "And here I thought—" she said, rallying, "I thought you'd still be hiding beneath whatever rock you slunk away to after leaving Frame Cottage."

"Now, Sherry, don't try to be arch. It doesn't suit you. It does, however, suit me. Straight down to the ground. That said—have you missed me?"

"As much as I'd miss a splinter under my fingernail. Now let me go, Dickie. You don't frighten me."

"Tsk, tsk," he said, shaking his head, even as he removed his mask, smiling at her with his perfect white teeth, with his clear, intense blue eyes. "You never could tell a decent lie, could you, Sherry? The so innocent, so beautiful, so incorruptible Charlotte Victor. How did you explain away our kiss, Sherry, considering that you'd wanted to kiss me? Surely our dearest Daventry didn't believe your little fib when you said I had taken advantage of you? No, of course he didn't. I counted very heavily on that, you know. How could Daventry believe you, when you'd never lied to him before, when you lie so very *badly?*"

"You *had* taken advantage of me," Sherry protested, even as he released her hand, backing up until she felt her thighs pressing against the stone balustrade that ringed the balcony. "I don't know how you did it, but you did. I also don't know *why*. I don't know why you and Edmund are doing any of this."

She shut her eyes for a moment, wishing the words back. Was she supposed to keep Edmund's name out of the conversation? Yes, she probably should have. But she was so upset! Thinking about seeing Dickie again was one thing. Having him standing here, right in front of her, was very much another.

He raked his fingers through his thick, midnight-dark hair. "Ah, yes. Edmund. You liked him, didn't you? I chose him especially, you know. Blond to my dark and all of that. He walked straight into your lives, took over where I had left off, as it were. But don't look so pleased to have found me out. You only know about Edmund because I wanted you to. Otherwise you wouldn't."

"You must have been overjoyed when he reported to you that Adam and I are—well, that our marriage isn't going well. That is what you wanted, isn't it? To destroy us, to destroy our marriage? It—it's the only thing I can think of, even as I still struggle to understand why you should be so mean."

How she longed to throw the truth in his face, tell him that, for all his planning and scheming, she and Adam still loved each other, probably loved each other more than before Richard Brimley had entered their lives. That their love was more real now that it had been tested, stronger. She wanted to see Dickie unhappy, let him know how it felt to lose.

But Adam had made her promise not to say anything.

She took a single step forward. "What did I ever do to you to harm you, Dickie? What did Adam do? Why would you go to so much trouble, trying to destroy us?"

He smiled, this devil with an angel's face. "Did it work? Edmund thinks it did. I think it did. Thank you, Sherry. I do so love when I'm proved right, not that I'm often wrong."

Sherry shook her head, trying to understand. "Proved right? What are you saying? Are you saying you only did this to *prove* something? What was it, Dickie, some sort of *bet* you made, betting you could destroy someone else's happiness? Did you and Edmund stand at the edge of a dance floor one night, playing your *game,* watching, selecting people whose happiness you deemed yourselves fit to destroy? Have you destroyed my life, Adam's life, over some horrible wager made between you and Edmund Burnell? Did it sicken you so much, to see how happy we were?"

Her hand went to the silly, ornamental dagger at her waist. She could kill. She would have denied it, would never have believed it before this moment—but she could kill. Kill Dickie. Kill the man who had nearly destroyed her life.

"Oh, wonderful!" he exclaimed as her fingers closed around the hilt of the dagger. "This only gets better and better, doesn't it? Anger, thoughts of doing murder— you've become a lovely vessel full of vices, haven't you, Sherry? All it needed was the opportunity."

Her hand dropped from the hilt as she turned away from Richard, unable to look into his happily smiling face for another moment. "What do you want?" she asked quietly, for the third time, the hundredth time, possibly the thousandth time.

She felt his hands on her shoulders, did her best not to flinch as he turned her around so that she was once more forced to look at him.

"Not what I want, Sherry," he all but purred. "It's what do *you* want? Just tell me what you want. I'm offering my help, Sherry. *Ask* me."

I want you to promise me you won't accept anything Burnell or anyone else might offer you tonight.

Why had Adam said that? How had he known Dickie would offer her his help?

Most especially if anyone offers you help. Say thank you very much, you'll think about it, but don't accept it.

Sherry smiled. It took everything she had, every ounce of will, of courage, but she smiled. "You'd help me? After breaking my life into little pieces, you'd help me pick up those pieces? Is that another part of the game, Dickie?"

"It could be," he answered, stepping closer, running the back of his hand lightly down her cheek. "Fascinating. I can't quite understand my reaction to you, little Charlotte Victor. But it was there, almost from the beginning." He leaned forward, gently kissed her mouth. "Tell me what you want, Sherry. I can give you anything. Anything and everything you want."

She felt it again. This strange attraction to Richard

Brimley. This unexplainable, unreasonable, certainly unwarranted attraction to the man.

"Tomorrow," she said, then cleared her throat, which had nearly closed shut on her. "I'll meet you tomorrow, all right?"

He kissed her again, spoke with his lips still against hers. She could smell him. She could taste him. He tasted of temptation. "I'll come to you. At two. We'll be together then, little doll."

"Get your bloody hands off her, you black-hearted devil!"

"Chollie," Sherry whispered, startled back to who she was, where she was. Why she was here. Dickie stepped away from her and she could see the gray-bearded Merlin charging toward them with all the force and rage of Buckfastleigh's Prize on the loose. "Chollie, no!"

"And so, good night. Ah, no, I believe that's Shakespeare," Brimley said almost jovially, putting one hand on the balustrade and then neatly vaulting over it, disappearing into the gardens below.

"Damn!" Chollie spat, pounding his fist on the balustrade. "Damn, damn, and blast!" He turned to look at Sherry. "Are you all right, sweetheart? Good. Go inside and stay there until Adam comes for you. Tell him I've gone hunting, all right?"

And then, even as Sherry opened her mouth to protest, he swung his legs over the balustrade and disappeared into the gardens. She heard the sound of running feet, soon fading away into the evening, and waited for a good five minutes, hoping to see Chollie coming back, before giving up and doing as he said and returning to the ballroom.

She'd not taken more than three steps when her elbow was grabbed and she was propelled, backwards, onto the balcony once more.

"Lady Jasper?" she asked, believing she recognized the woman's features beneath a small eye mask.

"Yes, yes, aren't you the smart one, though. Lady Jasper," the mishmash of white linen and chicken feathers grumbled, pushing at the bent halo that tipped drunkenly toward her left ear. "So? What happened?"

"I beg your pardon?" Sherry's head was spinning. She needed to sit down, preferably alone, and collect herself. She did not need Lady Gytha Jasper. She had to remember to pretend that Edmund Burnell was their friend, and not Dickie's accomplice. She had to remember, and yet she was so terribly confused. And tired. So afraid she might say the wrong thing if she said another single word.

"He asked you, didn't he?" Lady Jasper went on, almost as if Sherry hadn't spoken. "Hah! I can see it in your face. He did ask you. Just like I told that doubting husband of yours. Well? What did you say? Did you trade your soul away? If you did, I'm damned, you know. He thinks this sort of thing is funny," she said, indicating her costume with a disgusted wave of her hand. "I can't spend eternity with a fellow who thinks this sort of thing is *funny*." She gave her slipping halo another shove. "Which means, if you bungled this, dearie, I wouldn't cavil at tossing you headfirst off this balcony."

"You'll have to excuse me, as I don't have the faintest idea what you're talking about." Sherry's head began to spin, and her stomach didn't feel all that well, either, now that she thought about the thing. She had to think of her unborn child, she had to go somewhere and lie down. She certainly didn't need to be standing on this balcony, listening to a dotty old woman dressed up to look like an angel—or a chicken. "I—I need to sit down," she said, starting for the doorway to the ballroom once more.

For an old woman, Lady Jasper had quite a strong grip. She used it now, holding Sherry in place even as every last shred of Sherry's strength faded away, so that she collapsed against the edge of the balustrade. "Oh, all right. Ask your questions, Lady Jasper. I'll try to answer them."

The old woman gave a cackling laugh of triumph— perhaps she was a chicken, perhaps she would lay an egg, perhaps Sherry would faint, her head was spinning so, her stomach so queasy, near to turning.

"Let's start with what *you* know, dearie, and go on from there, all right?" Lady Jasper suggested. "Now, Daventry did tell you that Edmund's the Devil, didn't he? You do at least know that much?"

Sherry pushed herself away from the railing and sighed, feeling rather sorry for the old woman. "Lady Jasper, we've been through all of this. Your nephew is not the Devil. He probably only tells you that because it amuses him to upset you. He's a mean, mean man, to tease you so, but he is *not* the Devil. All right? May I please go now?"

"He's *not* the—" Lady Jasper sat down, right there on the balcony, her legs splayed out in front of her, her left wing snapping off against the balustrade. "Damn you, Daventry. You even took the book. You believed me. Damn you for not believing me. Now we're all lost. All of us . . ."

Sherry turned on her heels and all but ran back into the ballroom, catching the attention of one of the footmen and directing him to assist Lady Jasper from the balcony.

Then she stumbled into the ladies' retiring room and lay down on one of the couches, sure her queasy stomach would revolt if she moved another inch for the next hour, if she so much as raised her head from the pillow a maid placed there for her. Her only solace was that she had done what she'd been instructed to do if the opportunity arose. She'd gotten Dickie to come to Grosvenor Square tomorrow. Adam would be so proud of her.

Adam put the stopper back into the decanter after pouring almost half its contents into the base of yet another potted palm. He sat down once more, pulled a small gold timepiece from the small pocket cut into his costume, and checked the time.

Ten minutes. Edmund had been gone for ten minutes.

He quickly replaced the timepiece as the door opened and Burnell walked in. Smiling. Shaking his head. "Poor Lady J," he said, retaking his seat. "Woman's begun to molt. It's not a pretty sight, I can tell you." He lifted the decanter, measuring the level of brandy with his eyes. "Ah, I see you've been busy in my absence, Daventry. That's not entirely fair, you know. Now I'll have to drink twice as fast, just to catch up."

He poured himself a generous drink, then drank it down in one smooth movement, and with no more care than if it had been well water. "That's better. Now, where were we? Oh, yes. You were being silent, and I was being philosophical. At least I think I was. Maybe we should just keep drinking until someone comes by and scrapes us up off the floor. What do you think?"

Adam, slouching in his seat, looked across at Burnell, his eyelids at half-mast. "I know why I'm drinking, Burnell. But what's bothering you?"

"What's bothering me? I don't know, Daventry. Life? Yes, that's it. Life is bothering me. The whole thing seems such a waste of creation."

Adam took another sip of brandy. "A waste, Edmund? How so?"

Burnell shrugged. "You're born, you live, you die. In between, you do everything you can to prove you shouldn't have been born at all but, as you were, you might as well muck up anything and everything you touch along the way, just to prove you were here. That's how wars start, Daventry, did you know that? So that a man can prove he was here. Take Bonaparte, for one. Nobody will ever forget him, right?"

"They'll remember he lost," Adam agreed.

"They'll remember he was here. That's all that counts, in the end. Men are all alike, even those we want to consider to be the great ones. Perhaps, now that

I think on it, they're the worst of all. They're the ones who believe they're here for some purpose, some *higher* purpose, instead of why they're *really* here, which is no more than a failed experiment at best. Those are the ones who take everything to extremes and end by destroying all that they meant to be so wonderful, so glorious. Dangerous men, Daventry. Stay away from them. They can be amusing, but in the end, they just make you sick. All men make me sick. They're slothful, stupid, vain, proud, greedy. Destructive. All of them."

"And what are you?" Adam asked, grinning.

"Me?" Burnell grinned back at him. "I'm *drunk*, Daventry. Couldn't you tell?"

Adam pushed himself into a more upright position, reaching for his snifter. "I don't understand a *word* of what you're saying," he said, careful to slur his words. "But I'll drink to you nonetheless." Lowering his eyes, so that Burnell couldn't see any expression in them, Adam said, "But what about the ladies? What do they do?"

"They're slightly better, in some cases, and worse in others," Burnell replied, pouring more brandy for the both of them. "Just as vain, just as venal, just as greedy. But at least they're prettier, eh, Daventry?"

"Sherry's more than pretty," Adam said, slumping forward, to lay his head on his folded arms as he all but collapsed on the table. His crown toppled free, clanked on the tabletop. "She's sweet, and loving, and pure." He looked at Burnell. "And she detests me. I'd do anything, anything at all, to get her to love me again."

He flung himself backwards in his chair, glaring at Burnell. "I'd sell my soul to the Devil to have her back again."

"There is always that, isn't there?" Burnell said, a small smile playing around the corners of his mouth. "But how would one go about doing such a thing?"

Adam sat forward, jammed the crown back on his head, then grabbed at his snifter once more. He suddenly knew why Burnell had sent along these particular costumes, why he had chosen them. They had been meant as a reminder. "Good question, Burnell. Damn good question."

"It was?" Burnell pulled a comically confused face, frowned. "Good. Very nice. What did I ask?"

Adam spread his arms wide, waved them drunkenly. "There it was, Edmund, my friend. *Camelot*. A small Eden. Everything there, everything perfect. Everything happy. But how do you hold on to the perfect, Burnell? I couldn't do it. Arthur couldn't do it, and he was a king. How *does* anyone do that? Is it—is it because of what you said? That we always muck it up, no matter how we try?"

"I have no idea. Are you hungry?"

"Hungry? Me?" Adam shook his head, staring at the contents of his snifter. "I don't know. Maybe a plum?"

"Done and done, Daventry," Burnell said, and Adam looked up to see a bowl of luscious, ripe plums sitting in the middle of the table.

"How—how'd you do that?" he asked, reaching for one of the plums. "I don't understand. How'd you do that?"

Edmund leaned his elbows on the table, leaned toward Adam. "What would you say if I told you that *I'm* the Devil, Daventry? What would you say if I told you I could help you, miserable, ruined sot that you are? Get your bloody Camelot back for you? What would you say to that?"

Adam sat very still, staring at Edmund Burnell. None of this had been what he'd expected, but it had been what he'd feared. Deep inside himself, it had been what he'd feared. Now he had to get the hell—yes, the *hell*— out of this room. "I'd say . . . I'd say," he dropped the half-eaten fruit to the floor, very obviously belched. "I'd say plums and brandy don't mix well."

"Why I waste my time . . ." Burnell grumbled half under his breath, shaking his head. "Very well, Daventry. We'll continue this tomorrow, all right?"

"Continue what?" Adam asked, frowning. "Can you do anything else? My father, I remember now, used to pull gold crowns out from behind m'ears. Never figured out how he did it. Magic, I mean. Damn, Edmund, but I feel sick. Think I'll go home now. So sorry."

"And tomorrow? I could stop by, oh, around two? I think we have a lot to talk about, Daventry."

Adam blinked several times, burped again, then nodded. And then he stood, clapped both hands over his mouth, and staggered from the room, knowing he had to find Sherry at once, get her out of the ballroom, take her home, tell her the unbelievable.

Edmund Burnell's laughter followed him. The Devil's laughter followed him.

Here in this world he changed his life.
        —Sir Thomas Malory,
                Morte d'Arthur

Chapter Sixteen

"He's the Devil, Chollie," Adam gritted out quietly, pulling his friend into a small window embrasure as Sherry stood with Lady Winslow, saying her good-nights.

"Which one are you talking about, boyo?" Chollie asked in a whisper. "Burnell, or that Brimley fellow? He disappeared on me, you know. I followed him through the gardens after he left Sherry, and he disappeared on me."

He pulled out a handkerchief and lifted the bottom of his beard, dabbing at his wet mouth. "And I don't mean he outran me, neither, boyo. He was just there, and then he was just gone. Poof! Right in front of my eyes, and making sure I was watching him while he did it. Lady Jasper's right. He's the Old Boy, Old Nick. The Devil, boyo—" he whispered hoarsely, leaning closer. "The *Devil*."

"I know," Adam said under his breath, looking toward Sherry, more frightened for her than he could ever put into words.

"Now, I know you don't believe me, boyo," Chollie went on hurriedly. "I know you think he just got away from me, as if any *mortal* being could when I'm hotfoot on the trail, and it's sure I am that I wouldn't be so fast to swallow any of this if it were *me* the Old Boy was after, and not you, but—what did you say?"

"I said, Chollie, I know. Brimley's the Devil. Burnell's the Devil, too, for that matter. Or one of his infernal helpers, or whatever it says in that book. Not a club of devil worshipers, not just a twisted game played by bored men. The Devil is in this one, Chollie. The Devil is here."

"How? How did you come to believe Burnell's the devil? I mean Brimley. Damn it all, who do I mean, boyo?"

Adam couldn't resist a ghost of a smile. It was all so bizarre, so totally unbelievable. Especially, as Chollie had pointed out, when the person the Devil was after happened to be *you*. He'd rather any of a dozen other explanations, but this one, sadly, was the only one that fit. "I mean Burnell, Chollie. He produced a bowl of plums for me. Not one plum. A bowl of them. Then he sort of sat back and waited for me to ask him for something else."

"A bowl of plums?"

"A bowl of plums," Adam repeated. "A very large, golden bowl, Chollie, with at least eight or nine fat plums in it."

"Could be magic. A trick?"

"Can *you* produce a bowl of plums out of thin air at the drop of a suggestion, without knowing beforehand that plums would be what I'd want? Can you do that trick?"

Chollie hung his head. "No, that I can't, boyo, that I can't." He gestured toward Sherry through the crush of guests crowding the anteroom as the masquerade slowly dissolved into sad-looking, drooped feathers and sawdust-padded legs in ripping hose. She was just then being helped on with her cloak. "We have to tell her, boyo. You know that, don't you?"

Adam shook his head. "We have to tell her, do we? And how do you propose we go about doing that, Chollie? Tell her Brimley went *poof?* Tell her Burnell made a bowl of plums appear? Oh, yes, I can see how that's going to work, how readily she'll believe us." He squeezed one hand around the hilt of his sword. "Besides, I don't intend for Sherry to be a part of this anymore. I put her in danger tonight, more than I could have believed possible. She's out of this, Chollie, you understand, as of this moment. You are, too, if you want to be. I wouldn't blame you."

"Me? I could be knocking you down for that insult, you know." He pushed his spectacles back up the length of his nose. "Now come on, let's get ourselves back to Grosvenor Square and talk about this some more. Burnell must have done more than make a few plums appear. I want to know what he said. Everything he said."

Adam put a hand on Chollie's shoulder. "Thank you,

Merlin," he said lightly, to hide the fact that he was very close to being unmanned, thanks to his friend's loyalty in the face of such idiocy, such unimaginable terror. "The real Arthur, if there ever was one, never had a more loyal friend."

Chollie gave him a quick slap on the back as they went to join Sherry, Adam remembering to stagger a bit as he reminded himself he was supposed to look three-parts castaway. "Well, now, boyo, about this Arthur of yours. As I told you before, we tell it all a little differently in Ireland . . ."

Sherry was quiet all the way back to Grosvenor Square, pretending to doze off, but watching from her corner of the coach as Adam and Chollie exchanged whispers and more than a few meaningful glances. They'd already spoken at some length while Sherry had sat on a velvet bench in the reception area, waiting for their cloaks and while she said good night to their hostess, and their expressions had been hard, their hand gestures quick and sharp, like generals plotting a course of battle.

She let them have at it, both at Lady Winslow's and in the coach, too tired, too frightened, to participate.

But once they'd arrived, and Adam tried to convince her to go off upstairs with Mrs. Clement, she brushed past him and into the drawing room, plunking herself down with every intention of staying.

"Darling, please," Adam said, walking over to her. He held out his hand to help her rise, and she immediately tucked both hands under her arms, shaking her head. He unclasped the cloak at his neck and threw the thing onto a nearby chair, following it with the smaller girdle and sword. "God, I couldn't wait to be shed of that nonsense. Sherry. Enough. You've done what you could do, but now we have to think about the baby."

"I *am* thinking about our baby, Adam," she protested, looking up at him imploringly. "He'll need a father, and I believe that right now that father needs all the help he can get. Which is why I'm staying right here. Now, what are we going to do?"

"She's got you there, boyo." Chollie pulled off his wig and beard, sputtering a time or two because a few hairs had gotten caught in his mouth. "We at least need her to tell us a little of what happened, Adam, out there on the balcony." He looked meaningfully at Sherry, peering at her over the top of his glasses. "Only what Brimley said, you know, before he disappeared."

"Absolutely, Chollie!" Sherry agreed quickly, and not failing to understand the hidden message in his words. She turned back to Adam. "He asked me, Adam. He asked me if there was anything he could do to *help* me. Just as you said he might. Actually, you said Edmund might, but Dickie did. I fobbed him off with a promise to meet with him, here, tomorrow at two."

"Well, that should prove interesting. Edmund is meeting me here at the same time." Adam held out his hand once more. "Now, that's definitely enough for tonight. Go to bed, darling. Chollie and I want to talk about a few more things before we call it an evening. Right, Chollie?"

Sherry looked to Chollie. "Could you please leave us for a few minutes, Chollie?" she asked, smiling imploringly. "I . . . that is, there's something I have to speak to Adam about—privately."

"Are you sure you need to be doing that, darlin'?" Chollie turned to Adam, who nodded his agreement. "Very well, then. I'll just go on off down to your study, friend, and find my way to some wine."

"I'll join you there," Adam said, then sat down beside Sherry as Chollie walked out of the room, looking back over his shoulder a time or two, clearly reluctant to go. "Now, darling, what is it? Chollie said you were fine when he saw you, and that you told him later you'd had more trouble shedding yourself of Lady Jasper than you did with Brimley, who only had you to himself for less than five minutes."

Sherry nodded her head, bit her bottom lip. "Chollie—Chollie's protecting me, Adam," she said, looking at him, silently praying he'd understand what she had to tell him. "He kissed me, and Chollie saw him do it," she whispered. "Dickie kissed me. And I very nearly kissed him back. I probably did kiss him back. Just for a moment."

When Adam didn't speak, she rushed on, her words nearly tumbling over themselves. "He's mean, and he's evil, and he's everything I despise, and yet—and yet he *attracts* me in some way. I don't understand it, Adam. I *hate* him. As much as I love you, Adam—*that's* how much I hate him." She pulled the ornamental dagger from its sheath and brandished it in front of her husband. "I wanted to kill him. With this. Dickie laughed, as if he found that to be highly amusing . . . and then he kissed me."

She opened her hand and let Adam take the dagger from her, then slumped back against the cushions. "Then Chollie came, and saved me, and then Lady Jasper—"

Adam took her hand, lifted it to his cheek. "Yes, Lady Jasper. She had at you as well? Ah, darling. You have had a terrible night of it, haven't you?"

"You're not angry with me? Disgusted with me?"

"About Richard Brimley?" Adam shook his head. "No, darling. And I'll tell you why, someday. Just know that it wasn't your fault. Not at Daventry Court, and not tonight. I should never have included you in this scheme, but at the same time I felt sure you'd be the one who could draw Brimley out, into the open. I couldn't believe he was here all along, even if I do now. Now, tell me about Lady Jasper."

Sherry didn't understand much of what Adam said, only that he forgave her. That was enough, and her nerves, never so jangled as at the moment she realized that she'd allowed Dickie to kiss her again, finally relaxed. She could think clearly again.

"The woman's insane, Adam," she told him, smiling a little as he turned her hand over, placed a kiss in her palm. "She came at me just as Chollie was chasing after Dickie, demanding to speak with me, talking wild, saying impossible things. Edmund's the Devil, you know, to hear Lady Jasper tell it."

"He *is* the Devil."

Both Adam and Sherry looked to the doorway to

find that Chollie had returned upstairs, probably to check on Sherry, make sure she was all right after confessing to Adam about the kiss he'd seen on the balcony. "Chollie . . ." Adam began in warning, but the Irishman cut him off.

"No, boyo, don't you be stopping up my mouth for me. I got all the way downstairs, even poured myself a drink, before I got to thinking. And I figured out that Sherry has to know it all. You want to protect her, and I can understand that. But they're coming here tomorrow—he's coming here. Blast it, *one* of them is coming here—and we all, the three of us, have to put our heads together so we know what we're going to do about it."

Sherry shivered. "Adam? What's Chollie talking about?"

"Tell her, boyo," Chollie prodded. "Tell her now. About Lady Jasper, about the book. The poof, the plums—all of it. There's nothing else for it now."

Adam, sighing, took both her hands in his, squeezed her fingers. "All right," he said wearily. "First we get shed of these ridiculous clothes. Chollie, surely I have something that will suit you better than that ridiculousness you're wearing. Then we'll talk."

"Well, it's liking that I am," Chollie grumbled, already heading for the hallway and the stairs that led up to the bedchambers. "And he looks better than me, I suppose? That's what comes of putting a crown on a man's head, I say. Put on airs right along with the thing, and no mistake."

"And you'll tell me everything?" Sherry asked, as

Adam helped her to her feet, hating herself for doubting him, but he certainly hadn't been forthcoming up to this point. She leaned against him for support, as her knees seemed to have turned to jelly. *The Devil?* No. She couldn't have heard Chollie correctly. Things like the Devil appearing in someone's life—well, they just didn't happen, that's all.

"Yes, darling, I'll tell you everything. I promise."

". . . put my hands to my mouth and got myself out of there, pretending I was going to be ill at any moment. It wasn't very inventive of me, I suppose, or particularly brave, but it was the first thing I could think of. Besides, I believe I was rather sick. Looking across the table and suddenly realizing that you're looking directly into the eyes of the Devil can do that to a man, I've learned."

Chollie nodded rather energetically. "It was my knees, boyo, that all but gave me up for dead when Brimley grinned at me, waved, then disappeared. Poof! So, you're saying they're both the same man? The same devil, that is?"

"I think so," Adam said, as Sherry slipped her hand into his, sighed. "I know it sounds as fantastical as anything else we've been saying, but I believe that, when he left me to supposedly check on Lady Jasper, he took on the—the *person* of Richard Brimley and cornered Sherry on the balcony. Another few minutes, another poof or whatever, and he was Burnell again, and back with me."

He sat back, smiled. "You know, it's a good thing

it's the middle of the night. With Geoff and the rest of the household safely asleep, no one can hear us. Otherwise, we'd all be on our way to Bedlam by now, and be fitted up for our very own straight-waistcoats. Because we all sound insane."

"I still can't believe it," Sherry said softly, then looked at Adam. "Oh, I *do* believe it. I just can't believe it. Do you understand what I'm trying to say?"

Adam squeezed her fingers. "I understand exactly what you're saying, sweetheart. And I've been thinking back over the past few months, remembering more than one time when I thought about selling my soul to the Devil in order to have your love again. It's a good thing Burnell wasn't there to hear me, wasn't it? Because, not knowing he was the Devil, I probably would have grabbed at his offer with both hands." He frowned. "Or maybe I *did* summon him, or at least help to keep him close. I hadn't thought of that."

"We've all done it, boyo," Chollie said from his seat across the low table from Adam and Sherry. "We all, at one time or another, have wanted to sell our soul to go back, to change things, to put them right. But when itch comes to scratch, I don't think any of us would do it."

"Lady Jasper did," Sherry pointed out. "Or at least she says she did."

"I wonder about that, don't you, Chollie?" Adam pulled the book from his pocket, laid it on the table in front of him. "According to this, Lady Jasper had about as much chance of success in summoning the Devil as she did in marrying one of the royal dukes.

But she could have. If this book is right, and she was unlucky enough, she could have."

Chollie blessed himself, then made the sign against the evil eye, just for good measure. "You've been reading that thing, boyo? I wouldn't touch it. It's sitting at the bottom of a mile-deep bucket of holy water that I want to see that book, and no mistake."

Sherry reached for the book, then subsided into the cushions once more, without touching it. "That's it? It doesn't look all that dangerous. Just old, and small. But you found the names in there. Emma, and Rimmon?"

"Even Midgard, Lady Jasper's butler," Adam added. "Not that we'll see any of them again. Not now, now that Edmund has taken center stage, let us know who he is."

"And Dickie? He won't appear as Dickie again?"

"No, darling," Adam said, trying to reassure her, because he could hear the fear in her voice. "I don't think he will. Don't be afraid."

"I'm not afraid. I'm *angry*," Sherry told him and, if she'd never told the truth in her life, he would have known she was telling it now. His wife, his dearest, most wonderful Sherry, was about as angry as a person could be without actually exploding. "How *dare* he try to hurt us?"

"You're wonderful," Adam said, leaning over to kiss her. "Isn't she wonderful, Chollie?"

"Magnificent," Chollie agreed, still eyeing the book as if it might turn into a wild animal at any moment, a wild animal that would then leap straight at his throat.

"Um, could you put that thing somewhere, boyo? And tell me more about this taking of souls thing. You're saying Lady Jasper was wrong?"

"Not exactly, Chollie. According to the book, the devil doesn't so much *take* our souls as *we offer* them to him. She might have summoned him, but it was still *she* who had to do the offering."

"Not *we*, Adam," Sherry interrupted. "At least, not at first. He was after me. Dickie as good as told me so."

Adam set his mouth in a thin line. "How?"

"Dickie called me Charlotte Victor. Charlotte *Victor*, Adam," she said, spreading her hands as if that explained everything. When Adam shook his head, not quite seeing her point, she went on: "I believe that's how he thinks of me, and he couldn't think of me that way if he only met me after you and I were married. Because that's what you think, isn't it? That he saw us in London, then followed us to Daventry Court? I think you're wrong. I think he knew me before you did. He may even have arranged our meeting."

When Chollie murmured a quick, "Jesus, Mary, and Joseph," she turned to him, tipping her head as she looked at him sadly. "I'm sorry, my dear. It is frightening, isn't it, to believe that the Devil could plan something for so long?"

Adam was silent for a few minutes, as Sherry sipped tea, as Chollie got up and paced the area in front of the fireplace. "The chance meeting," he said at last, talking to himself, mostly. "The perfect roses." He looked at Sherry. "The snake in our paradise. Good God, Sherry, it fits. It all fits. Every last bit of it. Even Dickie's ridiculous story about his unfaithful lover."

Chollie held up his hands. "All right, stop right there. You've lost me, boyo."

But he hadn't lost Sherry, bless her. "Of course! He wasn't talking about a woman, was he, Adam? He was talking about his fall from Heaven, after he felt God had betrayed him! Betrayed him by creating us. Creating inferiors, loving those inferiors."

"So many things that Brimley said, that Burnell has said." Adam looked at the table, at the pieces of the sphere Geoff had left lying there. "Yes. It all fits. If you know where to put the pieces." He picked up the half-completed sphere and fitted another piece into it, smiling at Chollie, at Sherry. "And that's how we'll beat him."

"Now I'm more than lost," Chollie said, taking off his spectacles, dropping into a chair.

Adam couldn't sit still, so he got up, began to pace. "It's simple. So simple, it's complex. Hell isn't a threat or a punishment. Hell is a *choice*. Burnell can't steal or buy our souls, or even trade them for something—the way Lady Jasper feels she's traded hers. Lady Jasper—anyone—has to *want* to go to the Devil, has to *want* to let the evil out, if we want to be melodramatic, and Lord knows this calls for a bit of melodrama if we're ever going to believe any of it. Let the evil out, let the Devil in." He stopped pacing, looked at his wife, his friend. "Yes?"

"I'm not with you yet, boyo, but keep talking. I'll catch up."

"He's proud, arrogant. Pride has always been his weakness, coupled with that arrogance. That's why he's gotten so reckless. He can't fail. He doesn't believe he can fail. Because, to him, he's right. I watched him tonight, as I would any adversary, and I watched him grow reckless with his belief that he's winning, that we'll soon be begging him—begging him—to help us. But if we stay strong? If we don't give in to our own need to seek out the evil inside ourselves?"

"What evil? I'm more than lost now, boyo. Remember, you've been reading that book, not us. Sherry? What about you? Are you as lost as I am?"

Sherry looked up at Adam. "I'm sorry, darling. If you could explain? How would we choose evil? Selling my soul, which you say I can't do, in order to get your love again—that I can understand. But evil?"

"I wanted him dead, Sherry," Adam said, kneeling in front of her. "I wanted Richard Brimley dead, out of our lives. So, as you've told me, did you. *That's* the temptation we've been offered. Think about it. If someone were to have asked me, when everything between us was so terrible, what I would have wanted? I would have said I wanted to go back, start over, without Richard Brimley ever having come into our lives."

He felt Chollie tap him on the shoulder, and stood up once more. "So what you're saying, boyo, is that the Devil sent himself to ruin your lives so that you'd wish him dead and out of your lives—which would mean you let the evil out and would then be damned?"

Adam thought over what Chollie had said, then slowly nodded. "Yes. That's about it. He gave us each other, perhaps. He most definitely presented us with a sort of Eden, a sort of paradise. And then he tossed in the snake—Richard Brimley. To tempt us, and mostly, I believe, to once again prove himself correct. That mortals are inferior, not worth being created in the first place, not worthy of having *been* created in the first place."

He turned back to Sherry. "The *game*, remember? We've been partially correct, darling. This has all been a game, with us as the pawns. We're not the players, and never have been. Burnell has been the only player, right from the beginning. If we reject him, he loses, although in some twisted way, he also wins."

"He still wins? Well, it's not liking that, I am, don't you know," Chollie said, sitting down beside Sherry.

Adam smiled. He was beginning to feel much better. "Think about it another moment, Chollie. If he tosses temptation in our way and we choose to catch it, he wins. The soul that comes to him proves that we mortals aren't worthy of having been created at all. If we refuse him, reject him, he also wins. After all, Chollie, according to the book, his entire hope of Heaven depends upon people like you and Sherry and me rejecting him. If enough of us do, he might even regain his place in Heaven—although I believe there's little chance of that happening. Still, at the end of it, he'd like to think he's the master. But he's not. For all his pride, his arrogance, he's the *slave*. The slave of men, forever chained to *their* desires. You really ought to read the book, Chollie. It's quite interesting."

"My sainted mother had another saying, boyo.

When you sup with the Devil, have a long spoon. So I'll be standing a bit away from that book, if you don't mind. You can read, and I can listen. But that's as far as I go."

Adam took a deep, steadying breath, tried again. He wasn't at all sure of what he was saying, what he had read, but there was some small nugget of truth in there somewhere, and he had to find it. Find it, then use it.

"Look, Chollie," he said, trying again. "Burnell's not *trading* anything. He never was. Lady Jasper is wrong. It's a game Edmund plays. He tempts. We grab with both hands, or we walk away. Either way, he wins. He wins our souls, or he has a moment to *believe*, a moment to feel some shred of hope before the next person chooses evil. The Devil is the punishment, Chollie, not the judge." He took hold of Sherry's hands once more. "He can't take us if we won't go, Sherry, if we refuse him. If we love enough, are strong enough, he can't tempt us."

"Yes, and that's true *enough*," Edmund said, and Adam stood protectively in front of Sherry even as he turned to see the man standing in front of the fireplace. "But if I might correct you on one small point? Lady J didn't summon me; I go where I will, when I will. Just as I decided to appear here, tonight, gracing you with my presence—or damning you with it. Such a bother, you know, waiting until tomorrow."

"No," Adam said, resisting, doing his best not to betray how startled he'd been by Edmund's unexpected appearance. And he had to deny him, deny the Devil. He had to believe he'd understood correctly. "You may have some unearthly ability to appear when and where you want, but you also have to appear on demand. Lady Jasper *summoned* you. You are the slave and servant of man. She called, you came. Like a dog coming to heel."

"Oh, all right, Daventry, have it your way. I do admit to hearing her. Got a voice that could shatter the distant stars, the old besom. However, to get back to what I was saying, if I might? As you say, I *tempt*. It's up to man to refuse or be tempted. It's called precipitance, I believe. Lovely word. You drop yourselves— or I sometimes help drop you—into a situation, and you, in your fear or your greed or your arrogance or your slothfulness, whatever, act with rather undue haste to find the easiest way to solve your problems. *I'm* usually that easiest way. Resist temptation? Goodness, Daventry, you mortals cannot even resist a second serving of cake. You *race* to offer me your profound adoration, your most passionate and deepest allegiance. But, then, evil is quite an easy choice. It is, as you've found out, only good that is difficult. My congratulations."

"Thank you," Adam bit out, longing to do murder. But he wanted to keep Edmund talking. "How exactly did you get in here? I saw you produce the plums. You can also actually walk through walls, something like that?"

Edmund tipped his head to one side, smiled indulgently. "Now, really, Daventry, do you honestly feel you have to ask that question?" He took a step away from the fireplace, bowed to Sherry. "I've lost, haven't

I? Or have I? Surely there's bound to be something I can do for you, *slave* that I am."

He looked at Adam. "That really wasn't very nice, Daventry, you know. You read that in this book? How droll," he said, picking it up, looking at it. "I don't think we need this anymore, do we?"

As Adam watched, the book began to smolder, then burst into flame in Edmund's hand, disappearing a second later as if it had never existed.

"Now that was lovely, truly it was," Chollie said, rising to his feet, his hands bunched into fists at his sides, his chin jutting forward belligerently. "Would you be wanting to show us another bowl of plums now, or can we just get down to it?"

"Chollie," Adam said warningly, knowing his friend's Irish temper was swiftly getting the best of his good sense.

"I'll do this my way, thank you, boyo," Chollie said, lifting his fists in front of him and slowly advancing on Edmund. "Come on, you black devil, you. Going after sweet little girls and worried husbands. Let's see what you can do in a fair fight. Come on, come on. Ah, the pleasure it will give me to knock you down!"

"You keep him as a pet, don't you?" Edmund drawled, smiling at Adam. Then he lifted his hand, pointed a finger at Chollie, and the Irishman was suddenly flung, backwards, into a chair a good ten feet away from where he had been standing.

"You've killed him!" Sherry exclaimed, half-rising to her feet before Adam could push her back down.

Chollie was lying sprawled in the chair, his limbs limp, his eyes closed.

Edmund rolled his eyes. "No, I didn't *kill* him, my dear. I really, really don't know where I acquired this horrible reputation. He's merely sleeping, and will do so as long as I'm here. When he wakes, he'll remember very little about me. Nothing about tonight other than that there was a masquerade, nothing about any of what has been happening these past months—our little game, as you call it, Daventry. In short"—he looked at the now softly snoring Chollie—"and in long, the man is superfluous."

Sherry closed her eyes for a moment, tamped down her fear, her anger. Adam had been asking the questions, and receiving some frightening answers. Now, she decided, it was her turn.

"When did you choose me? How?" She shot a quick look at Adam. "Why?"

Edmund smiled, then indulged her. "I came to meet your very unhappy mother, actually, and saw you. That's the when and how of it, I suppose. But why? Ah, Sherry, you were simply too good to be true. Beautiful, innocent, depressingly honest. Oh, and before you start begging me to release your mother or any such drivel, let me tell you that my kingdom is not peopled with those who wish for something as silly as a better bed partner, or those who spit in the gutter or steal a loaf of bread." His smile was, for want of a better word, devilish. "We're overcrowded as it is, you understand."

Sherry laced her fingers together to stop their trembling. "But I was at Frame Cottage because of you, wasn't I?"

"Of course."

"I met Adam because of you, didn't I?"

"Adam. Always hated that name, Daventry. Do you wonder why? But, I admit, it did amuse me to pick you, and I picked you because of your name. I picked you, and then I placed Sherry where you could find her. Call me frivolous if you will, but I take my small pleasures where I find them."

Sherry reached up her hand and Adam took it, squeezed it. "You set the bull loose?"

"I did. My, confession *is* good for the soul, isn't it, if boring?"

"And the garden?" Sherry pressed, needing to hear more, so that she could at last believe.

"Mine, too," Edmund said, sighing. "But, before you ask, I had nothing to do with Geoff's accident. Or Baron Gilesen's, if you were about to ask that, too. Well," he added with a smile, "perhaps I had a little to do with Gilesen's. He annoyed me. As for Geoff? People most often create their own consequences, my dear, as I'm quite sure Daventry's headstrong little brother has learned."

Sherry sank back into the cushions, crushed by the weight of her new knowledge. "Then none of it was real, was it? Adam and I—we fell in love with a dream."

"Did you?" Edmund asked, and his smile made her shiver. "Let's think about that, shall we? I created the setting. A paradise, an Eden. Then I mixed in a little temptation, a little jealousy—that's all it usually takes." He looked at Adam. "Then I stand back and watch. I usually don't have long to wait. You're never happy, none of you, not even with perfection. You always want more, more," he said, pointing to Sherry, "or less. I don't understand that. That you'd want less, that you'd even question perfection."

Adam sat down beside Sherry, lifted her hand to his mouth, kissed her fingers. "No, you probably can't, Edmund. But we do. However, let's get back to you for a moment, all right? You must be rather proud of yourself, yes? I mean, you knew that Chollie and I had once been young and silly enough as to race blindfolded—you did know that, didn't you, as you *can* know the past—and then you used that against me. Clever. Very clever."

"Don't try to flatter me, Daventry," Edmund said, a thin white line appearing around his mouth. A vase on a far table exploded into a thousand pieces, so that Sherry gave an involuntary yelp, then buried her face against Adam's shoulder. "But, yes. I know the past, and I use it to my benefit. Wouldn't you, if you could? Isn't that what most mortals would happily sell their souls to do? And yet the past keeps repeating itself so very well. Especially by those who have been given perfection, just to be tempted by their need for more, and more. Adam and Eve. Cain and Abel—they were a special treat. Arthur and his Guinevere. I could go on, but I believe you understand. That's why I continued the game, broadened it. To have Sherry would be wonderful. To have you both? Ah, sublime!"

"But you don't have us, do you? Adam's right," Sherry dared, rallying. "You *can't* have us, because we love each other, and we don't need you or want you. We had the paradise you gave us and nearly lost that false love, but we're happier now, for all that you tried to destroy that happiness. Happier without that perfection. Our love is real now, and strong. How we must sicken you!"

The fire flared loudly in the fireplace, the flames burning white-hot for a moment before subsiding. This unexpected explosion was quickly followed by another as a jumbled mass of white feathers and heavy breathing burst into the room only to stop, resolve itself as the person of one Lady Gytha Jasper.

"Ah-ha!" she exclaimed, ripping a bent and broken halo from her hair and slamming it toward the floor. "I thought so. What are you doing here, Edmund? Have you taken them? Have they been so stupid as to hand themselves over to you?"

She looked at Adam, at Sherry. She frowned at the figure of Chollie as the Irishman snored on in his chair. "I am too late. I am. Oh, God help me!"

"God, my dear lady, has nothing to do with it," Edmund all but purred. "You'll sit down now, please. Over there, beside the Irishman."

"But I—"

He held out his hands. "No, no. Don't talk. Sit."

Lady Jasper shot a desperate look toward Adam and Sherry, which Sherry did her best to ignore, even as she felt herself succumbing to a small bout of sympathy for the woman. "But I—" Lady J said, then her eyes shot wide as her mouth slammed shut, reducing her to muffled mumbles. With her hands pressed to her shut mouth, she sat down beside Chollie, her entire body trembling with fear.

"You're horrible," Sherry said, even as Adam laid a hand on her arm, obviously to warn her to silence.

"Horrible? Really?" Edmund turned to her, walked slowly toward her . . . and there was Dickie. Sherry blinked, shook her head, opened her eyes once more. And it was still Dickie who stood where Edmund had been. Dickie. Smiling, and handsome, and with those strange, unforgettable blue eyes.

"Dickie?" she breathed, barely able to push the word past her numb lips.

Vaguely, just vaguely, she felt Adam touch her arm. "Sherry? What are you talking about? It's Edmund. See? Look at him. It's Edmund."

"He can't hear me, Sherry," Dickie said, holding out his arms to her. "It's only you here, only me. You know who I am?" He spread his arms. "This is who I am. Temptation. And he's wrong; Daventry is oh so very wrong. I can take souls. I can take his soul. You don't want that, do you?"

Sherry felt the tug, the invisible pull of Richard Brimley. His voice. His eyes. She tried to get up, wishing to confront him. That's all. Just to confront him. "You're wrong," she said, her voice trembling. "You can't take him. I won't let you."

She was held in her seat; strong arms held her to her seat, making it impossible for her to rise. She fought, frantic to be free. "Sherry! Don't look, darling. Don't listen!"

Dickie's arms were still reaching for her, urging her on. "Come, Sherry. Come near me . . . come to me. I'm the only one who can save him. I will save him, for you. If you come to me."

"Sherry! Sherry, stop! Damn you, Edmund! Let her alone!"

Someone was yelling. Someone was holding her.

But all she could see was Dickie. Dickie's eyes.

"Dickie?" Sherry pushed at Adam's hands, tried to be free of him. "Don't hurt him. Please, I'll do anything. Just don't hurt him!"

Dickie's smile was beautiful. Angelic. So warm, so caring, so potent. "That's it, little doll. Come to me . . . come to me."

Sherry shivered, shook her head violently. *Little doll.* How she hated that. She looked at Dickie again. His smile wasn't beautiful. It was mocking. He was laughing at her, toying with her. *Little doll.* No. No, she wasn't his little doll.

"Oh, Adam!" she cried, as Dickie's features melted back into Edmund, as Edmund reached into his pocket, casually took snuff, then turned away from her. "Oh, Adam, I almost went to him. I almost went to him!"

She tried to clutch at Adam for his support, but he moved away from her, jumping to his feet to confront Edmund. "Damn you, Edmund," he gritted out through clenched teeth. "Damn you to—"

"Hell?" Edmund finished for him. "Not very clever, Daventry, but then I suppose you might be feeling a bit overset at the moment. Wasn't that interesting? I gave her Dickie, but she resisted. So I gave her Edmund. But it was Dickie who proved the stronger." His smile was rather self-deprecating. "But not strong enough, obviously. As I said, Daventry, you seem to have bested me. Ah, well, it was a harmless amusement."

There was a long mumble from her left, and Sherry looked at Lady Jasper, seeing that the woman had nearly been able to turn her closed mouth into a smile.

"You said you only tempt, that you don't take," Adam said accusingly. "And yet you just tried to take my wife. Didn't you?"

"Well, of course I said that." Sherry watched as Edmund smiled, rolled his eyes. "And I lied, Daventry. I *lied.* Why on earth does that surprise you? You didn't really think you'd learned all my secrets from that silly book, did you? Understand all my powers, all my motives—all my desires? I love souls, Daventry. They're very tasty. There, is that what you want to hear?"

"Adam, sit down," Sherry begged, tugging on his coattails. "He lost; he has to leave. Let him go, Adam. For your love of me, let him go."

"You're right, darling," Adam said, reaching down to take her hand. "He can lie all he wants, but he still has to go now, has to play his game by our rules at last, bow to the inevitable. And he will go. Just as Shakespeare said: 'the prince of darkness is a gentleman.' " He lifted his chin, gesturing to Edmund. "Isn't that right?"

"Ah, dear Will," Edmund said, smiling. "The stories I could tell you—but enough. It is time I was gone, I suppose. I'd hoped to play a little longer, but then it will soon be Christmas here. My least favorite holiday, you understand. And I am rather bored. To you, I've been here for months, haven't I? That's how it feels when one isn't accustomed to eternity. For me, this was a blink of the eye, less than a blink, no more than a momentary diversion. One I'll soon forget." He turned on his heels, as if to leave, then turned back once more, looking straight at Sherry.

She lowered her gaze, afraid he might turn into Dickie once more, tempt her once more.

"Lady Jasper," he said rather conversationally. "Now there was a woman who didn't understand me. That horrid room, all those gargoyles and such. I'm not like that at all, you know. Beauty. I adore beauty. Untouched, unspoiled, untrammeled. A perfect rose. A glorious sunset." He spread his hands. "Beauty, Sherry. Simplicity. The way you enjoy it. The earth in all its glory."

He turned to Adam. "I was an archangel, Daventry. Do you know what that means?" He held out his hands, began ticking off his fingers. "Seraphim, cherubim, angels, *archangels*. And then the world became . . . cluttered." He shook his head. "Well, that's enough of that, I suppose. As you've said, I lost this time. I've lost before. Not enough to make me humble, certainly."

"Certainly," Adam said, as Sherry stood up, held his hand in both of hers.

Edmund raised his head, looked up at the ceiling, spread his arms wide. Flames seemed to flicker in every area of the room, although there was no fire, no heat. "Happy now?" he asked the ceiling. "You wanted me to suffer? You want me back? She brought me closer to both, and at the same time casts me farther from what we once had. She's only mortal, merely mortal, one of Your flawed creations. That I could love her *appalls* me!"

"Sherry, don't say a word, darling," Adam warned in a whisper. "He's taking his bows. It's almost over."

"Shut up, Daventry, I'm not that much of a gentleman," Edmund warned. "Now," he said, rubbing his hands together. "What shall I do? Shall I go now? Yes, I suppose so. I'll probably make a small stop along the way, however, to pick up a willing soul. So little challenge there, but she does want me."

Sherry found her tongue. "The duchess of Westbrook? Is that who you're talking about, Edmund? But—but she loves you."

Edmund shook his head, smiled indulgently as he looked at her. "You see, Daventry? Still so simple, so innocent, even after all of this. Does it amaze you? It amazes me. Come along, Lady J. I'll be taking you now."

Lady Jasper lifted her hands to her mouth, desperately tried to pry her lips open.

Adam stepped forward, Sherry two steps behind him. "I don't understand. Lady Jasper said if we thwarted you—her words, Edmund, not mine—that she would be free of you as well."

Edmund smiled, shot his cuffs. "That's true enough, I admit. Except that dear Lady J probably forgot to mention that she murdered her husband. Money wasn't enough for her, her title wasn't enough for her. So she killed him. People go to Hell for that, Daventry. Killing is not stealing a loaf of bread."

He smiled as Lady Jasper fell from the chair and began to crawl toward him. He looked down at her. "Poor dear. I didn't tell you that part, did I? But, then, I so enjoyed watching you get your hopes up, believing you could—what did you call it, Daventry? Oh, yes." He allowed Lady Jasper to clasp his legs at the knees; even patted her head. "You were going to thwart me, dear Gytha, weren't you? I think not."

"Adam, shouldn't we do something?" Sherry asked as Lady Jasper looked up at her imploringly. The woman looked so frightened . . . so *damned*.

"I'll leave her in her bed, just to save you the bother of having to deal with my rubbish. She'll have died in her sleep, poor dear. You see?" he said, arching his eyebrows. "I can be nice, if it suits me. And now for my exit. Should I just walk away, Lady J dragging behind? No, I don't think so. Besides, I imagine you're expecting some sort of dramatic leave-taking." He looked over at Chollie, snapped his fingers. "Wake up, Irishman. Even though you won't remember it, I believe you'll enjoy this."

As Adam pulled Sherry against him protectively, the flames shot up all the way to the ceiling, surrounding them. Lightning seemed to strike inside the room; thunder cracked and boomed with enough force that Sherry felt the reverberations inside her chest. She turned her face into Adam's shoulder, closed her eyes, clapped her hands over her ears.

And then there was silence.

"He's gone, darling," she heard Adam say as he put

his hands on hers, took them down from her ears. "After all of that, he's gone."

"Who's gone?" Chollie asked, standing up, stretching after his nap. "And would one of you be wanting to tell me why I'm sleeping in a chair and not in a bed? That will teach me to go to one of those masquerade balls, won't it? Drink too much, strut about looking stupid, and then fall asleep on top of it all." He looked at Sherry, at Adam. "Well? Isn't anybody going to say anything?"

"I am," Adam said, taking hold of Sherry's shoulders, pulling her close against him. "I love you, Lady Daventry. I love you with all my heart."

"And I love you, Lord Daventry," Sherry whispered just before his mouth closed over hers.

"There they go again," Chollie announced to no one in particular. "Never met two so silly with love. I suppose that leaves me to find my own way to my borrowed bed, in my borrowed clothes? Yes, Chollie," he then agreed with himself, "I suppose it does. That's just what I was thinking—it's time to go to bed. But you'd better have someone check that chimney someday soon, boyo, give it a good cleaning. It smells of brimstone and hellfire in here, don't you know. Do you hear me, boyo? Do you hear a single word I'm saying?" He took his spectacles out of his pocket, looped them over his ears, shook his head. "Ah, the devil with it!"

Still grumbling under his breath, Chollie picked up a single lit candle and walked out of the room.

Sherry and Adam never noticed that he had gone.

Epilogue

A Scent of Roses . . .

They say miracles are past.

—William Shakespeare

O embrace now all you millions,
With one kiss for all the world.
—Johann von Schiller

A warm September sun played over the gardens at Daventry Court. It shone down on the profusion of roses and other late-summer flowers just coming into bloom, and on the infant playing with her toes as she lay on a blanket spread on a small expanse of sweet grass.

"Oh, now, Julia, that's inelegant. Should we really let her put her foot in her mouth?" Geoff asked, frowning down at his niece.

Adam put his arm around Sherry as the two of them sat on their favorite bench. "I don't see why not, Geoff," he said, smiling at Sherry. "After all, we let you do it."

Sherry giggled, gave Adam a playful slap.

"Very funny, Adam," Geoff growled, then grinned. "She does look a little like me, though, doesn't she?"

"Only when she drools," Sherry quipped, then

clapped her hands to her mouth. "Oh, I'm sorry, Geoff. Truly. I can't imagine what made me say that."

Geoff stood up, brushing bits of grass from his knees. "I can. It comes from being married to this brother of mine. Well, I'm off. I promised Chollie I'd meet him at the tavern in the village. Seems he's been teaching some of the locals some rather bawdy Irish songs." He shook his head as he ambled off. "And you allowed him to be godfather to little Julia, here, along with me. Shame on you. Shame on both of you."

Adam reached out and broke a single bloom from the rosebush next to him, offered it to Sherry. "Happy, darling?"

She took the flower, sniffed its heady fragrance. "You know I am." Leaning her head against his shoulder, she went on, "It's so nice to see Geoff all but running about again, isn't it? There was barely the hint of a limp as he went bounding off to meet Chollie." She sat up once more as the baby began to make more fussing noises than cooing noises, kissed Adam on the mouth. "Your daughter's hungry, darling. I'll take her inside to feed her, then possibly go down for a nap along with her. Would you care to join me?"

Adam smiled. "That sounds like a remarkable idea, sweetheart," he said, helping her gather up Julia, who grinned at her father as he picked her up, handed her to Sherry. "In about half an hour?"

He watched as his wife and child went up the steps to the patio, then disappeared inside the house. He was a lucky man. A lucky, lucky man.

He heard a noise and turned around. He still started

at unexpected sounds from time to time. But, lately, not quite so often. He was getting his life back. Both he and Sherry were getting their lives back. Back, and better than ever.

"Good day to you, sir," Augustus said as he pushed a wheelbarrow along the brick path. "It took most of the summer, but the gardens is looking right fine now, aren't they, my lord? Won't ever be half of what we had last year, though. No, my lord," he said, sadly shaking his head. "We won't see another garden like that one, not none of us."

Adam patted the old man's bent shoulders. He looked around at the blooms, some of them perfect, some of them a little too small, or drooping, or too sparse on their bushes. It was a beautiful garden, but it wasn't perfect. It was real, and he loved it. "One can only hope we don't, Augustus," he said, smiling. "One can only hope. . . ."

After five long years away, the Prodigal son returns to his home, his heritage, and the wife he had left behind. . . .

Jack Coltrane reined in the huge black stallion at the crest of the hill, the exact place where, for good or bad, life as he'd known it had ended. This was the spot where he'd truly begun the long, hard journey into manhood.

He'd turned away from friendship, from love. Even hate had been discarded in favor of the day-to-day quest for the one thing he believed he needed. Money.

When had the struggle become more important than life itself? When had he changed into the man he was now, the hollow shell he'd filled with banknotes and properties and the belief that money was the answer to any question? Every question. Money, which bought him information, which equaled power, which equaled . . . surely not happiness.

1

Happiness was a child, skipping stones across a stream. Happiness was lying on your back in a freshly cut hay field, picking out faces in the clouds overhead.

Happiness was Coltrane House, as he wanted to remember it, as he longed to remember it.

Happiness was Coltrane House as he, Jack Coltrane, would make it again. Except that now Cluny and Clancy were dead, and could no longer be a part of Jack's tomorrows, as they had been such a large measure of his happiness in his yesterdays. They had left him, as he had gone away from them, and he hadn't been there to say good-bye.

Jack sighed inwardly as he heard the curricle pull up beside him and waited while Walter set the brake. The man was about to make some profound comment, Jack was sure, and the least he could do would be to listen.

"From the topographical description you've given me," his friend said a moment later, "I imagine I'm safe in assuming that this is the approximate location of the pinnacle of your youthful disgrace as a failed highwayman."

"Go to the devil, Walter," Jack said idly, shifting in the saddle. And then he smiled. A sad, yet faintly amused smile. "What a shambles we made of the thing. You should have seen us, friend. Everyone running, everyone screaming, shouting. My friend Kipp trying to be in three places at once, and none of them the right one for more than a second. And then Merry, coming out of nowhere like that. . . . God. I thought she was dead."

"And when she wasn't," Walter said smoothly, "you wanted to kill her. Completely understandable."

"I talk too much when I'm drunk," Jack said.

"That's true. You've said enough while in your cups that if your father, the Awful August, were not already dead, I should have had to skin him slowly with a dull knife within an hour of stepping foot onto English soil," Walter said, sniffing appreciatively at his one affection—the posy in his buttonhole. "As it is, I shall content myself with pissing on his grave."

"I don't deserve you," Jack said with a slow smile. "In fact, friend, there are moments when you truly terrify me."

"It's my great mind," Walter said. "Many are in awe of it, including myself, on occasion. That said, I believe it's time we part, as you must now gird your loins and ride down this hill. To Coltrane House, my friend, and to your bride. I shall remain here, rest the horses, and contemplate my place in this small, fateful dot in the universe."

"And who, then, shall guard my back?" Jack asked. "Remembering Merry, and knowing that Sherlock has undoubtedly told her of my arrival, I believe anything less than an accompanying regiment means I'm riding now to my death. Not that it appears you care what happens to me."

"The element of surprise still rides with you to some extent. She knows the attack is coming, but since you didn't give Sherlock a firm date for your arrival, she doesn't know when it is coming. She's on edge, frightened even as she prepares for you. Lacking sleep. Lacking comfort and peace. When the war whoop sounds, suddenly splits the air with its nerve-jangling terror, an opponent such as this does one of two things. She freezes to the ground, unable to react . . ."

"Yes?" Jack prompted as Walter bent to sniff the flower once more.

Walter smiled. "Or she blows a whacking great hole straight through you. In other words, my friend, do be careful, won't you? I've grown rather attached to you for one reason or another, none of which readily leaps to the forefront of my mind at the moment. Oh, wait, there is one. You've got a good heart, Jack. The only problem is that you misplaced it a few years ago. Perhaps you can ride down this hill now, and find it?"

"I never took you for a romantic, Walter," Jack said, uncomfortably shifting in his saddle. "I'll see you in an hour or so?"

The closer Jack rode, the more evidence of August's reign as master of Coltrane House came into focus. The house was a broken-down shambles.

And yet the fields surrounding Coltrane House were already planted. The considerable number of livestock appeared well fed. The tenant cottages he'd seen earlier were freshly thatched, the corn bins were still more than half-full. The sheep wandering the manor grounds beyond the ha-ha—how Merry had adored that silly name for a sunken fence—were fat and woolly.

"Sherlock's work," Jack breathed as he dismounted at the end of the circular stone drive in front of his childhood home. "I knew I could depend upon him to keep the estate profitable, just as he did when August was alive. But spend so much as a penny on the house? No, Henry Sherlock would never let Merry put out a penny that couldn't come back twice, even if the house collapsed around her. Keeping the estate, holding on to the land, that's what was and still is most important to Sherlock. Among other things," he ended, his jaw tight.

As he advanced toward the massive front doors of Coltrane House, Jack made one last assessment of the enormous building.

Money. Coltrane House needed money. Vast amounts of it. And that was just on the outside. God only knew what he'd find on the inside.

Jack's leisurely ride around the house had taken away any element of surprise for anyone who might have chanced to spy him out one of the hundred or more windows. He therefore decided Walter's suggestion of a war whoop announcing his presence would probably be seen in the light of being slightly overdone. So thinking, he approached the doors and lifted a hand to raise the badly tarnished brass knocker.

Which was as far as he got before one of the doors opened and he was staring down the barrel of a quite deadly-looking hunting rifle.

"You have five seconds to turn around and start running before I shoot you where you stand."

Jack refused to flinch. He raised one eyebrow, then slowly slid his gaze along the weapon until it collided with the figure of one very angry-looking young woman.

Who couldn't be Merry. Could she? Wait . . . yes. Yes, she could. There were the same huge sky-blue eyes. The same riot of curls, a darker red than he remembered, but just as wild, just as untamed. The freckles were still there, running riot across her nose and

5

cheeks, although he saw no evidence of her wonderful, wide smile. And, unless he was mistaken, she was dressed in one of his old shirts, an outgrown pair of his breeches, the riding boots he had worn at the age of twelve. God bless the child. She hadn't changed a bit.

But she had grown up, left the last of her childhood behind her. All her coltish awkwardness was gone, and she'd at last grown into her body, her long, once gangling limbs. She was beautiful. Unbelievably lovely. Tall, wonderfully formed, her posture graceful—or as graceful as one could be while wielding a rifle.

And she most definitely wasn't smiling. She wasn't laughing. She wasn't even throwing herself at him, doing her best to beat him into flinders for having deserted her.

She was simply staring at him. Looking at him without really seeing him, refusing to really see him.

Jack was just about to grab the barrel and pull the rifle from her hands when a voice from behind the door said, "Put it down, Merry. I've told you, shooting him won't do you any good at all. Poison, that's the ticket. It's slower, much more painful, and you're less likely to hang for it."

Merry's finger left the trigger just as Jack pushed the barrel out of the way and stepped past her, into the large foyer. "Mr. Bromley? Aloysius? Is that you? God, it's good to see you!"

"And me you, Jack," the tutor said, his watery gray eyes twinkling. "I believe you still owe me a paper on Homer's *Odyssey*, however. Have it on my desk by tomorrow morning, if you please."

Jack grinned, feeling some of his tension easing

away—at least as long as he kept his back to Merry, who still held the rifle even though it was now harmlessly pointed at the tiles. He knew what his former tutor was trying to say, and quickly agreed. "We'll split a bottle or two tonight as I tell you of my own odyssey instead, if that will suffice?"

"Done and done," Aloysius Bromley said, giving Jack a hearty slap on the back.

"If we're all done being sloppy?"

Jack turned to look at Merry once more. Look at his wife once more. Dear Lord, his wife? No. It was still impossible to think of her that way. In fact, it was impossible to think of her in any way at all. Because she was definitely no longer the Merry he always tried so hard to remember. The Merry he'd bounced on his knee, helped nurse through a bout of measles, taught how to tie her bonnet strings, inadvertently given a black eye when she'd failed to catch the ball he'd thrown her.

No, she was none of those memories. She wasn't the playmate he remembered. She wasn't the one who sat on the sidelines, cheering his every exploit. She wasn't the silly infant who dogged his footsteps night and day, learning from him, teasing him out of his dark moods, worshiping at his feet.

And she most certainly wasn't the same injured innocent his father had robbed of her inheritance, her freedom, by forcing her into a marriage that had destroyed Jack's hopes for her future.

"Merry?" Jack inquired, gesturing toward the main saloon. "If we might adjourn—minus this nasty piece, if you don't mind," he added, removing the rifle from her nerveless fingers and handing it over to the tutor, who took it gingerly.

Jack watched Merry's departing back as she whirled and stormed toward the main saloon, leaving him to follow in her wake if he dared. Good Lord, those old breeches of his had never fit him so well. "Do I dare follow her?" he actually asked Aloysius, who only shrugged before turning to pull his old body back up the stairs, to the safety of the schoolroom.

Aloysius hesitated halfway up the first flight, turning to look down at Jack. "She doesn't hate you, you know. She hates herself because she can't hate you. Of course, she doesn't know that, which is another way of saying that I believe you should watch your back, at least for a while. She's had five years to think up ways to make your life a living hell, and Merry has always been quite inventive, if you remember."

"But she was safe," Jack said, hating to hear the question.

"Many would sacrifice safety for happiness, you know, Jack." Aloysius shook his head. "We gave Meredith what she needed, never what she wanted. You'll be amazed at how she's grown, Jack. Amazed, and surprised, and most probably impressed. But I doubt you'll enjoy yourself these next weeks and months. Be gentle with her, Jack, allow her to hate you for a while longer. In time, she'll make you an exemplary wife."

"I don't want a wife," Jack said flatly. "And, if I did, it certainly wouldn't be Merry. For God's sake, Aloysius, we grew up as brother and sister."

Aloysius lifted one end of his long scarf and fanned

himself with it. "That may have been the way you felt ten years ago, Jack. But not by the time you left here, no matter how you might have still been lying to yourself, telling yourself that you knew what was best for her. So don't lie to me now, Jack, even if you need to delude yourself a while longer." He shook his head sadly. "You were always such an intelligent lad. I thought you might have learned something in the years since you rode away from here, your body bruised, your heart full of hate, of shame. Don't disappoint me, Jack. Don't disappoint me."

. . . and then there are Cluny and Clancy, late of Cluny and Clancy Traveling Shakespearean Players. Very late. Dead, actually, although they've stayed around, waiting for Jack to come home, to make their Merry happy again. They've been eavesdropping on the reunion. . . .

"Oh, that was cutting," Clancy said, looking down at Jack pityingly as Jack passed under the elaborate wooden arch he and Cluny were perched on, heading into the main saloon.

"Not cutting enough," Cluny responded hotly. "Doesn't want her? What makes him think she'll even have him? Still, did you see her? Did you see the pair of them, together again? Had you ever thought we'd live long enough to see such a sight? 'Eternity was in our lips and eyes, bliss in our brows bent.'"

"'Ay, every inch a king,'" Clancy said feelingly, randomly grabbing at another of Shakespeare's lines, his clasped hands pressed to his breast. "But we didn't live long enough to see them, Cluny. When are you going to remember that we're dead?"

"It doesn't matter," Cluny said, wiping a nonexistent tear from his eye with the sleeve of his burgundy-velvet doublet. "They're together again, and our long wait is finally over. "You want to see Jack again, Clancy? Oh, come one, I know you're longing to be close to him. Shall we join them then? Watch? Rattle the chandelier if they seem to be close to sword points?"

Clancy looked longingly toward the closed door. "So tall, so handsome, so immaculately turned-out. A gentleman of the world, Cluny, a gentleman of the world. He has become all that I've wanted for him, all that I've dreamed these more than twoscore years. I could watch him all the day long."

"I thought so," Cluny said, holding his nose and slowly floating down to the tile floor, where he landed with his feet a good two inches sunk into the tiles— even after six months as a ghost, landings remained a problem to him. Death had relieved him of his dependence on his cane, but there were times he believed that unlamented loss to be a mixed blessing. "If Merry lets us in, of course. You know how she can get. Welcomes us like the flowers in May most times, but when she wants us out, we're out."

"She wouldn't dare. Not today of all days." Clancy turned to walk through the now closed doors, into the main saloon. He stopped when his beaky nose collided with solid wood. "Saucy, stubborn baggage," he grumbled, then pressed his ear against the wood, frowned. "Can't hear a thing, Cluny. Come on, we'll go around outside, and peek in the windows.

"Can't," Cluny said, happy to share his knowledge

with the man who had believed himself superior to him, the man who, basically, was mentally superior to him, both before their deaths and since. "Once Merry has said no, it's no, and we both know it. We'll probably have more rules soon, too, once we introduce ourselves to Jack, and if he believes in us."

"If he believes in us? I never thought of that, Cluny," Clancy said, slowly walking away, his steps dragging as he headed toward the kitchens. He always went to the kitchens when he was unhappy, to smell the aroma of good food being cooked up by Mrs. Maxwell. "What will I do, old friend, if he doesn't believe in me?"

"He will, Clancy, he will. Just give him time. He's barely even home, and has his hands quite full with Merry at the moment, I'm sure." Cluny gave one last, longing look toward the closed doors.

Loath to leave this spot, he lingered a moment more, drawing on his love of Will Shakespeare, hoping to find the right words. "'For aught that I could ever read, could ever hear by tale or history—'" he broke off, mid-quote, as the sound of shattering pottery escaped the main saloon, then finished quickly, "'the course of true love never did run smooth.' Clancy!" he called out as he ran fast as he could to catch up with his friend, "wait for me!"

. . . *and wait for us, too, as we come along, to watch, to listen, and to enjoy the battle between Merry and Jack. It should prove worth the wait.*